Boots

A Puss in Boots Retelling

Boots

A Puss in Boots retelling

Copyright 2022 by Emily Luebke aka Julian Gresytoke.

All rights reserved. This book, and any parts thereof, may not be copied or reproduced without written permission of the author.

The scanning, copying, uploading and distribution of this work via the internet or any other means without permission is prohibited by law.

Cover design by AmerGrey. All rights reserved.

Also by Julian Greystoke:

Phoenix

The Wolf and The Hawk

Author's note

I first drafted Boots in 2016, which, from the vantage point of 2022, feels like another lifetime ago. After about a year or two of drafting and editing this little tale went into the query trenches. Unfortunately, it failed to find a home. I put Boots away to rest for several years.

I never forgot the story of a sassy cat and his human companions in their heroic quest to save their kingdom. It deserved to be taken off the shelf and given a chance to find a place in people's hearts. I took it out, brushed it off, and that is how you find it in your hands today. I may have come father as a writer in the intervening years, but I hope this little tale still brings you as much joy as it does me.

This book is dedicated to my grandfather, who would have loved it. To Kinshou, Nigel, and Jayne, the OG 3 who brought me inspiration and companionship every day. And to October, horse of my heart, upon whom Molly is based.

Part 1
The Shades

The first time Princess Joanna encountered the Shades she was eleven years old.

Joanna stood on the cushioned seat of her father's carriage, her body half out the window, black curls tangling in the wind. Her dark eyes shone with eagerness as the powerful horses charged up the country road.

The guards laughed and waved at her as they rode alongside. She stared jealously at the swords strapped to their saddles.

"Joanna, please come inside. We're getting near Carabas Castle."

A hand at Joanna's elbow pulled her back through the window. She plopped onto the seat beside Lyall, her personal bodyguard. The boy was the same age as she and looked as nervous as a bird to be in such a small space with the king. He perched on his seat, hands clasped in his lap, not even looking out the window.

Joanna pursed her lips at her father who pulled her down before he snapped the window shut. "Why shouldn't I look at Carabas Castle? It's on our land, isn't it?"

"It's on The Ogre's land." The king said, rubbing his bearded chin. He was giving Joanna that look she was coming to know as a *what am I going to do with you?* Look. "We should probably take this off the tour route, but the people in Strant village love to see us ride through."

"You brought me out here, why can't I look at the Castle?" She folded her arms and leaned her head against the carriage side, catching a glimpse of passing sky and trees through the window. The smell of growing things and good earth filtered enticingly in past the glass.

"Because I know you. One look at that place and you'll be forming wild schemes to liberate it. The captain of the guard has a job to do besides listening to a young princess's wild ideas."

"They're not wild ideas." Joanna huffed, fogging the glass. "They're sound military tactics."

Her father's expression changed to an indulgent smile and the carriage came to a halt. The smile vanished. "Why have we stopped?"

"Sire, something's not right!" One of the guards riding outside called. Joanna couldn't miss the urgency in his tone.

"Stay inside." Joanna's father put his hand on her knee before pushing out of the carriage. She knew he didn't mean for her to see him draw his sword, but she saw.

Joanna whipped around to face Lyall whose freckles stood out like pocks on his milky cheeks. His pale eyes were too-wide. "Do you have your sword?" She asked.

"Yes." He shot her a warning look as he reached for his hip. She'd taken his blade from him before on occasion, but Joanna didn't demand it now. She was distracted by the shouts of men and whinnies of horses. "Shades!" she whispered urgently, pulling both herself and Lyall to the floor of the carriage. "Draw your sword!" she commanded.

"I can't fight Shades!" Lyall spluttered, his voice breaking. He drew his sword just the same. He was a gangling boy, all too-long arms and legs as he fumbled clumsily with the weapon, trying not to strike the princess or himself. More yells outside, more horses screaming. Joanna heard her father's voice, shouting orders. Someone cried out in pain. She clenched her fists, fire raging inside her. If she was allowed to fight she could help. She could at least instruct the men as Father was.

Something heavy – a person? – hit the side of the carriage. Joanna gritted her teeth as she jostled into Lyall.

The window above Joanna broke and showered her in shards like glittering sand. She yelped, but managed to contain a louder scream. While Lyall looked terrified Joanna's heart raged with excitement alongside the fear.

The Ogre's minion crept in through the shattered window. Its body was long and stretched, like a shadow cast at dusk. This Shade was full bodied and so black she almost couldn't see through it. It held the vague shape of a man, with slender arms and sharp, grasping hands slithering down the inside of the carriage door towards them. It's eyes were twin holes, shining with the light from behind it. For the moment there was no mouth.

"Call for your father!" Lyall ordered, pushing himself in front of, and slightly atop, Joanna, brandishing his short-sword in trembling hands.

Before Joanna could open her mouth to yell, a sound that would surely have every guard and the king himself converging on the carriage door, the Shade slashed with its hand. Lyall had begun his training, but no amount of practicing with his father in a dusty field could have prepared him for this situation. He yelped as the Shade's claws, which looked as solid as smoke, but were actually keen as steel, sliced deep into his arm. His sword clattered to the glass strewn floor.

Joanna didn't think. She scrambled for the blade. Glass cut her knuckles as she scooped it up, shifted her body around the struggling Lyall, and thrust with everything she had. "RRRRAAAAAAAIIIIIIII!" She startled herself with her own battle cry, but it was effective. She drove her borrowed sword into the Shade's chest where it met with a faint resistance like tearing fabric. Teeth bared, hands slick with her own blood, Princess Joanna wrenched the sword upward, ripping the Shade from nape to the top of its head.

It made no sound but fell away, the two halves of its body flapping like a torn flag as its limbs lost purchase and it slid from sight.

Princess Joanna stood amidst the broken glass, gasping fierce breaths between bared teeth like a wild creature. She looked the part with her hair frizzing around her face and blood streaming down her hands onto her pale blue dress. Lyall, crouched on the floor holding his bleeding arm, looked up at her with mingled amazement and concern.

Inwardly she was aflame as she had never been before. No monsters were going to hurt her friends. Her people. Not now, not ever.

Later, much later, when she was back home in the palace, cleaned, dried, and bandaged, she strode up to the king and announced: "Father, I wish to have a sword tutor. Beginning immediately."

Part 2

The Cat

The cat thrashed and struggled for air as cold water pressed around him. The heavy burlap sack constricted, and he fought against it to no avail, his claws catching in the sacking. The human boys pressed him under, jostling one another for a turn. When the cat managed to force his head above the surface for a few seconds he could hear his tormentors' maniacal laughter before he was shoved down again.

He yowled at the top of his waterlogged lungs whenever he came up for air. He scratched the boys and scored a few good hits, even through the burlap, but his strength was failing. He was having a harder time scrabbling his way up for each choked breath and a fresh yowl.

One of the boys grabbed the thrashing cat's head and pushed it under. The cat guessed they had grown tired of being scratched and decided to end their cruel game in the only way they could—with a dead cat.

As he released what he assumed would be his last gurgling breath, unable to see anything but the darkness inside the bag, the grip of the hands around him changed. Instead of being held under, he was borne up and out.

He hacked water from his lungs and scrambled wildly to be free of the bag before the boys decided what their next cruel game would be.

He suspected it would involve rocks or sticks. He'd been around a few human children before, and they often relied heavily on rocks and sticks for entertainment.

The cat was too busy struggling to realize that the hands which held him now were not the small ones of the boys, but they had the strong grip of a young man. The cat finally got a full gulp of air and yowled at the top of his voice before lashing out at the human, whose voice joined his as claws met flesh and scored deep. The human dropped the thrashing bundle, and the cat wasted no time slashing at his soggy prison until he found the opening. He shot out into the bright sunlight and was away so fast that he doubted the human even saw which direction he went.

He was up the nearest willow tree and safely ensconced in the branches before he stopped, breathing in tense little pants. He shook himself at last and took stock. His usually lovely orange fur was plastered to his sides with the river water, and it stank like algae. He wrinkled his nose and twitched his tail angrily, wondering how long the scent would linger. He was not looking forward to the necessary grooming session. His heart fell to beating more normally now, and as he settled in to begin the lengthy process of cleaning himself, pawing water from his ears, he heard something else. Not the sound of the boys' laughter or complaining at the loss of their quarry. It was a young man speaking.

The cat was curious. His mother had often scolded him for wandering to explore when he was a kitten, but he would never sit quietly and clean his paws like his sisters. He walked out on a branch and peered down through the willow's hanging fronds to spy the human below.

The speaker, a male human, clambered out of the shallows where he seemed to have fallen. His simple, homespun clothes were sodden, and the cat noticed that there were several long scratches on the stranger's hands and forearms. The cat knew his own handiwork when he saw it.

"Of course my boots are ruined," the human complained as he made his way out of the river. He slipped on the slick rocks and stumbled several times, flailing his arms and sending showers of water flying from his soggy sleeves.

He had a thatch of excessively messy blond hair and the tough, muscled body of a laborer. The cat guessed he was a farmer. He'd known a few farmers, and they had all been kind enough to him. Most farms were interested in a good mouser, though the cat had never stayed at one for long.

He slipped to a lower branch, watching the man struggle. The human had reached the shore and sat to pour the water from his boots. He plopped down directly on top of a large thistle and yelped, falling to one side. The cat laughed in the way that cats do, with the gentle swishing of his tail and half closing of his eyes. Perhaps this human had been eager to gain some good luck by rescuing a cat, but it seemed his effort had been in vain.

"Gods," the man griped. "Da will never forgive me when he sees these." He pulled a boot free, water gushing out onto the bank. He shook the offending footwear, and the sole came loose, flapping wetly. "He just let me get them repaired." He jammed a hand into the boot and waggled his fingers out through the open sole, grimacing.

The cat finished his descent to the ground and slipped between the long fronds of the willow that bent over the river like a woman stooping to wash her hair. "Mau?" Said the cat.

The young man turned and looked around in confusion before his pale blue eyes came to rest. The cat sat on his haunches and took in his savior. The young man had a wide jaw, thick brows, and kind eyes that brightened when he saw the cat. "Hello," he said in a gentle tone. "Puss puss puss," he beckoned, as he extended a hand and twitched his fingers.

The cat spread his whiskers and butted his head against the man's hand, raising his tail to say 'hello' back.

"Are you alright, puss puss? Did those boys hurt you?" The man scratched the cat's ears, and the cat rewarded him with a purr because somehow this human knew exactly how to scratch. "Well," said the man, "you look fine. You're such a pretty color. Like embers on the hearth...or sunset maybe."

The cat loved being petted and he loved being complimented even more, so he strolled back and forth, allowing the human to stroke his swiftly drying coat and trilling encouragingly whenever the petting flagged. He didn't let himself draw too near, however. This soft-voiced man seemed nice enough, but the cat wasn't looking to get ambushed again. He stayed out of easy grabbing range as he let the stranger scratch.

"Do you belong to anyone?" The man asked, tilting his head, wet hair flopping messily over his high brow. "You're in good shape. Not skinny, and I don't see many scars from fighting."

The cat flicked his whiskers. He wasn't much for fighting. While other toms squabbled and shrieked over the most ridiculous quarrels, he kept to himself and nested down in barns to be cozy and comfortable. If he found another tom that looked to give him trouble, he just moved on.

"Would you like to come home with me, puss puss?" Asked the man, still petting. He only paused for a moment to pull his soggy boot back on.

This human did look like someone who needed the company of a cat. "Meow," the cat announced. *I shall stay for the moment, as you need me.*

"Very well, then." The man was clearly pleased. His kind eyes crinkled at the corners with sun-formed creases. He held out his arms to see if the cat would jump into them to be carried.

The cat looked the human up and down, skeptical. No. He would walk. The man's arms and clothes were still saturated with stinky river water. The youth chuckled, getting to his feet with a soggy squelch. The cat pinned his ears back in disgust and pity at the water that seeped from the ruined boots. He avoided the little puddles the human left.

"Oh no! Damn and blast!" The human cried. His attention was drawn to a basket lying on the ground, tipped on its side with contents spread on the grass. Several eggs had rolled away, and the loaf of bread was half-saturated. The cat took note of a large and wonderful smelling hunk of herb cheese, which the man picked up and attempted to brush the dirt from before jamming it back into the basket.

The human groaned his dismay as he collected up the eggs and found two had cracked. There were apples, which were bruised, and a crumpled packet of cinnamon. "Ma will not be pleased." The man raked his fingers back through his sun-yellow hair, making it stick straight up.

"Mrow row?" asked the cat, trotting over to an egg the human had not seen. The cat sniffed and determined that this one was unharmed. A pity. He would have liked to lick up the tasty insides. At least the wholeness of the egg would please the human.

The man came and bent down to pick up the egg with exceeding gentleness, as though worried he might squeeze too hard and shatter it. "Ma would never have sent me for the shopping," he confided, "but my brothers were busy with the mill today and Da's lungs are bad again—" His eyes went wide. "Oh gods! Da's medicine!" He dropped to all fours and began scrabbling around in the long grass.

The cat watched this absurd display for a few moments, then trotted around the fallen basket in a circle. He had no idea of any "medicine," but his keen nose had detected a blob of goat cheese wrapped in cloth. He nosed into the little packet, lapping at the crumbly cheese with relish.

The human made his way over, still on all fours. His eyes brightened, and he reached towards the cat, who hastily gobbled more cheese until he realized that the man was reaching for something else. A little glass vial which the cat had ignored, and which lay beside the food. "Well, I'll be! It's Da's medicine! Not even broken. You really are a lucky cat, eh?" He tucked the vial into a pocket. "You can have all that goat cheese as a reward!"

The cat purred loudly.

The young man finished gathering his things and placing what food he could salvage back in the basket. The handle was broken, so he was obliged to carry it in both arms, but surprisingly he seemed in good spirits as he began to walk towards the dirt road that lead out into the sprawling countryside.

The cat watched him go, licking cheese crumbs from his whiskers. He was almost dry and had a full belly so he should have been satisfied. Yet something about the man drew him up from his haunches. Without knowing exactly why, the cat began to follow his savior.

The human did not seem to notice the sole of his shoe flap-flopping as he went, or the fact that his sodden sock was turning from white to brown with the road dirt. Instead, he kept his head up and keenly alert. The cat had to admit that he had seldom seen a human so aware of his surroundings. The man was artful as he avoided rocks that might trip him or a gust of wind that threatened his patched, straw hat. He looked down at the cat and smiled, obviously pleased to be followed. "Alright," he said. "If you're going to come with me you need a name. What should I call you, eh puss puss?"

"Mer mew?" The cat responded as he trotted up beside the man. He looked up at his companion, curious. Humans did like to give one another special designations. When he was a kitten, the cat's mother had called him "The Orange One," or if she was pleased with him, "My Little Fire Cat," to tell him apart from his sisters. Now there were no other cats to differentiate himself from, so he had no need for a name. Perhaps this man had other cats? He was very skilled at ear scritches.

The man paused a moment, allowing the cat to walk on past him. The animal turned and looked up at his new friend, pricking his ears. *What is it?*

The man stuck out his chin in consideration. "You've got two white stockings on your hind feet," he pointed out. The cat sat down in the dust and squinted. "Socks?" The man said.

The cat sneezed.

"No? What about Stockings?"

The cat swished his tail sharply.

"Boots?"

The cat blinked slowly.

"Boots." The man tried the word a few times. "Here, Boots."

The cat perked up, standing to trot over to his new companion. "Rau rau?"

"Boots it is!" He jabbed his finger in the air and nearly dropped his basket all over again. "Now you have a proper name!" He seemed quite pleased with himself as he hugged the laden basket to him. The pair went companionably on their way.

The countryside was beautiful and open, dotted all over with windmills. The air was fresh, sweet, and just blustery enough to keep the blades of the mills turning. It was a perfect spring day, the cat decided, though he had only seen two other springs in his lifetime. He had made a new friend.

~~~~~

"What on earth is that?"

"A cat, Ma. His name is Boots."

"You named it?"

"Him, Ma. I named *him*."

The cat perched atop a wooden kitchen table, cleaning a paw as the humans talked in increasingly loud voices. The room was small, the walls made of stones that had clearly been plucked from a field several human generations past. Someone had painted them white, but this did little to hide the poor condition of the structure. The window by the door was missing a panel, the floor was packed dirt instead of boards, and not a single pot or pan was without rust. Nevertheless, the cat liked the place. He'd curled up in coal scuttles and manure piles; this house would do nicely.

"We cannot keep a cat," the woman said. She was a tall, tough lady with wide hips. She did not share the young man's kind eyes. Hers were steel grey and flinty as she shot a hard glance towards Boots, who hiked up his hind leg to lick his nethers in response.

"He'll kill the mice in the barn," the young man protested in his gentle voice. "And you know about cats. They're lucky."

The woman rolled her eyes and planted her fists on her hips. She had full lips and she pursed them now, scowling. "You and your superstitions. If there is magic in this world, Levi, it is never good or lucky. Where did you even find a cat?"

"Some town boys were drowning him in the river," said the young man apparently called Levi, sitting down on one of the five mismatched chairs at the table. Boots abandoned his spot for his new friend's lap, setting up a purr just to let this lady know that he intended to make himself at home.

To her credit, Levi's Ma softened. "Ogre take those boys, trying to harm an innocent animal. Still..." Her tone easily switched back to its previous frustration. "You can't be running around collecting sad animals, Levi. Not with how you get into scrapes. And look"—she nudged the basket on the table, with its broken handle, gnawed loaf of bread, and few remaining eggs—"because you had to save the damned cat, you spilled all my shopping. I knew I shouldn't have sent you."

"Would you rather I worked the mill?" asked Levi. Boots twitched an ear at the sharpness in Levi's voice.

"We don't have the money to replace all the parts you'd break." Ma threw up her hands.

"I did bring home Da's medicine in one piece," Levi pointed out, and he fished the little bottle out of a pocket to set it triumphantly on the table.

"Well," Ma's eyebrows shot up. "I didn't dare hope!" She plucked the vial from its spot and examined it for cracks. Boots waited for her to say "well done" or "good job," but she did not. He laid his whiskers back in disdain and watched her with the inscrutable judgment of a cat.

"Is Da doing better?" Levi asked, sitting forward. His chair gave a sad little groan. The cat readjusted himself cautiously. This human was not a small specimen, and the cat had no faith in the integrity of this chair.

"As well as can be expected." Ma's lower lip quivered, but she covered it quickly, her scowl returning as fierce as ever as she tucked the medicine vial into a nearly empty spice rack hanging on the wall. "We'll give him some of this with his dinner, and I'm certain it will help."

"The apothecary says to give him two drops in his tea instead of one," Levi selected one of the bruised apples from the ruined basket. "She had to dilute the mixture more than usual. The thyme she uses grows primarily on The Ogre's land, she says, so everyone is having trouble getting enough for their potions and medicines."

"And I suppose she charged us full price? Did you even try to haggle?"

"There was a good deal of glass and valuable medicine in that shop, Ma," Levi answered flatly.

Ma clucked her tongue, but said nothing more. She turned back to a stew she had bubbling anemically in the small, sooty fireplace. Boots rubbed his face against Levi's chest.

"Ma..."

"Hmm?" She didn't turn.

"About Boots..."

"What boots? Did you ruin your boots again?"

"Er-" Levi glanced down at his tattered footwear, then tucked his feet further under his chair. "No, Ma, I mean Boots the cat."

The woman heaved a mighty sigh worthy of a wind goddess. "Fine. Keep him. But I don't want to have to feed him."

"Merwow!" Boots announced loudly. *Madam! I am the finest mouser in this or any other county. You insult me by insinuating that I cannot feed myself.*

The woman turned and gave the orange cat a hard look before a little smile twitched the corner of her lips. "Got some voice on him, eh?"

"That he does," Levi agreed, a faint grin to match Ma's creasing his features. Levi stood, catching Boots up in his arms. As he moved to leave he caught his foot on the leg of his chair and went sprawling. The cat leaped clear with a chirp of surprise, but Levi landed hard on the packed dirt floor with an "Ooof!"

Ma only half turned and rolled her eyes again before focusing on her stew. Levi got to his feet with a grunt, dusting off his britches. He turned to right the chair, and a leg fell off and rolled into a corner. Ma groaned. "Just go, Levi. Go find your brothers and tell them dinner is almost ready before you destroy my kitchen."

"Yes, Ma." Levi set down the chair and it groaned as though it were considering losing its remaining legs. "Coming, Boots? I'll show you around." He led the way out the front door which was propped open to let in the day.

"Mer, yow," said Boots as he trotted after his new friend, equal parts alarmed and impressed at the young man's ability to fall down and break things at the same time. He knew humans to be clumsy creatures, but this one seemed to go above and beyond. The cat might ordinarily have rubbed against Levi's legs as they walked, but he suspected this would only result in more tripping and him getting stepped on, so he kept well clear.

Boots enjoyed the smell of hay and animals and cornmeal which settled over the dusty yard. There was a low, stone millhouse across the yard, where two oxen were yoked to walk around and around in circles all day, grinding corn and wheat into meal. The cat spotted fat bags of flour waiting to be loaded into a cart for market.

To the right of the millhouse stood a barn, which looked in poor repair, though the beams still stood strong, and the roof was in one piece. The cat could already scent all the mice hiding inside, and his mouth watered. The foolish little creatures thought themselves safe and they were in for a rude surprise indeed. Boots resolved to stay at least long enough to help these people clear up their rodent issues. He flared his whiskers in anticipation.

"What on earth is that?" A voice boomed.

"Why does everyone keep asking me that? Clearly this is a cat. His name is Boots, and he's mine," Levi said.

The cat looked around to see another human approaching with three sacks of flour draped casually over one massive shoulder.

Boots' eyes went wide, and he tilted his head back to take in this new specimen. He had thought Levi tall and muscular enough, but this new human was far beyond anything the cat had seen. The giant had dirty blond hair a few shades darker than Levi's, and the same sun-creased features. Boots guessed this one to be older than Levi, and he could smell the familial blood they shared. Brothers, most likely.

The enormous human tossed the flour sacks into a waiting wagon as though they weighed nothing. He suspected this human could crush a cat with his bare hands if he had a mind to.

Boots stuck up his tail and strutted around, sniffing the dusty yard as if he hadn't noticed the human behemoth. It was best not to let large creatures know you were intimidated.

"What do you want, Levi?" the huge man asked, going to fetch more bags from the stack beside the millhouse.

"Ma says that dinner is almost ready," Levi followed his sibling and pulled a flour bag onto his own shoulder. As soon as it rested there several stitches burst open at one corner, leaking yellow corn flour all over the back of Levi's shirt and the ground.

Boots flattened his ears in dismay as he watched the lazy stream of powder fall to the dirt. Levi spun and looked down, spotting the trail he'd left and gritting his teeth.

"Give that here," grumbled the giant brother, snatching the bag from Levi, as though further contact might cause the flour to burst into flame. "I don't need your help. I'll finish up here and go inside. You go find Brodie."

"Right. Fine." Levi's shoulders slumped. "Where do you suppose Brodie is?"

"Where do you think?

Boots glanced into the millhouse, where the pair of oxen circled their wide, stone mill wheel, grinding away. This big man was like one of those pullers. Huge, dull, and unambitious. Boots turned to follow Levi again.

"Don't mind my brother," Levi said to the cat. He walked around the mill, leading the way behind the squat barn. "He's not so bad, really."

For an ox, Boots kept pace. He could hear the mice in the barn smelling him and running for their lives. He grinned and couldn't stop his tail from giving a few satisfied swishes. Let the mice tell their friends and family that a new cat was on patrol. It wouldn't save them.

Levi and Boots rounded the barn. Behind it, a few old barrels sat in disrepair beside a stack of straw bales covered in canvas. Boots wondered why they were back there, glancing at a broken wagon wheel that leaned beside the straw. Before he could look at Levi and meow his curiosity, motion behind the bales caught his attention. He trotted ahead of Levi to find two more humans, a male and a female, wrapped in one another's arms, faces pressed together in a kiss. They didn't seem to notice Levi or the cat, distracted as they were by grabbing at each other's body parts.

Boots flattened his whiskers. Human displays of affection were bizarre at best and these two were especially enthusiastic in every moment of it.

Levi leaned against the straw bales and a sly grin spread across his face. Seconds later the bales toppled, seemingly on their own, falling towards the lovers and sending them staggering. "Hey Brodie. What are you up to?" Levi raised a thick eyebrow, peering around the man to see his female companion, who blushed and swatted at her skirts in a futile attempt to straighten them. "Good evening, Mari."

"Hello, Levi," the girl said. Even the cat could appreciate that Mari was a comely country lass, with a sturdy build, fair face, and proud hips. She was the sort that all the male humans chased.

"What do you want?!" snapped the man, furiously tucking his shirt into his britches. Though he was clearly country-bred as well, judging by his tan-lines and lean muscles, even the cat could tell he was decidedly handsome by human standards. His face was chiseled, his hair a shining gold. His eyes were a merry, dancing blue that the cat was certain charmed any female who looked into them. Mari seemed loath to tear her own gaze away.

"Ma sent me to get you, Brodie. It's time for dinner."

The handsome man grumbled as he reached for the woman's hand as if to lead her away. "Leave off. I'll come to dinner when I'm good and ready."

Levi folded his arms. a cheeky grin flickering on his lips. "If I leave now, I might tell let slip to Ma what her son was doing behind a barn with Miller Stanton's only daughter."

"You wouldn't." Brodie blanched, and Mari glanced around as though she feared a parent might be hiding in the corn field, ready to box her ears or whatever it was that human parents did to their unruly young.

"I wouldn't on purpose, of course." Levi's little smile didn't waiver. "But you know me, Brodie. I'm a bad liar, and I might just let something slip. With my luck it'll be right when Ma is in a foul mood."

"Curse you, you rat!" He turned from Levi and gave Mari a quick kiss. "I'll see you soon."

"Good day, Mari." Levi dipped his head respectfully to the young woman.

"Good day, Levi," she smiled prettily, her cheeks dimpling. "Fine looking cat you have there." She kissed her fingertips, pressed them to

Brodie's lips and walked off towards the back fields with just enough sway to her hips to keep both the human males watching her.

When the cat decided this ogling had gone on long enough, he gingerly bit Levi on the ankle. The man looked down questioningly at the cat, who butted his calf. *We have a task, remember?*

"When did you get a cat?" Brodie straightened his shirt and finger combed his mane of sun colored hair out of his face. While Levi's hair stuck up at odd angles, Brodie's fell perfectly into place as though by magic. Boots wondered how this sibling could be so graceful while the other broke chairs just by sitting on them.

"I found him this afternoon" Levi said.

Brodie frowned at Boots for a moment, then let the matter drop. Having straightened himself up sufficiently, he strode off around the barn, Levi and Boots in tow. "Not a word to Ma," Brodie muttered as he passed his brother. Levi made a crossing motion over his heart, though his eyes flashed with mischief.

~~~~~

Boots found dinner in the Miller household to be a pleasant affair. As much as Ma fussed about having to feed Boots, she turned a blind eye when Levi, and even his brothers, dropped tasty morsels.

The mysterious "Da" Levi spoke of remained locked away in his little room. Occasionally Boots could hear someone coughing behind the rickety, wooden door. Whenever this happened, everyone in the family stopped moving, tense, until the coughing subsided.

It seemed that Levi was just as much of a disaster around the dinner table as he was everywhere else, and Boots suspected that half of the treats that fell his way were not intentional.

When the meal was finished, Levi stood carefully, looking down to address the cat. He patted his leg with his fingertips and headed for the door. "Come on then, Boots. Bed time."

Boots trailed at the man's heels into the cool dusk. He wondered why Levi did not follow his brothers to the rickety stairs that ran along the outside of the house and clearly led to their room on a upper floor. Ma and Da seemed to sleep in the large bedroom downstairs. The one with the closed door, from which the coughing had emanated.

Levi led the way across the sandy yard to the barn with its aging walls and sturdy beams. Inside Boots could hear oxen moving in their stall. There was another animal as well. Her big voice boomed with excitement. ***Levi! Levi!***

The cat had met a few horses before, but never got too close. Any animal with clubs for feet deserved their space. Still, this horse was shut behind the door of her stall, so her deadly limbs could not reach him. "Hello, Molly." Levi hurried to pet the horse on her thick neck. Her coat was a pale blue roan, and her mane and tail were so light that they were almost white. The cat guessed she must have been a gorgeous animal in her prime, but old age had reduced her beauty somewhat. She was greying, over-plump, and her upright ears were filled with tufts of fluffy fur. Her eyes were intelligent and bright ,and she watched the cat with interest.

"Here we are, Molly. This is Boots. He's our new friend," Levi introduced as he fed the horse some molasses grain from an open barrel beside her stall.

Hello, horse, said the cat.

Hello cat, said the horse.

So—Boots bumped his head against Molly's soft nose—*this human...*

This human, agreed Molly, blowing her warm breath all over him. *He is a good human, if a bit clumsy.*

Levi had turned to a bale of hay sitting beside the stall door. Rather than open it with the knife that was hanging from a peg, the young man tucked his knee into the hay and tugged the strings away, opening the bale like a fan. *Does he live in this barn?* Boots asked. *Not in the human house?*

He does. The horse dipped her head to eat as Levi tossed two flakes of hay into her wooden feeder. She took a big mouthful and huffed out the chaff. Levi chuckled fondly and patted the horse's neck again, then walked away into the dimness at the other end of the barn. He lit a lantern there, and the cat followed, watching his new friend apprehensively. He wasn't certain how Levi would do with fire. Levi was careful to light the taper over a large barrel of water, then he closed the lantern securely and set it down beside the barrel.

"Here we are, Boots." Levi spread his arms to indicate the room which Boots guessed had been an animal stall converted to a living space for him. There was a low bed at one end below the loft, as well as a small table, a desk, and two stumps as chairs. The table had wide, thick legs, and its surface had seen many spills and stains. All in all, the space was cozy, but Boots wondered again that the human did not stay in the house with the others of his kind. "Mew?" Boots asked.

Levi let his arms fall to his sides and smiled ruefully. "I know. It isn't much. As my brothers and I grew, we got too big to all fit into the bedroom in the house. I, as the youngest, was moved to the barn. I suppose it was really because I tend to..." he paused, considering his words. "I tend to make messes."

"Meow," agreed Boots, twitching his tail as he showed himself around. The place was well tended and only smelled faintly of animal dung and hay. For a cat it was certainly suitable, even if it seemed a strange spot for a human.

"I might have had the loft—" Levi pointed upwards as he sat at his desk, pulling out a few pieces of paper from a slot at the front. He spoke to the cat as he might to another human. Boots swished his tail in appreciation and leaped nimbly onto the desk. "But I don't do well with ladders." Levi tidied his papers. "Look at this, Boots," he gestured to an ink well, beside which sat a wood handled pen and a few short charcoal pencils. "Try to knock that ink over. Go on," Levi challenged.

The cat eyed the ink well dubiously, but already had the undeniable feline urge to swat it with a paw and send it skittering across the desk surface. This notion warred with the equally powerful desire never to do as he was told. So, by way of compromise, Boots crouched down and rubbed his head against the ink well. To the cat's surprise, it barely budged.

Levi laughed and scratched the top of Boots' head, making the cat stand up tall. "It's weighted and wider on the bottom than ordinary ink wells. Even I have a hard time spilling it." The human looked so pleased with himself that the cat was obliged to swat him in the face with his tail. "See, Boots," Levi went on, taking several pieces of paper with drawings on them from a drawer. "I'm designing all sorts of things that are safer to use. If I'm ever going to be any help around here at the mill, I need to be able to handle things without breaking them. Da won't be around forever and..." the man's exuberance left him in a rush, and his shoulders sagged. He looked into Boots' yellow eyes and sighed.

The cat stared back and blinked once before washing a forepaw and wiping his muzzle. When Levi spoke again his tone was determined. "Of course, Da will live a good while yet. I got him new medicine and all. It'll give me some time to implement my designs. I've had a few of these since I was young, but I think I've started to refine them, and soon we'll have money to try them."

Boots moved on to cleaning the other paw as the human chattered away, showing the animal one picture after another. They were all nonsense to Boots. Cats don't have much interest in things that come in only two dimensions, and Boots was growing eager to be about his new mouse catching duties. Of course, he would not show it. Instead, he washed all four paws meticulously and picked his claws with his teeth to ensure that they were battle ready.

Levi sketched on a fresh piece of paper for a while. He dripped a great deal of ink and smeared it with hand and sleeve, but still seemed pleased enough with the results. When he finally retired to his sturdy bed and was snoring lightly, the cat went about his deadly business.

Boots caught five mice that night, and one vole. He left the plumpest of the mice on the foot of Levi's bed as a gift and consumed the rest with gusto. Then he sat on the wall of the horse's stall and tidied himself up, feeling full and pleased.

Good hunt? asked Molly.

Boots stretched languidly, extending his claws and plucking at the wood of the stall. *The mice will spread word of the mighty new hunter who patrols the barn, and my efforts will become more difficult, but I enjoy a challenge,* the cat said with a grin, before retiring to a hay bale for a nap before morning.

As the pale fingers of dawn threaded their way into the dusky blues of the night sky like a lover combing their beloved's hair, a distant morning bell began to toll, and the cat stirred.

He turned to Levi, who slumbered on like a useless lump. Levi was not an easy sleeper, and he had turned himself all around so that one arm hung out over the side of the bed and the other was somehow propped at an odd angle behind his head. His face was smooshed down into his pillow, and one leg hooked over the foot of the bed at an angle. Yet he slept on. As the cat strode over to get a better look at this lazybones. He noted that there was a shallow lip around the bed so Levi could not easily fall out. *Clever enough you might almost be a cat*, Boots mused. *Almost.*

With a hop, Boots was atop Levi's still form, balancing expertly. The man had twisted and turned so that the blankets were all wrapped around him, but Boots picked between them and avoided the young man's other leg, which was tucked against his chest, before reaching Levi's face. Boots planted a paw firmly on Levi's cheek and sang his most proud and pure note. "MEEEOW!"

The youth woke with a start and was momentarily trapped in the net of his own making as he struggled against the blankets. Boots bounced out of the way, pleased that his technique had yielded such quick results. Tugging free of his bonds at last, Levi blinked at the cat, who now sat imperiously between the man's legs.

Levi looked around his little room, rubbing at his chin. The hair on his head was a mess of alarming proportions, and Boots was certain that if his Mama cat could have seen Levi, she would insist on grooming him herself. "Mi," he proclaimed in disgust.

"Are those the morning bells?" Levi listened, letting his hands fall to his sides. "Gods, I never wake up on time to hear the bells! Ma won't believe it. Thank you, Boots." He gave Boots three, good, full-body pets before swinging his legs over the side of his bed. Boots present from the night before was flung to the floor when the human wakened so vigorously. Levi's bare feet made contact with the mouse. "Ach! Uhm... oh..." Levi reached down and picked up the fat, lifeless creature by the tail. "This... is this from you, then?"

Boots puffed up his chest and spread his whiskers with pride.

"Well, thank you so much," Levi said, a thin smile twitching his lips. "I will just... treasure this outside, shall I?" He hurried to the door of the barn for a few moments and returned without the mouse. "It was lovely. Thank you, Boots."

The cat grinned all the wider, twitching the end of his tail. He could get used to this life. No human had ever showed him this level of attention and kindness.

Levi moved about, getting dressed and pulling on his bedraggled boots in a haphazard manner that made the cat wonder how the human got anything done. Levi clucked his tongue in disgust as he reached inside one boot and his hand came right out through the sole. He pulled it on as grimly as a soldier accepting his fate. "Maybe today I'll go into town and find someone who can repair these cheaply. Don't tell Ma."

"Mew," agreed Boots, following as his new friend headed for the house., The sole of his boot slap-slapped.

~~~~

The brothers returned from town late in the evening with good news. They had managed to sell their wheat flour to the baker for a good price, though Boots could tell Ma thought they could have gotten more. The best news of all was that they had secured the baker's business, so he would use their flour in his delicious cakes and breads.

Boots gathered that this too was a good thing. Brodie and Fergus had even used some of their freshly acquired credit to bring back sweets for the family. Boots was allowed to lick a bit of buttery frosting from a plate after dinner.

The only sadness that prevailed was that Da was unable to join his family for the meal. He had "taken a turn" and decided to lie down for the rest of the evening. "Let me bring him a piece of cake," Levi begged. "Please, Ma. I'll be so careful! I'll give it to him and leave right away. I won't have a chance to break anything or knock anything down."

Ma was in the best mood Boots had seen her in. She had even poured herself and her two elder sons some wine from an aged-looking bottle. None was offered to Levi, nor did he ask for it. Boots had been kicked by enough drunken humans to be glad of this.

"Alright. In and out. Be careful." Ma handed a plate with a small piece of cake to Levi, who took it as though she had offered him spun glass and precious jewels. He rose with meticulous slowness and headed for the little bedroom, Boots following on his heels.

Da's room was dimly lit, the walls close and the ceiling low. It reminded Boots of a cave he'd been forced into during a particularly bad rainstorm. Boots stuck close to Levi's feet. He didn't like the smell of this room: the odor of long sickness, herbs, and human sweat. He put his ears back, but soldiered on.

The only furnishings in the room where a small nightstand and a wide, low bed. Boots could make these out well enough, though the lighting was poor. Someone had hung a blanket over the window so not even the sunset could shine through to illuminate the figure wrapped in blankets on the bed. "Da?" Levi asked in a whisper, squinting.

At first there was no sound but labored breathing. Then a few hacking coughs rattled the air and Levi moved nearer, obviously concerned. "Da, I brought you some cake. I don't know if you could hear, but Brodie and Fergus did well in town. We have the baker's contract!" He inched nearer to the bed and set the plate on the nightstand with the gentleness of one settling a fragile babe.

"Levi," the man on the bed rasped. "Come here for a moment, son."

Levi hesitated, no doubt remembering his mother's warnings. Boots could hear Ma laughing jovially in the next room. The sounds seem to decide the young man as he sat down gingerly on the edge of the bed and took his father's withered hand in his two strong ones. Boots jumped up to join them, nestling himself into Da's armpit and purring encouragingly. "What is it, Da?" asked Levi. Do you need me to fetch your medicine?"

"No, no," the man spoke words that were half coughed from between chapped lips. "I wanted to speak to you before I... before I can't speak any more. Wanted to tell you—" His body convulsed with a fresh bought of hacking. Boots snuggled closer so as to be as comforting as he could. Levi glanced towards a cup of water sitting beside the cake on the nightstand, clearly weighing his desire to fetch it with the certainty that he would only spill it. Before he had to make up his mind, Da collected himself and went on. "I wanted to tell you a few things, son, but I think there is one, most important thing you should know about yourself."

Levi leaned closer, concern bringing his brows together again and forming a furrow between them like a little scar. "About me, Da?"

"Yes. You should know before I send you out into the world unprepared. Your Ma doesn't want me to tell you, but I must."

"What?" Levi asked more urgently, both hands now gripping his father's.

"Before you were born, when your Ma and I were a young couple, just starting out as millers, and she was pregnant with Fergus, an old peddler woman came by. The woman asked for shelter from the rain, which we gave her gladly. Though the house was not yet finished, it had a roof and walls to call our own and a fire to warm us." Da's voice grew surprisingly steady, as though his desire to tell the tale gave him strength. "The woman was an interesting person, indeed. She told us many stories of her travels and shared with us that she was a magic worker. One of the few left in the kingdom. Ma was skeptical, but I believed her. Maybe I could sense the magic." The old man gave his son's hands a weak squeeze, and Boots nuzzled his nose against their fingers. "I asked the mage woman for a blessing for our child. That he might be born big and strong, so as to help us work the mill. Your mother scoffed and said she should also like him to be handsome so that he could find a good wife. The magic woman said that, for a fee, she could see that our first son would be strong, our second handsome."

Levi's breath seemed to catch as he stared at his father with an intense gaze of deep blue. "And your third child?"

"The mage told us we must not bear a third child. She said that too much magic in one place is unpredictable and this magic would rebound upon the third child and curse him. I did not understand at the time. I'm not certain I understand now." Da looked so wan and lost that, were it not for his raspy breathing and the occasional blink, Boots might have thought him already dead.

Finally the man pressed on. "I paid the woman, though Ma only laughed. Of course after that we had two fine sons, just as the woman had promised. Fergus, the uncommonly strong and Brodie, the astonishingly handsome. Then Ma became pregnant with you. There was nothing we could do; the mage woman was years gone, never heard of by us again. Ma assured me that it was all just a story, anyhow. It was coincidence that Fergus was growing so tall and tough and that little Brodie was already the talk of the village for his looks. And then you were born, Levi, as you are. Cursed."

"Cursed?" Levi rocked back a bit and his brows rose, then creased with uncertainty. "What are you talking about, Da?"

"We didn't understand it right away, but soon it became evident that you were plagued with ill luck that could not be cured." Da's watery eyes searched his son's. "So there. You see. I had to tell you, so you could understand. So you would not have to face the world not knowing any longer."

Levi took a long breath and said nothing for some time. He even ignored Boots when the cat batted at him with a paw, trying to bring him back to reality. Finally, when it seemed that Da might have fallen back asleep, Levi whispered, "Da, I... I've always suspected something like that might be going on, but I thought I was mad for thinking of it. That curses were only in stories, but now...now I know for certain. The way I am...." He exhaled a breath his shoulders going slack, as though this revelation had hauled a great weight from them.

Boots licked a forepaw and thought he himself might be angry if he found out all his siblings received special blessings and he didn't. Then again, mama cats would certainly know better than to make deals involving magic.

"You suspected?" For the first time the old man looked incredulous, cocking a bushy eyebrow.

"Well, yes," Levi admitted, shrugging. His voice was solemn, perhaps a bit sad, but not defeated. "I have never met anyone as clumsy as me. I break things just by standing near them. I have never successfully climbed a ladder. I once managed to trip while sitting down."

Da laughed, a choking, rusty sound. Boots watched Levi's face. The cat wondered if he should have guessed this as well. Sometimes even the animals spoke of magic. A long ago and far thing that was whispered of, but no one took seriously. The old ones, such as the turtles, claimed to have seen magic, but there was little proof, and Boots might have scoffed as any skeptic would. Not this time. No one had as much bad luck as Levi seemed to without something being afoot.

Da watched his son with quiet, smoky eyes, deep in consideration of his unlucky offspring. Levi's face was just as lost in thought. Boots thought if he meowed just then, he could startle both humans at once. Finally, Levi spoke again, brows deeply furrowed. "Da... do you suppose that the woman who gave you the blessings and the curse is still alive somewhere?"

"Oh, son," Da shook his head jerkily. "I looked for her when you were young. You were toddling around destroying everything in your wake, and your Ma was on constant vigil to keep you safe. I searched far and wide, but already the magic was gone from our land. I couldn't find anyone who had even a scrap of magic in them to help you."

"The Ogre has magic—"

"*No*, son. Not The Ogre."

Boots pricked up his ears. This was a new word, "ogre". He wondered what sort of creature it might be.

Since he came to our land, he has been nothing but dangerous to any who approach him. Our own king dares not oust him from the castle he stole."

Levi's expression changed again. This time Boots could almost see the gears working behind the young man's eyes. Machinations whirring into being. "But Da, if I was cured of my bad luck, I could help you around the mill! Fergus and Brodie wouldn't have to do all the hard work, and they wouldn't be so grumpy all the time. Think of it, Da!"

"I am." The man scowled, deep creases forming on his wan face and around his sunken eyes. "I am also thinking of my son being slain by The Ogre's minions before he even reaches that castle. No, Levi, you must not—" His words fell away into a fit of coughing. His eyes watered and his whole body shook. The cat was obliged to scoot out of the way. Between bouts of hacking, the man tried to squeeze out a few more words as his son looked on with concern and uncertainty. "Levi, I need to tell—this mill—your brothers—"

Ma burst into the room like a soldier breaching a wall mid-battle. Clearly, she had heard Da's desperate coughing. "OUT, Levi!" she snapped.

Levi stood and shuffled from the room with as much speed and care as he could manage. He slammed his shoulder into the door frame but did not seem to notice. Boots trotted at his heels. As much as the cat pitied the old man on the bed, he preferred the lively, if unlucky, company of the son.

Once outside the room, Levi was faced with his two brothers, who stared at him as though the coughing they could all hear behind the door was their youngest sibling's fault. Levi bent and scooped up Boots, then left without a word to Brodie and Fergus.

Boots was carried across the yard towards the barn. Levi was marched, obviously lost in his own thoughts, not looking where he was going. By the time he reached his little room the human had tripped and nearly fallen three times, and somehow managed to kick over a bucket of water and clunk his head on a low-hanging beam that should have been easily avoidable.

Levi plopped down on his bed, little noticing the pink bump forming on his brow and making no effort to pick up the spilled water bucket.

What's the matter? Molly lifted her head over the stall wall and watched the human with concern.

Da explained some things, the cat said from his position still cuddled in Levi's arms. Boots gave the horse a quick overview of the situation.

Hmmmm, I see. The horses bobbed her head. *Magic at work. I once knew a horse who swore there was still a bit of magic in the land. Claimed he could smell it.*

The cat yawned and cuddled down into Levi's arms, closing his eyes. *Yes, well, I wasn't the least bit surprised to learn it was magic all along. You know how humans are? My mother cat said that a human will always serve himself, and in the most complicated of ways. They never think anything over first.*

The horse let out a snort and Levi jumped, looking up for the first time and smiling wanly towards Molly. The horse twitched her ears forward. *I've heard that cats are the same way*, she said.

Boots opened one eye lazily to glare at Molly. *Just because we can achieve more than most animals doesn't make us self-centered. We simply know ourselves and what we are capable of. Just because we can leap farther doesn't mean we don't look where we might land.*

Molly wrinkled her velvety nose. *Speak for yourself, Boots. I have seen some very foolish cats.*

Boots opened his other eye, grinning slyly. *And I've seen some very intelligent horses...once. A long while back.*

Molly stamped a rear hoof, but Boots could tell that she was only pretending to be angry. One thing was true of most of the horses Boots had met in his travels; they all had an excellent sense of humor.

"What do you think...?" Levi spoke, startling the two animals. They looked at him in silence for a moment, wondering if he had somehow been able to interpret their conversation. That was nonsense, of course. It was a rare human who tried to understand the speech of beasts, and none could fully master it. "Da said it was magic that made me so accident prone. So magic could undo it, right?" He looked from cat to horse as if for an answer.

Molly stared back with her big, chocolate-brown eyes, and the cat began purring and snuggled more securely in Levi's lap. Levi seemed to take this as all the answer he needed and went on speaking. "I might go to try to see The Ogre right now, but I can't leave the mill. Not with Da so sick. Ma and my brothers might not like to admit it, but one day this mill will be partly mine. When I was young, my brothers and I asked him if Fergus would inherit because he's the eldest. Da said he could never bring himself to divide us like that, so one day he would leave the mill to all three of us so we might run it together and look after Ma. Perhaps once Da is better and everything is settled, I can see about going to visit The Ogre. Then we won't need to spend the money on expensive parts for the mill." He nodded to himself, then to each of his four-legged companions.

Going to see The Ogre? Molly cocked her head. *Even I know that is a bad idea.*

How bad could he be? asked the cat.

I don't know, but I suspect our Levi will not be able to face him.

Levi sat down on the stump before his desk and pulled out his pen and un-tippable ink well. He selected three sheets of paper and began to draw. The cat leaped onto the desk and watched as the nonsense lines arched gracefully across the pages. "I know what you're thinking," Levi said, dipping his quill again. "How does he do this without stabbing himself in the eye with the pen?"

Boots quirked one side of his whiskers. He hadn't been wondering that until it was mentioned, but now he was interested, ears pricking forward and tail swishing languidly as it hung off the edge of the desk. "Mer mer?"

"Practice," Levi announced with a flourish of the pen that would have sent his ink well clattering to the floor if not for its special design. Boots was impressed, which he demonstrated by sitting on Levi's stack of clean papers and refusing to move.

~~~~~

Night brought rain with it, which would have spoiled Boots' good mood if he hadn't had a nice barn to hunker down in. The mice foolishly came in for cover, creeping through the cracks and crannies to their deaths.

Boots' catch was even better than the night before, and he was feeling optimistic about improving his numbers when he heard something outside. He climbed down from his perch in the loft, depositing his latest kill on a haphazard pile he was making in the middle of the floor. Molly had snorted disgusted protestations and called him a *filthy predator*, but he didn't mind. She turned her backside to him and made her own rude gestures with her tail.

Boots laughed as he trotted past her.

Beyond the open door of the barn, the cat could see little through the downpour. He flattened his ears to think of all the nights he had spent sleeping outdoors on nights like this. As he squinted with disdain at the fat droplets his keen eyes caught sight of something else. A shape, low and graceful, definitely animal, moving about near the house. It was pale grey, almost white, and seemed to flicker—one moment visible, the next gone from view. It paced back and forth below the window on the first floor. Ma and Da's bedroom. The cat tilted his head, trying to get a better look at the creature.

"Mew," he said, very quietly. The sound was muffled by the rain.

Molly's keen ears heard him, and she turned in her stall. *What is it, cat?*

Do you see that animal? Boots asked, gesturing with his nose towards the house.

The horse squinted, then her ears laid flat, and she bared her teeth. *I do know that creature, though it is not an animal as we are. You are young cat. Have you never seen a human die?*

A human die? Boots cocked his head, still watching the shape trot back and forth below the window as though on sentry duty. *What does that have to do with anything?*

You don't know of the gods, do you? I have lived many years and known several owners. My last owner died, and I saw that beast. She flicked her muzzle in the direction of the house. *That is a wolf god of Death.*

A what of the what? Boots huffed. *If that is a god, as you claim, then why make himself visible to me and you?*

The horse tossed her head. *No one knows. Whatever the reason, we **can** see them, and you are seeing one now. The wolf comes alone or with a pack to take the human soul away to the afterlife. Animals know the way, but humans need a guide. The wolves are kind to take them.*

Boots watched for a long time in silence. A second shape joined the first. Now two, flickering, almost transparent wolves stalked below the window. *Could I...could I chase them off?* the cat asked twitchily. He had scared away much larger animals than himself when the need arose. The fur on his back was beginning to stand up, unbidden.

Not these wolves, Molly answered, her dark eyes watchful and sad.

Boots might have considered what would become of his soul if he should die, but an animal never ponders his own death until he is in the jaws of the creature that intends to eat him. *What do you suppose the afterlife is like for them?*

I don't know.

Why do gods take them?

Someone has to. The horse blew out a gust of warm air, clearly growing weary of the conversation. Horses were good indicators of when someone should be afraid, so Boots sat, relaxed and watchful.

And the humans don't see the wolves?

Not until after they die.

Huh. Boots wrapped his tail neatly around his feet. He could sit deathly still when it suited him. He might have been mistaken for a statue cat.

Finally, something stirred. Behind the closed shutters a white light shone through the cracks. Not the tentative, orange light of a candle; this was something else. The light began to pour out through the cracks in the shutters like molten silver. Molly made an annoyed sound and swished her tail. *It would have been much easier if the silly humans had left the window open.*

Boots didn't blame them for closing it. No use letting rain in. Horses, he knew, favored rain. Another reason to doubt their sanity.

The white light slithered out, pouring to earth, then rising again like a cloud of steam. The wolves stood back and watched intently, ears cupped forward, plumed tails still. With aching slowness, the white vapor formed itself into a shape. The figure of a human, though without detail or face. The cat couldn't even tell if it was male or female, and it had no smell at all. Come to think of it, neither of the wolves had an odor either.

This made the cat edgy. Everything had a smell. To encounter a creature that did not was like meeting someone with a blank hole where their face should be.

The human shape put one hand on each of the wolves' heads and they took off running, much faster than animal or human could ever run. The cat trotted to the edge of the doorway, just clear of the rain, trying to see as the person made of white light and the two wolves vanished from view. He thought he heard the faint sound of joyous laughter, and all three were gone. Boots turned to the horse once more. *That's it?*

That's it. She nodded, then lowered her head to fall back to sleep where she stood.

The cat wrinkled up his nose and huffed. They hadn't been all that impressive really, those wolves. Cats were far more special. Boots sat down and groomed for several minutes to settle himself before returning to his hunt.

~~~~

The next day was chaotic. All of the humans were very upset and rushing around, or sitting down with their heads in their hands. The cat was accidentally stepped upon several times, and he eventually retreated to the barn and sat in the rafters. He reflected, as he sat, on his time as a kitten. One of the old cats had died and the clan was obliged to eat the corpse before it was of no use to anyone. Humans were not so practical. Da's body had to be taken out of the house and swaddled in canvas. A special cart draped in black fabric came to collect him.

They bury the bodies, Molly watched the proceedings from her stall.

What? Why? Boots asked.

I don't know. Perhaps they believe there is some badger god in the earth that will take the body away? Molly blew the chaff from her breakfast hay out of her nostrils.

Humans are very strange. Boots shook his head. *What do horses do with their dead?*

Leave them be, of course. They will return to the grass to nourish it, and the predators will eat the meat so the rest of the herd may live.

Practical, Boots affirmed, letting his tail hang down as he watched the house. The special carriage that bore Da away had left, and things seemed to have quieted down.

Hmmmm, Boots mused. *I do feel bad for poor Levi. He loved that "Da" person and certainly didn't want him to die. Perhaps I should go inside and sit on his lap, so he feels better.*

Molly tilted her head to look up at the cat with one eye. *That might be wise. I would go myself, if I could get free of this stall, and if horses were allowed into the house.* She laughed at her own joke.

Boots ignored her as he jumped skillfully down from the rafters using another beam, the top of Molly's stall, and an upside-down bucket.

Then he trotted lightly across the yard and paused in the open doorway to the house. While the night had been rainy, the day dawned bright and sunny once more, with only a few threatening clouds on the horizon.

Boots heard the humans speaking in low voices. All four of them were around the table. Brodie had his arm about Ma, whose face was stained with tears. Fergus looked somber but collected, and Levi had his head on his arms and his arms on the table.

Boots picked his target and scampered across to jump easily onto the table. No one seemed to notice so Boots strode up to Levi and butted his head against the human's. "Mer mer?" No response. Boots jammed his wet nose between Levi's fingers, "Mer raaah!" he announced. *I am here!*

Levi raised his head and looked at Boots with blue eyes rimmed red and welling with tears. Still, he reached out and petted the cat's head. "Hello, little pal." He straightened slowly. Boots took up the space where Levi's head had rested at once, butting fervently at Levi's arms to cheer him up. What could be better comfort than such a fantastic cat? Boots reasoned.

It seemed to work a bit, and even Fergus reached over and gave Boots a quick pat.

"What now, Ma?" Brodie asked, his voice shaky. "What of the mill?"

"I expect your father left it to you boys," sniffled Ma, "as he always said he would."

"It won't be the same without Pa," Brodie said.

"We'll manage," Fergus's tone was gruff, clearly trying to hide the emotion in it. "Don't worry, Ma. We'll all take care of you."

"Yes, of course we will, Ma," Levi held out the hand he was not using to pet Boots and clasped Ma's.

Ma burst into tears and Brodie held her tighter. Fergus followed suit.

Soon the whole family had wet faces again, and Boots was obliged to go from person to person, rubbing against arms and swishing his tail in faces to offer his condolences. Cats did not mourn in the same way as humans, but he understood their sadness. The cat who had died when he was a kitten had been a wise elder, and well loved by the clan, so all were sad to see him go. But, of course, they were also practical.

Little work got done at the mill that day, and no one seemed worried over it.

Mostly they sat at the table, ate, drank strong smelling drinks (except Levi who had water and milk with herbs in it) and talked about Da. Times they had all gone fishing as a family (Levi had fallen in the water). Ma spoke of how she and Da had met as lovestruck youngsters in mill country. Fergus shared a time he and Da had spent the whole night awake watching falling stars after the rest of the family had fallen asleep.

Boots noticed that quite a few of the stories also included Levi disturbing the activities with his bad luck, and Da having to fix it, or work around it, or rescue his unfortunate youngest. The time Levi had gotten his hand jammed between two mill gears; Levi held up his right palm to show the faint scars were still visible. The time that Levi had tried to work the plow and the straps had come unbuckled. The oxen had run away, and it took all three boys and Da to find them and bring them home after the beasts had eaten a hefty portion of someone else's corn crop. The time that Brodie and Fergus learned to work the mill, driving the two oxen around and around on their little path, and how Levi had stayed inside with Ma to learn to make corn husk dollies. He'd still managed to cut himself with the husks. Even these stories were told with fondness and warm smiles tinged with tears.

When evening finally wrapped its gentle arms over the land, the cat followed his human friend back to his room in the barn, where Levi collapsed onto his bed without even working on his drawings. Levi rolled over, faced the wall, and curled up like a cat himself. Boots hurried over to insert himself into Levi's arms, so that this sad position might become a cuddle pile instead. Levi hugged Boots and buried his face in the cat's thick, fire-orange fur. "I'm going to miss him."

Boots licked Levi's ear.

"I knew he wasn't going to get better, but I kept hoping. Da would never give up. How could he? If *he* gave up that means that I could give up." His eyes appeared, meeting the cat's. Boots allowed the eye contact, even though it put him on edge. "I can't give up, Boots. I own part of the mill now. I have to find a way to make it work."

"Mer mer," Boots agreed and put his paw on Levi's cheek for emphasis.

~~~~~

"The horse?! What, just the horse? Just Molly?"

Boots was sitting on the kitchen table again with the humans all around him, though this time he did not go from person to person giving them the comfort of his magnificent company. Instead, he perched stoically beside Levi, who was the only one who was upset this time.

A tall, lean man in fine clothes had appeared that afternoon. He perched across from Levi on Da's old chair, several papers spread before him. Ma said he was the "lawyer" from town, and he was there to discuss Da's will. The cat was uncertain what any of that meant, but it made everyone hurry to sit around the table again and look anxious.

As the humans discussed the situation, Boots tried to ignore the smell of the stranger. Too clean, like he never lived a life. The oil with which he greased back his grey streaked hair had a distinctive odor as well, like boot polish. The man settled little glasses on the end of his long nose like a bird on a branch.

Boots eyed the pages spread on the table, half expecting to see more drawings like Levi's, but these papers were covered in rows of neat, little markings. "William dictated his will to me some months before his death," the lawyer said, his tone placating.

Boots wondered who William was, but soon decided the lawyer-man must be referring to Da. Perhaps all humans had more than one name, just as Boots had been called "The Orange Kitten" by his mother and was "Boots" now.

The man went on to read out the will in detail. Boots stopped paying attention. He found a small knot in his fur near the base of his tail and spent considerable time combing it free with his teeth until Levi startled him by shouting. Boots had never heard Levi shout, and it made his tail poof out. It took the cat a moment to rally himself and focus in on the conversation.

"You can still stay here, of course," Brodie was saying. "Like Ma. You'll always have a home-"

"I don't want to just 'always have a home'!" Levi snapped. "I was supposed to own part of this mill, just like the pair of you!" He turned to the lawyer and, in the motion, managed to spill not only his cup of water, but Fergus's as well. Levi ignored this, as his enormous brother heaved a sigh and mopped up the spillage. The lawyer snatched the papers clear of the liquid. "You must have read it wrong," Levi told the little man. "I'm supposed to have part of the mill, just like my brothers. Da must have meant to give me Molly as well, as a personal gift because she likes me so much. That's all."

"I'm afraid not, lad," said the lawyer, managing what he must have imagined was a sympathetic expression, but which the cat thought made him look gassy. "Your Da planned on giving the mill to his three sons once. When you were much younger, but a while back, we revised the paperwork."

"But...but why?" Levi sputtered. "Da told me it would be all of us!"

"Levi," Ma said, her tone soothing. Boots shot her a glare as he dodged being swept off the table by Levi spreading his arms in annoyance. "Sweetheart, there's something Da and I never told you—"

"The curse. Yeah. I know." Levi stood up, was too close to the table, caught the edge and toppled the whole thing. Boots dove off just before the table edge hit the floor. Cups went flying, one cracked, though it was made of wood. The lawyer stood blinking, utterly dismayed, the front of his crisp jerkin covered in splattered water and his papers all over the floor.

"LEVI!" Ma shouted. "Settle!" Her tone was so commanding that Boots was reminded of his mama cat and plopped his own backside on the floor. "Da told you about the curse?"

"Wait...curse?" Fergus asked. He and Brodie righted the table as casually as they might a fallen bit of cutlery.

"You two were given blessings, I was saddled with a curse as third born," Levi explained, voice still too loud. The lawyer was backing towards the door, clutching his remaining papers to his chest. "Da told me before he died. I'm cursed with bad luck because I had the *bad luck* to be born last."

The two older brothers took in their youngest sibling, recognition dawning on their faces. Boots saw years of them caring for Levi in their eyes. Of a little brother who broke everything he touched and hurt himself at the simplest tasks. "What blessings are we supposed to have received?" Fergus asked, looking at Ma for confirmation.

Ma was staring at the water-speckled floor, her expression sorrowful and lost.

"Look at yourselves," said Levi frustratedly. "Fergus, you and Brodie both work the mill, but you're twice his size and throw sacks of grain around like they're filled with feathers. And Brodie; haven't you noticed the eyes of everyone in the village follow you everywhere? How the women, and some of the men, practically throw themselves at you?"

Both brothers looked at one another, as though seeing each other for the first time.

"I suppose," Brodie raised his eyebrows, "that it does make some sense, but there's not supposed to be any magic in the land anymore."

"There was when you were young." Ma's voice was tight. She wrung her skirt in her hands, not meeting any of her sons' eyes.

"And if Da knew you were cursed, Levi, it would also make sense that he wouldn't leave you part of the mill. If something happened to us, there would be no way you could run this place by yourself." Fergus folded his massive arms.

"I could!" Levi asserted, clasping his hands and trying to stand still so as not to overturn anything else. Boots walked to his human friend and rubbed his body along Levi's leg to try to settle him. Boots could feel Levi's anger through his skin like a charge of electric energy. It was a foreign and highly unpleasant sensation, but the cat determinedly butted his head against Levi's shin.

"I have all these ideas to make things safer, easier for me—"

"I'd best be going," the lawyer said. He was standing outside the open door and looked as though he had already begun to walk away before deciding he should inform everyone of his departure. "Here is a copy of the will for you. Please, come to my office if you have any questions," the man said, passing Ma a disheveled stack of papers without reentering the kitchen. "I wish you all a good day!" He turned and rushed off, springing onto his gangly horse and cantering out of the yard without a backward glance.

"Now you've frightened the man off with all this curse talk." Clearly Ma was still in a scolding mood. She had her hands on her hips, and her scowl might have convinced a charging bull to back down. Boots wondered if all mothers, mama cats and humans alike, learned to make the same face. He moved to hide behind Levi's legs to be out of Ma's line of sight.

"I know in my heart that Da meant the best for you, Levi. Just as he knew I could not take care of the mill myself if Brodie and Fergus were not here. Da loved you, and wanted you to be safe and happy. You'll always have a home here, a place to stay and family," Ma said.

"I have a horse." Levi spat back. "Da gave me an aged horse who can barely pull a cart. That is what I have!"

"You love Molly," Ma said.

"I also love this mill!"

"It isn't going anywhere," Fergus' voice tinged with impatience. It was clear to Boots that, since the eldest brother had gotten exactly what he expected from Da's will, he did not mind one bit what became of his youngest sibling's share. "Da must have known that Brodie and I will already have enough trouble between us, figuring out how to work things out around here, especially once we get married and have families of our own."

"Well, good for you. At least you'll have something to leave your children. I can give my sons bleached horse bones." Levi glared around at his family with a face like a storm cloud.

Ma clucked her tongue sympathetically, but Brodie smiled, his eyes sparkling with mischief. "With your luck, Levi, you'd have only daughters. Pretty ones."

To Boots' surprise, Levi also cracked a smile before he schooled his face back to a scowl. He was silent, staring at the floor for several minutes before he spoke again, letting his hands fall to his sides. "I...I have to go think about all of this." He stooped down and scooped the cat into his strong arms.

"Take all the time you need," Ma said, granting her youngest son a warm expression at last.

Levi turned to leave and hooked his foot on the table leg. The wood groaned, then snapped. Boots wondered, as he watched the scene play out, if a nail had become loosened, or the wood was beginning to grow brittle with age. The table fell towards the now absent leg with a lurch and everyone let out a collective moan, but no one seemed surprised or even angry as Levi continued his walk towards the door with a mumbled "I'm sorry."

Boots was pleased that they made it across the yard with a minimum of destruction.

Once they were in the barn Levi crossed to Molly's stall and spent several moments petting the horse's face and soft nose. Boots wasn't completely pleased with this, as it meant no one was paying attention to him, but he decided to let it slide for the moment. Levi was very sad after all. The cat clambered out of Levi's arms and onto the man's shoulders were he draped himself like a shawl, tail wrapping around his friend's neck.

When Levi had finished speaking with the horse, he went to his little room, nearly tripping over a hay bale on his way, but managing to catch himself before he tumbled completely. Boots was obliged to dig his claws in a bit, but Levi didn't seem to notice.

Boots was nearly jostled from his human friend's shoulders again as Levi sparked into a flurry of motion. Levi went to the squat dresser in which his clothes were kept. Boots noted, as he clung to Levi for dear life, that all of the dresser handles had been reinforced. Levi pulled the drawer so hard it fell to the floor at his feet. He knelt, gathering up his clothes and tossing them on the bed. Boots continued to cling, watching with concern. *What on earth is he doing?* he asked the horse.

I don't know. He's never done this before. Molly peered over her stall wall to watch as Levi moved with feverish energy.

He emptied the other dresser drawer in the same fashion. Once the clothing was all lumped onto his bed he grasped the corners of his patchy quilt and pulled it all together like a giant, ungainly sack. He tied it decisively at the top and stood back, nodding at his creation. Boots stared. If the human wanted all his things bagged up why didn't he just go fetch a grain sack or two?

Levi moved again, and Boots nearly fell off. He was obliged to swing his tail wildly for balance.

Levi went to his desk and pulled out all his papers. He wasn't careful, and they fluttered everywhere. He scrambled to collect them and a few tore, but he ignored this and settled them all in a pile on top of his desk. He rushed to a nail on the wall, where bailing twine was hanging, and pulled a few pieces free. After several failed attempts, he managed to tie his papers into something approximating a neat bundle. He crossed to the bed again, shook the pillow out of his pillow case, and tucked his pencils, pens, empty ink well, and a corked bottle of ink into it, then tossed it and the papers onto the bed.

He stood back, surveying his strange collection like a farmer looking over a well-tilled field.

Boots decided he might be best served to get off of the madman's shoulders. He jumped to the desk and cleaned a paw, trying to look calm as the human turned and strode over to where Molly's tack was hanging from pegs at the far end of the barn. He took down her halter and lead. He didn't even speak soothingly to Molly as he slipped the halter over her head. He led her out of the stall, and she stood quietly when he dropped the lead.

Boots hopped to the floor and went to stand beside the horse. *Why do you let humans lead you around by the face?* he asked, as he watched Levi rush to his bed and scoop up his strange bundle of blankets and clothes. Halfway to the horse, the knot came loose and everything spilled onto the dusty floor. Levi sighed and knelt to collect it all once more.

Horses have an arrangement with humans. Molly answered Boots' question. *We allow them to lead us, and to use our strength to pull their loads. In exchange they give us a place to stay and food to eat. If we are injured or sick, they take care of us.*

Cats don't need any help from humans, said Boots, who had to dart out of the way as Levi nearly stepped on him when he scrambled to fetch the canister of ink-setting powder, which had rolled their way.

The horse might have retorted, but Levi had managed to collect everything again and tie the bundle once more. He stood and plopped his strange blanket bag onto Molly's back and arranged it so it draped evenly on either side. She turned her head and plucked curiously at the fabric with her dexterous lips.

"There we are, girl," Levi announced, pride in his voice. He went for his pillowcase bag and slung it over his own shoulder. "Come on, Mol, we're leaving."

Leaving? The horse swiveled both ears in his direction.

Levi picked up Molly's lead rope and led her out of the barn into the muted sunlight of a cloudy day, Boots trotting along beside her. He looked up at Levi and tilted his ears to the side. Clearly the human had gone insane.

"Stay here, girl." Levi let Molly's lead fall to the dusty yard, where she remained still and obedient. He dropped his pillowcase bag beside the horse and marched into the house. Boots scurried in after him, his feline curiosity peaked.

For once no one was about in the little kitchen. Levi rushed to and fro, grabbing a loaf of bread, a few pieces of fruit, and a hunk of questionable smelling cheese that made Boots wrinkle his nose. Levi also selected one plate, one wooden cup, and a small skinning knife with a dented blade.

For a moment, the man hesitated, looking at the small collection on the table with uncertainty in his eyes. Boots wondered if humans had etiquette about stealing food. The cat rules on the subject were complicated and had several hundred bylaws regarding sharing, taking, dispensing and hoarding. The young man's gaze was drawn to a few pieces of paper that had drifted into a corner, unnoticed from when the lawyer had visited. Levi's jaw tightened visibly and his eyes flashed flinty grey. He snatched up his food and exited without a word.

Boots rode backwards on Molly's rump, watching the mill grow smaller and smaller. It was not too late for the cat to jump down and scurry back to a home of food, shelter, and warmth. He turned and looked at Levi's back as the human urged Molly into a trot. Levi's shaggy blond hair was still a mess, flopping against his broad shoulders. This clueless, cursed, unlucky man was leading the way to gods-knew-where, to what dangers Boots could only imagine. Perhaps it was time to jump from Molly's back.

Boots remembered the cold grip of the water and a cruel fingers of the boys holding him under. He remembered the feeling of being freed from the bag, of being given a chance to live again, and of cuddling in human arms. This human's arms.

"So then, Boots, you're staying with me?" Levi asked, looking over his shoulder at the cat.

"Mer mer raw," said Boots. *Yes. Yes, I suppose I am.*

Part 3
The Miller's Son

"This was a mistake." Levi was soaked through, and his clothing clung like a second skin. He shivered so badly that his back scraped the ragged bark of the tree he was crouching against, leaving little scratches he knew he couldn't do anything about.

Each day away from home was a fresh disaster. He had made good time at first, knowing he had to outdistance his family. He avoided the village, instead heading down unknown paths that plunged deep into farm country and would eventually lead him north towards larger cities.

He had expected bad luck in his travels, but it still caught him by surprise. He sat glumly in the relative shelter of the tree, failing to stay dry. Since he had left home, it had poured rain every day. His ink bottle leaked, spoiled the pillowcase, and coated everything else that was inside. He'd done his best to rescue his papers, tucking them under the blanket pack on Molly's back, but they soon became damp as well. Levi's boots completely gave up on even resembling footwear, and he was obliged to go barefoot. He'd eaten all of the food he had packed, what hadn't gotten too soggy to consume, and had spent that morning foraging for berries and nuts, of which he had only found enough to fill his hand. He avoided the mushrooms, as he was less certain of them. Da always insisted Levi memorize every berry, and now he understood why.

Without knowledge there was only luck, and Levi's luck wouldn't come to his rescue.

"Brodie was right," Levi mumbled, as he licked the last of the berry juice from his palm. "I won't survive the curse to break the curse."

"Mer mew?"

Levi leaned his head back to look for his cat. Wet hair stuck to his forehead as he caught a flash of fiery orange fur amidst the green. Boots peered down from a sheltered branch cranny. The cat seemed to have a better time staying dry than Levi, but then again, Boots didn't have the bad luck of always sitting in puddles, or having the branches above him shift in the wind to dump collected rain water over his head.

"I need to find something to eat," Levi answered his pet, as though Boots had asked a question. "It's all well and good for you and Molly. You can hunt and Mol can eat the grass, but what about me?"

"Mew," Boots squeaked before his face disappeared from view.

"I can't hunt. You know I can't." Levi tucked his legs up against his chest, trying to get his trembling body under control. "It would be a disaster if I tried. If I used a bow the string would break, or I'd shoot an innocent farmer who just happened to be passing by, or I'd enrage the deer so it would attack me." He looked up again, awaiting Boots' reply. When none came, Levi sighed and rested his chin on his knees.

He could just make out Molly's silhouette moving quietly in the rain as she grazed. He wished he cared as little about the weather as she did. She seemed to enjoy the wet. "I know complaining doesn't solve anything. I've had good ideas about how to solve my troubles in the past. I just need one now. Of course, usually when I think up my ideas it isn't raining on me." He longed for his drawing desk back home. His warm little room with a soft bed. A roof overhead and family to take care of him. Ma would make a creamy mushroom and leek soup, and there would be sweet cornmeal bread to dip in it. Levi's stomach gave a disgruntled growl, and he winced.

Even without table and paper, Levi's mind struck out in the direction of solving each fresh dilemma. He needed food, and shelter that was more substantial than a tree. He had to find these in such a way that he did not sabotage himself with his own bad luck. Perhaps the otter goddess of water and joy could be prevailed upon to help, he mused, as another splash of rain fell onto his head from an overburdened branch. He scooted to a different spot, tucking himself up in the wide tree roots. Maybe the falcon god of hunting would look in on him. Or the rabbit goddess of cunning.

His thoughts of animal gods veered off into consideration of rabbits in general. He knew there were rabbits in the area because he had found plenty of their droppings in his hunt for berries and nuts. He had no hope of hunting the rabbit himself, but perhaps he could find another way. If he could set a snare and get away from it quickly enough so his bad luck would not ruin it, perhaps he could catch a small animal.

Levi stood, grimacing as cold water slithered down his spine. He moved to where he had sheltered his belongings as best he could on the other side of the tree. The twine he had used to tie up his now soggy paper was in one piece and looked sturdy. If it ever stopped raining, he could dry the paper, but for now he had need of the twine. He slipped it free as carefully as he could.

Levi stepped out into the downpour, surrendering to being drenched.

He walked several yards from his shelter-tree to a thick bed of clover, where he had spotted a large number of droppings, and squatted, blowing water from his lips and blinking it from his lashes. His hair flopped in his face, but he pushed it back with a palm and arranged the twine. He had never set a snare before, but he saw it laid out before him in his thoughts as he positioned a whippy sapling and tied a little noose in the twine. This was just like his plans and schemes for the mill, except simple enough that he didn't need to sketch it.

He knew rabbits came out at dusk and that even with the rain they would not be able to resist the lush patch of clover. He had nothing for bait, but hoped the especially lush greenery would be enough to attract a few unwary bunnies.

After some struggle, Levi arranged his snare the way he wanted it and rushed away, not even minding when he tripped over a protruding root and fell face down in the mud. Falling was better than his snare breaking.

Tucked under his tree once again, he tilted his head back, letting his hair fall away from his eyes to see that Boots was still perching in the crook of a thick branch. At least the cat looked comfortable. "Now then, Boots," Levi called conversationally, "about this curse."

"Mi," Boots made a little sound as if to indicate that he was listening, even if he wasn't about to come down.

"This curse needs to be lifted with magic, and the only one who has any magic around here anymore is The Ogre. So, the way I see it, I need to go to The Ogre and ask him to break the spell."

"Mer?" Boots made a harsher sound.

"Da told me about The Ogre. There's a story about him, just like the stories they used to tell about the old gods." Levi began reciting, his father's rolling, husky voice like a song in his memory. "When my Da was a boy there was no Ogre. Those were good days, so they say. Yes, indeed. There was enough magic in the world that everyone could have a little piece, though some people had a good deal more. The animal gods roamed the land, helping the people, or playing pranks on one another. But then The Ogre came. Monstrous and terrible. No one knows where he came from, but The Ogre wanted all the power for himself, and so he stole it away from us, and he stole a castle too. Inside he hid and called the magic to him until there was none left in human hands. The king sent soldiers to banish The Ogre, but because he had all the magic, The Ogre defeated them easily. Now The Ogre lives, to this day, in the castle Carabas, though none have seen him in many years, and all the magic users of old either lost their power completely or left our kingdom behind." Levi finished. The story was warm in his chest even though the rain froze his outsides.

"Mer mer." Commented Boots.

"Yes. I know. No one goes to see The Ogre. He's supposed to be evil and cruel and have horrifying minions. But what if he's not? What if he can be reasoned with? What if he doesn't mind a peasant like me coming to speak to him because I could never do any harm?" Levi paused. The rain water coursing down his body was in serious danger of washing away his resolve as well. "Or, with my luck, one of his minions will kill me before I even get near his castle."

"Mi meow." Boots chirped in probably agreement.

Levi snorted. "You're very encouraging." He caught some water on his hand and flicking it towards the cat, who was perched far too high up for it to reach.

Man and cat sat for some time under the tree. Levi shivered and thought about warm fires, and Ma's soup, and how foolish he had been for leaving home. Boots fell asleep on his branch, and Molly grazed. The rain pelted them all relentlessly. Levi wondered if the crops were alright back home. Would all this rain stress their roots? If there was enough flooding the plants could be washed away and with the new contract from the baker, the mill couldn't stand a bad year for wheat and corn.

He knew that no matter how Ma wept, a part of her, however small, was probably pleased to be rid of her unlucky son. She could use real chairs at the table. She could bring out whatever good dishes remained that Levi hadn't already shattered, and leave a knife on the table while she cooked without worrying Levi might cut a finger off. He looked at the scar at the base of his thumb and winced. He'd managed to do that with a blunt knife, and there had still been blood everywhere.

Brodie and Fergus would recover quickly. They'd spent their lifetime supervising their troublesome little brother. It would be good to have some freedom at last. Levi folded himself up even more tightly, trying to find some scrap of warmth that hadn't been leeched away. Brodie and Fergus would run the mill flawlessly, even without the improvements Levi suggested. They'd buy a newer, better horse, and everything would be well.

A piercing squeal caught Levi's ear through the rain, yanking him from his wallowing. His head snapped up, hair hanging like a soggy curtain in front of his eyes. He scrambled to his feet and rushed from his tree shelter, heading for the patch of clover where he had set his snare, gripping his mother's battered, third-best skinning knife.

When he reached the clover he might have cheered, but clapped his free hand over his mouth as he spotted the plump rabbit struggling in the brush. It was caught in the snare by both a rear and a foreleg. This gave it good potential to break free if it struggled enough.

Levi crept closer, knife bared. He'd never killed an animal before. Certainly he had watched at a distance when Da skinned rabbits and plucked chickens, but he had not been there when Da had done the actual killing.

The little creature struggled and squealed. He looked into its small, dark eyes and sighed. His grip on the knife slackened and he dropped dejectedly to a knee. He couldn't do it. He was doomed to eat nuts and berries until he died, malnourished and mourned only by a horse and an orange cat.

That very orange cat appeared out of nowhere in a flash like fire. Levi had never seen Boots move so fast. The cat streaked across the green and smashed into the snared rabbit in a flurry of fur and yowling. There was a great scrabbling of limbs and Levi could hardly tell what was happening, but a few moments later the rabbit lay still, the cat crouched over its body.

Levi inched nearer, wondering if Boots would claim the catch as his own. Instead, Boots backed away from the rabbit with a look of disdain on his feline features. It was clear that he was not the least bit concerned with his act of violence, but with the rain which now soaked him as well.

With a sneeze and an unhappy yowl, Boots was off again, heading for the shelter tree. Levi laughed, the sound strange in the rain and the quiet. He squatted and freed the rabbit from the snare, careful not to break the twine as it would be useful for future endeavors.

It took Levi some time to skin the creature, and when he finished he thought it was the saddest looking specimen he had ever seen. Twice he dropped it in the mud, but both times he held it out into the rain and washed it clean. He'd mutilated the pelt beyond recognition. It would be useless for selling, but perhaps he could fashion an ugly pouch out of it, if it was ever allowed to dry. He'd also nicked his finger with the knife, but it was dull, so the wound was shallow. Of course, the dullness of the blade made the skinning process all the more challenging.

Boots watched from high in the tree and refused to come down, even when Levi offered him some of the meat.

"You don't need to sulk." Levi addressed the foliage where he thought he saw yellow eyes peering down. "You probably saved me from starving to death, if I can figure out how to cook this rabbit." There was no response. Even as he spoke the fresh kill slipped from Levi's hands again and landed with a "splort" in a mucky puddle. He sighed, extracted it, and held it out into the downpour.

With the mangled rabbit in hand Levi began to consider what he was going to do with it next when the rain became a drizzle, then stopped. Levi let out a sound that transcended ordinary laughter. It was almost a yelp. "Boots! Molly? Do you see this? My bad luck is fighting me so hard it turned into good luck! I needed to clean the rabbit in the rain, so the rain stopped!"

He kicked up his heels in a ludicrous dance he was glad no one except his animal friends could see.

When Levi had finished capering around like a drunken idiot, Boots deigned to join him on the ground. Levi planted his hands on his hips and watched the sun roll out from behind the clouds as if it were waking from a nap.

Riding a gleeful high, Levi returned his focus to his catch. He snagged a handful of leaves from the tree to finish cleaning the rabbit, then he settled it on a stone to set about his adventures in fire starting.

Boots strolled over and sniffed the pink, freshly skinned rabbit with interest and finally helped himself to the little pile of entrails Levi had left out for him. Levi couldn't stop grinning, even when a cloud of black flies homed in on his kill—biting black flies that left Levi with several itchy welts.

Boots stood well clear of them as they buzzed industriously around Levi's head.

"Thank you again for helping me with the rabbit, Boots," he said, flashing the cat an undaunted smile and swatting uselessly at a fly.

With no flint and tinder, Levi made a valiant attempt at starting the fire by rubbing two twigs together, but he knew this endeavor was doomed before it began. He'd only ever heard about this being done, and no matter how he tried, all he succeeded in was breaking a lot of sticks.

Levi tossed down his most recently snapped twigs and glared at Boots, his smile finally faded like smudged charcoal. "I don't suppose you know how to start fires as well as kill rabbits?"

"Mer mer," said Boots, sniffing the rabbit, which was laying across a flat rock. The air was growing humid and the sun seemed over-bright. Levi was damp with rain and sweat as he rocked back on his heels and scowled at the corpse on the rock.

"Alright." Levi exhaled the word as he rose, flexing the kinks from his knees with a grimace. "No fire. It looks like we will have to do something else with our rabbit. We're not giving up."

"Mew mer mer." Boots raised his tail, ears forward as Levi plucked the rabbit from its rock.

"No, you may not eat it. We're going to make better use of it than that, alright?"

Levi took the kill over to the horse who was still grazing as though she had not even noticed the rain had stopped. Molly wasn't thrilled about the dead thing so near her, nor was she thrilled about it hanging from her makeshift saddle bags. She tossed her head and flattened her ears, shifting away in clear protest. Levi followed doggedly until she heaved a resigned sigh and stood still so he could attach the rabbit, dropping it thrice in the attempt.

Levi rested his hand on Molly's flank and wished for a breeze as he struggled to ignore the leaden weariness in his limbs. He felt like a soggy, old rag from his Ma's kitchen, in desperate need of a wash. He raked his fingers through hair that clung in stringy clumps, and closed his eyes.

He had to think of his triumphant return, to imagine himself standing proud and tall as he surveyed all the improvements he had made to the mill. They'd lead to contracts with other bakers—fancy ones in big cities, who would clamor for his finest flour for tarts and pies, rather than to make the coarse country bread from back home. Just as a smile began to work its way onto his lips, the biting flies found him. Molly tossed her head, knocking him off balance, and he fell into a pile of her scat.

~~~~~

The dejected man and his animal friends trudged on, though they did not have to do so for long before Levi spotted a small farmhouse a short distance from the road. Wooden fences in need of repair barely contained a herd of goats, who looked up and bleated curiously at him. Levi smiled, his dire mood lifting when a kid bounded over and swished her little tail, ears pricked forward in greeting. "Alright, Boots." Levi turned and addressed the cat, who was once again astride Molly's rump like a prince on his steed. "Let's ask at this house if we can barter for the rabbit."

"Mew," said Boots, in what Levi chose to believe was approval.

Levi led Molly off the road and down the long, muddy path that led to the house. This farmstead looked a great deal like a smaller version of Levi's own home. The house had thick fieldstone walls painted white in an attempt to make the place look tidier. The roof was well thatched, but in poor condition. It did look better than some of the straw-roofed homes Levi had seen since he left his own community.

The goat pasture ran along the path, and the herd of goats rushed to follow in a clump of curious faces and big, goofy ears. Levi had to stifle a laugh at the kids, who easily fit under and between the slats of the fence, darting in and out as if flaunting their freedom to their parents.

As he drew nearer the house, Levi made out a squat well and a small figure beside it. He squinted. There was a little girl in a dirty brown dress and stained apron sitting in the dirt, playing with what appeared to be a corn dolly and a little goat figure made from twigs. She looked up then and saw Levi, her eyes going wide in alarm. She scrambled to her feet, clutching her toys and shooting glances over her shoulder.

"Whoa," Levi told Molly, who came to an obedient stop. They were still some yards from the house, but he didn't want to frighten the girl further, and he had no idea what his bad luck might do to their little home. "Hello there," he called, raising his hand in greeting.

"M-my Da is out back," the little girl said. She pushed a thick, black braid behind her shoulder as she shifted from bare foot to bare foot.

"That's alright," Levi said, holding his hands at his sides, palms towards the girl to signal he had no weapons. "May I speak to him, or you? I don't mean any harm to you or yours. My name is Levi, and this is Molly and Boots."

The little girl cocked her head to the side, peering around Levi at his horse and— "KITTY!" she exclaimed, dropping her toys. She took a few excited steps towards him but thought better of it. Instead, she balanced forward on her toes as though she might take flight. Her eyes sparkled as she stared at the cat.

Levi plucked Boots from his perch, setting him on the muddy earth and giving him a little nudge towards the child. "Go on, Boots. Go say hello."

The cat shot a withering look towards Levi, which the human was certain was meant to strike his heart with fear. Instead, he just chuckled as the orange cat sidled over to the girl, clearly trying to make it look like this was his own idea. The child's face broke into the most open and earnest smile Levi had ever seen as she dropped to her knees and scooped a long-suffering Boots into her arms. She nuzzled her face against Boots's and the cat looked ready to mutiny, but didn't struggle. Levi let out a breath of relief. He knew Boots was a good cat, but he hadn't been certain how Boots would handle a child after his experiences on the riverbank. The end of Boots' tail twitched with obvious frustration, but he allowed the girl to cuddle and coo.

Levi turned back to Molly and took down the rabbit from her pack, showing it to the girl. "Can I barter with your Da for this?"

The girl looked up, blinking at Levi as though she had forgotten he was there. "Da is in the back woods. He won't be home until dark." She winced. Clearly, she was not supposed to tell him that.

"Well, would you like to surprise him with a fresh rabbit for dinner when he gets home?"

"Who skinned that?" She wrinkled her nose.

Levi's mouth twitched as he attempted to remain serious. Even a small child was judging his rabbit skinning skills. "Never mind that. The meat is still good, and it's fresh caught this morning."

The little girl pursed her lips and wrapped her arms more tightly around Boots, who continued to glare daggers at Levi. "What you want for it?" she asked.

"Do you have any food? Cooked food I mean? I've uh... I've had rabbit every day for weeks and I need something new to eat before I go mad."

The girl looked apologetic. "I'm not s'posed to cook or use the fire."

"Ah. I see." Levi's shoulders drooped. "You don't have any leftovers from your meal?"

"No, ate it all." She hung her head. Then she raised it again, eyes shining. "Wait! I know what you can have. Do you like goat milk?"

"Love it!" Levi brightened. Instantly his mouth began to water, and his shriveled stomach gave an excited grumble.

The girl nodded and let Boots slip from her arms, then rushed into the house. Levi heard her clattering around, and she came back out a few moments later carrying a tin of milk, a wide wooden bowl, and half of a thick piece of bread. She marched up to Levi, clearly having decided to trust him, and thrust her offerings at him. "Rabbit, please." Her expression was the serious one of a seasoned trader, and Levi had to fight not to laugh again.

He handed over the creature, and the little girl looked it over with a practiced eye. "I suppose it isn't too terrible."

"Thanks," Levi muttered in reply, plopping cross-legged onto the ground, watched keenly by goats the entire time. The herd studied Levi even more scrupulously than the girl had.

Levi poured the creamy milk into the bowl and dipped the bread hunk into it, allowing the milk to soak in. Then, finally, blessedly, he sank his teeth into the first proper meal he'd had since he left his home. The milk spilled down his chin and Levi didn't care. The thick, seedy bread might have been stale, but the milk softened it perfectly. His stomach sang a gurgling hymn of joy.

Boots sidled over and peered up at his human friend. "Meow!"

Levi, whose eyes were half closed with pure ecstasy, looked around at the cat and sighed. He dipped the bread again and slid the bowl of milk towards Boots with his foot. Boots swished his tail in appreciation and dug into his own meal.

Levi finished off the bread and drank down the rest of the milk from the tin the girl had brought, as Boots lapped up what remained in the dish.

The girl dropped the rabbit off in the house and returned to take in the scene as though she were studying a strange creature that had wandered into her field. She squatted, dark eyes intelligent and intrigued. Levi handed back the bowl and tin as Boots sat down to wash his face and paws.

"Thank you." Levi meant it with every fiber of his being.

The girl took her things back and looked up at him, strands of dark hair falling over her small, dirty face. "You're welcome, mister," her brows came together as she considered Levi. "Do you... need somewhere to stay? Da won't mind, now that we're friends." She was addressing the cat more than him.

"No," Levi gave her his best confident smile. "I have a little way to travel yet. I was glad to meet you so I could trade." He might have stayed a bit longer, but there was a gentle pulling sensation building in his chest. His bad luck threatened and he didn't want to press things. Any second the sky could open back up and this girl did not deserve to get soaked, or to have to take the goats back into their little barn by herself.

In the end it wasn't rain that sent Levi on his way. The goats, in their curiosity, burst a board on the fence and scampered around the yard. Levi offered to help gather them, though he had never dealt with goats before, but the little girl just gave him a smile that wrinkled her small nose. "Naw, they always do this. I'll catch 'em." She glanced at the broken slat. "Huh. Da just fixed that part of the fence. I thought it would last longer."

Familiar guilt rose in Levi, and he stepped away as though she'd caught him holding a hammer, pulling the fence apart. He might as well have, he thought darkly, keeping both hands clasped behind his back so as not to touch anything. "That's a pity. We really should be going, I suppose. Thank you again for the food."

"Wait!" As the goats rampaged around the yard behind her, and a few even let themselves into the house, the little girl trotted up to Levi and picked up Boots, giving the big cat one more hug as he hung from her arms. "Goodbye, kitty!" she kissed him between his ears.

Levi struggled heroically not to laugh at the look his feline friend was giving him. It clearly said, *the things I do for you, human.*

~~~~

Levi made decent travel time the next several days. His luck dogged him, and it took him a while to figure out what path it would take now that he was away from home, but he managed. His bare feet were an issue, so he cut pieces from his blanket and tied them to his feet, which made for better going.

Levi and Boots became even better at their game trapping. Levi would set the snare and, when an animal was caught, Boots would rush in and finish the job.

This method worked surprisingly well, and soon Levi had rabbits and even a few pheasant to trade at the various farms he came upon. He no longer tried to skin the kills, and people marveled at how the prey had barely a mark on them. Of course, there were mishaps: Levi broke more than his share of snares, got struck in the face by the whippy branches he used, and was once bitten quite hard by a rabbit.

The weather remained problematic, alternating between rainy and too warm, with sticky humidity. Levi had to keep reminding himself, as he trudged under a blistering sun or tried to keep dry at the side of the road, that late spring weather was bound to be unpredictable. There was a chance that his luck wasn't the sole reason, though most times he suspected it was.

After a little over two weeks of traveling, Levi and his animal companions found themselves on paved roads more often, and passing through towns rather than small villages. He knew this meant they were drawing nearer the capitol city and the royal palace, though he had no idea exactly how far out he still was. He'd picked up from those he questioned on his way that if you went east for a few weeks from the royal palace, you'd come upon the lands of The Ogre.

Levi recalled Da's stories of how The Ogre was a terrifying creature that even the bravest quailed to look upon. "Well," Levi muttered to the horse, "He will look however he looks, and I will react however I react, but if I can break the curse, it will be worth it."

Pushing away images of enormous, club wielding creatures with green skin and tusks, he returned to his favorite fantasy about his victorious homecoming. Ma enfolding him in one of her warmest hugs. His brothers clapping him on the back and cheering, saying that they would fetch the lawyer to change the paperwork so Levi could be a full partner in the mill. For a moment his fantasy also included Da, healthy and smiling.

As this painful thought caught in his mind, Levi snagged his foot on an uneven paving stone, grunting with surprise and frustration. He stumbled, lost hold of Molly's rope, and veered off the road and directly into a thick patch of stingweed.

"Blast!" Levi huffed, scrambling to be free of the twisting, red-tinged vines.

Molly stood above him on the road, rope dangling as she cupped her ears forward, clearly questioning why he had taken such an ill-advised detour. Boots, on her back, yowled his agreement.

Levi hauled himself from the ditch and sat down at the edge of the paving stones to examine the damage. The roadside was pleasantly wooded, and a gentle breeze picked up. He supposed this was a decent enough place for a break, were it not for the unfortunate plant situation.

His blanket-wrapped feet had fared well, all considered, but his shins and calves were beginning to go red and blister, and his fingertips to sting. Levi grimaced and leaned back, casting a doleful look skyward. "I suppose I went a good while without anything bad happening to me, eh?" Levi's chest tightened as if in answer. Some days he swore he could feel his bad luck pull at his ribs, mocking him. He focused his breathing, watching the gently rustling trees and letting the motion of the branches and the play of the shadows hypnotize and settle him.

"Mer mer," Boots jumped down from Molly's rump and scurried over to his human, butting his head reassuringly against Levi's arm.

"I know. I know, Boots. These sorts of things happen." Levi tried to ignore the burning and itching that was crawling steadily up his legs. "We had too good a time in that last town. I was able to barter the quail we caught for some good, strong cord, which will work better for the snares." His tone turned bitter and gestured to his legs. "I should have expected this."

"Mi mer," Boots agreed, still rubbing his head and side along Levi's arms.

Molly, deciding that her human might be a while, strolled off to find some grazing at the other side of the road, away from the stingweed. Levi watched her go and made no move to collect her. "When I was young and wandered into a patch like this, Ma put mud on my legs to make them feel better," he commented to Boots. "Maybe we can find a stream nearby, or it could start raining again." He looked up once more at the clear blue of the sky between the branches, unblemished by a single cloud. "Or perhaps not."

Sudden hoof beats, fast-moving and thunderous, made Levi sit up and look around. He could not see past a bend just down the road but was certain it was where the rhythmic sound originated.

He only had time to scramble to his feet before a carriage careened around the corner on two wheels, panicked horses, eyes rolling white and wild, charged on with no heed for what might be in their way. The driver clung to his seat at the front of the vehicle, the reins flapping loose as he held on for dear life.

Levi threw himself into the ditch and the carriage crashed past him, nearly running him down before one of the wheels sprang free and ricocheted off the road. The naked axle end, like a piece of exposed bone, sparked against the paving stones.

He ignored the burn of stingweed as he scrambled to the lip of the ditch to watch the scene play out. He also checked that Molly had had the good sense to flee. She had, and was peering out from a stand of aspens on the other side of the road. Boots joined with Levi in his mad dive, then climbed a tree and glared down at the proceedings with an expression worthy of Ma.

Levi's panicked breaths hitched as he watched the carriage totter to the side, then fall into the opposite ditch, dragging the horses back at an awkward angle. They screamed in dismay and alarm pawing for purchase on the damp turf. The people inside the carriage did the same. The driver was thrown clear and landed with a cruel thud beside a tree and lay still.

For a moment there was an eerie stillness, broken only by the clattering of struggling horses.

Levi thought he could hear his own heart beating just as loud. He was about to pull himself from his hiding spot to go help, when something else caught his attention. Beyond one of the wheels, which spun lazily several inches off the ground, a shape emerged.

No. Not emerged: formed. It gathered itself together into a mass of semitransparent blackness like a shadow cast by nothing. Twin eyes opened in a vaguely human shaped head, eyes like holes that let the light through from behind the creature. Once it was fully formed, the shadow scrabbled around on the carriage as though seeking to reach the people trapped inside. Levi could hear its long, claw-like fingers rasping against the wood paneling and metal latches.

Another shape materialized, the same as the first. It slithered across the carriage and stretched long-fingered hands to pry at the door handle. Luckily, it was a very fancy carriage and had glass windows.

Levi sat, frozen as though he'd been turned to stone. He couldn't even find the will to hunker further down into the ditch. Some rogue part of his mind was not satisfied to focus on survival and struggled to identify these monsters. He recalled a few stories he had heard as a youth—tales of mages who could conjure servants from stones, or make animals walk upright and speak. These shadow beings were nothing like the amiable magical creatures from the tales.

Levi had no weapons. No chance against...whatever these were. His hand closed around a clot of earth as though he might throw it. Likely that would be his last act on earth.

The screaming of the terrified horses and the people inside the overturned carriage steeled his will, and he stood up just in time to see a dozen riders crashing down the road towards them at top speed. It was back into the ditch for Levi or be crushed by hooves. He rolled and caught himself more skillfully this time, then crawled to the lip of the ditch to take in the newcomers.

These people were dressed in gleaming armor and wielded swords and spears. One carried a tall flag, which Levi recognized as bearing the emblem of the king: a red stallion against a green field, the animal's mane flying. Levi only recognized the flag because he had seen the image on bags of grain as a child.

In the lead of these king's men rode a woman, also clad in armor. Levi had to look twice to make sure he hadn't imagined her. Her leggy, bay horse surged forward, and she stood in the stirrups, leaning over its neck, her face a mask of ferocity. One sword was pointed before her over her mount's head, and she clasped a second blade in her other hand.

The shadow creatures noticed the oncoming fighters and bodily split themselves like tearing paper, once, twice, so that there were six of them. They seemed thinner, like tree shade on a sunny day, but they swept along the ground with alarming speed towards the oncoming chargers.

Horses were reined in, and riders hurried to dismount. The lady was somehow more striking on the ground. Clearly, she led these men, though they all towered over her. Her twin, curved blades glinted keenly, and her expression was just as deadly.

She slashed at the oncoming creatures, letting out a roar worthy of any warrior hero of fables. The lady's men followed her in formation, all of them wielding swords and tall shields.

The monsters recoiled as the lady sliced them with her blades. Where she hit their wispy forms, they were torn like cloth and sunlight shone through the wounds. Bits of their strange flesh floated away like ash on the breeze. The woman did not stop, but allowed one swing to carry her into another, moving as though she hardly wore armor at all. Her black hair was contained in a braid that was pinned up to the back of her head, but had worked itself free and whipped behind her as she went.

The king's men were equally efficient and ruthless.

Levi's mouth hung open. He had never seen a battle before and perhaps everyone fought like these people. Perhaps it was not so uncommon for a woman to be as fearsome as the men. He couldn't tear his eyes away, even to make sure Boots was still safely installed in the tree.

The human fighters forced away the attackers, who slithered and skittered over the ground in ragged tatters. The blobs of black came together into a single mass of twisting shade, like a patch of nighttime the sun had forgotten, and retreated entirely.

The men rushed to the overturned carriage and began struggling to free and calm the distressed horses as well as to pull the trapped people from inside. Some went to see to the fallen driver. The woman stood back, hands on hips, watching her men work with a stern eye. Now that she was no longer shouting battle cries, Levi was able to take in her face. She had brown skin and a round face with dark, intense eyes. Levi wondered who she might be, as she sheathed her twin swords. They hung low on her hips, supported by crossing belts.

"Who are they, Lyall?" the woman asked. Levi noticed her accent was unexpectedly cultured.

"The prince's entourage, I'm afraid," reported one of the warriors, who stood with a booted foot braced against the carriage as he struggled to help a lady from it.

She was an older woman, and so laden down with skirts and corset that she was having great difficulty wedging herself through the door.

"You should be afraid!" the woman snapped as the tall man called Lyall heaved her free and onto the road, where she continued to bluster. "What were those creatures?! I have heard of bandits in the area, but this sort of thing should not be happening so near the palace!"

"Servants of The Ogre." The armored lady sighed, brushing a few curls of loose hair from her sweat-streaked face.

The carriage woman blinked a few times in obvious confusion. "I…I had heard that you left the palace and rode out with a group of soldiers, but I thought that was only for show…to put on a good face for the people. Now I see the rumors are true."

"My father isn't proud of my extracurricular activity." The warrior woman dipped her head, but a smirk played on her lips. "I am fulfilling my duty as Protector of The People." She leaned closer, eying the carriage, "where is the prince, if you don't mind my asking?"

"Ahead of us, I expect." The flouncy woman huffed, trying to wipe strands of sweaty hair from her neck and collect them back into her elaborate bun. "He left from the palace, while we came from our estate. Let us hope that such an evil fate as this has not befallen him too."

The warrior woman furrowed her brow. "Doubtful. Shades rarely come this far so for them to attack two travelers would be unheard of."

"Who's that?" Someone else spoke, and Levi realized with alarm that a young warrior with messy black hair and a scar on his lip was pointing at him. Levi had been so interested in the scene playing out that he had almost forgotten he was there himself.

As the man called Lyall hauled a lady's maid and a finely dressed gentleman from the carriage, Levi found himself being hoisted from the ditch by two other soldiers, then brought before the armored lady.

She folded her arms and looked up at him. Though he stood at least a head taller than she, Levi felt smaller, so intense and dominant was her gaze. "Well then, who are you now, my lad?"

"L-Levi," Levi looked around at the soldiers. Those who were not helping with the carriage had gathered to stare at him. "I'm a miller," he added awkwardly. He had never introduced himself to anyone more socially important than a village midwife or shop owner.

"Levi The Miller." The warrior woman rocked back on her heels, hands on her hips. "What were you doing in that ditch, Levi the Miller?"

"Hiding. Trying not to be struck by a carriage," Levi felt endlessly pathetic. He was deeply aware of his clothing, not only covered in mud, but coming apart at the seams. He grimaced as he remembered the rags he wore instead of shoes. Any exposed skin was showing angry red with the stingweed rash. He wished more than anything that he could slip back into the ditch and become one with the muck, so these fine people would forget him.

"Merrar!" Boots appeared at Levi's feet, standing before the human as though to claim Levi as his own. The cat met the woman's eyes with an equally steady and dominant gaze.

The woman's full mouth twitched in a smile. "A friend of yours?"

"Yes," Levi said, allowing a shy grin to break free as he peered through the fringe of his bangs. "His name is Boots. That's my horse beyond the tree line over there."

Molly watching them all with her ears pinned in disgust, though she didn't draw closer. Some of the war horses stretched their necks curiously in her direction, and she glared at them.

"Your Highness?" the man in fine clothes who had been helped from the overturned carriage spoke up, stepping forward to gingerly touch the warrior lady's shoulder.

Levi's vision swam for a moment, and he staggered back in alarm, then threw himself to the dirt before the woman. "Highness!" Royalty? What was one supposed to do with royalty? Kneeling was a good first step, but then what? His mind raced. Should he kiss her hand?

She wore leather fighting gloves. Was he to wait for her to remove them? He crouched in a panicked huddle on the ground.

"Lyall," the woman called, a hint of annoyance in her tone.

Firm hands gripped Levi's shoulders. He looked up into the face of the man who had pulled the people from the carriage. A long face with very blue eyes and a straight nose. Blond hair was bundled back into an efficient tail, though many strands fell loose.

"Come on then, lad. Settle down. Princess Joanna doesn't like people to fawn over her. In her position as People's Protector, she is not to be bowed to. Do you understand? Not unless you see her at the palace."

Levi tried to clear his head, avoiding looking at Princess Joanna as though eye contact might burn him alive where he stood. See her at the palace? He had no idea of ever being able to look her in the face again, let alone finding himself at the palace. He allowed 'Lyall' to stand him up and dust him off a bit. "Gods! What happened to you?" The soldier raised one of Levi's arms, which bore a spreading, angry rash.

"Stingweed in the ditch." Levi shrugged.

The princess—gods it was still alarming to think of her that way—made a single gesture. A bearded man with light brown skin and dark hair pulled back in a tail looked up from crouching over the fallen cart driver. "He'll be alright," he assured the Princess as he crossed the road to stand before Levi. This man was armed and armored as well, but wore a white tabard with the crude image of a doe emblazoned on it. The sign of a healer.

Though Boots watched with suspicion, Levi stood in stunned silence as the healer looked him over.

The princess, blessedly ignoring Levi for the moment, spoke in low tones with the people from the carriage. They were clearly upset and kept making wide, expressive gestures. Princess Joanna was doing her best to calm them down. Levi could hear her voice, steady and reassuring under the shrill tones of the fine lady. Several of Princess Joanna's men, having dragged the carriage from the ditch, jogged off down the road to collect their scattered mounts. Another gathered up the wheel, examining it curiously.

"Do you suppose it can be repaired, Rylan?" Lyall asked the healer, conversationally.

"I should hope it can!" the woman from the carriage squawked. She was reminding Levi more and more of an old hen he had known growing up. A speckled creature who would even boss the roosters. "We cannot very well walk to the palace. No doubt the prince is already there and worried where his guardians and bride-to-be are."

Princess Joanna stiffened. Levi could read her tension, even through her armor. Lyall winced.

"I am not his bride-to-be yet," the princess ground between her teeth.

"At this rate you may never be," the lady huffed, straightening her voluminous skirts. "We simply must get the carriage put together. I cannot walk, and I certainly cannot ride in this gown."

Lyall snorted with amusement, and Levi glanced at him. The blond warrior's thin lips twitched in an ill-concealed smile as he murmured to Levi and the healer, "Knowing Jo, she is about to suggest a duchess strip down to her underthings and ride."

"Oh, there's no need," Levi spoke before he could think better of it. He took his arm back from the healer's gentle grasp and stepped around him towards the carriage, nearly tripping over Boots, who was sitting on his feet. The cat yowled and bounded out of the way. "Let me see the wheel?"

The black-haired soldier held it out to him, but Levi did not take it. He suspected that if he did, one of the sturdy spokes would snap for no reason. "Hmmmm, yes. This wheel is steel reinforced. It weathered the ordeal just fine. If we reattach it, it should make the journey to a proper wheelwright. What does the axle look like?"

He squatted to examine the carriage as the men stood aside to let him see the end of the axle where the wheel was meant to attach. "Here we go. The cotter pin snapped. You see, this helps the wheel stay in place." Levi reached down and plucked a piece of metal about as long and thick as his forefinger, from the dirt. It had been sheered in half by the force of the wagon's jostling weight. He stood back, realizing that everyone was staring at him, feeling a blush rush to his cheeks to match the rest of his reddened skin.

"Erm, who is this again?" asked the fine gentleman, thin brows raised.

"Levi The Miller," Princess Joanna said.

Levi made the mistake of looking at her, and the moment he met her eyes, he thought he might fall down to bow again. He could not wrap his head around the fact that he was standing on the same road as a princess.

She spoke as though she had not noticed Levi's mouth hanging open. "He seems to know a deal about cart wheels."

"Oh, I've had a few break on me, and not been so lucky as to have the steel reinforcement." Levi shrugged, fixing his eyes on the paving stones.

"So what do we do?" asked another young soldier, eyeing the pin.

"We can replace it for now. That'll get you into town at least. I need thick wire if you've got it." Levi said.

The soldiers scrambled around in a flurry of motion, digging in saddle packs and pouches. Levi kept still, arms at his sides, and tried not to meet Princess Joanna's intimidating gaze.

"How about this?" The healer, Rylan, held up a long, thick needle. "It's used for holding bandages together."

"That might just do." Levi nodded, but did not take the needle. He hoped no one noticed his hesitancy to touch anything. "We need to bend it at the end so it comes back on itself."

"Right!" A red haired solider went to his pack and returning with some tools that Levi recognized as farrier's gear. "Give it here." He held out his hand, and Rylan placed the pin on his palm.

The man went to work bending the needle. Levi edged away, trying to keep an eye on the work while still getting his bad luck as far from it as he could. The man finished and held it up. "How's this?"

Levi gave a few instructions for modification and the pin was finished. The men gathered the wheel and popped it back on the axle, then slid the pin into place. It was small for the opening, but held.

"Go slowly," Levi cautioned the carriage driver, who was sitting nearby, freshly bandaged and watching the scene play out. "If you keep it to a walk, you should make it to town."

"Oh, I will," The driver said, voice still shaky.

"Well then," Princess Joanna said, a smile dimpling her cheeks once more, "it looks as though we were lucky to have you around, sir Miller."

"Lucky?" Levi mumbled, the word hanging potently in the air.

As if to punctuate the word, the strap on the healer's satchel snapped and the heavy bag fell to the road with a plop. Several vials of powders and liquids tumbled out and scattered on the road. One cracked and left a trail of greenish medicine in its wake.

Boots darted after another, trapping it with a paw and sniffing it curiously. "Blast!" The healer scrambled to gather his things. "That strap was brand new. What happened?"

Levi backed away, almost tripping on his cat. Boots huddled possessively over the bottle he'd captured, patting it with his paws. Rylan, chuckling at the feline's antics, retrieved the bottle. "Essence of mint," he explained, wagging the bottle at Boots. "Cats love it."

"I had better be on my way," Levi said as the soldiers went about hitching the horses back to the cart.

"Nonsense!" Joanna dismissed his words with a wave of her hand. "We'll rest here for a bit once the lady and her entourage are on their way. You must sit and have a meal with us."

Levi fumbled over several answers, none of which he allowed to pass his lips. If the princess told you to stay and eat with her, did you have any grounds to refuse? Even if your bad luck would probably spoil the meal?

"Highness," the woman from the carriage said, her eyes narrowing. "Won't that make you even later to the palace to meet the prince? He's already been waiting."

Princess Joanna turned on the woman, her shoulders once again set in a hard line. Some of her men shot each other knowing looks. "My soldiers and horses are tired after the fight to save your skins. They will have a rest, and we will return to the palace when we are ready and able."

The woman made several flustered "hurumph" noises, but allowed herself to be handed into the carriage by the gentleman, who Levi guessed to be her husband. Last came her docile maid.

Levi watched as the driver, who was looking very much recovered, climbed up to his spot and flicked the horses into motion with the reins.

"You should have no more trouble from the Shades, but I will send Varric and Liam with you as protection," the Princess said, signaling the dark and ginger haired men. The pair looked the freshest and had clearly been at the rear of the Princess's battle formation. They trotted their horses up to ride on either side of the carriage.

"We shall see you at the palace soon!" the woman called, drawing one of the windows down so she could stick her head out. "The prince will be most interested to meet you."

"Grand," grumbled Princess Joanna. Levi barely heard her, and he was certain that the fine lady had not, as her carriage lurched into motion to carry her and her people down the road once more. "Now then." The princess laced her fingers and stretched them, looking over her men with a practiced eye. "Shall we have a bit of a rest?"

Everyone agreed with shouts of "Yes ma'am!" and "I'm done in from that little skirmish."

Levi watched, trying to stand on the fringes of the group. He could tell that none of the men were actually tired. They strode about enthusiastically gathering firewood and chatting in loud voices.

The tall man called Lyall came to stand beside Levi. Boots looked up at the stranger before apparently making his choice and weaving back and forth between the man's legs. Lyall smiled and bent down, as best he could in his armor, picking the cat up as gently as he would a baby. "What a fine cat." He tickled Boots under the chin. Boots set up his loud purr at once.

"He is that," Levi agreed nervously.

Lyall had a gentle smile which made Levi feel a little better. "You have no need to be shy around the princess. You're the reason she rides out like this. Not for those nobles, though that is a side effect. She rides as The People's Protector. As second born, it is her right."

Levi had no idea what that meant, but he decided not to comment on it. Instead, he nodded and watched a man set up a fire beside the road, well away from the patch of stingweed. Joanna supervised like a foreman at a worksite.

Levi wondered if he could sidle away without anyone noticing. The last thing he wanted was to flaunt his bad luck around someone as important as this. Never mind that he had no business even breathing the same air as a royal, even if he wasn't looking so shabby and pathetic. If he was the proud owner of a mill, he'd be able to hold his head up, but at the moment he was a nobody.

"Here you are, lad." One of the soldiers led Molly over to Levi, who took her reins automatically. The horse still looked grouchy, ears pinned and lips tight.

"She doesn't seem too keen on our lot." Joanna strode over and jabbed a thumb towards her own horses with a grin.

"No," Levi tried shakily to imitate the princess's smile. "She probably wants to boss them like foals."

"Ah, a lady after my own heart." Joanna petted Molly's face, and the old horse butted her nose against Joanna's forearm. "Lyall, look at these!" The Princess exclaimed over the pair of pheasants hanging from Molly's makeshift pack. "Not a mark on them! How did you manage that?" Princess Joanna cocked an eyebrow at Levi.

"I snare them," Levi mumbled, watching as the woman took the pheasants down to study them more thoroughly. One did have some dusty and bent feathers, as it had fallen onto the road more than once, but otherwise both birds were in excellent condition. Levi planned to barter them in the next town he came to.

"Snare them?" Princess Joanna's eyes met Levi's, and he quickly dropped his gaze, balling his hands into fists to hide their trembling. "That is impressive." She held one of the pheasants up for Lyall to see. "You can see where the neck was broken, but it's a clean break. Not like you normally get with a snare. These are great looking birds!" She turned her attention back to Levi, "what will you take for them?"

"Er, what?" Levi blinked.

"My father loves wild game. If I bring him back these lovely pheasants, I'm certain it'll put him in a better mood," the princess said, reaching for her belt and the small money pouch which hung there beside a sheathed dagger.

Levi wondered why the king would be in a bad mood to begin with, but he knew better than to ask. Instead, he pondered the coins the princess held towards him. "I...I usually barter for the game, I don't really know how much they're worth," he admitted. He didn't want to go overboard on the price, even if she was the princess and could spare it. It seemed like a bad idea to overcharge royalty.

"Hmmm," Princess Joanna cocked a hip, her armor clanking with the motion. "Alright. How about we barter...a fresh tunic and some boots?"

Levi supposed he might feel more confident around her if he wasn't dressed like a vagabond. Lyall had already gone to one of the horses and opened a pack, tugging free a pale blue tunic and some very nice boots, identical to the ones the soldiers were wearing. As the tall man fetched these items, Boots climbed up to perch on Lyall's shoulders, watching the other men with the same imperious expression he always wore when riding Molly.

Lyall returned and offered the boots and tunic. The boots were considerably sturdier than anything he had ever owned. These were clearly made by a palace cobbler, not some peasant who had learned a few tricks with leather and sinew, and thought they might try their hand at shoe-making. He wondered, as he admired the thick soles and fine lacing, if these would last him longer before his luck caused them to fall apart. The leather was soft and supple. He realized he had been staring lovingly at the boots for several moments. "Yes," he said before he could catch himself and wonder if the two birds were worth the exceptional footwear.

~~~~~

Half of an hour later found Levi sitting with the princess and her people around a small fire. The men had tossed a few potatoes into the embers to cook while others speared pieces of fruit-and nut-filled traveling bread on long sticks, holding them out to the fire to toast.

Levi munched on one such hunk of bread. Though he was careful to sit as far from the fire as he could, as he was still on the lookout for signs that a bout of disastrous bad luck might strike. For the moment there was no familiar tugging sensation in his chest, which he usually noted when his luck was about to be at its worst.

Boots made the rounds, endearing himself to one soldier after another. Even a big fellow who reminded Levi of a slightly less gigantic version of Fergus, who had tried to remain uninterested in the cat, was soon tickling boots' chin and sneaking him little pieces of cheese and dried fish.

Levi listened quietly to the conversations of the men. They griped about a saddle getting old or a blade in need of sharpening. The healer commented with a wry smile that he had never seen someone as covered in stingweed as Levi. "Most people avoid those plants on sight."

Some of the other men chuckled at this and Levi raised his arm to shyly show off the rash, coated in a thick layer of healing salve.

He knew perfectly well he did not belong among these people, but wearing his new tunic and fine boots let him imagine he did, if only for a while.

"Those Shades were awfully far west," the big soldier commented, stabbing at the fire with a twig. He had the tan-skinned look of a farmer.

Levi looked up. The way the man had said "Shade" made it sound as though he saw those monstrosities all the time.

Princess Joanna grimaced. "Cade, must we discuss this in front of—?" She tilted her head in Levi's direction.

Cade looked down, chastised, black hair flopping over deep-set eyes.

"Mer mer!" Boots announced, his tail waving like a signal as he sought out more snacks.

Princess Joanna watched the cat and smiled fondly, then met Levi's eyes. He dropped his gaze at once. Surely you weren't supposed to make eye contact with royalty He cleared his throat, trying to find the words that were trapped just behind his teeth. "I *was* wondering what those creatures were. I thought I heard someone say they were 'minions of The Ogre'?"

Joanna and Lyall passed a look between them, and the princess answered. "Yes. The Ogre sends them out to cause trouble for local farmers, disrupt trade and give me and my men something to do." Several of the soldiers let out little whoops of agreement.

"Are they...what are they?" Levi asked.

"Magic, I suppose," Lyall answered. He nudged a potato further into the embers with the toe of his boot.

"There isn't any magic in these lands," Levi said. He was curious how she would respond.

"You've heard the legends, I imagine," Princess Joanna replied. "Tales of how we once had magic here and how The Ogre stole it all? Well, that may or may not be true, but one thing is certain; he at least has some. His Shades don't need food or rest. They can attack us using their own bodies as weapons."

"But they're not especially difficult to defeat," Lyall cut in, no doubt noticing Levi's alarmed expression. "They usually don't come so far west. The Ogre keeps them close to home most of the time. I guess these ones were determined. They might have followed the carriage for days waiting to strike and decided now was the time."

"They're not very smart, the Shades," one of the other soldiers added.

Everyone spoke so casually of the monsters. Just thinking of those dark creatures clinging to the carriage and trying to claw their way inside made Levi's skin crawl. He tried to shake the image of them with their hollow, see-through eyes and the way they changed shape and joined together or split apart.

Lyall agreed with the soldier. "Very true. They don't make plans or change tactics. They only do as they're told. We were on our way back from a patrol and were planning to meet up with and escort the duke and duchess to the palace anyway. When we saw the Shades trailing them, we knew we had to move in."

"It saved us from having to escort them," Joanna commented. "I wasn't looking forward to it." She plucked one of the toasted hunks of bread from the fire and tossed it between her hands until it cooled. "So then, Miller. We were also lucky that you came along and knew a thing or two about reattaching cart wheels. What brings you out so far from mill country?"

"I..." Levi stuffed food into his mouth to give himself time to think. He couldn't very well admit to his true quest, which he was beginning to think was even more futile than he had expected. "My Da recently passed away and—"

"May the wolves guide him home." The princess a hand over her heart, which startled Levi. Then she made a sign with her hand, a tribute to the wolf gods of death. Some of the other men did as well.

"Wolf gods?" Levi asked.

Princess Joanna dipped her head, smiling sheepishly. "I know the royal family is supposed to follow the Father God and Mother Goddess these days, but if I am to be honest with you, Miller's Son, I think we were foolish to completely abandon the animal gods of old."

"Jo," Lyall hissed, and Levi raised an eyebrow. "We probably shouldn't bore the folk of your kingdom with your personal...proclivities?" He ended the sentence like a question, but the princess nodded.

"No, no, I don't mind at all!" Levi raised his hands. "My Da and I still believed in the old gods as well. I grew up hearing all the stories."

Princess Joanna's face brightened. "Really? Which was your favorite?"

"Oh, any of the tales about the Cat God of Luck." He hesitated. "I uh...I recently discovered that my family was somewhat concerned with luck. For"—he cleared his throat —"various reasons."

"Have you heard the one where the cat god tricks the horse goddess of war?" Princess Joanna sat forward, her eyes sparkling in the firelight.

Lyall chuckled, shaking his head but not bothering to interfere. Some of the other soldiers grinned and nudged one another.

"Yes!" Levi answered as Boots jumped up to sit on his broad shoulders, tail wrapping around Levi's neck like a fuzzy necklace. The cat had seemingly eaten his fill and was ready for a cuddle. "The horse goddess was angry because the cat was using his luck to get out of all of his godly obligations, so she wanted to punish him. She said she would pound him to dust with her mighty hooves."

Princess Joanna laughed, a strong, confident sound that might have rattled the trees. Levi startled, then blushed, looking down at his hands in his lap. He'd never heard a woman with a laugh like hers. The girls around the village tittered and giggled behind their hands, usually while watching Levi's handsome brother. When Ma laughed it was a fast, low sound that included more than one silly snort. This woman sounded like she could laugh at her enemies and see them retreat as if it were a battle cry.

"Right!" Princess Joanna gestured enthusiastically, and Lyall was obliged to dodge her arm. "I remember now! The cat followed the horse to war without the horse knowing. She was trying to aid the human armies in their fight, but the cat kept making each side have good or bad luck in turns so no one could win, and the horse could not figure it out until, finally, she was so fed up she stamped her hoof so hard she split the land right in two. One army was borne away from the other as the lands drifted apart and the sea spilled in. That was how the Horsehead Sea was created. The cat revealed himself, and the goddess was forced to acknowledge his cleverness and swear not to strike him with hoof or teeth if he would leave her work alone from then on."

"I love that story!" agreed Levi, beaming. "There are so many great ones!" He took another bite of the bread, the warm, oaty flavor filling him with a feeling of home and safety. Then he fumbled and dropped the rest of the bread in the dirt, where it rolled and came to rest beside an anthill. In seconds the greedy ants were out to help themselves.

"Rotten luck," Lyall said, passing Levi another piece.

Levi carefully took the offering and chuckled once, a dry, mirthless sound. "You have no idea." He turned back to the princess, whose expression was distant as though she were remembering more tales from her own childhood. It was strange to think that the child of the king and queen might have listened to the same stories as a country lad.

Levi quickly devoured the hearty bread before he could drop this as well, though he was careful not to choke on it. Then he looked to the princess again, finding it was easier to hold eye contact. "I'm about to sound ignorant, but what are The People's Protectors?"

Princess Joanna rested her arms on her knees, her armor shifting with a clatter as she explained. "There hasn't been one until a few years ago. I'm certain you know of my brother, Alroy, the crown prince?"

Levi nodded, wishing he had more bread to stuff into his mouth. He knew a woefully small amount about the royal family. He knew there was a king and queen, who he'd been told took care of their people. He knew they had children, but he hadn't even known how old those children were.

They had little use for kings and queens out amongst the mills and fields, aside from faces stamped on coins. He couldn't even be certain the coins he had seen bore the faces of the current rulers. He kept all of this to himself, instead reaching up and plucking Boots from his shoulder, settling the purring cat in his lap.

The princess went on, little noticing Levi's embarrassed expression. "My brother is first in line for the throne. I'm second born. As a female I'm destined for a matrimonial fate. But"—she shot a cocky grin towards Lyall, who returned it with a quirk of his eyebrows—"If I was a second *son* I would have a responsibility to the people. To learn to fight, to ride out with the guard and protect the land from bandits or any other threats. In time of war I would serve as a general."

Levi nodded as though he understood. His Da had never mentioned anything like that, and certainly not that a princess might take on the role. Yet, as he studied the short, curvy woman, he knew she could defend him in combat, certainly better than he could defend himself. Then again, she had swords she knew how to use, and he could accidentally slice his own artery with a letter opener.

"My father wasn't excited about the idea," Princess Joanna admitted.

"Not excited," Lyall scoffed. "You argued with him for two years to let you hire a fighting teacher, and then you had to convince him you weren't going to die the moment you left castle grounds. You'd battle harder against him than most of the Shades we've faced. Not to mention all the work your mother put in to soften him to the idea. And then you had to win all of those martial competitions to show that you weren't going to die the moment you encountered a foe and then—"

"Alright, Ly. Hush!" The princess raised her hand to the soldier, who fell silent, but did not look at all admonished. Princess Joanna turned back to Levi and shrugged. "Let's just say that my father took some convincing, but I finally got the position. Of course, rather than fighting bandits I spend all my time trying to keep The Ogre's grubby grasp off of our land."

Levi flinched. He watched as her eyes darkened when she spoke of The Ogre, hooded by thick, black lashes. He looked down at his hands and arms, slick with the salve the healer used to stop the itching of his stingweed encounter. There would be more stingweed. More rainstorms that lasted for days. More inability for him to help his family or even fend for himself. He had to break the curse, and he knew no other way besides magic.

Levi cleared his throat, and a few of the soldiers jumped, but the princess was paying attention again. "I've been living in Mill Country all my life, so I don't know much about...worldly...dealings." He fumbled his words, feeling like a country idiot and wishing he could shut back up. "We know that The Ogre seems to have magic. Do you suppose there is magic anywhere else in the kingdom?" He suspected he knew the answer, but hoped against hope that such a worldly person as the princess might have some other lead.

"I'm afraid we have it the same all over." It was Lyall who spoke. "We've all heard our parents talk about magic, and how they or their grandparents saw it being worked by humans, but since then, no one has seen or heard anything of magic aside from The Ogre."

"You ride out to fight The Ogre's minions, so I guess the king and queen are not excited about The Ogre either?"

"I should say not!" Princess Joanna snorted, eyes flashing. "Not only did The Ogre steal all our magic, when he arrived he also helped himself to the castle and lands that belonged to one of the finest families in the kingdom. That was when my grandfather was king. They still aren't certain how The Ogre ousted the family Carabas from their home and holdings, but I believe it was because we had been living in peace for so long, they had a minuscule guard on hand to protect them."

"Right," Levi said. He didn't want to go on, but he couldn't think of anyone else who would be able to answer his questions. "Does anyone go to see The Ogre now? Perhaps to talk about a truce or something?"

The princess barked her abrupt laugh, and a few of her men chuckled as well. "No one visits The Ogre! My father is not a warlike king and would be happy enough to let The Ogre sit in his stolen castle and stew, but these days he has been claiming more and more land."

"Stealing it," Lyall corrected.

"I see," Levi said, still looking down at his hands. They were still red and puffy, and he wasn't looking forward to dealing with them once the healer's salve had worn off.

"Don't worry," Princess Joanna said, and Levi looked up without thinking, his hair flopping over his eyes. He shoved it back with annoyance, aware that now it was probably sticking straight up and making him look shabbier, despite his new tunic and boots.

The princess leaned towards him, patting his knee with her hand, reassuringly. "The Shadows will leave you be, don't worry. As we said, it is rare for them to be in the area, and I know they were specifically after the duke and duchess. The Ogre has his sights set on my father's castle next, I know it, and he has been slowly reaching out to see which threads he can pull to make the whole tapestry unwind."

Levi wasn't certain he grasped the metaphor, but nodded just the same.

Lyall stood up, working out the kinks in his joints from sitting so long in armor. He extended a hand, and the princess took it, rising with a clatter and squeak of metal on metal. "We had best be moving along, Jo."

"You're right of course," the princess replied, though her brows came together in a annoyed scowl. She turned to Levi, extending a hand to him. "Thank you for your help and pleasant conversation, Master Miller."

Master Miller. Levi's heart gave an unexpected little flip. If only he could live up to that title. He'd settle for anything at this point besides "muddy peasant," but "Master Miller" was a dream, especially coming from a princess. He was so overcome with the notion that he forgot his nerves and took her hand for a firm shake.

Lyall shook Levi's hand as well. "Good to meet you friend."

Levi shook a few more hands feeling slightly overwhelmed as the princess moved to mount her horse. Without thinking, Levi extended a hand to help her up. Something in his chest shivered, and her stirrup snapped. Slipping sideways she fell, landing in a clatter of armor.

Her horse sidestepped, snorting at looking down at her with confusion. Molly, who stood beside Levi, nipped at the princess's bay, which made him prance all the more.

"Oh, gods! I'm so sorry!" Levi spluttered, every instinct urging him to help her up, but his own experience forcing him to step away from her. To his endless surprise the princess was laughing, and her men joined her. Levi stared in utter bafflement.

"Bit of a spill?" Lyall was already mounted, and he looked down at his princess with an amused expression on his refined features.

"Damned stirrup broke. Leather must have been getting ratty," the princess said, tugging the stirrup off her foot and throwing it aside, where it hit Levi in the shin. He didn't make a sound, not wanting to draw more attention to himself. No one else knew that he had been the reason she fell, but he knew.

Boots meowed with concern and leaped down from Levi's shoulder. He trotted over to sniff at Princess Joanna.

"Are you hurt?" Lyall asked, single eyebrow raised.

Princess Joanna, still grinning ruefully, waved him off. "Not a bit. I'll be sore later, but all that was damaged was pride, and I suppose Mother would say it's good to let that happen to you every so often. Builds character or something like that." She scrambled gracelessly to her feet. She went to the other side of her horse and climbed up using the remaining stirrup. "There we are." She arranged herself in the saddle, tucking the reins neatly into her fist.

Levi marveled that she could go from falling on her backside in the dirt to sitting tall and dignified in a matter of moments. "Now all of you will have something to talk about in the mess later."

"So we shall," chortled one of the men.

Levi stood out of the way, uncertain and shy all over again. He didn't want these people to go. He wanted to ask them a thousand more questions. What would The Ogre do if he approached? Why were the princess and her men seemingly the only people fighting his minions? Would he ever see any of them again? The cat, obviously finished feeling sorry for Joanna, strolled back over to Levi and wound himself around his human friend's new boots.

"Here, lad" the healer rode over on a stocky grey mare as the warriors began to move into a formation two riders wide with Joanna and Lyall in the lead. The man passed Levi a small canister. "More ointment for you. If you run out use a bit of plantain. It grows hereabouts."

"I know the plant," Levi assured the man, taking the canister of salve as though receiving an egg rather than a metal tin. If the healer noticed the added care, he didn't comment.

"Chew the plantain a bit then put it on your rashes. You got a bad dose of stingweed poison, so it might take quite a while to fully heal." Gathering his reins, he turned his horse's head and took his place at the end of the formation.

"Thank you!" Levi called.

"Best of luck to you, Master Miller!" The princess raised her arm to Levi, "and thank you for the pheasant!"

Levi let another rush of giddiness wash over him at her words, even if he knew that no amount of wishing him luck would help.

Princess Joanna dropped her arm and at the same moment urged her horse to move. The animal exploded into a canter, and the rest of the riders surged after her, somehow keeping their formation trim and neat without a single animal out of place. Molly, excited by the motion but too old to follow at such speed, lifted her head and whinnied before turning to blink at Levi as if to ask what they were to do next. "We go see The Ogre," he answered, ruffling her forelock. He felt a little silly talking to the horse after having spent over an hour in the company of human beings.

"Going to see The Ogre," Levi muttered to himself. Those shadow creatures the princess had fought came from The Ogre, and that notion was terrifying. Yet when he looked down at his rash covered arms, or remembered how a simple touch from him had caused Princess Joanna to fall, he steeled his resolve. She rode all over the kingdom. She would know if there was magic anywhere else.

No. The curse had to be broken, and it had to be The Ogre who did it. He'd have to risk those creatures if he wanted to succeed. That was the nature of heroic quests, he told himself as he trudged on along the wide road.

As he led his horse, cat perched on her back, out of the tree line and into farm country, his mood was strangely high for someone who might be walking towards his death. He had a good meal inside him, a new shirt on his back, and boots that were infinitely superior to rags tied around his feet. If he had dared to show outward happiness, he might have whistled, but he didn't want his luck to get any ideas.

It was past noon, and for a little while, a pleasant breeze played through his messy hair as Levi led Molly past farms that were increasingly larger and more prosperous. Their outbuildings were made of wood rather than field stone and the houses sometimes had two stories.

Levi saw more people as well. People working in fields, riding down the road on horses and in carriages, leading animals out to pasture. He was passed by a low wagon with three massive pigs in the back who studied him with small, intelligent eyes. It was a pity to watch them go. They were clearly being taken to market, and they had no idea that their happy lives of rooting in the muck were coming to an end. "They'll feed their family well," he commented to Molly, as though the horse shared in his sympathy.

"Meow wow mi!" Boots announced, and Levi glanced at the cat, then turned to follow the animal's gaze. The cat was staring at something, eyes wide and attentive.

"By the gods," Levi exhaled, taking in the countryside that spread before him as he crested a hill. He'd been too busy enjoying the smiles and nods of passersby to take in the full sprawl of the farm country. Lush fields, square patches of every shade of green spread into valleys and over smaller hills as though someone had draped a quilt over the land. He could see the homes, dots of color like flowers against the green, pastures of happily grazing sheep and goats, and orchards that stood out in clusters. The breeze picked up, and Levi was taken by the scent of young crops and distant animals.

He turned to the left to take in more of the glorious scene and stopped when he saw a castle perched atop a distant hillside. He could make out the tiny banners that fluttered from the battlements. "Look at that!" He pointed, and Boots jumped to his shoulders, taking a few steps down Levi's outstretched arm. "That must be where the princess lives! It's so big! Can you imagine living somewhere like that? You could get lost trying to find your way to breakfast. I certainly would."

"Mer mer!" Boots trilled imperiously, as though he could easily imagine himself living in a palace. He dug in his claws as he tried to get all the way out to Levi's hand. Levi didn't stop him, as he was accustomed to cuts and scratches.

Levi watched the palace in the distance, half expecting to see Princess Joanna riding out from it, taking her troop of fighters across the land in a heroic parade. "She certainly wasn't like any of the ladies at home, was she?" he commented to Boots as he pulled the cat from his arm and tucked him under one instead. The cat hung contentedly, paws dangling. "Maybe that's just how princesses are. I mean, I certainly never met one before. Nor will I again, I imagine." He continued his turn, enjoying the patchwork of green fields dotted with multicolored homes and barns. People here could afford to paint their houses something besides white.

"Now that we have the palace in our sights, we know how to get to The Ogre's lands. Just head east." Levi filled his voice with more confidence than he felt. His insides were full of anxious fleas, all jumping at once.

Boots let out a squeak and jumped lightly from Levi's shoulder to Molly's back. "You're right, Boots," Levi said, taking Molly's lead rope and shaking himself free of intimidating thoughts. "We have a bit of a walk ahead of us, don't we?"

He was on his way once more. The sun was at its zenith, and the heat was growing. The salve the healer had given him was rubbing off on his new shirt. Before long Levi was sticky, itchy, and dry-mouthed, but he tried to keep up the good mood he had so recently acquired.

He chatted with his animal friends, little minding when he passed people working in their fields as they looked up and eyed him in confusion.

"Think of it, Boots. Once the curse is broken, we can stop home to say hello to the family. Considering that we're close, personal friends of the princess now, I'm certain we can secure a mill of our very own in these lands. We'll have a house with two stories and fields of grain that are tended by our hired hands. Well-paid hands, of course. I'll oversee it all as Master Miller. Come to think on it, I'll own several mills, not just one, and have managers under me who see to the small details, but everything will run smoothly thanks to my ingenuity. Then my family can come live with me in my fine house, and there will be enough room for everyone!"

"Mer mer," Boots agreed, looking pleased, if a bit warm, on Molly's broad rump.

~~~~

It took Levi almost a week to reach the foot of the hill where the Ogre's castle stood. The fact that the dark, squat castle belonged to the magic thief was all the more obvious when Levi saw how the few farmers living near The Ogre's land behaved. They shut their houses up tight and glared when they saw Levi, as though he might be one of the Shades. There were few carts and horses on the road, and what paving stones remained were ratty and broken from years of disrepair.

Eventually there were no farmers at all, only fields of weeds growing hearty and tangled. Levi had no one to trade with for his meals, and the fields provided little shade or shelter from the heat of the sun, nor from the rain that periodically plagued him.

The sun and rain seemed to be taking turns harassing him, though he was able to find a few patches of vegetables, growing where once they had been cultivated, and helped himself. He strolled across fields, easily climbing or even stepping over what remained of the fences. By then, he was mostly finished itching from his stingweed experience, though he lost the little canister of salve the healer had given him on his second day of walking. He had managed to hunt up some plantain, as instructed, so he was not completely without relief.

While Levi trudged along—hungry, too hot, or rained upon, and looking steadily more bedraggled once again—Boots and Molly were having a lovely time. Of course the cat did not fancy the rain, but the fields they walked through were filled with fat mice, and Molly never had to look far for grazing.

Levi wished he could just put his head down and chomp on the weeds and shrubs like the horse.

"With my luck," he mumbled, "The first patch of plants I'd eat would be more stingweed. Hello, what's this now?" Levi stopped and examined a wooden sign at the side of the path. It was cracked, moss was growing on it, and it had started to list to one side, but the painted words were clear enough.

"BEWARE OF OGRE"

"At least we know we're in the right place. Who do you think painted this?" Levi crouched in front of the sign. "The farmers? The Ogre himself? I wish I knew what to beware exactly. Will I be attacked, or warned off with magic? We haven't seen any sign of those Shades the princess fought. Maybe they don't hang around here..." He raked his hand back through his long bangs, aware that they now stuck up at dramatic angles. He reached out to wipe some of the moss away in the hope there might be more writing hidden on the sign somewhere, and the hunk of wood with "OGRE" on it fell off into the grass with a soft plop.

Boots marched over and sat on the fallen piece of sign, grinning a cat grin.

Levi chuckled. "Now it looks like we should beware you, Boots."

"Meow!" Boots agreed.

"Come on, you two," Levi said, taking Molly's lead rope and beginning his trudge afresh. "We're almost there." Levi looked up past the fields full of twisted thorns and thick stalks of feral corn grappling with grapevine. Still no sign of a single enemy. He could make out the castle more clearly now and noted that it was more of a mansion than a proper, defensible castle. No moat, no great wall or high cliff, but the dark stone looked sturdy, and Levi imagined The Ogre could fit quite a few guards or soldiers inside.

A bizarre feeling of confidence filled him as he followed what remained of the road towards The Ogre's keep. Nothing had attacked, chased, or attempted to eat him yet. He'd half expected The Ogre himself to charge from the castle. He imagined a lumbering beast with rippling muscles, claws as long as Levi's hand, and deadly sharp tusks.

When no such creature materialized, and the unseasonably warm day went on uneventfully, his determination intensified. He was here to see The Ogre and get his curse broken, and if he could not, well, at least he would have done something that no one else had. Not even the heroic princess.

It didn't take long at a steady walk to find himself standing before The Ogre's gate. The wall around the castle would have been nothing to an invading army, but looked quite formidable to a miller's son. He craned his neck back, taking in the evenly laid bricks, and the metal spines along the top. The gate was constructed of tarnished metal with thick bars and no obvious hand or footholds for climbing. Of course, climbing would be out of the question for someone who could seriously injure himself falling from a step stool.

Levi reached out, wondering if The Ogre would have any need to lock his gate. Apparently he did, because the gate didn't budge.

Levi looked back to his animals as though they might have some idea what to do next. Boots still sat on the horse's rump, looking disinterestedly towards the mansion with low-lidded eyes. Levi considered walking along the fence to see if he could find a gap or weak spot.

He gasped in pain as his arm was unexpectedly jerked. Molly had spooked, tossing her head and yanking his shoulder. Boots fell onto the ground with an annoyed yowl. He darted away into the long grass and, with a final effort, Molly pulled free of Levi's grip and joined the cat in his retreat.

"What in the gods' names?" Levi gasped. His skin prickled like someone had run a finger up his spine. In his chest, something stirred like a waking cat, and he turned back to the gate in confusion. His mouth fell open. The latch was undone, and the gate was standing ajar.

He glanced over his shoulder towards Molly, who stood several yards away and clearly had no intention of coming closer. "Alright...everyone be calm. I think there must be a mechanism. Wait, I'll show you. On the other side of the gate there'll be gears and chains and a pulley. Maybe the line even runs underground all the way to the house so they can open it for guests without needing to come out." These explanations spilled from his lips as his eyes frantically searched for a mechanism. The horse did not seem convinced.

"Wait..." Levi breathed, "Wait, could this be magic? I've never seen magic worked on a gate before." Fledgling excitement stirred in his chest. "We came here seeking someone with magic, after all."

He rested his fingers against the gate and gave it a little shove. It swung open further, emitting a faint squeak. With his heart thundering, he stepped inside, pausing to wring his hands and look up towards the bleak windows of the heavy stone building.

He turned back and looked at Molly one more time. The horse was still standing with her ears pointed in his direction as if to say, "you can go in there if you want, but I will be staying here." Normally, she'd have begun grazing and be ignoring him by now. There was still no sign of Boots. It was unnerving not to be urged onward by a demanding meow.

A gravel carriage path and a swath of overgrown yard was all that stood between Levi and the huge front doors. The grass reached Levi's waist, and he imagined snakes or very large spiders lurking inside. Or perhaps the shadow creatures slithering between the stalky grass blades.

He made his halting way towards the imposing front doors.

As nothing had decided to attack him, Levi dared to stop for a moment to admire the stonework of the castle and wonder what tools the builders had used to get the big, square stones so evenly matched. These had not been plucked from a field and mortared into a wall like puzzle pieces, as was common practice in the countryside.

Much of the building was overrun with thick, leafy vines, and Levi knew that eventually those crafty plants would worm their fingers into the mortar and start to erode even the excellent stone itself. Perhaps he might point this out to The Ogre to earn himself some favor before he asked for magical assistance.

Levi folded his arms protectively over his chest as he considered the front door, which was nearly twice his height and almost as wide. He knew the doors must be latched and wondered if he should try to locate a side servant entrance. As he leaned out to look down along the wall for other methods of ingress, he spotted a pull chain beside the big door. Tentatively, he wrapped his hand around the cold links. This might be his last chance to flee. He could return to his animal friends, perhaps head back into the farm country and try to make a life for himself.

The chain broke off near his hand, and he nearly burst out laughing as he looked at the faintly rusted links dangling across his palm.

There was nothing for it. He reached up to the remaining chain and gave it a firm yank. There was the jangle of a distant bell before the rest of the chain snapped and coiled to the ground at Levi's feet. He wondered if he should try to put the chain back up, in hopes that The Ogre wouldn't notice.

The door opened of its own accord with ponderous slowness and the cry of weary hinges. Levi shied back before he could be struck by the door, but quickly recovered himself, standing up and brushing his hands on his pants like a youngster come home after a day of playing in the dirt.

If Levi had expected the inside of the castle to be dimly lit and dungeon-like, he was surprised. The massive room that spread before him was unnaturally bright, brighter than the outdoors had been. An elegant carpet spread before him across a black and white marble floor.

Now he was reduced to an awestruck child as he took in the grand entry hall. He'd heard of such places in fine homes. Guests would gather, greeted by servants, before being ushered to ball rooms, or dining rooms, or wherever wealthy people liked to spend their time. Usually, in the stories, a woman dressed in lavish silks would dramatically descend the main stairs, much to the awe of some waiting prince. There was no sign of any fine gentlemen or elegant ladies in this particular hall.

Levi took in the shining floor, as smooth as undisturbed water. The walls were painted white with vines stenciled expertly along door frames and windows, and the banisters of the grand staircase that spread before him at the other end of the room were hewn from red oak and polished to a sheen. He still wasn't entirely certain where the light was coming from. The tall windows? The golden chandelier, which was covered in hanging glass beads like captured raindrops? No, none of the candles were lit. It must have been sunlight that somehow illuminated every nook and cranny. But how could the muted light from the tall, slim windows reach every corner so efficiently?

He couldn't help himself, he wanted to know how it worked, to figure out the puzzle as he stepped into the room. "Mirrors," he mumbled, absently reaching up to touch one of the thick curtains which hung all the way to the floor. The fabric was finer than any clothing he had ever owned.

In this grand hall he felt like a clot of dirt picked from someone's boot. "It must be done with mirrors."

"No mirrors. Magic."

Levi whipped around, flushing with nerves and wishing he had a hat to take off.

Across the room a short, well-dressed man stood smiling without showing any teeth. He had smooth, sallow skin, so pale it was almost grey, and narrow, intelligent eyes that were green as a field in summer. His hair was pitch black and combed slickly back from a widow's peak.

The man folded long fingered hands before himself and looked expectantly at Levi.

"M-magic?" Levi asked, not certain if he should bow, shake hands, or flee. This couldn't be The Ogre. Probably a servant. This was working out better than he had dared hope.

"Yes, my dear lad. Magic." The small man stepped closer. He carried himself like a lord. Upright with his shoulders back and measured stride. Levi imagined himself trying to walk that way and almost chuckled as he saw himself toppling over backwards in his mind's eye.

The stranger, hands still clasped, strode up directly in front of Levi, and he found himself shrinking back. He knew that he could probably do some real damage to this skinny fellow if he wanted to, but he was unnerved by this man for no reason he could put his finger on. Maybe it was the unhealthy pallor of his skin, or the glint in his eyes that warned of something deeper.

Levi took a backward step, and the man scrutinized him as though studying an interesting beetle that had waddled across his path. He almost seemed to be sniffing Levi.

"Er... I... I wanted to see The Ogre?" Levi managed in a cracking voice.

"Did you, now?" The man leaned back, looking Levi up and down, one elegant eyebrow cocked. "What's your name, lad?"

"L-Levi."

"Levi? That's all? No surname?"

"Miller?" Levi shrugged. "Where I come from most people are known by their jobs."

"Interesting," said the man, though he did not sound interested. He was still staring at Levi in a way that made the miller's son want to grab the thick curtain to cover himself. He wished again that Boots had come with him. The cat was always good at breaking the ice in awkward situations.

"Why have you come to see The Ogre, Levi Miller?" the man asked.

Levi hesitated. He hadn't spoken to any humans about his curse, and even though this person seemingly knew about magic. He set his jaw. He hadn't come all this way only to pretend everything was fine. It was ow or never. "I have...I have a curse placed on me. A curse of bad luck, and I want it broken. I was hoping The Ogre could help."

Both elegantly slanted eyebrows shot up, creasing the man's parchment smooth forehead. "A curse? Really? How novel! I've never seen one of those up close! No wonder you have so much magic clinging to you. It won't come free! It's like it's part of you."

"What?" Levi tried to move away again and found his back against the wall.

The man was smiling again, still without showing any teeth. "It's why I let you in. I could sense the magic on you, even miles out. I couldn't understand it, so I allowed you to come to my castle." The man's thin mouth twitched. "Do you suppose there are more like you, Levi Miller? More people with magic bound to them like this?" He reached up and placed slim fingers against Levi's chest for a moment before withdrawing his hand and looking curiously at his fingertips. Levi wondered if some of the sweat and grime on his clothes had come off on this person's clean hand.

"Er..." Levi's mind strayed to thoughts of Fergus and Brodie. His brothers, not cursed but blessed. Did they have magic bound to them as well? He decided not to mention them just yet. "I don't know."

"Hmmm," the man rubbed his fingers together, pursing thin lips. "Sometimes I can feel little pockets of magic still out in the kingdom, but beyond my reach. They will not come to me as the other magic did."

"Wait." Levi raised a hand, already regretting the question he was about to ask. "You...you're The Ogre?"

"Ah, please, call me Simon." The man gave a dramatic bow, sweeping an arm back elegantly, his other hand pressed to his chest.

Levi did not try to mimic the artful motion and dipped his head instead. He glanced towards the big doors. They had slid shut behind him without his noticing.

"I know what you're thinking," the man said. "This is The Ogre? With a title like that shouldn't he be a bit bigger? More horrifying?"

"Er—"

"Ah, but you see, I am a mage. The most powerful mage in the lands, even before." He cleared his throat, his mouth twisting into a grimace for a moment before his smiled returned. "I have one of the rarest magical gifts there is. The power of transformation. I can transform ordinary things into whatever I please. Give life and a fresh form to a common cup, or knife, or shadow. I can also transform myself. Would you like to see?"

"Uh—"

"Alright. Stand back. I don't want to frighten you. I assure you that what you see before you in a few moments will still be me. Merely Simon wearing a powerful disguise."

Levi did try to step back, but the wall was firmly behind him. He cut a glance toward the window, wondering if he should risk jumping through. He knew he'd end up cut to ribbons by the glass, but perhaps he wouldn't be killed.

Luckily the man moved away from him to the center of the room. Then, raising arms adorned in fine, forest green velvet, the man spoke a few words and began to transform as easily as one might pull on a shirt. He seemed to stretch in all directions, outward and upward. His limbs grew thick as tree trunks. His torso was a mass of rippling muscle, etched with widening scars. His face was transformed as well, boiling for a moment in a roil of churning flesh that made Levi's stomach turn before finally settling into a new shape. Prominent cheek bones, a wide jaw, and small, sunken eyes, still green and shining with cleverness. Massive tusks protruded from the creature's lower jaw, and it stood, apelike, balanced forward on its knuckles. Its skin had the same green hue and velvety texture as the man's coat.

Levi pressed himself against the wall, but did not feel as frightened as he thought he should have. His mind seemed to have decided that, rather than be completely terrified, it would go numb, offering no suggestions as to a plan of action. Thus Levi stood, staring and unmoving, breathing hard and fast. There were flashes of memory as he recalled monster stories he'd heard as a child, but what good were tales when you were actually meeting a true ogre?

After watching Levi with his small eyes for a few moments, The Ogre seemed to decide he had made his point and changed back. He shrank down to his previous, human size with much greater speed than when he had transformed outward.

He stood, elegant and gentlemanly, before Levi again. This time he did show teeth when he smiled. Levi noted that they were very white, and his eye teeth were sharp. "Simon" spread his arms. "There? How was that for an ogre? I hope I didn't frighten you too much. I seldom get the chance to show off my abilities these days."

Levi wanted to say something. Anything really. No words came. He was an utter simpleton faced with an impossible magic, and he was handling it as a simpleton might. He scolded himself in his head, but no amount of internal admonishments would allow him to form words.

"I see I have frightened you," said Simon, a kind tone coming to his voice. "Believe me, lad, that was far from my intention. I merely wished to show you that I am indeed The Ogre that you sought. I have no intention to harm you. Especially as you are so fascinating to me. You and your curse. What was it?"

"Bad luck." Levi finally managed to force his lips to move.

"Bad luck." Simon put his knuckle to his lips as he considered. "My, that is rather vague. Why don't you come have dinner with me and tell me all about yourself?" He turned, indicating one of the doors, which was white and painted with golden vines and delicate, raised leaves made of thin metal. "I would love to know all the details of your predicament, and it may even aid me in freeing you from it."

That was the fire Levi needed to get himself moving again. His legs came back under his control and he began to walk along with the man towards the indicated door as if his body had decided to take control, since his mind could not be relied upon. He knew he was out of place in his filthy clothes, and he was aware that he must smell terrible.

He tried to flatten his messy hair, which he guessed looked like a pile of straw. He saw no mirrors to check his appearance in, nor to explain the brightness of the room. He ached to find the mechanisms, the cause and effect, some fragment of his world where things made sense and people did not transform into monsters.

He supposed that he would have to give up his own world and surrender to this strange one. He could certainly stand it long enough to get his curse broken. That was it. He had to focus on breaking the curse. Everything else was secondary and things seemed to be going his way for once. He'd found The Ogre with ease and was already making friends. This was good.

He was led into a hallway that was just as brightly lit as the front hall had been. The walls here were vibrantly colored and along the corridor hung paintings depicting trellised gardens and happy people cavorting in grassy parks. Levi kept himself away from these, and any of the delicately painted vases he passed as he followed his host. Only once did he catch his foot on the carpet and lose his balance.

He grabbed at the wall for support and instead found himself grasping the thick frame of a painting. He snatched his hand away as though scorched lest he damage the precious item, and allowed himself to fall instead.

"Oh dear! Are you hurt?" Simon turned, looking down at Levi with what appeared to be genuine concern.

"No, no." Levi chuckled dryly. "I just tripped."

"Does this happen often?" Simon extended a slim hand for Levi to take.

Remembering what had happened when he tried to help Princess Joanna onto her horse, Levi took the offered hand with the utmost gentleness and picked himself up with no help from the man.

Simon looked at Levi with a cocked eyebrow, but didn't comment, turning and continuing to lead the way down the lavish hallway. Several more doors along the walls indicated the vastness of the castle. Levi had never been inside a building with so many rooms. The largest he had ever seen was the inn in the village, and that only had three sleeping rooms, a main one, and a kitchen in the back. He knew he could be lost in seconds if he tried to wander this place on his own.

The corridor was not so long, but it seemed to Levi, in his constant effort not to touch or bump anything, as if it went on forever.

At the end stood another finely decorated door. Simon pushed it open to reveal a dining hall. Levi gasped. It was everything he had imagined from the stories and so much more. The long table of polished, red-hued wood, the crystalline plates and goblets all perfectly set. The shimmering candelabras and lavish wall hangings depicting running stags and blooming gardens. There were little tables to the side where servants would arrange the meals before presenting them to their waiting masters and their guests. Levi put his hands firmly at his sides and stood still as stone, almost afraid to breathe amidst all this finery.

"Come, sit," Simon urged, striding into the room and pulling out a chair.

"Those legs look... thin," Levi managed, eying the chair with concern. It was a beautiful piece of furniture with carved arms and legs that looked like coiling waves. The seat itself was green velvet bedecked with needlework vines creeping up its surface. All very excellent reasons he should not sit down. "My bad luck makes it so that I...break most everything I touch."

"Does it?" The Ogre considered for a moment. "Well, my magic can help a bit, perhaps." With a wave of his hand and a whisper the chair transformed into a sturdy cabin chair with fine, thick legs and no adornments. "How's this?"

"Better, I think," answered Levi with awe and relief. This magic wasn't frightening or harmful. It was useful. He was already feeling silly for having been alarmed by doors that opened themselves.

He took his seat and looked nervously at the delicate plates set before him until Simon transformed these into wooden plates. They were still far finer than any Levi had kept at home, and he grinned gratefully. In spite of the fact that he stuck out like a lone fence post in a field, The Ogre did not seem to notice.

"There we are. Much better. Now dinner, and we can discuss that curse of yours," Simon announced cheerfully and clapped his hands twice.

Levi turned to see two shadows cast by the candles and the tall windows at the far end of the room coil themselves upward in a decidedly unnatural way. He shrank back as the Shades crept up the walls until they stood as tall as men and formed themselves into wavering, human shapes.

Levi couldn't help but cast a look over his shoulder in an effort to see who was casting these impressive shadows, but there were only himself and The Ogre sitting in the room. Levi turned back to see the Shades detach themselves from the wall and begin to glide about.

He swallowed and gripped the arms of his chair, recalling the creatures that had attacked that carriage—how they had clawed relentlessly at the carriage doors and windows, like foxes trying to oust a chicken from its pen.

"Don't be afraid of my servants." Simon spoke in a reassuring voice. "I can use my powers of transformation to make these shadows into my loyal workers. They don't mind a bit, as they have no minds of their own."

Levi watched with mounting suspicion as the Shades slipped noiselessly from the room, sliding through the cracks instead of opening the door and leaving behind empty brightness where they had been.

Levi realized with a start that he finally understood why the front room and hallway had been so oddly well lit. There had been no shadows where there should have been many. When Simon called them to task, they left nothing behind. A shiver ran up Levi's spine and his knuckles went white as he gripped his chair arms. Most people feared darkness, but the unearthly lightness of everything in this place was unsettling as well.

Levi licked his lips, feeling as though he was expected to say something. "I uh...I have heard of these Shade people causing some...trouble down in the farmlands beyond your land," Levi tried to sound nonchalant. He pried his fingers from the arms of his chair and instead fidgeted with the corner of a silky napkin.

"Have you now?" Simon asked. He gave no sign of insult on his smooth features. Instead, he settled his own napkin in his lap and looked indulgently at Levi. "I admit that keeping track of all these Shades can be a challenge. They do get away from me and perhaps people see them and become frightened. They wouldn't mean to harm anyone of course, but being brainless they might occasionally do something I would not condone. What have you heard?"

"N-nothing much!" Levi spluttered, then grimaced. A miller's son had little need for guile, and he hated that he had not gained any new skill at it in his travels. "I heard a rumor that some Shades attacked a carriage, that's all." He hesitated, then added, "And that the princess drove them off."

"Ah yes, Princess Joanna."

"You know her?" Levi's eyes widened and he sat forward.

"Well, of course. She *is* the second born to the king and queen of these lands! I should say I know of her at the very least. I have never met her in person, but I quite admire her little campaign to rid the land of evil, even if she is barking up the wrong tree with my Shades. I'm certain that they were only misbehaving, and I am quite glad she sent them packing."

"So, it was an accident then?" Levi asked.

"Yes, quite." Simon nodded once, sharply.

The Shades returned to the room using the door this time and carrying with them wide trays of food. Levi might have died from the heavenly scent alone, even before roast mutton with leeks and carrots was set before him, surrounded by little, colorful potatoes and slathered in cream sauce. He thought he might like to smash his face directly into the food and eat like a ravenous dog. He completely forgot the horrifying Shades that battled the princes. His stomach overrode his brain as he took in the spread with wide, childlike eyes.

"I thought we would skip the soup and salad courses, as you look half starved." Simon said, smiling warmly.

"Thank you, sir!" Levi was unable to tear his eyes from the steaming perfection being settled on the table.

"Never mind that 'sir' business. Please, just call me Simon," the mage said, still wearing an unpracticed, but amiable expression. He folded his hands and watched expectantly as Levi stared at the food.

Levi looked up, mouth-watering, but still patient. "If you don't mind my asking, do you say a meal blessing?"

"Hmm?" Simon cocked his head.

"Well, my family usually forgot our blessing, but when we remembered we said one to the Mother Goddess and Father God. Sometimes I would say a little one to the animal gods too." Levi blushed, wishing he hadn't mentioned it. People who were raised in polite society probably knew exactly how to handle meal blessings wherever they visited. He clasped his hands in his lap, knowing he must look like an utter bumpkin.

Simon laughed. A light, tittering sound that reminded Levi of dry leaves in a breeze. "Ah, yes. We do not usually bother with meal blessings in this house. I do not put much stock in these Mother and Father characters that are so popular these days, and I am not fond of the old gods in the least." Simon's lip curled when he spoke of the animal gods. His features seemed to fold into that bitter expression much more readily than into a pleasant one.

"Not fond of them?" Levi asked, half wondering if this meant he might begin eating immediately. He had met plenty of people who chuckled at his fondness for the old gods, but most dismissed it as whimsical fancy. No one had showed disdain against the animals themselves before.

"Yes." Simon was still scowling, though he had begun to pick at his food, which Levi took as his cue to begin. "They are greedy little creatures who can hoard magic for themselves if they choose and never share it with the world."

Levi had already stuffed a sizable chunk of mutton into his mouth and found the savory, soft meat to be the best thing he thought he had ever tasted in his entire life. It was all he could do not to let out a little moan of happiness. He hardly even noticed as the cream sauce spilled down his chin. He snatched his fine napkin and tried to delicately dab his mouth as Simon was doing. Instead, he dropped the napkin into his food.

"Never mind." Simon smiled indulgently again. Like he'd found a new pet. He snapped his fingers and one of the Shades slid over and plucked Levi's messy napkin from his plate, then passed him a new, crisply folded one from a small stack on a preparation table. "Now then," Simon said, sitting forward. "Tell me all about your bad luck curse. How does it work?"

Levi took a more manageable bite of potato and chewed thoroughly before he spoke. "The bad luck mostly focuses on me and whatever I am trying to do. It can be small things, like stubbing my toe or bumping my head, or it can be disastrous, like causing me to break important things." He thought of all the time he had tried to help with the mill work. He could lift and carry almost as well as Fergus. He was strong and fit and a hard worker, but it little mattered when every tool fell to pieces in his hands. "My family eventually got tired of me ruining everything I touched, so I wasn't allowed to work around the mill much." Levi's broad shoulders sagged.

"Can your bad luck reach other people as well?" Simon asked. His green eyes were bright.

"It can. Usually if I am making physical contact with that person. Or if I am standing too near them for too long. Then I start to ruin their things by giving them bad luck." He thought of the healer's broken satchel strap and how the princess had fallen while trying to mount up, all thinks to him. "Things near me will break without warning as well. I've ruined fences by standing beside them, and bags of grain split open when I walk past. Mostly my luck stays on me, or near me."

"Fascinating!" Simon's eyes sparked with hungry interest and he tented his fingers over his plate. "Can your luck be deadly?"

"I suppose it could," Levi shrugged. "When I was little, it would make me get sick far worse than my brothers were. I got hurt all the time." He held up one of his hands, which was etched with little scars. "I have more on my arms and torso. Something came to Levi then, and he wondered that he had not considered it before. He supposed that it was because no one had ever asked him about his curse. "Animals," he said.

"Pardon?" Simon sat up straighter and shot uneasy glances around the room, as though seeking the animals Levi had mentioned.

"No, I mean, my luck doesn't seem to affect animals. I guess I never thought of it before, but I can be near animals as much as I like and nothing bad happens to them. Otherwise I'd be laming horses left and right, and my cat would never catch a single mouse!"

"Cat?" Simon squirmed in his chair. "You have a cat? Is it here?"

"No. He's outside. He must have decided to do some hunting. Otherwise, he is almost always at my side. He's a good friend."

"Good friend," Simon scoffed. "Cats are no one's friend."

Levi thought to respond, but decided better of it. Plenty of people disliked cats, and there was no need to argue about it with the man he hoped could remove his curse. "So..." Levi said instead, after another hearty bite of his meal. "What do you think? Can you break the spell on me?"

Simon shook his head jerkily as though to clear it, then fixed his emerald gaze on Levi once more. "I am uncertain. I have never dealt with someone quite like you, though I have long hoped to solve the mystery of those people I could sense in the land with magic trapped inside them. I suggest you stay the night in my castle, and I will consult my books to see what I can gather for you tomorrow." A hunger had replaced the nervous glint in the mage's eyes.

Levi ignored it.

"Alright." He agreed without pausing to think. The lavish food alone made this place worth any creepiness and strange shadows. Simon seemed nice enough, and willing to listen and help, which was a rarity to say the least. It conjured memories of Da, sitting in the sunset-warmed yard and listening to young Levi share the adventures, or misadventures, of his day.

Levi knew he should be cautious, but already he was daydreaming. What could he do with no bad luck to hold him back? He pictured himself riding to each of the mills he would own, supervising and sharing his ideas and drawings for improvements with his foremen. In his imaginings, the princess would come by and wave to him like a friend, and he would wave back, and everyone would be impressed and ask him how he knew the royal family. Then another thought struck him. "Simon, I also have a horse waiting outside your gates. Can I put her in your stable?"

Simon's jaw tightened noticeably but he planted a drawn smile on his face. "Alright. So long as you see to her. My Shades are no good at that sort of thing. Also, so long as you never bring her near me."

"No, of course I wouldn't if you did not want me to," Levi raised his hands in a calming gesture, caught the edge of his plate, and flipped it so dramatically that gravy splattered the wall and potatoes rolled to the floor. "Gods! I'm so sorry!" Levi gasped, attempting to sweep up the mess with his new napkin.

"Never mind, never mind. It's alright." Simon's smile became genuine as he gestured for his uncanny servants to clean up. "I understand, lad. It's the curse. Not your fault! Please, sit back and be at your ease. My Shades will have everything tidy in no time at all."

Levi did sit back, mostly because he didn't want the Shades to touch him. He had no idea what that would feel like and had no desire to find out.

Once they had tidied away his spilled food, they retreated behind the servant door and returned with a fresh plate. Levi marveled that they were able to make the food so quickly. Maybe Simon used his powers to transform uncooked meat into cooked. What did magic taste like? Could he tell if he ate something that had been magicked?

Transformed or not, the food was delicious, and Levi's stomach still felt like an empty sack, so he resolved to keep eating.

Once Levi had settled back to his meal, Simon asked a few more gentle questions about his curse. Levi surprised himself with how much he knew and understood about his affliction. He hadn't even known it was a curse until recently, yet he had inwardly recorded all the information he could about it so he could live his life. He recalled his childhood being so much more challenging than his adulthood. He had thought it was because all childhoods were challenging, but as he spoke he understood it was because, as he grew, he got a handle on his curse without realizing it.

After the meal was finished, Simon led Levi out to fetch Molly and set her up in the stables beside the main house.

Levi clasped his hands behind his back, uneasy in the hallways. Very few shadows rested where they should, against floor or wall. Most were absent and Levi wondered where they could be. He imagined more of them attacking carriages or getting into scraps with Princess Joanna and winced in worry.

After beautiful hallways and uncertain silence, Simon opened a plain looking door onto the outside. Levi blinked in the natural light. They had come out on the northern side of the castle, and Levi could see the front gate off to his left and Molly standing patiently in the field beyond, enjoying the long grass and hearty weeds.

Simon excused himself with a terse bow. "I'll leave you to it. I must retire to my study and begin my research. One of my Shades will show you to your room when you have finished."

"Will your Shades leave Molly alone overnight?" Levi asked, awkwardly mimicking the bow. He knew the horse wouldn't enjoy an evening filled with spooky creatures slithering around her.

"They have no need to go to the stable, so of course *the animal* will be left to itself." Simon said, wrinkling his nose when he said, "the animal." Then, with a curt nod, he turned on his heel and briskly marched away into the depths of the castle, shutting the door with a snap.

Levi made his way across the wide, stone yard to the overgrown lawn and the front gate. It opened with a simple push of his hand. No magic or mechanisms required this time. Molly looked up as he approached and huffed a happy greeting, lipping his arm affectionately.

"I missed you too, sweet girl. Come on, I have a nice stall for you to sleep in tonight. You've eaten enough grass that you shan't need any hay for dinner, which is good because I think hay left around here would be moldy by now." Levi paused and looked around. "Have you seen Boots?"

The horse swished her tail and nipped at a few long stems of grass.

"Boots?" Levi called. He cupped his hand to his mouth and tried again. "Boots! Here, puss puss! Come on, Boots! I have a nice soft bed waiting for us tonight! Come on, puss puss!"

No response from the swaying weeds. Levi's shoulders drooped. What if something had happened? Had the frightened cat fallen into a hole or been attacked by a Shade? In all this wild, overgrown country, Levi could imagine weasels, badgers, or wild dogs that would attack a cat. He knew that it would be useless to search. Even if an ordinary person could find Boots, which did not seem likely, he knew he never would. He tried one more time, scanning the terrain, now overlaid with the crimson glow of sunset. "BOOTS! Come on, Boots! They have mutton and a soft bed inside! Come on!" No grass parted, no orange fur stood out against the weeds.

Levi heaved an unhappy sigh and took hold of Molly's rope. He made his way slowly towards the stable, keeping his eyes open for Boots as he went. This meant he could not watch where he stepped, and he tripped several times.

Molly helped him stay upright by throwing her weight to the side as he toppled. He patted the horse's neck. "Thanks, girl."

The stable was in a serious state of disuse, and Levi had to find a broom and chase away thick cobwebs before he led the horse inside. He knocked over several things as he swept, but there were no lit lanterns or sharp objects, so he didn't worry about it. Once he had selected one of the oak walled stalls that lined one side of the long stable for Molly, he searched up some straw for her to bed down on. He took this outside and opened the bale, shaking it and kicking it around to get the dust out.

Once the straw was as dust free as he could make it Levi put it down in Molly's new stall and led her inside, slipping her halter from her face and hanging it on a peg. The peg fell out and clattered to the floor. Levi chuckled. "Sometimes I still forget." Molly blinked lazily at him in agreement. Levi set the halter on top of a wooden box instead.

He wandered the stable for a bit until he tracked down a tack room. What remained inside was in poor shape, but he dug a curry comb and brush with bristles that hadn't been chewed by mice, and a hoof pick that wasn't completely rusted through. He wondered how old everything was. His father always told him that The Ogre had arrived when he was still young. How old had Simon been when he showed up and began siphoning away the magic? As he brushed Molly and cleaned out her feet, his hands itched to sketch images of the castle as it must have been in its heyday.

Levi pulled open Molly's blanket-pouch and dug around to make sure nothing new had broken or spilled. He also took out a thick pack of paper, which he had bartered two rabbits for to replace the ruined stuff from home, and a few pencils. He'd given up on his pen and ink because he hadn't been able to keep the ink from spilling on everything no matter what he tried.

"Alright, Mol." Levi petted the horse a few extra times, half expecting to look up and see Boots seated on her back. He dared a glance and, of course, there was no cat, so he heaved a sigh and slipped out of the stall, carefully latching the door. Satisfied that the latch wasn't about to fall apart from his touch, he left the stable, striding out into the paved yard.

The sun was nearly set, and the courtyard was darker than expected, thanks to the surrounding walls. He never would have thought he'd be excited to see spreading shadows that looked perfectly ordinary.

Levi knocked tentatively at the little side door, uncertain what the protocol was. Seconds later the door opened, and a Shade loomed on the other side. Levi shuddered and tried not to look at where a face should be. He could see right through the two "eyes" straight to the wall beyond, and there was no nose or mouth at all. Levi wondered if the Shades could see in the conventional sense, or if some magical power allowed them to find their way.

The Shade raised a wispy arm to indicated that Levi should follow it. Levi swallowed. "Er, yes...of course. You'll take me to a room where I can stay the night?"

The Shade nodded, its head rippling like cloth.

Levi shuffled after the creature, though he found himself wishing that he could spend the night in the stable with Molly. He didn't fancy a night in the grand castle filled with shadows that could come alive at any moment. He wasn't sure which he found more alarming, the lack of shadows in corners where they should be, or seeing them alive wandering the castle.

More hallways, some stairs, and several terrifying moments with fragile decor later, Levi found himself deposited in a room that might have seemed plain to someone like Simon, but was downright lavish to the miller's son. The walls were papered in robin's egg blue, accented with white fleurs-de-lis. There was an enormous bed heaped with fluffy blankets, a standing wardrobe carved of beautiful mahogany, a dressing table with mirror, and, near the fireplace, a large claw-footed tub already filled with warm water for bathing. Best of all, on the far side of the bed, stood an elegantly carved desk, where Levi hurried to set down the papers and writing tools he had clutched to his chest.

This done, he found himself afraid to move farther. He'd tracked some muck from his boots across the floor and had no desire to make more of a mess. He half expected every shadow to transform into a creature that would attack him, but none did.

After a few minutes of standing still, breathing in his new situation, Levi decided he need to stop being such a bumpkin. He slipped off his boots and set them by the door. Surprisingly, they were still in good condition, and, while they had been tight at first, they were now better molded to his feet than any footwear he' ever owned. And they reminded him of his pleasant time with the princess and her men.

He turned to explore the room. He opened the wardrobe and was confronted with a plethora of crisp shirts and neatly hanging trousers. Nothing fancy, but serviceable and sturdy. He touched one of the shirt sleeves, half convinced that the garment would come apart at the seams the moment his fingertips brushed it. It did not. The stitching work was excellent and looked as though it could take punishment.

It reminded Levi a bit of how Ma had sewn his clothes back home. He caught a glimpse of himself in the mirror and flinched. Even the tunic the princess had given him was hanging off him like a potato sack after days of hard wear. It was a wonder anyone took him seriously. His skin was tanned by the sun and his hair such a disheveled mess, it surprised even him. The beggars back in the village would have mocked him. He tried to drag his fingers through his hair and met with painful tangles.

Levi stripped, tossed his old clothes aside, and eased himself into the waiting bath water. As weeks of road grime washed away, he wondered if he could accidentally break the bathtub. To his surprise, nothing cracked, the water didn't turn icy, and he was able to find the soap and a rag to give himself a good scrub.

He lay there for a long time, up to his jaw in pleasant lavender scent and warmth. He hadn't realized how much his muscles ached until the water eased his pains away. He might have fallen asleep, but knew better. No need to nearly drown himself in a bathtub.

Once the water had gone completely tepid and all the pleasant smell was gone, Levi began the ungraceful act of getting out of the tub. The edges of the tub and the stone floor below were slick. As he fiercely gripped the side of the tub, he almost wished one of those shadow creatures would appear to help him out. Almost.

It took three tries to convince himself to throw his leg over the side and climb free of the water. His hand slipped with a jerk, but he managed to keep himself upright. With both feet firmly on the floor he gratefully wrapped himself in the plush towel that hung on a rack beside the tub.

Heaving a breath of relief, he took an unwary step and brought his foot down on a bar of soap which had somehow ended up on the floor. The soap flew one way, Levi the other. He flailed for anything to steady himself, toppled the towel rack and heard it break, smashed his shoulder into the tub, and landed on the stone floor so hard his teeth clacked together.

Levi lay for a moment in a pathetic heap, feeling like an idiot. His shoulder throbbed, and all his sore muscles were screaming again as though they had never stopped. "Ow," he muttered.

He hissed as he sat up, taking stock of his position. The towel rack was ruined.

"Meow?!" A warm, furry friend was rushing over, all concern and flared whiskers.

"Boots?" Levi asked in amazement as his cat avoided a few puddles on the floor and trotted to his side. "What on earth? Where did you come from?" He looked around as he petted Boots. "How did you find me in this big place?" Smell, Levi supposed. He didn't like to think about the odor coming from his pile of old clothes. "Boots, Boots, I'm fine!" he chuckled as the cat looked him over like a concerned mother, trilling and prodding with his nose. "You've seen me fall loads of times."

"Mer mer mer mi!" The cat scolded.

"I'm sorry for whatever it is I seem to have done." He got hold of his towel and stood with a grimace. "I will admit that wasn't one of my better landings." He checked his shoulder and saw a thick red bruise already forming. "This'll last me a while I suppose." He sat down on the edge of the bed and Boots jumped up beside him, butting Levi with his head several times.

"Where were you anyhow? You made me worry." Levi crossed the room to the wardrobe.

"Mew meow!" Boots followed Levi around the room.

"Fair enough," Levi said, doing as he was bidden and giving Boots a thorough chin scratching.

Having finished he picked out a long, white nightshirt from the wardrobe and put it on. He hadn't realized how much he'd been looking forward to sleeping in clean clothes. Not to mention the joys of not having rocks jabbing him in the spine every night.

Not ready to commit himself to the plush bed just yet, Levi crossed to the desk and sat down, spreading his papers before him to see which were in the best condition. He weeded out those that were too damp or crumbled. Once he had chosen a relatively flat piece, he took up one of his pencils and began to draw.

He wasn't certain why. It came like a compulsion, like a welcome memory. He stretched a curving line across the paper, relishing the 'hush' sound of each stroke. He hadn't been able to draw on his travels, and he hadn't realized how badly he'd missed it. This piece of him had been missing, and he'd found it again.

He tried to sketch the Shades, but couldn't get them to look right. He knew he wouldn't have much luck with trying to draw Simon either. He wasn't good at drawing humans. Several crossed-out blobs later his pencil strokes began forming the distinct lines and artful arches of the castle as he had seen it coming up the road. He lost himself in trying to get the slope of a roof just right and working out the foreshortening on the gate, letting his mind be consumed in the work and nothing else. In the margins of the drawing, he wrote what sort of stone was used here or there, and what he suspected the shingles on the tower roofs were made from.

"Mer mer?" Boots, who had been sniffing about the room, jumped up onto the desk and plopped down in the middle of Levi's drawing.

Levi blinked, sitting back as though snapped out of a trance. "Sorry, Boots, I think I was just feeling a little homesick. We're close though, Boots. Really close. Simon is going to figure out how to break the curse, and I'll be free to live my life and do whatever I please. I'll be a normal person at last!"

"Meow," Boots declared, swishing his tail across the paper and smearing the pencil lines. Levi sighed, stood, plucked the cat from his art and set him on the floor, then folded the drawing neatly.

"Come on, puss puss," Levi called as he crossed the room. He examined the bed for a few minutes, hands on hips. It was an excellent bed, but a little too high off the ground for his liking. He took hold of the mattress and pulled it from the bed onto the floor beside it. He arranged the blankets and pillows into a sort of nest and flopped down. Even without the bed's springs the mattress was unbelievably soft. "This is no straw mattress under the loft." He spread his arms and legs, unable to reach the edges. Who needed this much space to sleep?

"Boots, help me! I might never be able to get up!" Levi pretended to flail in the downy covers.

The cat watched with amusement, then strode onto the mattress and settled himself on one of Levi's legs. Resting spot chosen, the cat set to grooming a forepaw.

Levi sighed and lay still, draped over the mattress. Everything that had happened that day finally came crashing over him. He'd been stumbling along, one thing to another, but now that he was finally sitting still his thoughts took their turn to race. He'd done it. He'd found The Ogre and not only made friends, but talked he strange man into helping him. Perhaps his luck had decided to take a little break, or perhaps it couldn't do anything to The Ogre.

It did seem impossible to be here.

Surely he wasn't really in this soft bed in a castle. He had to be laying in a ditch somewhere, perhaps slowly freezing to death. This was all an elaborate hallucination. Where did someone like him get off marching up to a monster's castle and asking for help?

Well, if this was all a dying dream, it was a good one. The cat purring on his leg tethered him to what he hoped continued to be reality as he drifted into slumber.

Levi's dreams were invariably nightmares. He supposed this to be another facet of his curse.

Tonight he dreamed of the Shades, and of The Ogre taking the form of the giant beast from the entry hall. *The Ogre shuffled towards Levi, and the Shades gathered around, trying to grasp at Levi with pointed, too-long fingers. They plucked at his clothes, which were once again the sad rags he had left home in. Levi looked desperately for an escape route as the creatures closed in. All the doors and windows were gone.*

He was locked in an extravagant room, and all he wanted to do was leave it and return to his dirty little home. Distantly he heard his mother calling, tears in her voice. "Levi! Levi, come home, sweet one! Please!"

He opened his mouth to call to her, to his brothers, even his father, but his mouth was filled with lavender scented bath water that spilled down the front of his shirt.

The Ogre leaned low, maw gaping and filled with deadly tusks. The Shades clawed Levi's skin leaving long gouges. Levi flattened himself against the wall and whimpered. As he searched one last time for a way out, his eyes went wide.

A white cat with eyes the color of sunset sat watching the scene with a calmness that Levi suddenly shared. His panic was gone, his breathing steadied at once. He little noticed the grabbing hands or The Ogre's hot breath as the cat blinked at him.

There was a flash of silver light that expanded through the room like crashing water, washing the Shadows away and blinding Levi before he woke up with his usual start.

He had managed to roll off the mattress and onto the floor, jamming his already bruised shoulder. He spent a few moments thrashing in a tangle of satin sheets trying to extricate himself and determine where he was. Everything came back to him slowly—his time spent with The Ogre, Simon, and why he was sleeping in this lovely room instead of under a tree. "Boots?" He looked around for the cat. "I'm sorry if I kicked you. Boots?"

Once again his feline friend was nowhere to be seen. Boots almost always returned from hunting in the night to curl up with Levi again before morning, but Levi wasn't overly worried this time. After yesterday, he knew that the cat could vanish and reappear as it pleased him. There was, after all, a great deal of castle to explore, and Boots was nothing if not curious.

Levi went to the wardrobe, keeping an eye out for tripping hazards, and selected some clothes. A loose shirt and comfortable britches suited him well enough, but he also slipped into a vest with intricately stitched patterns like leaves on the front, and a lot of brass buttons.

He checked himself in the mirror, standing back so he couldn't break it, and raised both eyebrows in surprise. He did cut a dashing figure. If only his mother could have seen. On a whim he pulled back a handful of his hair from his brow, tying it off with a strip of leather and letting the rest hang to his shoulders. It would be messy again in seconds, and he might have to cut the leather out that night, but it was worth it for the morning. Today could be the day he'd be free of the curse at last! That thought made his chest as light as if someone had filled it with clouds.

He crossed the room in such a flurry that he fell twice, but each time scrambled to his feet as fast as he'd gone down. He reached the door and wrenched it open, leaning out onto a lavishly carpeted hallway. He looked left and right, but saw no one. He fixed his gaze on the shadow cast by a small table across the hall. Clearing his throat and feeling immensely stupid he mumbled, "er... excuse me?" No response. "Excuse me?" He tried again, then exhaled a long, frustrated huff of air. He'd never find his way around this place. "With my luck I'll end up locked in a broom cupboard."

"Good morning! Glad to see you're up! Did you sleep well?"

Levi's whipped around, to see Simon striding towards him, arms open in magnanimous greeting. He wore another green coat, different from yesterday's but just as fine, with gold stitching and buttons. Even his cravat, pinned in place with a golden pin, was dark green. The color did nothing to compliment the pale grayish pallor of his skin, but Levi didn't comment.

Chatting animatedly about the weather—"It's already shaping up to be a gloriously sunny day!"—Simon led the way down to a breakfast room. Levi had never imagined having a separate room for certain meals, but there he was. He also didn't like how much glass there was here. Tall windows to let in morning sunlight and crystalline fixtures everywhere.

Levi enjoyed delightful porridge out of a transfigured wooden bowl, and managed to lose not one, but three hard-boiled eggs under the table. Simon just laughed.

At the end of the meal, when fresh strawberries in thick cream were brought out, Levi reached for his fork without looking and slit his thumb on the knife he had purposely left unused. He hissed and stuck his thumb into his mouth.

Simon leaned forward on his elbows and studied Levi. "I must say, it is a wonder with such bad luck that you still have both your eyes. Are you still in possession of all your fingers and toes?"

"I do have some scars. Lots on my hands and feet." Levi held out his free hand. It was etched across with white lines. An intricate map of an unfortunate history. "My family was attentive, and I learned how my curse worked without even realizing it." Levi thought of how nerve-wracking it must have been for his parents to take care of someone like him. He knew Fergus and Brodie were fed up with it. They'd spent their lives having to look out for a brother seemingly destined to injure or kill himself in a plethora of ways.

"Come, then!" Simon was on his feet and placing a hand on Levi's arm. "Come down to my study and we'll discuss my findings about your curse."

Levi jumped up too fast and bumped the table. The legs groaned in protest, fit to break, but The Ogre was ready with magic. In seconds the legs were transformed to be sturdier. A rampaging bull would have had trouble breaking them.

Levi marveled at the ease of it. Living with someone with the power to fix all of Levi's mistakes was a dream almost equal to being cured.

Levi was practically bouncing with anticipation and nerves as they made their way through fine halls and down a winding set of stairs that seemed to lead into the heart of the earth.

The study was in a sub-level of the castle, deep underground. The Ogre opened a door onto a circular room. Levi had never seen so many books in one place. They were on shelves, stacked in towers on the floor, and draped open on every surface. To his surprise, the shadows that were cast here by a plethora of candles and lamps were entirely where they should be. Not a one showed any sign of springing to life. Lingering shadows were normally unnerving, but now he found he preferred them to the eerie front hall and passages.

"Welcome, welcome!" Simon spread his arms to indicate the room. "This is where I do all my magical work and study. I figure out new spells and learn all about my gift."

Levi moved cautiously about, taking in the towering shelves and breathing the loamy scent of earth and old books. He peered at the nearest stack of tomes and resisted the urge to pluck one from the top and take a long whiff of the yellowing pages. Instead, he let his fingers drag over a textured cover. The pile rocked dangerously, and he withdrew his hand.

"I never had many books as a child." Levi admitted, almost to himself. "I loved the ones we had. I can read," he added hastily. Many of the farm folk in their area learned reading and basic mathematics skills at the local schoolhouse, though Levi had been taught at home. He'd loved to study the pictures best, and he wasn't a speedy reader, but he knew how well enough. Each book was like a little pocket world waiting to be cracked open.

Inhaling tensely, he dared another step into the room, scooting around a shorter stack. The topmost book was open, and he tried to subtly squint at the words. The writing was so tiny and the style so intricate that he began to doubt his reading abilities after all, so he retreated to stand near the door.

Simon moved to the middle of the study, where a large mahogany desk waited, covered in papers and open books both large and small. He leaned against the desk on his fingertips and looked across at Levi. "I did a great deal of research last night regarding your...affliction."

"Thank you, sir," Levi said, clasping his hands.

"I have good news and bad news."

"You can't break the curse?" Levi's heart plummeted like a stone. He'd known there was a good chance the curse was impossible to break.

"You're correct," the man said, somberly. "However, I have discovered that *you* can."

"I what?" Levi looked up, hope springing to life again.

"A curse of this nature can only be broken by the one who bears it." Simon tapped his fingers on one of his open books.

"Alright!" Levi clapped his hands enthusiastically. "What do I do?"

"That's the spirit!" Simon grinned, showing his strangely sharp teeth. The Ogre selected one of the small books from his desk. It had neither title nor mark on the soft leather cover. "There were many types of blessings and curses in the days of old. Often with different methods for breaking. To cure a curse of this nature one must show kindness and goodness to the world. Tell me, Levi, have you spent much of your time helping people? Doing good deeds?"

"Er..." Levi swallowed. "I want to, but Ma...my mother doesn't want me to help anymore because I break everything. It's the same with my brothers." A thought struck him. "I rescued my cat from drowning shortly before my Da died!"

Simon's eyes flashed and his face tensed. "Well, I doubt saving a *cat* would do you much good. Foul little creatures."

"Why don't you like them?" Levi asked before he could think better of it.

"Because of them." Simon, still wearing a disgusted expression, set down his smaller book and took up one with large pages covered in beautiful, watercolor illustrations. He held open a page and aimed it towards Levi. Drawn elegantly in ink and pale colors was a cat sitting beside a riverbank. The animal was porcelain white and had piercing eyes the color of sunset.

Levi didn't need to read the caption to know what the animal was. He'd seen similar drawings in his children's books, along with such scintillating captions as "See the Cat. See the Cat sit. Sit, Cat, sit." There was something else about the illustration that drew him, a feeling of safety he couldn't quite place. "You hate the cat god?" Levi asked.

"I'm...not fond of any of them." He flipped through the book, scowling at each illustration as though the creatures there had personally wronged him.

Levi wondered if Simon believed the animal gods were real. As he grew up Levi thought of them more as charming legends rather than factual beings. The venom with which his benefactor glared at the watercolors made Levi wonder. Perhaps only mages could see the animal gods. Perhaps that was why people stopped believing in them. Then again, no one had ever seen the Mother and Father gods either, and people enjoyed worshiping them.

He burned with curiosity, but didn't dare question further as Simon glowered at the pages. Finally, the man tossed the book down on his desk, propped on a small stack of other books so Levi could see. The page was open to an image of seven wolves with silver-blue eyes. The death gods in their full pack. "These are the worst," grumbled Simon, smacking the page with the back of his hand.

"I suppose no one enjoys the idea of death," said Levi tentatively, secretly admiring the illustration. Whoever had painted it had captured the elegant motion of the ethereal wolves and managed to make them look welcoming rather than threatening. No easy feat when it came to the creatures who took your soul to the afterlife when you died.

"I have no fear of death," Simon scoffed. "No, these selfish mutts take and hoard magic all for themselves." Simon's eyes flashed dangerously, and the air around Levi prickled as though statically charged. "When someone with magic inside them dies, like you, for example"—Simon gestured to Levi, who flinched—"The wolves come to collect your soul *and* your magic. I believe that the magic should be put back into the world, but instead the wolves get to decide how it is distributed. I know they have been keeping it to themselves, hoarding it all away in their realm."

Levi decided it would be unwise to mention that The Ogre had also personally rid their land of a great deal of magic, aside from whatever was trapped inside Levi.

As if to remind Levi of his own special brand of magic, he stepped backwards fractionally and struck the open door beside him with an elbow. The top hinge squealed, the pin broke, and the door lurched to the side and hung crookedly. Levi's cheeks went scarlet, and he tried to make himself small, which was a futile exercise.

"Oh dear, are you alright?" Simon snapped out of his anger as though he had never shown it, his expression becoming soft once more. With one hand he snapped the book of animal gods shut, and with the other he flicked magic towards the broken door. Before Levi's eyes, the hinge shifted back into place, the pin repairing itself and sliding easily into the hinge.

"I'm fine," Levi mumbled, hugging himself so as not to accidentally swing an arm towards anything else. He heaved a weary sigh. "To break my curse I need to be kind?"

"Yes," Simon nodded, closing a few more books on his desk.

"Er...this may sound stupid, but...how? Do you need any help around your place?" He glanced tensely at the books, imagining the disaster that would ensue if he tried to tidy up.

Simon laughed and shook his head. "I'm afraid not, my lad. It'll take far more than a bit of housework to break your brand of curse. Fret not, I came up with an idea for you last night."

Levi's heart gave an excited flutter. Guilt prickled at the edges of his mind. He'd been avoiding people when he could, and those he met he did business with and then hurried on his way. He never offered someone a snared pheasant or rabbit for free, only for trade, no matter how poor the farmer might look. Levi admonished himself and vowed to be more selfless as he watched Simon rummage in the stacks and tug out a folded map.

"Here we are!" Simon spread the map unevenly onto the desk and covering books with it. "This is our kingdom,"

Levi leaned forward to see, still keeping to the relative safety of the doorway. He'd only seen a few maps in his life. There was one of mill country hanging in the general store back home. Just mill-farm after mill-farm with little to distinguish each except the names of the owners printed on them. This map covered far more territory. Mill country was a blob near the middle and a little to the south. None of the farmers' holdings were outlined, and Levi couldn't have pointed out where his own home was. Still, he imagined he could track his progress north and east to where the royal palace stood, decorated with flourishes and the king's flag. He could make out The Ogre's castle as well. It looked so near the royal palace on the map.

"Here." Simon pointed to a location so Levi was obliged to come, haltingly, into the room for a better view. Simon had a slim finger resting against a twisting river, which cut directly down the countryside, dividing the kingdom nearly in two. This was the Serpent's River.

Simon explained, "recently, right here, an important bridge was des—...washed away in some flooding. The palace has hired some of the local farmers to repair it, but I am certain you could be of help. This river connects my own land with those of his majesty and has been commonly used for trade from the neighboring kingdom of Ferda."

"So I should go there and try to help them rebuild the bridge?" Levi recoiled. "I don't...I don't think that would be a very good idea. With my luck I'll—"

"Do you want to break your curse or not?" snapped Simon, folding the map roughly so the creases didn't match up.

"Well, yes, I just—"

"You what? You think it will be difficult?" Simon's voice took on a stony edge. His eyes flashed, reminding Levi suddenly of a green snake he had once seen slithering through the grass in search of bird eggs. "You told me yourself that you have a good handle on your issues. Certainly, it will be challenging, but if it were easy, you would have broken your curse on your own by now."

Levi opened his mouth, then snapped it shut. Simon was right. Of course he was. "How long do you suppose I'll have to work with them before the curse breaks?"

"I can't be certain." Simon's voice was more level, and he slapped the ill-folded map into a thick book with marbled pages. "I've never broken a curse like yours, and my research findings were spotty at best. It seems you're a rarity, Master Miller."

When Simon called him "Master Miller," Levi did not get the same warm feeling as when the princess had said it. "Did any of the people you read about break their curses?"

Simon blinked at Levi for several moments as though he had been staring through the young man. Levi wondered if Simon thought he was particularly stupid for asking. Simon's lip curled, but he answered in his gentle voice. "Yes. I found a journal of one afflicted like yourself. He broke his curse, using kindness of course."

"Alright." Levi nodded determinedly, more to convince himself than anything. "I'll try it. I'll go help with the bridge, and I'll stay to help until I break my curse, if I can."

"Keep in mind it might take more than one act of kindness," Simon added.

"Hmmm, yes. I guess that makes sense." Levi worked to keep his rising unease from showing on his face. He could do this, surely. He had to do this.

"Don't worry, lad." Simon stepped towards Levi and reached up to squeeze the miller's broad shoulder, "I'll help you. You may return here every night and enjoy meals each morning before you set out on your worthy quest."

"Thank you!" Levi said, and meant it with all his being. To have someone helping him. To finally have someone give him answers. It was all he had dreamed of and hoped for since he left home.

~~~~~

Because Molly had no pack to carry this time, Levi decided he would ride her out in search of the bridge. Simon had not allowed Levi to take the large map from his study, but instead made a special one on a piece of fabric which was less likely to be ruined in the unlucky man's grasp. It only showed the route to the river, with no frills or unnecessary landmarks.

Levi rummaged around in the stables for some time before coming up with a longer rope to use as reins for Molly. He didn't dare try one of the old bridles he found there. The leather was so aged and stiff he knew it would snap the moment he pulled it over Molly's ears. He also did not bother with a saddle, which were in the same poor condition as the bridles, but instead used the stone mounting block in the stable yard to climb onto her.

Molly bobbed her head in annoyance at having the weight of a human on her back. Levi patted her neck and arranged his cloth map over her withers. "Now, now, girl. I know. You're not used to something so heavy. It's because I've had a good breakfast, that's all." The horse snorted and swished her tail sharply.

Levi rode Molly towards the gate, the *clop-clop* of her hooves reverberating in the silent yard. As if on cue, he looked up and caught sight of Boots, balancing atop the fence. The cat met Levi's eyes and yowled his greeting, raising his tail like a flag.

"Catch any good mice, Boots?" Levi called to his feline companion as he steered Molly over to the wall. The cat jumped lightly down to Levi's shoulder and rubbed his face against Levi's jaw.

"Mer mer," the cat said conversationally.

"Ah, I see." Levi nodded as Boots alighted from his shoulders onto Molly's back to return to his accustomed seat on her rump.

With a little cluck of his tongue and pressure with his heels, Levi asked Molly to walk on, heading for the gate.

~~~~~

It was midday when Levi caught sight of the wide, slow running river stretched like a basking snake across the fields, and heard the voices and clatter of the building project. Simon had told him that the bridge was at the edge of his land. Levi guessed a faster horse, well ridden, could have made the trip in only two hours.

As Levi approached, he saw the work was well under way. Stones of varying sizes had been brought to the bank and were sorted into piles. Three teams of impressive oxen stood to one side, yoked together but enjoying a meal of lush grass. The wide stone-boats that they had hauled to bring the largest rocks from the fields to the riverbank were detached and out of the way.

Levi's brows went up. These creatures made the oxen at home look like dainty dairy cattle. The horses the laborers had ridden to work grazed a short distance from the riverbank, swishing their tails in the sunlight.

The river was running calmly. A gentle breeze caressed its surface, and the workmen likely knew they had to take advantage of the quiet. They'd already built up the centering. The wooden construct that would help form the stone arch of the bridge looked like a halved wagon wheel sticking up out of the water. The workmen were divided into two crews, one on each bank of the river. They would work towards one another from opposing banks until they met in the middle. Two wide, shallow boats also floated beside the beginnings of the bridge, the men standing inside helping to position stones and ferrying workmen back and forth as needed.

Levi only knew the basics of bridge building, but he was able to take in the project at a glance. The mechanical part of his mind that loved puzzles and projects came to life and he found himself eager to get stuck into the task.

Levi left Molly in a field, far enough from the other animals to stay out of trouble, then he walked over to where the nearest men were hauling stones closer to the bridge. Boots trotted along at his heels as though he fully expected to find employment as well.

The men looked up as Levi approached. He gave them his best smile and spread his arms in a gesture of greeting. "I was wondering if you might need a little extra help today." He decided the best plan was a direct one. The sooner he got down to helping, the sooner he could break the curse.

The men looked at one another then back at Levi with raised eyebrows. They seemed impressed. After all, though he wasn't much help around the Mill, Levi still shared the general build of a miller's son and sibling of people like Fergus and Brodie. He hadn't gotten their blessings, but he was still their kin. One of the men straightened and wiped sweat from his brow with a grimy hand. "Those are mighty fine clothes for someone who came to work."

Levi cursed inwardly. He'd been so pleased about his nice clothes that morning. His father would have thought him a frivolous idiot.

With a few quick motions he yanked off the vest and then the shirt, matching most of the other men. Someone whistled. Levi glanced down at himself. His arms and hands were the most noticeably scarred, but he had many old cuts on his ribs and a few on his back. There was a nasty scar down his shoulder from when, at eleven, he had fallen from a ladder onto a hay hook. When Ma had rushed him to the healer, hook still in him, she had wailed and wailed how it might have stuck him through the eye. Levi wasn't allowed near ladders after that.

He cleared his throat, self-conscious.

A weathered looking man with a thick mustache took pity on the newcomer. "Right. Now that you have your fancy duds out of the way, what say you help us move some stone?"

Levi grinned with relief. "Yes, sir! Just show me where to put it."

Levi enjoyed the weight of the cool field stone on his shoulders, the grit under his finger nails. The men were good company and chatted as they worked. Many of them were local farmers who volunteered their days to the project. Two were overseers paid by the palace specifically to supervise. A few more were hired builders. Levi liked to listen to them, though he kept quiet himself.

Everyone adored Boots. They dubbed him their mascot, and he sat in the wagon with their bank's foreman, Roland. Everyone joked that the cat was their new foreman, and they would listen to no one else's orders. For his part the cat meowed enthusiastically whenever someone came near, as though passing out instructions. If someone took a break in the shade and a cool swig from a waterskin, Boots was their companion and received a petting for his time.

The men chuckled and bobbed their heads as they passed saying, "Yes, Master Boots!" or "Right away, Sir Cat!" This clearly pleased Boots, and he ruled with an iron paw over his new underlings.

However much Levi was enjoying the task and the camaraderie, he knew in his heart it couldn't last. The bad luck started innocently enough. Levi tripped and dropped one of the rocks he had was carrying. It was one of the special, tapered "builder" rocks that would make up the arch of the bridge. It split as soon as it hit the packed earth.

Levi apologized fervently, and the man with the mustache, a fatherly farmer named Danno, patted his back and told him it was an accident. Levi wished that were true. Only an accident meant that it might not happen again, but the faint pulling in his chest told him otherwise.

He moved to a different job as soon as he was able, shifting less important stones that would make up the body of the bridge.

Levi dropped more rocks. He began to bump into people. Twice, other men tripped or slipped, dropping their own stones when they walked near him. Levi tried to stay farther away from the bridge itself. He knew, as the hot day dragged on, that his bad luck was beginning to seep from him and into those around him. His chest ached now with the threat of the magic that lay curled like a spider inside him. How long before he brought the whole project down? He swallowed.

Acts of kindness. He repeated in his head. *Acts of kindness to break the curse.*

When one of the oxen snapped its yoke and charged off into a field the foreman called for a rest. The bridge was beginning to look more like it should. The arch was nearly finished and the springers were set firmly against the bedrock of the riverbank. They had been able to use the good foundation of the previous bridge to start from, so they had not needed to dig out a new one.

"Bedrock is best, of course," Roland explained to Levi as they all settled down for a late afternoon meal. Those on the opposite side of the river relaxed into their own meal and conversation. Levi had brought food from The Ogre's castle without losing it somewhere along the way. The small loaf of bread was looking a little squished and the cheese somewhat misshapen, but everything was still edible.

Boots wandered amongst the men, insinuating himself into their mealtime with his usual, gregarious nature. The workers shared bits of cheese and ham with the orange tom.

"When I was a boy we had this little calico. Fierce as a wildfire, she was. Never saw something so small bring in so many mice. Rabbits too!" said a younger man named Andrew as he passed Boots a healthy portion of his dried meat.

"That's nothing!" proclaimed an aging farmer with a flourish of a chicken leg. "I had a cat could take down a hawk on the wing!"

"You never did!"

"I did! The hawk would swoop low thinking to have my cat, Tim, as a feast. Well, old Tim would turn right around and grab that bird! In a scuffle of feathers and fighting, he'd bag himself a hawk! Did it more than once, did old Tim."

The foreman, Roland, settled down near him. He was tan-skinned, a bit older than Levi, with dark hair and a wide smile that dimpled both cheeks. He explained the building project as Levi listened with interest. "You see, if there's no good bedrock on a riverbank, we anchor the bridge with wide, flat stones. We dig out the bank and sink them in, but it's not as sturdy. Fortunately, we've got bedrock here."

"I see," Levi said, intrigued. Already he was planning to sketch everything he was learning when he got back to his room. It was fascinating watching the bridge come together in spite of all his inept stumblings. "Will you use mortar to hold the stones in place?"

"No." The foreman shook his head, sweat dampened hair falling in his face before he swept it away with a calloused hand. "We may use pinning stones if two "builders" don't match up properly, but we're trying to do that as little as possible. We're using a dry build for this bridge. That way if the water rises too high with the spring rains it'll wash between the stones instead of tearing the mortar away."

"Did they use mortar last time?" young Andrew asked, taking a bite out of the tomato he had brought.

"No, and that's the odd thing," Roland frowned. "By all accounts the old bridge was washed out in one of the bad storms we had earlier this year, but there was no reason for it I can tell. I saw that bridge myself on many an occasion, it was fine and sturdy. It should have outlived us all."

"Yeah," Danno agreed. "My grandad helped build the old one. He said it was the best job he ever did."

"Well, it came down, and it's our job to set it right." Roland slapped his thigh with finality.

"Is this an important bridge?" Levi asked, enjoying the hearty, oaty bread The Ogre had sent with him. How had the mage known Levi's favorite kind?

"I should say it is," the farmer with the hawk-catching cat answered. He was a middle-aged man with a bent back from years walking behind a plow, and his skin was leathery as the oxen's hides. "That bridge connects the two halves of this farmland. This river—"

"Serpent's River," one of the men piped up helpfully, only to be glared down by the farmer.

"The Serpent's River divides our kingdom from north to south. Here is where it narrows, and the farmland beyond is vital for trade in and out of the kingdom. There are other bridges, of course, but none so convenient for the farmers as this one."

"Doesn't...doesn't this road run right beside The Ogre's land?" Levi asked, trying to keep his tone casual. He doubted he had succeeded when everyone turned to look at him and several of the men spat on the ground. Most people spat when they spoke of The Ogre, though, of course, none of them had met the man.

"The Ogre might claim that land is his, but it still belongs to the king." Harshness edged into Roland's voice. "He might think he owns this road, or even this bridge, but he doesn't scare us. We'll keep on farming this land, and the princess can keep chasing off his Shades for as long as it takes."

Levi sat forward, excited about the subject of Princess Joanna, when a swarm of biting midges descended on them all.

The men were forced to cram what was left of their lunches into their mouths and spend several minutes dancing around, swatting madly trying to discourage the bugs. Levi swatted and stamped along with them, but he knew why the flies were there. He could almost feel his luck barreling down towards him like charging horses. If he were at home, this would be the point when he would absolutely stop what he was doing and go to sit away from everyone else.

The Ogre's voice in his head kept him from fleeing. *An act of kindness could break the curse.* He had to ride it out. Just endure until he was free.

So Levi went back to work.

For a while longer, all that happened was a few more stumbles on Levi's part, though he noticed that the other men on his side of the river were getting clumsier too. Roland blamed it on the heat and instructed any who slipped or tripped to sit down and have a drink of water.

Levi soon found himself at the water's edge with three such, sipping cool water from a clay cup and hoping if he sat still enough he couldn't do any harm.

It began with Boots. The cat perched atop the nearest rock pile and let out a disgruntled yowl when one of the men moved him aside to get at the stone he needed. Levi turned to see what had upset the cat and, in the process, extended his arm to support himself. Young Andrew, who Levi hadn't seen coming carrying a large stone, caught his shin on Levi's arm. In seconds the man overbalanced, and with a cry of dismay, toppled over Levi and into the river.

Someone yelled.

Levi drew up his legs and wrapped his arms around them, instinctively making himself small. He heard mother's scolding voice in his head: *"What have you done this time?!"*

Andrew didn't surface immediately. Roland rushed to the bank with a tree branch, jabbing it into the river. The fallen man did not grasp the branch and the foreman swore, eyes wide with fear.

Levi didn't think. He was even a little surprised as he tipped himself into the cool river. The last thing he heard before his ears were filled with thick silence was Boots' throaty meow.

Ma and Da had insisted Levi learn to swim. They lived near enough to the river that they knew their unlucky son would find his way there before long. As dangerous as it was a teach him, Da had insisted it was even more so not to.

The water closed around Levi, and he opened his eyes, peering into the murk and ignoring the sting. Because the river had been slow running for a while and the plants had gotten a foothold. Everything was tinted a vibrant, healthy green.

It took Levi a moment to locate Andrew below him, trapped at the bottom. The rock he had been carrying had lodged against his leg and caught him fast. Andrew's chin was turned up, pale face slack. Had he already taken in too much water?

Levi swam powerfully downward. He aimed for the rock and crashed his shoulder into it, the jarring impact lancing all the way down his spine. He ignored the pain, shoving mightily against the stone. It budged. He tried once more, grunting, air bubbles billowing from between his clenched teeth.

He sensed rather than saw that at least two other men dove in behind him. They were struggling to pull Andrew's arms as Levi worked on the stone. He wished one of them would come help him, but he had no way to communicate. Instead, he gave his next attack everything he had.

As he slammed into the rock again, his arm glanced across a chipped edge. Now he was bleeding into the water and running out of air. *One more try*, he told himself doggedly. *One more try.*

He lunged as best he could, kicking wildly with his legs, worried he had struck one of the other rescuers in his fervor and then not caring, because this time the rock moved just enough to free Andrew's foot. Those swimming above Levi pulled the unfortunate man free.

Levi let the stone fall back into the niche where it so clearly wanted to rest. He turned, striking out for the surface. As he rose towards the shimmering light he instinctively reached up to grasp at anything that would help him out of the water. His lungs seared with pain, and he knew he was seconds away from passing out.

He grasped one of the stones of the bridge and it shifted under his hand. Before he knew what was happening rocks were falling through the water on top of him. The last of his air left his lungs in a gout of bubbles, and he knew nothing more.

~~~~~

Pressure settled on Levi's chest, firm and aching, but far away on the edge of his perception. A nagging annoyance. His body was heavy and he was vaguely aware that he must be lying on the ground instead of in the water, but he was still far away, still lost in a world where no air found his lungs. Were there stones holding him down, or was he made of stone himself? Was he even alive at this point?

What finally snapped him from that foggy place, and back to cruel reality, was a sharp pain on his hand.

The pressure against his chest exploded into full blown pain, and he curled up, retching river water over the grass and his own arms.

People were patting him on the back and all speaking at once. It took his fuzzy mind a few moments to piece together what they were saying, or even who they were.

"There we go, lad!"

"That's it. Get it all out. Good job!"

"Easy, son, easy now!"

Finally, the people stopped patting and Levi finished heaving, flopping onto his back. His mouth tasted like death, and he wished someone would pass him a waterskin because if he tried to speak he might vomit up his stomach like an empty sack. His lungs burned, his arm throbbed, and his head felt stuffed with wool.

He blinked around at the men. Roland was kneeling over him, a hand on Levi's shoulder and a serious look on his face. "Easy now. You hit your head pretty bad down there. Go slow."

"MEOW!" Boots was there, front paws on Levi's chest, pink nose right up against Levi's. Levi realized that the sting on his hand must have been a bite. He lifted his heavy limb to check and sure enough, little pinpricks of blood shone against his skin. Boots had chomped down hard on the webbing between his thumb and forefinger.

Roland smiled. "I've never seen an animal so worried in all my days."

Levi could only stare dumbly at Boots for a long moment, a messy sensation of happiness mingling with the throbbing of his various injuries. Then he blinked a few more times and looked up to see the men all standing around. Most of the workers from the other side of the river had come over in their wide boats as well.

He found Andrew, very much alive, and sitting up a few feet away, being seen to by the foreman from the other bank.

Roland gingerly lifted Levi's arm, examining a long, jagged cut that ran from wrist to his elbow. The man grimaced as someone handed him some rags to clean the wound.

Levi tried to ignore the sting, looking past the men towards the water. His heart plunged like a stone to the bottom of the river. The bridge was ruined. All their hard work of the day, lost to the water. His simple action of grasping for the stones had sent most of them tumbling out of sight blow the rippling surface, reducing the bridge back to its bare anchoring stones and the wooden arch, like the bones of some long-dead creature. Some of the fallen stones could be salvaged surely, with enough time and effort, but there would be no more work that day, and another man was injured. There was a lot of blood on Andrew's leg where he'd been pinned by the rock.

Levi gritted his teeth, but not against the pain in his arm or head, or because Boots was digging his claws into Levi's chest, but because he knew he had caused all of this. His bad luck. His act of kindness turned against him. If he sat on the bank much longer, who else might he injure or maim?

"Whoa whoa, easy now! Where do you think you're off to?" Roland asked, trying to finish tying the bandage on Levi's arm as the youth levered himself to his feet, dropping Boots in the process.

The cat gave an angry chirp and pouted, tail high.

"I have to go." Levi staggered. Kind hands caught him and his guilt grew even stronger as he looked at their concerned faces. "I'm expected back. I'm late..." He was doing his best to get a handle on his tongue. The world was shifting as though he were standing in one of the little boats.

"Now then, lad," Roland said, gripping Levi's shoulder again. "Hadn't you better go back with one of the fellows to their place? I'm sure that'd be better."

"I live not half a mile away," The older farmer offered, "and the missus will be more than glad to see to you."

"NO!" Levi said, too loud and too firm. "I live—" He paused, blinked, fought to keep his mind on track. "I don't live far, and the horse knows the way. My family is waiting." For a moment, he was so muddled he actually believed himself. He envisioned Molly taking him home to the little mill house. Ma sitting him down to see to his hurts as his brothers listened to the tale of his adventures.

He looked at the kind farmer, who smiled at him with concern on his sun-washed features. The man's poor family would never suspect the disaster that would befall them if Levi stepped foot in their house. He backed out of Roland's grip and held up his hands. "It's alright. I'm fine. I'm so sorry about the bridge."

"That wasn't your fault." Danno gave Levi a sympathetic smile. "You jumped in to save Andrew after all. How were you to know that stone you grabbed wasn't secured? Why, it was good luck that we were able to haul you out when we did, and managed to get all the water out of your lungs."

Good luck? Levi thought darkly. He could still feel it, like a cold hand on the back of his neck holding him down. The creeping presence of his bad luck. An enemy he'd known all his life. He shuddered, and someone must have thought him cold because they handed him his fine shirt.

Still fumbling for excuses and followed all the way to Molly's side by the concerned workmen, Levi finally managed a retreat. The last straw was Andrew calling out thanks to Levi for saving his life. Levi's stomach clenched so hard that he thought he might retch again.

He wanted to shout back that it was his fault. That his bad luck ruined everyone's hard work and nearly killed a man. Instead, he grasped Molly's withers and fumbled his way onto her broad back. She grunted as he clumsily flailed, almost falling off her other side.

Roland reached out steadying hands and propped Levi in place. "You're sure you have to go?"

"Yes." Levi kicked Molly up into a trot, trying his best to stay on as she bounced. Over his shoulder he called to the baffled men, "I'm alright! And I'm sorry!"

Boots loped along beside the horse, yowling with annoyance until Levi deemed them far enough from the work crew to slow down. The cat climbed a fence post and bounded lightly onto Molly's rump, where he did not stop yowling. Levi took his lecture without comment. He hung his head, messy, damp hair falling completely over his eyes. His shirt, soggy with river water, stuck to his skin and smelled like something that had rotted, unnoticed, under a cupboard for months.

About halfway back to The Ogre's castle, it began to rain.

~~~~~

"My dear boy! What happened?! You're a mess!" Simon fussed over Levi so much that it was almost humorous. Simon had taken one look at Levi's bedraggled self standing in the main hall and pulled the youth into a lavish anteroom. He plopped Levi down on a couch.

Levi had managed to get Molly to the stable and even brush her down before he had dragged his leaden limbs to the main house. Somewhere in between he'd lost Boots. Probably the sulking cat had remained in the stable rather than walking back across the rainswept yard.

As Simon fussed, Levi imagined his Ma looking him over, hands on hips. Da would try to make Levi laugh with some stories as Ma fixed him up. Even his brothers would stand by to make sure he was alright.

Simon clucked his tongue as he addressed the large bump on the back of Levi's head. Levi had only tried to examine it once himself, and a simple touch had shot an arrow of pain through his head and neck.

He'd have fallen off Molly if the horse hadn't deftly shifted to counterbalance him. "Have you had any dizziness? Blurry vision?" Simon asked, his cool fingers gentle as they explored the bump.

"Yes," Levi admitted, clasping his hands between his knees and following the patterns in the fine carpet with his eyes. A wide vine of gold swirled and wove like a river through a forest of plush black and red. He wondered how long it would be before the couch he was sitting on collapsed, or a bit of log fell out of the fire and started the whole room aflame.

Simon called on his magic. Even Levi could feel it collecting around The Ogre's slim hands. A white, cool magic like frost. The curse inside Levi tugged faintly as though it too wanted to join the rest, but it was tethered tight and bound up inside Levi so expertly that it could never escape.

Simon put his hand against the back of Levi's head, and it was all the young man could do not to make an audible groan of relief as the relentless throbbing and dizziness faded away, leaving his head clearer than he could have hoped.

With his head mended and The Ogre seeing to his cut arm, Levi finally spoke, his words a sad mumble. "It didn't work."

"Mmm?" Simon's eyes flicked up from where he knelt beside the chair, the young man's arm in his hands.

"My act of kindness. It didn't work. My bad luck came and ruined everything."

The Ogre's expression was nothing but gentle concern, like a father whose child had fallen from his first pony riding lesson. "Well, I shall do more research and meditation to get a feel for the magics at play here. Perhaps we missed something." He didn't sound the least but daunted.

"Maybe," Levi sighed, thinking of the men and how they'd all be so worried about him and so clueless as to what had destroyed all their hard work. Would they wonder why he did not reappear the next day to help them rebuild? He hoped poor Andrew's leg would heal quickly.

Levi's arm gave a twinge, and he looked up in time to see Simon's magic knitting the cut's jagged edges back together as though they had never separated. "Do you think *you* could go to the bridge and fix it?" Levi brightened. After seeing how well the magic could heal a wound, he thought surely it could repair a fallen bridge.

Simon shook his head solemnly, taking up Levi's discarded bandage and tossing it into the fire. "The people do not trust me. Anything I might repair with magic they would tear down out of fear. They cannot understand."

"But if I went with you maybe? They liked me. What if I told them—"

"No, Levi," Simon's tone was indulgent. "They would never accept my help. They only know me as the monster who stole all the magic from their land, even if I try to explain that I cannot help it." He gave Levi a sad and soulful look. "You see, I never meant to 'steal' any magic. Magic is drawn to me. That's all. It wants to be near me, to be used by me."

Levi watched the small man move about the room, clearing away his damp boots. He looked down at his arm, flexing his hand. It was unnerving to see no sign of the jagged cut that had marred his skin minutes before. He'd seen magic worked more times than anyone else he knew, but he still wasn't used to it, and wasn't certain he liked it. He glanced up through the fringe of his hair.

Before The Ogre had come along, lots of people supposedly used magic. Simon didn't try to deny that he was the reason for its absence, but if he couldn't help it...

Levi's mind was too weary and befuddled to ponder this further. His eyelids were heavy and all he wanted to do was curl up in his bed like a cat and sleep for a year. He moved to stand, but his balance was still off. He reached for the arm of the couch to steady himself and instead grasped one of the stiff, embroidered pillows. As he stumbled he swung his arm, still grasping the cushion, and launched it onto the hearth where it immediately caught fire.

Before Levi could make a move to put the fire out Simon flicked his hand. The cushion stopped burning and repaired itself. The singed stitch-work zipping itself back into place as though an invisible seamstress was at work. Levi thought the finished product looked better than the original.

Simon picked up the pillow and tossing it lightly back to the couch. The mage was still smiling kindly, if only with his mouth. "Go on, before you fall down. Off to bed."

Levi had to be guided to his room by one of the Shades so he wouldn't get lost, but thanks to his weariness he didn't mind, even when the creature left him by slinking up against the wall and becoming an ordinary shadow again.

Safe in his room, Levi thought to tumble right into bed, but as tired as he was, he wasn't ready. He sat down at his desk and hunted up the stub of a pencil. Finally letting his heavy muscles ease, he settled in to draw bridges. Even as he drew, his mind's eye cast back to the wreckage he had caused. His hands worked automatically as his thoughts rolled over like the river, wondering how the men might salvage their ruined project.

Most of them were farmers, so coming back to start the bridge over would mean less time they could spend on their fields. Levi knew all too well that a year of poor crop yield could spell disaster for a family.

With only a few bridges clumsily sketched and notes on what he had learned scribbled illegibly in the margins, Levi set his head in his hands, palms against his eyes, and let out a frustrated moan.

Something brushed the back of Levi's bare ankle. Warm fur and the tickle of whiskers. "Boots?" There was no orange cat staring back up at him with corn-yellow eyes. Levi's brows came together. He'd been certain a cat had brushed against his leg.

"Mer Mow?"

There was Boots at the door, strutting into the room as though he owned the entire castle. "Still 'Sir Cat'?" Levi asked, cutting one more look at his leg where the phantom cat had touched him, before rising and crossing to his mattress nest. He plopped down heavily, catapulting several pillows across the room. He left them where they fell, instead letting Boots walk back and forth across his lap, chattering to him in cat language.

Without thinking he began to talk as well. He wondered aloud what his family was up to, or what Princess Joanna was doing at her palace, or if he could get his drawings of cats to come out right. He leaned his back against the billowing cushions, speaking more and more slowly as sleep overtook him. Boots kept the conversation going with meows and chirps as the human began to snore.

~~~~

"You found more?" Levi asked, hope rising.

"Yes." Simon sat at his big desk. The study was just as Levi had last seen it, but now he risked coming further inside. He reasoned that if he started something on fire or cascaded all the piles of books to the floor, Simon could have everything as good as new in no time. The mage plucked a pair of delicate reading glasses from his nose and scrutinized Levi. "I tracked down the account of a young woman who was cursed just as you are."

"With bad luck?" Levi moved towards the desk, managing to topple two piles of books.

Simon sighed and went on. "Yes, as I said. This account says she angered a certain, very touchy witch and found herself with bad luck for all her days. She became determined to break the spell, and she found that, after many acts of true kindness, the curse was finally broken. With this account, and the journal I found before, I think we can definitively say that kindness is the way."

"How...how many acts of kindness?" Levi asked, clasping his hands into nervous fists. His bad luck pressed at the center of his chest like knuckles against his breastbone. He wished Boots had come down to the study with him, but the cat had once again disappeared.

Simon scanned the two books before him, one a small and leather bound, the other hefty and official looking. Levi didn't dare go nearer to the desk to peek for himself. There was far too much breakable equipment around. The Ogre flipped through a few pages, a frown creasing his features. "Neither tells me precisely. The journal recounts some acts in detail, and others he mentions in passing. He may have left others out completely."

"Quite a few acts of kindness then?" Levi's heart plummeted.

"It would seem so." Simon closed both books with a decisive *snap*. He fixed Levi with a serious look. "Don't worry, lad. I'll do my best to help you. I have my own theory that the larger the act, the more it contributes to the breaking of the curse."

"What if I just ruin everything instead?" Levi could still taste the bitter tang of the river on his tongue, even though he had eaten breakfast.

"Perhaps it is the intent that counts?" Simon mused, standing and moving towards a large, silver orb that was propped up on an intricate metal stand concealed behind several tall stacks of books in the middle of the room.

Levi drew closer, cautious. Around the orb on the floor was drawn a circle with a star inside. It was difficult to make out more as books and papers almost concealed it entirely. Simon was speaking again, and Levi's attention snapped back. "Otherwise the woman would have had the same trouble as you and would never have been able to break her curse."

"Maybe..." Levi said, letting his hope inch back in. He tried his best to renew his daydreams of running a fleet of mills. Right now the simple pleasure of not endangering everyone he met was just as tempting a dream.

"Do not fret, my young friend." Simon's mood was already turning from somber to cheery as he spread his pale hands over the silver orb. "I'll use my magic to find you more people in need, and we'll have this curse broken in no time."

Levi watched with awe as fluttering images appeared on the surface of the orb. Brief flashes of landscape, and then of people, going by too fast for Levi to understand, but he supposed Simon must. There was no sound to accompany the images, which was a little disconcerting.

The mage's delicately arched brows came together with concentration. Levi waited, arms folded, enthralled by the magic as it prickled in the air around him. The curse inside him tugged then nestled comfortably in, like a cat into a lap. His magic was perfectly content to remain. *Don't get too cozy*, Levi warned it.

"Aha!" Simon announced, waving a finger in the air, his expression clearing. "Come here and see, Levi. I have found your next assignment!"

Part 4

The Princess

Joanna didn't take the most direct route back to the castle.

Lyall gave her "the look," which she knew meant she should see to her 'responsibilities'.

"But my responsibility is to the people." She leaned towards him in her saddle and giving him her best warrior's grimace. "And with carriages being attacked so far west, we cannot be too careful."

He rolled his ice blue eyes, immune to her pleading. "We've seen to the people, now we had better get home before your father sees to you and you're never allowed to leave the palace again."

"Fine." Joanna's hands twisted more tightly around her reins, and she nudged Willow to a trot, followed by her men in formation.

The princess and her contingent of fighters made their way through the prosperous city of Longmark, which nested at the foot of the large hill where the palace towered. People greeted her as she passed. Children pointed and waved, workmen raised tools in salute, and wives looked up from their chores and smiled knowingly. Joanna sat straight and impressive in her saddle. Her bay gelding showed her off well. A tall horse did wonders. Most of these folks had no idea how pathetically average their princess was physically, as they seldom saw her on foot.

A few children began to bounce eagerly alongside the formation, one waving a little flag with a crude patch bearing the princess's unofficial symbol—a mailed fist grasping an upraised sword.

"Did you fight loads of Shades today?" a girl asked, jumping so enthusiastically that her hair flopped over her face.

"Oh yes, but I sent them packing!" Joanna raised her chin, knowing that the setting sun shone brilliantly off her armor, adding to her heroic visage.

Even as she soaked in the admiration her mind was still whirring. She wondered that the Shades had come so far from The Ogre's land. The people of Longmark had never seen one of the creatures in person, only knowing of them through the reports and stories family brought from the outlying villages.

Joanna shook her ponderings of Shades and Ogres from her mind and continued to nod graciously to her people as she led her party up the main thoroughfare. Her family might disapprove of her "shenanigans" (as her father called them), but all over the kingdom the farmers, the millers, the smiths, and cowherds saw their princess riding out to fight Shades. They were coming to know her for what she was, their Protector.

"I cannot stop today!" she called over her shoulder when a local pub owner tried to entice her in for a visit. "I have business with His Majesty."

Chuckles behind her told Joanna that the villagers had seen the fine carriages bearing the emblems of another visiting prince. She grimaced. She was glad the villagers all knew her, but wished that didn't mean that everyone knew her business as well. She cut a glance towards Lyall, who smiled thinly back.

Joanna put her finger and thumb in her mouth and let out a whistle. Her company formed into a column three wide as they trotted their horses up the well-paved road to the palace gates. The massive, four-inch-thick main door stood open, and the portcullis before it was resting at half. Tall enough to admit horsemen, but not raised fully to indicate a feast day when the common folk would be allowed inside.

The wall guards peered down at Joanna and her troop as she passed below them into the large, open courtyard. Joanna felt like she was riding into a giant's embrace. She had to fight the claustrophobia homecoming always brought, as freedom and open fields were replaced with judging eyes and stone walls. Her hands twitched with the urge to turn her horse and charge out towards the grass and trees and freedom. Instead, she closed her fists all the tighter on the reins, the leather of her gloves squeaking faintly. Lyall, who was still riding beside her, reached over and rested his hand atop hers.

Stable hands appeared and they hurried to take the princess's horse. Someone else pushed a mounting block over, so she could dismount easily in her armor. This she did with a faint sensation of embarrassment, recalling an unplanned dismount earlier that day that had involved a broken stirrup and her landing on her backside. It was lucky there were so few there to see it and she had covered for it well enough. "My saddle needs repair," she informed the hand in a hushed voice so her men wouldn't hear. She didn't need to remind any of them of her blunders.

Once she was on the ground, Joanna turned to her horse and pulled the two pheasants hanging there free. She passed them to a servant. "I want these prepared for my father as soon as possible." It was a pity she was too late for the lovely birds to be used for that evening's meal, but they might still go a little way towards softening the blow of her disobedience.

The servant nodded and hurried away, holding the birds with appropriate admiration for their condition.

As their horses were led on to be groomed and fed, and her soldiers hurried towards the barracks for their own meal and a pleasant evening of cards and drinking, Joanna and Lyall strode to the doors of the palace.

Joanna absently patted at the frizzy mess that was her hair, which was struggling out of her bun, and struggled to shake the fog from her mind. At the last moment she turned to her departing men and called, "Well done today. I'll be certain to get your new orders to you soon. Until then, see to your armor and be vigilant."

"Yes, ma'am," the men chorused, saluting her with fingertips to their brows. Joanna turned back and smiled up at Lyall, who was considerably taller than she, now that both were on even footing. "How long before they start drinking and forget all about maintaining their gear?"

"Ten, maybe twenty minutes," the blond man speculated. "You know they won't overdo it, but they worked well today and will want to celebrate."

"I suppose I can't blame them." Joanna sighed as the big doors swung open, pulled by servants, and she and Lyall clanked their way inside. "I just wish—"

"Jo, you can't supervise them every moment." Lyall pulled off his gloves and handed them to another servant. Though the lanky man was below Joanna in station, he stood above the other staff as body servant to a royal. It was power Joanna seldom saw him flex.

Joanna little noticed the servants and guards around her hustling to and fro, intent on various tasks. She did take note of a new banner hanging in the main hall. She lifted an eyebrow at the image of a grey wave with a horse emerging from it. The animal had a horn on its head and fins where hooves should be. "Must be the symbol of my latest "husband to be," Joanna commented as she stopped before the banner. "Pity they don't know what a horse looks like."

"Be nice," Lyall cautioned, though his thin lips twitched.

"Someone should rescue the poor animal. I think it's drowning." This time her words were met by a satisfying snort of laughter from her best friend.

"Let's go, sassy boots," Lyall waved her on towards the wide, elegantly carpeted stair. With a little smirk she did as bidden.

She and Lyall made straight for their rooms, which adjoined. As they walked, she could feel the eyes of passing servants and guards following her. She knew not everyone agreed with her tendency to ride out to fight bandits and Shades, though they were all wise enough to keep their opinions to themselves, unlike her father. Joanna was a great source of gossip for the staff. Well, she mused, at least she kept them entertained.

Joanna slipped into her room, closing the door and leaning against it as she drank in the lavish, but homey surroundings, complete with massive canopy bed carved of oak and decorated with vines of gold. There were wall hangings worth a farmer's yearly earnings and carpets it took four servants to roll up and take outside for airing twice a year. The elegant decadence was only disrupted by the inclusion of armor stands and a gleaming weapons collection. Joanna kept her everyday swords down in the armory with everyone else's, but she had received a number of decorative blades as gifts from well-meaning relatives who thought her warrior tendencies skewed more towards an aesthetic than the practical.

Pushing herself from the door and taking in a cleansing breath of the faintly perfumed air, she strode into the room, already unbuckling one side of her breastplate. She could hear Lyall's armor clattering to the floor in his room, separated from hers only by the wall behind her bed. As her bodyguard, it was his duty to remain as near to her as possible.

"Jo! There you are! Your father has been sending servants in here every half hour wanting to know if you were back yet!" Hana, Joanna's maidservant, rushed in from the adjoining bathing room. The woman was only a few years older than Joanna and had been with the princess all her life, first as her mother, the nurse's, helper, and then as Joanna's proper handmaid. Currently her fond features were formed into the exact expression worn by hunting hawks.

"I'm sorry, Hana," Joanna muttered as she attempted to free herself from her breastplate. It required her to open all the buckles on the right side to open the armor like a door, but the shoulder buckle was impossible to reach if you were the one wearing the armor.

Hana strode over, deft hands unbuckling with the skill and ease of any squire. The taller woman had long since picked up the skills befitting a knight's helper as well as a lady's maid. She could whet blades, polish armor, and maintain leather as well as any man.

Joanna spotted a small, open book beside the window. While Joanna was off "gallivanting" (another of her father's terms) Hana was allowed free use of the princess's rooms and personal library. Especially as Joanna had little interest in books if they didn't include diagrams of battle tactics. Joanna knew her maid must have been furious to have her reading time interrupted again and again by the king's lesser servants popping in to ask after the absent princess.

"Did you have a successful hunt?" Hana asked in her conversational way, as she expertly stripped off metal plates until Joanna felt more like a human and less like a metal barrel with legs.

"Reasonably. Caught some Shades near the Blue Marsh and then—" She paused, a light shudder rippling through her. "You'll never guess who we met on the road."

"Oh, I can guess." A smile started on Hanna's lips. Hana had an angular face with a slightly pointy nose and brown eyes that might have been called beady, if someone was feeling cruel. Joanna knew those eyes could be as kind and gentle as any sister's.

"A carriage rolled in around noon with a certain lord and lady aboard who were very...shall we say, cranky? They claimed that they had met you on the road and went on at some length about your appearance and manner. Seems they found you all together 'unsuitable.' That was their word."

"How did Father take it?" Joanna was stripped down to her thick, padded gambeson, worn under the plate and chain mail. Hana unbuttoned this and pulled it off like a coat. Beneath Joanna wore a simple, breathable tunic, which was saturated with sweat.

Hana wrinkled her nose as she tugged off the tunic, and Joanna removed her own leggings. "His Highness was not pleased, but he was as gracious as ever." The maid said, holding Joanna's sweat-soaked clothes away from herself between two fingers. She carried them to the wicker hamper she would later take down to the washrooms. "At least there's no blood this time."

"There hasn't been any in quite a while," Joanna countered. She glanced down at herself. Her warm brown skin marred only by a single, white scar that ran from the bottom of her rib to her navel. That had been a bad day, and poor Hana had nearly fainted. Joanna began to undo her breast binding as she recalled the battle that she had nearly lost. How the bandit sword cut deep. It was more luck than skill that allowed her to parry the second blow that would have killed her. These days there were fewer bandits, and far more Shades to contend with.

She handed her equally sweat-soaked breast band to Hana. To wear her armor comfortably she had to bind her chest. While the princess was stocky and well-muscled, she had a curvaceous figure that was concealed when she wore her full kit. And she found an unbound large chest was not conducive to riding and fighting.

Now she would transform herself into the young woman her family knew. No more hard edges and keen lines; only softness and grace were allowed in her father's dining hall.

Joanna finished stripping and headed for the bath, her hair still in a messy riding bun. The tub, in a small anteroom, was already filled and waiting with delicately scented water with apple blossoms and salts. Hana only had to add a few buckets of hot water to bring the bath back to a comfortable temperature.

The princess enjoyed the transformation she could make from warrior to woman. She loved seeing the awe in people's eyes when they had spotted her astride Willow, fully kitted out in armor and blades, then viewed her again in her royal regalia. She smiled to herself as she thought of it, slipping into the perfect water. The delicate, feminine odor of the flowers and salts caressed her, and she sighed as she relaxed down into the tub.

Hana settled in on a stool beside the bath to pull pins and ties from Joanna's hair and then began diligently working out the myriad tangles. "I wish Father would just let me cut it," Joanna complained as Hana's quick fingers worked. The princess's black hair was naturally curly, and as such, protested being worn up with every tangle and knot it could manage.

Hana didn't reply. Both women knew the king would throw an absolute fit if his daughter, already the source of so much shame, appeared without her hair—her "crowning beauty." Joanna thought grumpily that if he liked it so much, he should have to wear it for a few days.

"What do you do out there, stick your head in tree thickets?" The maid held out a twig, which she had just plucked from Joanna's curls. The princess did not answer, but let herself sink deeper into the perfumed water and wished she could drift off to sleep.

Once Joanna and her maid had scrubbed away all the sweat and grime accumulated through days on the road, the ladies went back into the main room. Hana brought out the princess's gown for the evening and laid it on the bed with a flourish. Joanna cocked an eyebrow. "Is the visiting prince really so handsome?"

"Oh yes." Hana passed Joanna her underthings.

"Are you decent?" Her bodyguard called through the door that adjoined their rooms.

"Never!" she called back, grinning as she finished with her undergarments. Hana rolled her eyes.

"Can we be serious?" Lyall's muffled voice asked.

"She's fine!" Hana answered before Joanna could sass back.

The princess folded her arms and sent her maid a pout before she turned to look Lyall over. He stepped into the room with a flourish and a beaming grin. "Ooo!" She raised both eyebrows. "You're dressing smart tonight. I warn you, I have it on good authority that the visiting prince is very good looking."

Lyall was bedecked in blue tunic with darker coat, a color which contrasted flawlessly with his pale skin and sun-blond hair. He had pulled his hair neatly into a tail, this too tied with blue. She was jealous that he could prepare so quickly, while she took an hour if she and Hana worked as fast as they could. The man settled himself languidly on Joanna's bed, watching the princess pull on her corset, which Hana began to lace for her.

Even as he lounged Lyall wore a serious expression. "I wanted to talk to you about the skirmish today. Our formation was alright, but a little sloppy in places. We could do better. The men need to learn how to dress the line mid-charge. I was talking to Liam about it and he says a few of the lads have been skipping mounted formation practice with the horsemaster."

Joanna exhaled as the corset tightened around her, making her chest and hips even more pronounced. The corset was like armor of a different sort. "I know. Half the trouble is that I'm asking the boys to do something I've only ever *seen* done. Not to mention some of them aren't natural horsemen."

"Must we talk about this now?" asked Hana. She shot Lyall a warning glare. "This is the part of the evening when I take over as her second-in-command and brief her about the battle ahead."

Lyall tipped back his head in a laugh, flashing perfect teeth. "I'm sorry." He raised his hands in surrender. "You have the floor, good madam."

Joanna tried to join in Lyall's amusement, but she knew what lay in store for her tonight. Awkward dinner, awkward dancing, awkward conversation. "So you saw him, Hana?"

"Briefly," Hana fetched the dress and sweeping it up over Joanna's head. It was a complicated gown, deep red and decorated with silver droplets in cascading lines down the bodice. Pearls dribbled from every hem: drops of dew on spider thread. The collar was low to further accentuate the princess's "assets," and the skirt was full and flouncy.

Hana had, as always, been briefed with practical information about the night, and she rattled it off dutifully. "His name is Prospero."

Joanna snorted and Hana prodded her in the ribs.

"He is the third and youngest of King Aelfric's sons. His family is responsible for a small, seaside kingdom that bears the distinction of being the highest exporter of sea fish and fishing vessels. They have a two notable shipyards, which supply the surrounding coastal villages."

"Father's getting desperate," Joanna grumbled. She let Hana put on her necklace, which was silver and bedecked with tiny diamonds. It looked like she was wearing a chandelier around her neck, and it was almost as heavy. One of the jewels hung so low on her chest that it vanished into her cleavage. Hana began arranging silver decorations in Joanna's cascading curls

"He's looking farther afield, and we're down to third sons now." Joanna commented.

"What's next?" Lyall leaned back and grasped his knee. "Servants? Tailors? Butlers?"

Joanna groaned. "I will never understand how my father can see me lead soldiers out to battle with Shades and still have the notion of attaching me to some man so I can fulfill my 'wifely duty.'" She spat the words as though they were olive pits. The idea of being someone's wife, and the physical expectations that came with it, roiled in her stomach like bad eggs.

She plopped down at her vanity where her jars and canisters of makeup were artfully arranged. "If father would just get the idea! How hard is it to understand? You know me Lyall, and you too Hana. Even Mother has finally come around, but then there's Father still clinging to the notion that I just need to meet the right man." She fluttered her lashes dramatically at herself in the mirror then stuck out her tongue.

"As I said, this Prospero is very handsome," Hana seemed determined to finish her report. "At least there is that."

"I'll have someone nice to look at tonight." Lyall's grin spread lopsidedly.

"Does Joshua know you ogle other men?" Joanna tried to arrange her jewelry so it fell more artistically, like a waterfall over her collarbone. The necklace kept flopping more than draping, so she turned to Hana for help.

"Joshua understands that if I happen to see another handsome face here at court, it is all part of my duty as your bodyguard to keep an eye on it. He knows I would never act upon it." Lyall drawled.

Joanna wrinkled her nose at her friend in the mirror. She painted her full lips with deep crimson. She dusted her eyelids with brown powder and touched her lashes with charcoal to darken them further. She brushed her cheeks and bosom with rouge and stood up, turning to face her friends for approval.

Lyall looked her up and down then nodded. Hana fussed a bit longer over the way the skirt fell.

"We did meet a nice miller lad on our travels today," Joanna mentioned to her maid as the woman tugged this or that place on the dress.

"He was a rather fine specimen in that rugged, work-a-day way that country folk have," Lyall agreed.

Hana tilted her head. "Did you fancy him better than any of the princes you've met?"

"No, Hana. A nice miller for *you* I mean! I know you've had your eyes open for a husband, and don't pretend you haven't." Joanna planted her hands on her hips. "None of these palace servants suit you. Why not look farther afield?"

"Into an actual field." Lyall snorted with laughter.

Hana blushed and looked down. "I'm sure that miller was a very fine gentleman, but—"

Before Lyall or Joanna could further playfully embarrass the maid there was an insistent knock on the door. Lyall rose with the grace of a heron and reached the door in three long strides. Joanna envied her friend's legs. She always had to take two steps to each one of his.

Lyall didn't open the door fully as he conversed with whoever was on the other side. Joanna watched his back as if she could see through him to the servant beyond. Lyall finished with the brief talk and shut the door again, possibly in the face of whoever was standing outside it. For all his sweet and gentle nature, Lyall could be abrupt if he didn't like someone. He reminded Joanna of a hound her father once owned. The animal adored the family and been endlessly loyal and sweet, but with strangers it had been nothing but bared teeth and tucked tail at all times.

"My father?" Joanna asked, knowing the answer.

"The king is curious if you plan to join them for dinner." Lyall affirmed with a faint smirk.

"Right then," Joanna stood, checking herself in the mirror. Someone who had seen her on the road wouldn't recognize her now. As children Lyall had poked fun at her when she wore the fine dresses *"oh you're a girl today, eh?"* Joanna smiled at the memory.

Hana was still not satisfied and flitted about Joanna until Lyall made an urgent sound in his throat and the princess gently swatted her maid's hands away. "This will have to do. At least Father cannot say I didn't try to look presentable."

"That is true," Hana agreed, smiling warmly at her mistress. "Though you kept him waiting as usual."

Joanna had once used a sloppy appearance to chase away one of her suitors, and her father was so upset she'd had to listen to lectures for a week afterward. These days she was sure to dress in her finest. She had other ways of ensuring the men who came calling for her hand never took it. She turned towards her door, hesitated, and moved back into the bathing room for the object she had left behind beside the tub. She returned in moments, slipping on a white ring in the shape of an amber eyed cat that, when worn, appeared to chase its tail around her finger. She nodded towards Lyall and Hana before heading for the door, her bodyguard in tow.

"Go easy on the poor prince," Hana urged. "He's only a third son."

"No promises," Joanna called over her shoulder before the door closed between them.

~~~~

"Ah, Daughter. There you are." The king was wearing his most steely smile. It took every ounce of his effort to paste that grin on his lips when he saw his daughter. It was a look the princess was used to receiving. Her keen attention didn't miss the warning glance the king shot towards Lyall before his face returned flawlessly to one of pleasant cheer.

"There she is indeed." The sour tone of the woman beside her father made Joanna inwardly flinch, but she kept her back straight and her expression docile. She could wear a mask too. Her mother had taught her how to smile in a certain way, to incline her head just so and pacify angry heads of state with a flutter of her lashes. Of course, she had never actually tried any of these moves on heads of state, but she liked to imagine she could. If all else failed, she knew where the swords were kept.

The duke and duchess who had accompanied Prince Prospero watched Joanna with mingled interest and mistrust. She knew they were trying to reconcile her in their heads. The last time they had seen her she'd been armored, dirty, and shouting. Joanna took a moment to arrange the pearls that cascaded down her dress to give their guests time to process what they saw.

"Greetings, Father," she said. She used her most feminine, demure voice, and she could sense Lyall's barely contained amusement behind her shoulder, where he stood like a sentinel.

"Your mother and the prince are waiting," the king replied coolly. He was dressed in one of his favorite coats of dark, forest green. He had slightly lighter skin than Joanna, but they shared the same eyes, so deeply brown there were almost black, as was his hair which fell to his shoulders in loose curls. The king managed to control these with liberal use of oils, which gave his hair a slightly damp appearance, but a pleasant smell.

"We asked to meet you before we went in for the meal. We wanted to ensure that you would be...suitably prepared to meet our charge," said the duchess, who looked completely recovered from her ordeal on the road. Not a single hair was out of place, and her makeup was flawless. The duke stood beside her, tall and lanky, also looking as though he had never in his life allowed his shoes to touch road dirt.

Joanna bit down on a snide remark. She could still feel Lyall's silent chuckling behind her and wished she could subtly kick him in the shin. Instead, she smiled with all her charm. "I hope you find me sufficiently changed." She spread her arms to display her dress.

The king seemed to have had enough at last, though Joanna was uncertain if it was enough of her glares or of the duchess' scrutiny. "Alright, shall we enjoy our dinner?" He gestured towards the dining hall. The motion caused several servants, standing surreptitiously in corners or behind pillars, to rush into practiced activity. They opened doors, beckoning the way with the same pasted-on smiles to match Joanna's.

Joanna's footsteps echoed on the marble floors of the dining hall, resounding from the high ceiling, which was ribbed with white beams carved with intricate designs that reminded Joanna of waves. She cast her eyes up to those beams so she did not have to look at the family portraits that lined the walls. She hated the ones of her. She never looked good in paintings, and her frown increased in each one as she aged. Joanna could feel her portrait selves' judgmental eyes following her around the room.

The table in the dining hall was unreasonably long and took up the bulk of the room. It was meant to accommodate visitors and representatives from many different kingdoms, but these days hardly anyone visited unless they were trying to win Joanna's hand. As usual everyone was bunched up at the far end making Joanna imagine the table was a boat that was poorly balanced and would soon flip, drowning all aboard.

There was a mad rustle of chairs being pushed out as her brother and her newest suitor stood, and she wondered if it would have been better to have Lyall announce her. She cut a glance towards her father, knowing he was eating this up. Deny it as she might, Joanna enjoyed all eyes falling on her. She glided towards her seat with an artful smile, making certain to move her hips so her skirt rippled alluringly.

Servants scuttled about pulling out chairs and pouring the first drinks of the evening into long stemmed glasses. They knew better than to touch Joanna's chair. Lyall always saw to her at table, sweeping the chair out with practiced elegance. She stepped in, collected her skirts, and sat as he moved the chair under her. It was like a dance, and they had gotten very good at it.

Joanna knew the prince must be watching her, but she kept her eyes down, arranging her skirts. Let him goggle for a bit before she rewarded him with some eye contact.

The queen was seated to the left of her husband, who took his place at the head of the table with Joanna taking the next spot. Their body servants stood dutifully behind them, awaiting any gesture or whim. The guests were seated to the king's right, across from the family: Joanna's older brother, the Crown Prince Alroy, and his wife, the gentle Kathleen.

Kathleen flashed Joanna a quick smile. She had pale skin and blue eyes to contrast Alroy, who, like the queen, had warm, dark skin and umber eyes to match. Joanna wondered what their children might look like. She would not have to wait long as Kathleen was already carrying Alroy's firstborn, rendering Joanna even more superfluous as a possible heir to the throne.

Finally, Joanna dragged her gaze up to Prince Prospero. Just as she expected, he'd been staring. His eyes were hazel with flecks of green, and he was tan, though she recognized that it was not only natural coloration, but also exposure to the sun that warmed his complexion. This made her curious. Princes seldom spent enough time outdoors to acquire a sun-kissed appearance.

"Prince Prospero of Thalassos, may I present my daughter, Princess Joanna." The queen spoke for the first time, and a rush of warmth spread through Joanna when she heard her mother's steady, authoritative voice.

"Please, call me Prosper." The prince's voice was soft and low, and Joanna couldn't help but think of the sea where the young man lived. He was watching Joanna with interest that was not as unpleasant as it could be. She'd had been ogled and leered at across the table by enough men to recognize when someone was merely intrigued. Already she could tell that this young man was a cut above the usual fare. What a pity she'd have to ruin his dreams and send him packing.

Before Prosper could say anything more, the duchess launched into a lengthy oration. She addressed the king, rattling off a list of the assets their kingdom brought to the table with this match, as well as hopes for what Joanna could offer. As this boy was the third son, he did not stand to inherit much, and as Joanna also stood no chance of taking the throne in her own kingdom, her father and the duchess fell to hashing out how this marriage could be advantageous for them both.

"Naturally this would open trade between our two kingdoms for the foreseeable future, not to mention the advantage Thalassos could offer as a lookout, should an enemy attempt to strike from the sea. As it stands you have little connection at all with the borders of this continent, especially with the Storm Sky Mountains," the duchess pontificated, gesturing with her fork.

"Of course, our landlocked situation may seem indefensible to you," the king said, already leaning towards the duchess.

Joanna rolled her eyes. Her father loved this part. Rattling on with her suitors or their entourage about the benefits of marrying her off. Their kingdom was admittedly isolated, separated from many of the other kingdoms by the Storm Sky Mountains to the northwest. Her father always minimized that issue, expounding instead the virtues of the fertile farmland their kingdom boasted.

She tuned out of the talk and picked at her hors d'oeuvres. She was unable to talk to Lyall, who stood stiffly behind her chair. No food would be set before Joanna unless it was by Lyall's hand, passing under his keen gaze first. Once she'd lobbied her father to allow Lyall, who was family in all but blood, to sit at their dinner, but she had been countered on all fronts by tradition. Even Lyall himself said he preferred his post. He always ate as lavishly as the family after their meal was over.

A warm, slender hand settled unexpectedly atop Joanna's. She looked up to see her mother's gentle smile. "How was your work today, dearest?" the queen asked in a whisper. She hardly needed to be quiet, as the king and duchess nattered on loudly enough to be heard at the far end of the ridiculous table.

"It went well enough," Joanna replied, chasing a cherry tomato around her plate with no intention of eating it. She knew Prince Prosper was still watching her, but she did not reward him with eye contact this time. "The Shades are getting more and more prevalent and spreading farther afield. Today they made it all the way to the King's Road. It's like The Ogre means to snap up all our land from under our noses and we're letting him."

"Are you certain he's not merely reacting to you?" the queen questioned, tilting her head to look her daughter in the face. Her glossy black hair fell in stylish loops that Joanna envied. "You've been riding out for three years, and his Shades have also become more troublesome in that time."

"I began riding out when I started overhearing the reports from the farmers of the Shades harassing them and blocking trade roads," Joanna corrected her parent.

"Perhaps The Ogre would settle down if you left him alone."

"He'd get along well with Father." Joanna harrumphed, flicking the tomato so hard it skittered across her plate and stopped at the very edge. "No, Mother, I don't think he's reacting to me. I think he's decided he's tired of his little, stolen castle and useless lands. He wants to expand. We should spend less time trying to marry me off and build ourselves a proper army so we could just put an end to the issue."

The queen clucked her tongue. "Now, now. I doubt such extreme measures are called for to deal with one ogre. But"—the queen's eyes narrowed as she took in Joanna's steely expression—"I can see you're deeply concerned, so I will speak to your father again." She sat back, popping a little piece of goat cheese into her mouth. "He won't like it."

"He never does," Joanna sighed. She sat straighter and gestured to her plate. Lyall's hand came down and plucked it from the table at once. She knew her friend was listening to the conversation and wished that he was allowed to add to it.

Joanna made the mistake of letting her gaze drift up to meet Prosper's across the table. His expression was contemplative, as if trying to read the behavior of a potentially dangerous animal. She gave him a quick, well-trained smile, and his mouth flickered in a replying grin. He had a pleasant smile, and it brought charming creases to the corners of his eyes. Further proof that he spent his time in the sun. She risked darting her eyes towards her father and the duchess and wrinkled her nose.

Prosper's quick smile was back in a flash, accompanied by a minuscule nod of agreement. He paused as his own servant settled a salad before him, just as Lyall did the same for Joanna. The princess noticed her suitor's personal servant for the first time. An odd contrast to his master, this man was short, plump and balding. She suspected that he was a high-level house servant at Prosper's palace and had been selected to join the prince on his journey. He didn't look as well dressed as he should, nor as well trained. Where Lyall might interpret a twitch of her hand or a nod, this man practically had to be told what his master needed.

Joanna tuned back to her father's chatter for a moment, catching him extol the virtues of their land's excellent soil and astounding wheat yield. Once, the king would have bragged of his daughter's accomplishments and suitability as a bride. Dancing, horseback riding, an extensive education. These days he didn't bother. She watched him with annoyance prickling her like needles under her skin. She was just a means to an end. *"Marry my strange daughter and you'll have access to good farmland and a wealth of crops."*

Joanna plucked half a walnut from her plate and flicked her wrist to launch it towards her parent, but before she could another hand came down on top of hers. Alroy's. Her brother gave her a stern look and shook his head. Joanna replaced the walnut atop her food and scowled at her food for the rest of the meal.

After a dinner Joanna hardly touched, and much more negotiating on the part of the king and duchess, it was time for the two "intended" to bond. Another pointless tradition her father insisted upon.

The party rose and made their way in relative silence down carpeted halls to the waiting, cavernous ballroom. It was mostly empty, save for a small cluster of musicians that had been tuning up and chatting while the royals ate. Now they snapped to attention; all conversation dropped as they poised bows over strings and watched expectantly for their cue.

The elaborate chandeliers were aglitter with tiny points of flame, and the dance floor's reflective marble surface was gleaming like still water. The family situated themselves at one end of the room on a raised dais to watch and commentate as Joanna and Prosper were supposed to dance before them and "fall in love." Joanna had a hard time not rolling her eyes repeatedly as her father spoke to the musicians, selecting what he deemed the perfect song. Only Lyall's presence beside her kept the princess from shouting, throwing up her hands, and declaring the whole situation as pointless as it truly was. Instead she was able to turn to make occasional faces at her friend so no one else would see.

Once the king was satisfied with his musical selection, he stepped back to his seat. The first gentle notes of a popular tune flitted invitingly across the ballroom. Joanna finally met Prosper's eyes. Watchful again. He seemed to quietly study each new situation before reacting. She could appreciate that quality as one she lacked. Still, as she looked up into the face she supposed must be attractive—and at the youthful body and slender build she knew Lyall was appreciating silently behind her—she felt nothing.

Her entire puberty had been a confusing mess of family assurances that soon she would begin to feel drawn to men or women. That desire would find her. But it never happened, and she had no idea what that attraction was supposed to feel like.

Now that she too had made a thorough study of her counterpart's features, she held up her hand, straightening her back and stepping in with her right foot, feeling rather than seeing Lyall leave her. He would watch with the other servants standing along the walls, waiting in case she should call for refreshment.

Prosper stepped forward as well, touching the wrist of his extended arm to hers. He looked a bit uneasy, but clearly knew the dance well enough as they stepped in, stepped out, switched arms, spun away and back together. This dance because it was commonly known through most kingdoms, with some variations.

Prosper did a workmanlike job, never missing a beat, but also not managing to add any flourishes of his own. Joanna was so familiar with the steps that she might have done them in her sleep, and she began throwing in her own, still hitting all the important motions. And extra skip here, an added flourish of her skirt there.

Prosper looked so intent on the dance that Joanna had to fight back a smile. She wished she could turn to Lyall and giggle. *"He's so serious. Look how serious this one is!"*

"I believe we are also supposed to talk at some point here," the prince finally ventured as he was once again moving with Joanna, their outstretched wrists touching. Even with his sun-kissed tan, her skin was a few shades darker and made a warm contrast to his.

"I suppose we are." Joanna replied, hiding her amusement. "I also suppose you have been warned about me?"

Prosper put on an exaggerated expression of surprise, widening his eyes, his mouth forming a little O. Joanna's lips twitched involuntarily as she tried to maintain her poise. The dance brought them around for a twirl, which he nearly flubbed. Composing himself, Prosper answered. "The princess who rides out in full armor? The one who rescues carriages and fights monsters? That princess? I may indeed have been warned." He was smirking. His hazel eyes twinkled as he spun away from her then back together again.

"And you've been warned how many suitors I have seen off before you?" She cocked an eyebrow. It was a warning.

"I had not been given exact details, but for your family to seek me, the prince of a land so far from your own, and my being a third born, I expected you to have some sort of crippling deformity or to be on death's door for your family to wish to marry you to me."

"You're very blunt."

"I am." His eyes were still alight, and Joanna found herself unable to contain her smile any longer.

"Blunt is good. I won't have to beat around the bush with you." The dance moved them apart for a moment, and Joanna sneaked a glance towards her father. He was watching them, tapping his fingertips on the arm of his chair in time to the music.

No doubt he was replaying in his mind the many times his daughter had chased away every prince he had sent before her. It was difficult enough getting anyone to come to a land plagued by an ogre, and then to have a daughter so bent on never marrying; her father must wonder every day what he had done to displease the gods. Joanna idly spun the cat ring around on her finger. Perhaps it was the animal gods who had cursed the man, when he converted to following the Mother Goddess and Father God.

"So what more do you need to tell me, princess?" Prosper asked as the music swept them back together once more. Wrist to wrist.

"That I don't intend to marry you. That I intend to put you off by whatever means I must. I hope, with you, it might be logic."

"Logic?" Prosper's brow rose. "I am prone to occasional fits of logic." Concern flashed across his features. "Tell me, is there something you find unsatisfactory about me?"

"Not in the least. You seem very nice and intelligent."

"Blunt and intelligent," Prosper mulled. His eyes held hers, unflinching. "I suppose that will have to be good enough. I find you to be beautiful and very interesting. I wish I could get to know you better."

"And I you." She meant it. This man had potential as a friend. A rarity indeed. He was taking this all quite well, and she tried to read something deeper on his earnest features. What else could he be up to? "Come." She grasped his hand.

The song was not finished, but she led him from the dance floor. Her father's voice rumbled behind them, shouting something. Joanna ignored him. She guided the confused Prosper out onto one of the small balconies, which were situated behind thick, velvet curtains on the western side of the ballroom. They looked out over the twinkling city and the rolling farmland beyond, illuminated by the stars and washed over by creamy moonlight.

Pleasant summer breezes ruffled Joanna's hair as she slid her hand from Prosper's. Suddenly awkward, she wrapped her arms around herself. Her biceps were tight under her hands, and she idly wondered if she could beat Prosper at arm wrestling.

"You have a lovely kingdom," Prosper commented, moving past her to lean against the thick, stone balcony railing, the wind playing in his own dark hair.

"Yes," Joanna agreed. She discreetly craned her neck, checking the curtain for any signs of the servants her father might send to spy on her. How long could Lyall stall them? Turning back to Prosper, she raised her chin. "Now it's time for the logic I told you about. My truest mission and desire in life is to keep my beautiful kingdom safe, which I cannot do if I am wed to you." She paused for his reaction, and when he said nothing, she launched into the explanation she rarely bothered to give. She told Prosper of the danger of The Ogre, his encroaching borders and his Shade warriors. How it would have been her duty, if she had been a second born son, to deal with this and any other threats to the happiness of the people within their kingdom. She assured him, on no uncertain terms, that she fully intended to continue serving her people in that capacity and that there would be no marriage in her future, no matter how understanding the husband.

Prosper listened and his expression remained one of contemplative watchfulness. He did not interrupt, though when she spoke of The Ogre, his brows came together. When she finished he studied her for a moment longer.

She had rattled off her story so powerfully that his gentle voice was a stark contrast. "I understand. About loving your kingdom, I mean. I love mine too. I'm the third born of three sons. I have a younger sister as well. I'm what you might call useless to my family." He chuckled dryly. "Fortunately, I learned to be helpful elsewhere. I go down to the seaside. I lend a hand to fishermen on land and aboard their little vessels. I'm a wind mage so—"

"Wind mage?!" Joanna spoke too loudly and shot a glance over her shoulder. Lyall had positioned himself in the balcony entrance and had clearly heard her, his head inclining in her direction. She was uncertain if anyone in the palace had heard, but her friend gave no warning gesture, so she looked back to the prince.

"Yes." Prosper looked confused, then he held out his hand, palm down before her and flicked it in a side to side chopping motion. Joanna was struck in the face by a gush of wind. She blinked in astonishment and almost laughed aloud. "I'm sorry," Prosper said quickly, grasping his hand as though it had done something wrong. "That was supposed to be gentler."

Joanna gaped at the prince, her mouth hanging open for a beat before she collected herself. The only magic she had ever witnessed was that of The Ogre's Shades, and she was immediately torn between demanding to see more, and bustling Prosper out of the palace and her kingdom as fast as she could.

"Didn't my father warn you? Didn't anyone tell you about The Ogre and what he does?" Joanna asked urgently, eyeing Prosper with a combination of concern and fascination. Perhaps there should have been fear as well, but instead she stood forward on her toes, overcome with curiosity.

"I've heard the rumors like anyone. That your ogre steals magic. Back home we didn't think it was possible." Prosper was still looking at his hands as though he wasn't certain they were his. Joanna resisted the urge to grasp them and check them over herself. Could this man twist the winds around his fingers as someone might tangle thread?

Joanna leaned so far forward in excitement that she overbalanced and stepped awkwardly, drawing Prosper's attention back to her. She explained as best she could. "I've never seen it personally. They say The Ogre leeched all the magic from our land before I was born. We have no mages here. No one has even an ounce of magic in them."

"I thought those were stories. Exaggerations." A crease formed on Prosper's brow. "We live so far from you, our stories of your kingdom come second and third-hand. I'd never imagined there could be a land without magic." He was looking at her with concern now. As though he'd suddenly realized she didn't have a nose. Like she'd told him her people lived in a world without trees. Without water.

"They're not exaggerated, I assure you." Her mind raced. Could she feel the magic in his hands if she touched them? "We haven't a shred of magic, and while you're here, you might be in danger too. Have you felt...have you noticed anything off about your magic? I don't know how it works." Joanna's voice came in a rushed whisper. She cut another glance towards Lyall, who had angled himself to listen. He reassured her with his eyes that their conversation was still private. Perhaps the king hoped against hope that his daughter was engaging in a romantic conversation at last. She had never rushed anyone out to the balcony to talk before.

Prosper sighed and leaned his lower back against the balcony rail, folding his arms. "I suppose I have been feeling a bit under the weather. I thought I was getting a cold from the journey."

Joanna squinted up into the man's eyes. He seemed healthy enough, but already her thoughts were a tangle of possibilities. How much power did he have? How much had The Ogre already stolen? What would happen to Prosper if all his magic was taken and how much more power would The Ogre gain? Would Prosper get his magic back when he left their lands, or would it be lost to him forever? "I don't think we should take any chances," she said. "You need to go before something...I'm not certain what…happens to you. Go back to your sea and your ships. You're in danger here, mage. Tell my father anything you need to. Tell him I struck you, or I'm a spiteful shrew, or you cannot stand the sound of my grating voice—whatever you need to."

The prince's mouth quirked in a sly grin. "Is this another method of yours to be rid of me? I was warned you have many techniques. Should I be concerned, if this attempt fails that you will tip me off the balcony?"

Of course the first mage she'd ever met would be charming. She surprised herself by wishing this man could stay, so she could bombard him with a million questions. Perhaps if she understood magic, she might be able to combat the Ogre, and Prosper would act as her advisor. With a growl of frustration, she set her jaw. "I'm being completely honest with you. Your power is in danger here and that is all there is to it."

"Your father must have known—"

"My father doesn't care." Joanna threw up her hands, aware she was growing more agitated by the minute. Her dress flounced dramatically as she paced one way, then back to face Prosper. "He wants me married off and out of his hair. He's probably hoping that you'll whisk me away back to your seaside kingdom before you even notice the magic The Ogre has taken from you. If my father even believes in The Ogre's ability at all. He claims he does, but I'm not so sure." She was a little breathless from her rant. Her cheeks warmed with embarrassment as she looked back into Prosper's eyes and saw a twinkle of amusement there, along with an appropriate amount of concern.

Joanna clamped her mouth shut, willing herself into silence so the prince could ponder her words. Why was everyone else so slow about making decisions? She wanted to grab his hand and haul him right back to his rooms to pack, but instead she squeezed her biceps and did her best to appear calm and logical. The man turned and looked out over the slumbering kingdom with its lush fields and stands of verdant trees. He held out his hand and twisted it in a stirring motion until, before Joanna's eyes, the dust and a small smattering of leaves that had settled on the railing were caught up in a funnel of wind no larger than a cat. It swirled just beyond the edge of the rail. Joanna and Lyall watched, hypnotized.

When Prosper stopped moving his hand, the funnel of air was gone and everything that had been caught in it dropped away to the courtyard below. Joanna thought of some poor guard getting a little shower of dust, leaves, and a stray twig pattering against his helm. Even seeing such simple magic ignited a fire of curiosity and excitement inside Joanna, and it was all she could do to bite down on a fresh bombardment of questions.

Prosper leaned down with his forearms against the rail, staring after the fallen dust, still thoughtful.

Joanna couldn't contain herself any longer. She held out her own hand, imagining she could feel the pull and current of the winds. Call them to her will. "How does it work?" she asked. "How does magic work?" She turned her hand over, looking at her calloused palm. Her hands always gave her away as a fighter. Little scars, rough patches from gripping rein and sword hilt. Her nails were trimmed short, unladylike and efficient. Could a mage's hands look like this?

The prince met her eyes again and smiled. She must have seemed like an eager child to him, and she didn't care. "Magic comes naturally to those who are born with it. When you're a mage, the magic lives inside you. Mine settles in my hands most of the time. Sometimes you inherit it from your parents, but more often it just crops up. As if the gods bestow it at random. Usually, as soon as your family realizes you have the gift, they get you tutors or send you to a special school."

"How strong are you? Could you cause a storm that would crush enemy ships? Could you stop a storm from coming inland?" Joanna grasped her skirts, crushing the little pearls under her fingers as she watched Prosper's hands. He had callouses too.

Her heart gave an excited flutter, and she admonished herself inwardly. *Try to look a bit less excited about the magic that will be stolen from this poor man.*

Prosper chuckled, his eyes crinkling pleasantly again. "I have never known any mage who would attempt such a thing. Perhaps in a true emergency, but it's dangerous. The first thing they teach you is to know the limits and rules of your power. Magic... it has give, but also take. 'Magic begets magic.' For each thing I do, there will be a reaction. Like throwing a pebble into a pond. You hardly notice the little ripples and they seldom reach shore, but if I toss a rock that uses all my strength to lift, it'll make a wave. If I raised up a storm at sea I might cause a drought over my own lands. Or perhaps there will be a deadly lightning strike. It's impossible to know exactly what reaction you'll get, but the more you stress your magic, the higher the chance that it will have a negative or deadly consequence."

Joanna soaked up everything he said like a child seeing the sky for the first time. "And you're limited to the magic you have inside you?"

"Yes." Prosper nodded, absently clasping and unclasping his hands. "Normally whatever magic you allow to flow out of you finds its way back to you. It's yours until you die. Like your spirit. I have heard of people magicking others, like blessings or curses. Those are forbidden in our land; they might just be stories. Supposedly you push some of your magic into someone else and you seal it inside, like a pearl in an oyster." He held up his hands, pressed together at the wrists, then closed his fingers to imitate the sea creature.

"But The Ogre could take all that away," Joanna warned. "Because your magic is only yours, there's a good chance it might not come back!" Could Prosper lock some of his magic inside of her? Just a little. Something that could help her win the fight with The Ogre. She shook the notion from her head. "Can you feel The Ogre taking your magic at all?"

The mage sighed, then nodded, resolute. "I can sense something. I wasn't certain if I truly felt it, or if I imagined it. Since I came here, I have felt a sort of tickling sensation. Like someone trying to pluck something invisible from my palms. Distracting, nothing more." He hesitated, his eyes still locked on Joanna's, searching. "Perhaps you are right."

"So you shan't be marrying me?" Joanna asked, just to be certain. Best to get one issue out of the way at a time.

Prosper's laugh was sweet and gentle. "It's alright. The whole marriage thing was basically a pretense anyway. My family fully expect me to come home as wife-less as ever."

"So my reputation does precede me, even all the way to the sea."

Joanna heard Lyall stifle a chuckle.

"My father only agreed to this meeting because he has been meaning to open trade with your kingdom. My aunt is a skilled negotiator, as difficult as she might be, so she was a natural escort for me. I was only one possible trading chip for the enterprise. My mother and siblings didn't even bother bidding me goodbye."

"Good," Joanna said, then flushed, "I don't mean it's good that your parents are using you as a trade incentive.... Mine too, I suppose."

"I know what you mean." Prosper raised his hands in a calming gesture.

Joanna's muscles were taught as a bowstring, as if she were astride her warhorse charging into battle. Her mind kept drifting to the thought that someone magical was standing right in front of her and she couldn't let him stay, as much as it hurt. She wanted to ask him every possible question. To sit with him for days and learn everything. She had no idea how important magic was to a person's life-force, and she didn't dare risk him staying longer than he had to. "You should tell your escorts that you need to go." Her voice sounded choked.

"Right. I'll inform my aunt." Prosper nodded curtly, his expression firm. The prince turned and strode past Lyall, back into the ballroom.

Joanna lagged behind, stopping beside the bodyguard.

"That might have been the quickest you have ever gotten rid of a suitor." Lyall leaned down to speak quietly to her as they watched Prosper cross the room. "Your father looks thrilled."

"You heard him. He's a mage." Joanna fidgeted with the pearls hanging from her dress.

"You did the right thing encouraging him to go. We don't know enough about The Ogre and his power to risk the prince staying."

The pair stood by as Prosper interrupted his aunt, who had once again bent the king's ear over affairs of trade relations. Joanna wondered what the young man was saying, but suspected he was playing ill as he coughed and put a hand to his own forehead.

Joanna shook her head sadly. "I liked this one. Not to marry of course," she put in hastily, as Lyall shot her a look. "He'd be a good friend and ally. Perhaps when we sort out this ogre problem for good, he can come back and teach some of our people how to use magic again."

"Perhaps." Lyall said.

Prosper got his aunt and uncle on their feet and was hustling them from the room with remarkable efficiency. The king's stare was ice. She held his gaze for only a moment before she snatched Lyall's arm, positioned him as though he were escorting her, and guided her friend out of the ballroom, as far from her disgruntled parent as she could get.

~~~~~

"Perhaps he should have stayed a bit longer. You don't know how quickly The Ogre steals magic. We could have studied it. Maybe figured it out." Joanna shifted on the balls of her feet in the packed sand of the practice yard. Lyall, dressed in leathers and wielding a wooden sword and shield, struck down from overhead, catching one of Joanna's twin, wooden swords.

The princess let out a grunt of exertion, shifting her body to knock his blow away. Both combatants were already soaked through with sweat and smeared with grit. Even on mornings after a late night of fending off suitors Joanna insisted on never missing a chance to keep her skills sharp. Fighting always helped her order her thoughts, and she had plenty of thoughts to order today.

"You always come in from above because you're taller," she griped. "When will you learn that I expect it and block?"

"When I can no longer do this—" Lyall faked high, then dropped to a knee and swiped his sword well under Joanna's guard, smacking her firmly on her thigh, which, like his, was protected with padded leather.

Joanna grunted in annoyance and brought the wooden blade in her left hand down on her friend's shoulder. Not hard, but enough to get the point across. "There! See how you like it!"

"If your leg was chopped off you would be too distracted to do that," Lyall pointed out, disengaging and rubbing the muscle where his neck met his shoulder.

"A single swing would never chop my leg clean off." Joanna slipped out of her fighting stance and settled her two swords against a nearby bench. She reached into the water bucket perched at one end and helped herself to a tin cup. Her hair clung in itchy curls to her forehead and the back of her neck, so she finished her drink by dumping the rest of the dipper-full over her head.

"You keep coming back to the topic of magic." Lyall joined her at the bucket. She refilled the cup and handed it to her friend.

"So I do." A smirk played on Joanna's lips. "Keen of you to notice. I just hope I made the right decision about Prosper." The mage and his entourage had left earlier that morning with the duchess complaining to anyone who would listen about the inhospitality of it all.

Prosper held fast, proclaiming that he simply had to be away and could not stand another minute in these lands.

"Why don't you just ask your father how The Ogre steals the magic? He might have heard something about it from your grandfather." Lyall pulled his hair from the leather band that held it, stray strands sticking to his high brow. He tried to retie the tail, but his hair kept falling loose, so at a gesture from Joanna, he knelt in the sand before her, and she stepped behind him to gather his hair and tie it back.

Joanna looped the leather band expertly around her friend's hair before knotting it. She tapped Lyall's shoulder to indicate she was finished, and he stood, turning his sky-blue gaze on her.

"You know I can't ask my father that sort of thing. Or anything at all. He always turns it around to lecture me about duty and family and, well, you've heard the speeches."

Lyall sighed, but nodded, moving back to where he had left his practice sword and shield. Having been with Joanna since childhood meant there were very few fatherly lectures he hadn't heard.

"JOANNA!"

Joanna's insides clenched as though a horse had kicked her in the gut. She turned to see her father, surrounded by servants bearing water goblets, a fan, and suspending a cloth on poles as shade for their king.

"What?" she snapped and caught Lyall's wince out of the corner of her eye.

"How did you do it this time? Did you tell the cook to put something in the prince's food? Is that why he took ill so quickly? Did you take him to the balcony to show him all your horrible battle scars? How did you do it, Joanna?"

"Logic, Father," Joanna turned to her parent and raised her chin.

"Logic?" The king stopped short of entering the practice yard and glowered down at the sand as though a river stood between himself and his daughter.

"Yes." Joanna grabbed up her wooden swords again, facing Lyall who looked uneasy. "He was a mage, which I suspect you knew. You also know what happens to people with magic around here. I told him about it, and he decided to go home."

"He wasn't ill?"

"No. He was informed." Joanna raised a sword, and Lyall tapped it tentatively as his signal to start the bout.

"Joanna, stop. Speak to me like I am your father! for once," the king entreated, moving around the practice ring to try to get into her line of sight. His servants scrambled to follow him with the shade cloth.

"If you want to have mages here, we need to deal with The Ogre, just as I've been saying." Joanna took a few easy swings at Lyall, gauging him. He blocked, but was giving her a look she knew well. Her best friend's disapproval stung far greater than her father's, but she ignored both and stepped to the side, watching for an advantage.

"All you are doing is riding out and slaying a few Shades. I think you like the glory and acclaim you garner from it. The Ogre is still there in the castle he stole, minding his own business." The king pointed out.

His words were no doubt meant to dissuade her with her own failings, but perhaps he had forgotten who he was speaking to,

"You could get me a new fighting teacher. There is only so much Lyall and I can do with the knowledge we have." Joanna faked to the left, then moved in, her sword clattering against Lyall's shield as she bent her knees and tried to jab in at his side with her offhand sword. Her slim companion dodged and brought the pommel of his own sword down on her back. He struck hard enough to make a *thump*, but not enough to cause pain. "You see?" Joanna snapped. "I need better training."

"And then you could defeat The Ogre and all his magic? If I got you a new teacher?" The king folded his arms over his elaborate doublet, which was decorated with gold chains and shimmering jewels. One trade route that was as strong as ever was that between their kingdom and Ebb, which was renowned for its gem mines.

Joanna's previous battle master had been a retired fighter her father hired from another kingdom, who wanted to earn a bit of coin in his golden years. He taught Joanna, Lyall, and any of the guard who cared to learn, but he grew too old and retreated to the countryside where, as far as Joanna knew, he was still living peacefully. The job was never refilled, due in no small part to Joanna's taking to fighting so strongly, and her simultaneous assertion that she would never marry. She suspected her father regretted "creating a monster" when he indulged her.

The King tried again. "I let you follow your dreams, your whims. I let you ride all over dragging your reputation through the mud—"

"My reputation as People's Protector, you mean? Because I think that's going well. I save their farms and homes from being ripped apart. From having their animals slaughtered by Shades."

Her father dipped his head as though walking into a heavy wind and forged on. "You need to think of your family, your duty, your place in this society. The god and goddess say that marriage—"

"You know I follow the old gods!" Joanna flourished her blades in a showy gesture before she stepped in, switched direction, and slammed her shoulder against Lyall's shield. This time she caught her friend off guard. He overbalanced and nearly fell. He scrambled for purchase in the sand and managed to block her incoming blow by inches.

He exhaled tightly and struggled to recover his stance.

"Joanna," the king groaned, looking skyward, not really addressing his daughter so much as begging his gods for assistance.

"The people need me, father. Or, to put it in terms you care about: you've all but lost contact with Narhime on the other side of The Ogre's lands. Wouldn't you love to work with them again?" She knew she'd hit on something. As a peacetime king, his true love was with bargains and treaties. She'd used to visit his office when she was a child and would wander, lost and awed, through his collection of maps that sprawled expansively across tables and all four walls. All the maps were marked with indecipherable trade routes and notes about each and every kingdom.

Her father fixed Joanna with a steely gaze, but she could see his mind was working. He ground his teeth and spat the words, "you know I won't stop you from riding out, but you also know that I will continue to try to find you someone you like. If only you'd give them a chance." He'd tried a few times, when she was younger, to put her under house arrest. She'd jumped from two windows, bribed any number of guards, and escaped from solitary confinement in a locked room. The only result of her imprisonment was his not knowing where she was. At least when she took her soldiers into the countryside, she reported to him first. She knew it drove him mad, but it was a bargain that had to be struck.

"If you want to throw men at me, how about more soldiers? It's difficult to get things done with only fifteen."

He didn't answer, but his look clearly said, *I shouldn't have allowed you the ones you have.*

Joanna snarled and whirled on Lyall, crashing against him again, shoulder to shield. She parried aggressively as he tried to strike her free sword arm. Locking hilts, she twisted her wrist in a maneuver she seldom managed, but this time it sent her companion's sword flying from his grip. Then she whipped her sword point up and past his shield to rest against his collar bone.

Lyall, panting, nodded to indicate he acknowledged her win. She stepped back, her blood hot with the wildfire of combat. This was what she was made to do, every muscle and bone singing with the blows of her twin blades. She heard her father make an annoyed noise, and it took a great deal of willpower not to look at him again.

"Joanna, I am running out of patience."

"No. You're running out of men you can convince to marry me. Prince Prosper was from the farthest kingdom you have ever considered. Where next? Going to get me a prince from the eastern snow plains? Do they even know we exist?"

The king rolled his eyes, a decidedly un-kingly gesture, but one that Joanna knew well. "Are you going to be this difficult when Alroy is king?"

"You mean when the good sibling is in charge?" Joanna snorted. "The one who thinks just like you do, and who you've trained his whole life in your own image? I think it's safe to say that, yes, I plan to be exactly this difficult."

"Your brother and I argue too," the king said.

"About trade agreements. He never flouts tradition." Joanna fumed, breathing hard even though her swords hung loose in her grasp.

"I know you hate the idea of marriage, Joanna, but would it really be so terrible? You'd still be you."

"And what am I? Am I born to be useful to you and no one else?" She gestured with one of her swords. "I found my own way to be useful, Father. I'm the Protector of the People. Or I'm trying to be. Until I defeat The Ogre, I'm only half-way there, at best." She winced at her own words, catching a cautious look from Lyall.

The king huffed "That's not what I meant, and you know it. You have Lyall to keep you safe, but the closer you ride to The Ogre's lands, the more dangerous things become."

"I have *myself* to keep me safe." Joanna's lip curled in disgust. She spun on her heel to face Lyall, raising her sword. He refused to meet it, keeping his practice blade low.

"I'm not sparring with you like this," he said, eyes flicking to the ground.

Joanna fumed. "Both of you? Teaming up on me now?"

"No," Lyall spoke flatly, letting his shield slide from his arm to the sand.

"I want you to be safe. I only have two children." The king tried again, his own temper audibly riding just under the surface. Her father was much more calm and collected than Joanna. He was always a pillar of strategy and steadfast peacefulness, but he laid down orders as if from the gods and expected them to be obeyed.

"You already have a grandchild on the way. Your family line is safe." Joanna said.

"I don't care about the family line being safe. I want you to be safe."

Joanna's skin prickled. She hated—HATED—when he used that tack. How could she come back at him from here? "Then stop trying to sell me like a horse at market!"

"Jo." Lyall's voice was a whisper, but it was also a warning. Her friend knew she was dangerously close to saying something so stupid and damaging that would have her and her father in a boiling feud for weeks.

Joanna almost rounded on Lyall, but fought down the roar that rose in her chest. Once, thirteen-year-old Joanna had let her temper loose on her bodyguard. It had ended with both of them miserable and not speaking for weeks.

"I'm going on patrol," Joanna announced, setting aside her practice blades with a rigid calm.

"Oh? For how long this time?" The king asked, also managing to keep his tone casual.

"I'm not sure. I want to ride my usual patrol route at least. With so many Shades about these days, I want to be certain none of them try anything." She walked to the bench and picked up one of the rags draped beside the water pail, wiping sweat and grit from her face. "We only got to Lark this time before you recalled me to meet with Prince Prosper—whose family's carriage was attacked by Shades, may I remind you."

The king glowered, but did not answer.

"Don't worry, Father. I won't get hurt and I'm sure I shall be back just in time to meet whomever you entice to come calling for my hand next."

The king watched her for a moment longer with the expression of one scrutinizing a difficult puzzle. Seemingly unable to come up with a solution, he nodded and turned to go. Lyall bobbed a bow after the ruler then shot an uneasy glance at sparring partner. "You put me in a tight place sometimes," he said, when the king was out of earshot.

"Oh?" Joanna set about unbuckling her practice armor. The breastplate of padded leather fell to the sand and a servant, who was sitting nearby in the shade of a small apple tree until called for, rushed over to gather it up. She handed the young man the arm pieces as well, and he scurried away to hang them all in the small practice armory pavilion.

"I can't be seen to correct you in front of your father, nor can I vocally side with you or him because the other one will tear me apart later." Lyall worked his straps loose and slid his chest armor free.

"I would not tear you apart!" Joanna protested, stung. Lyall looked directly at her, both eyebrows raised, and she found herself unable to keep a straight face. "Alright, perhaps I would. I'm sorry. I shall try to keep my arguments with my father to a minimum. Perhaps only holy days."

Lyall lobbed a bracer at her. She swatted it out of the air and laughed. The servant looked peeved as he picked up the bracer and shook off the sand.

"Ly..." Joanna cocked her head at her friend. "Can I ask you something I've always wondered about you?"

"Why am I so handsome?" He raked a hand back through his sweat-streaked hair.

Joanna shook her head. "Why...? Why do you follow me? Why are you contented to be my bodyguard? I've offered you titles, a knighthood…hell, land of your own, and you always turn me down." She plopped onto the bench to unlace her greaves.

"Trying to be rid of me?" Lyall landed beside her, eyes cast mournfully skyward. A faint smile flickered, but when he answered his voice was level and serious. "Joshua asks me that too. I suppose I'll tell you the same thing I tell him. Putting aside the fact that you're my best friend, I've always known this is the life I belong in. Like you've always known you should be the People's Protector." He nudged her shoulder with his. "Some people want greatness. Glory. They seek it, sniff it out, never stop searching for it. Some of us aren't built that way. I like a simple life. I like knowing my job and that I have a purpose. Some people might think it's odd to wish to be a spoke in a wheel, but without spokes the whole carriage collapses. Sure, sometimes my job means I have to follow along with your crazy schemes, but that hasn't gotten me killed yet. I wouldn't have it any other way."

"Are you being honest with me?" Joanna leaned back, studying his angular face in profile: long, straight nose; deep-set eyes; features she would know in the blackest night and could describe without a thinking.

"For once, yes." His roguish grin was back. He elbowed her playfully. "C'mon Jo. Don't let your father get to you."

"It's not just him," Joanna admitted. "I'm jealous you already feel like you're where you belong. Every time I ride out in that armor, trying to look like a champion, I know I'm constantly on trial. I can't slip. I can't let go for a second because I have to show everyone what I am. Prove that I'm a true guardian. And the men…" Joanna rolled her eyes.

"They love you and you know it."

"As long as I keep winning, keep up the image of the fierce warrior princess they can be proud to ride with."

"They watched you fall off your horse and land in the dirt." Lyall pointed out, eyebrow cocked.

"That wasn't ideal. I just hope the things I do to impress them outweigh my stupid mistakes."

"Jo…" Lyall's eyes softened. "I really don't think– "

Joanna sprang to her feet, new energy infusing her muscles. She didn't want to let Lyall reassure her that her men were loyal or that the people loved her. No, she needed to know it for herself, and to do that she needed to keep proving that she was worthy to everyone, from the king to the lowliest farmer. "Let's go, Ly. We have a kingdom to protect!"

Lyall sighed, rocked to his feet, and followed Joanna out of the practice yard.

~~~~

The party reached Glen Hollow a week and a half into their ride. The city was east of the castle along the direct route towards The Ogre's lands. Joanna wondered if the thriving city had once been a little village more suited to its simple name, as she guided Willow down a wide, paved street.

The buildings here had two stories and were freshly painted and maintained. Flowers stood out in bright window boxes to add color and character to each street, and the people milled around them in clothes that had never seen the stains of field labor.

Though it was only nearing midday, Joanna and her men were headed for one of the large inns near the town square.

As she turned in her saddle to admire a particularly fine-looking wolfhound walking with some hunters, she looked up into her own men's pleading, puppy-dog eyes. She tried to contain her amusement. "Be back before sundown. We'll meet at the Iron Bull tavern near the city heart." She nodded to Avery, the youngest of her troop, whom she knew was eager to be off to a neighboring farmhold to visit his sweetheart. "You too. Go on."

"Thank you, Highness!" The youth attempted to give her a sober, soldierly look, but instead grinned like an idiot. She had hand-selected Avery, and several of her other men, from her father's guard, and the smallish, clever-eyed lad thrived much more readily with her than surrounded by stodgy, older guardsmen.

She turned to Lyall. "That goes for you as well, Ly."

The tall man had already dismounted and was putting his riding armor away into special saddle packs. "Never fear, Jo," Lyall reassured her as he pulled a fine, embroidered doublet from another pack, laid it against his saddle to straighten any creases, then slipped it on. "I know you want us all accounted for so we can leave at dawn." He spoke more for the men than her, a not-so-subtle reminder of what their leader expected.

Joanna swung her leg over Willow's back and landed gracefully. She hoped her men took note of her clean dismount this time. She strode over to Lyall to help arrange his sleeves so they billowed. She reached into his pack and pulled out delicate leather gloves that were definitely not for riding or fighting, holding them out to him.

None of the men made notice of the princess helping to dress her bodyguard as though she were the servant, but a few townsfolk did, and they raised eyebrows as they passed. One young woman gawked openly from her window.

"Any plans for what you'll be doing in town?" Lyall asked as he allowed Joanna to do up his buttons. He must have known that this stop was more for them than her. So near to the royal palace there would be little chance anyone would have news of The Ogre or his Shades.

Joanna shrugged. "We can't risk being complacent. It's possible The Ogre's managed to extend his reach yet again." Joanna tugged the bottom of the doublet firmly, then smoothed it, admiring the intricately stitched patterns.

"Worth keeping your ear to the ground." Lyall stepped back and struck a pose, his mind clearly not on the matter at hand. Joanna knew he was fighting to keep from beaming at the prospect of spending a day with his sweetheart.

"We'll talk about this when you get back." She patted his chest. "Though I think I've decided on my employment for the day. Seeing what rumors I can drum up."

"Good idea," Lyall met her dark eyes with his light. She loved when he smiled with his whole being. He almost seemed to glow from within.

"Get out of here." She slapped him on the shoulder. "Go see to that man of yours."

Lyall, with an added skip to his step, strode off down the street. Joanna chuckled to herself as several women noticed her bodyguard and fluttered their lashes, to which Lyall was endlessly oblivious. "Alright," she turned back to her men, all of whom were fidgeting in their saddles. "You are free to go about your day. Liam," she addressed the red-haired man who acted as farrier in their group. "Are you able to see that the horses are settled in the city stable?"

"Yes, ma'am," Liam nodded. He fondly petted his own mount, a short-bodied, brown mare who seemed unimpressive, but who could easily keep pace with the larger steeds. Joanna guessed that Liam would happily spend his day touring the city stables if he was allowed.

The horses seen to and her men off on their various pursuits, Joanna found herself standing with Rylan, the healer. She knew he had drawn a short straw. With Lyall gone, it fell to one of the other men to stand in as bodyguard. "So, you're going to protect me, then?" she asked Rylan, grinning.

The healer snorted. "I'm just here to put anyone who angers you back together again." He gestured to the healer's pack slung across his shoulders, which none the less hung conspicuously beside the sword at his hip.

"Well then, I suppose I shall have to protect you." Joanna rested her hands on the pommels of her twin swords, slim belts that crossed over her midsection holding the blades in place.

"I would appreciate it." The healer dipped his head. Rylan was a gentle soul who had once been wed, but lost his wife to illness before she could bear him any children. The man vowed never to love again. While Joanna did not understand the romantic angle of it, she could still appreciate the loyalty. Rylan had a round face and a skin that was closer in tone to Joanna's, a trim beard and kind eyes. "Where are we off to?" he asked.

"The square to start, I suppose. It's market day, so it'll be busy," Joanna said. Rylan fell in beside her. "I want to keep my ears open for any rumors or mention of The Ogre, unlikely as it is this far west."

Market day was bustling as ever. Joanna and Rylan bought some sweet bread and ate as they walked, weaving through the crowd that hardly bothered to make way for their princess. Some knew she preferred to walk peacefully amongst them, and still others, especially the children, had no idea who she was and extended her no special courtesy.

"Ma, why isn't that lady wearing a dress?" asked a little girl, tugging her mother's sleeve as the woman scrutinized a basket of fresh carrots. "Ma" didn't look up, and the girl continued to gape openly at Joanna in her leggings, jerkin and armor.

"It's because riding horses is difficult with skirts." Joanna stopped and leaned down, smiling.

"Oh." The girl stuck her knuckles into her mouth, considering, then popped it free. "Why have you got shiny metal on you?"

"To protect me when enemies try to hurt me." Joanna tapped a fist against her breastplate.

The girl took in her princess like a jeweler appraising a gem and finding it unsatisfactory. "You've got swords too."

"I do. Those are to hurt the bad people who might try to hurt you."

"My brothers say I'm not allowed to play swords. I have to stay out of the way. Girls aren't to use swords." The child's voice was accusatory, as though she had caught Joanna doing something she shouldn't and planned to tattle.

"Of course you can learn to use swords." Joanna planted her hands on her hips. "Your brothers just don't want you to learn because you'll beat them."

The girl considered this for a moment before raising her round chin and grinning Her mother began to move on, drawing the child with her.

"Don't tell your brothers what I told you." Joanna winked. "If you want to learn to fight, find someone who will teach you no matter what it takes, then go home and show your brothers how well a lady can use a sword."

"Okay!" squeaked the girl, doing a little hop-skip to keep up with her mother. "An' I won't wear dresses anymore either!"

Joanna straightened and her own smile faded as she caught Rylan's serious look. "What?"

"It may seem kind of you to encourage a poor girl like that, but you must know that you're giving her false hopes. Her father can't afford to fund her wild pursuits, and there's no one who will train her with a blade. The reality is that she'll grow up and face the same matrimonial fate you're looking to avoid."

Joanna's temper flashed and she pivoted on the older man. Her instinct roared in her to tell him off for speaking to her like that. She managed to tamp it down when she caught the earnest look in his deep brown gaze. Painful as it was, he was right. Yet, as she remembered the little girl's hopeful smile, she knew she'd encourage her all over again. "Well, once I'm officially The People's Protector, I'll do something about that."

To her surprise Rylan's face creased with a warm smile. "I believe you will."

The pair moved on, weaving through the crowds, stopping to purchase a piece of honeycomb each or some turnips for stew on the road. Joanna couldn't help but wonder, as she kept the quiet company of the older man, if this was what it was like to stroll with one's father.

Joanna had never seen her parents step foot in a marketplace. The king never left the palace without carriages and servants galore, and this only on special holidays.

Joanna listened to the drone of the crowd. Farmers spoke of the unusually rainy spring and how it affected their crops, or how a fence pole had rotted in the mud and the cattle had run loose. Families discussed their days. Their children ran unchecked through the streets, shouting and playing. People haggled, and sellers shouted the merits of their wares.

Rylan stopped to drop a few coins on the counter of a trinket seller. He turned to Joanna and held up a little wolf carved from soapstone. "See, not everyone has forgotten."

Joanna gingerly took the charm and admired it as the pair made their way towards the edge of the crowd. The creature sat on its haunches and looked at her with eyes made of blue beads. Its tail curled around its feet and, for a creature that represented death, it had an almost friendly expression on its angular features. She passed the wolf back to her friend, and he slipped it into his pouch. "Did they have any cats?"

"Sadly no. One horse and quite a few hedgehogs. The god of solitude is not very popular so he doesn't sell I imagine."

"I suppose not."

Joanna paused to look up at an impressive building casting its heavy shadow over them. Smooth arches and decorative statues adorned the front. The stone was new, not tarnished with weather like the surrounding buildings. It had obviously been costly to build, with marble imported from a mountain kingdom. It had been funded by the royal coffers. It was topped by a peaked steeple adorned with male and female figures, robed and twined in one another's arms, though with their heads turned to stare judgmentally down at the milling crowd. There was still a little disturbed dirt around the building's foundation where the tenacious grass had yet to grow in. Joanna grimaced. "Looks as though they finally completed it."

"It did take them a while. Good thing the God and Goddess are ever patient." Rylan said, folding his arms and eyeing the structure.

Joanna had not gone out of her way to fill her troops' ranks with soldiers who still preferred the old gods as she did, but she knew Rylan wore a chain with three silver running wolves under his tunic front. She idly spun the cat ring around her finger. "The animal gods didn't need such elaborate temples."

"People built them little shrines in the woodlands, I'm told," Rylan shaded his eyes with a hand as he followed the structure upwards to its impressive peak. "Or set out little offering tables in their homes."

Joanna flinched under the unending gaze of the mother and father gods, staring from every stained-glass window and piece of statuary, always holding hands, or wrapped in one another's arms, eternally inseparable. "Many of the gods forbade worship in man-made structures. I read a book about monks following the law of the various wild gods, roaming the lands and spreading wisdom rather than holding mass in certain places." She frowned, folding her arms as she watched a priest slip out from a smaller door to the right of the main one. The woman was garbed in cream-colored robes which were decorated with twin golden figures rising up from the hem. "I suppose this means the people of Glen Hollow have decided to give themselves over to the new gods?"

Rylan nodded soberly. "That's modernity for you, Highness. Time marches on and beliefs change." He tossed his wolf trinket and caught it on his palm.

Joanna watched the charm rise and fall as he tossed it again. "People are starting to think of the old gods as curiosities. Something to make art of, or to put in picture books for children."

"Some still believe, I'm sure." He tucked the wolf away in his medicine pouch.

"The God and Goddess didn't catch on here until The Ogre," Joanna sighed. "I have occasion to talk to princes from other kingdoms. Several still believe in the old gods."

"Yes, and in the mountains they believe in giants that formed the world, and I've heard that by the sea they worship seafoam. Everywhere is different."

"They don't really, do they?"

"Do what?"

"Worship foam?"

"According to what I've been told...by a man in a tavern, so I admit my information is likely faulty," Rylan admitted.

"I should have asked Prince Prosper while he was here." Joanna snapped her fingers in mock frustration. "Oh well. I suppose there's not much we can do about this." She gestured to the temple. "If this is what the people want, it is what they want."

Joanna glowered at the structure a moment longer as the priestess began watering some of the young flowers planted beside the front entrance.

Just as Joanna turned to go, her eye caught on something in the crowded square. Though poor and wealthy mingled easily on market day, her gaze rested on a man who stood out in his raggedness. He was covered in road-dirt and skinny as a fence rail. What was worse, he carried what at first appeared to be a bundle of cloth in his arms, but Joanna quickly realized it was a child.

She darted into the crowd without hesitation, a confused Rylan on her heels. The ragged man was trudging, bloodshot eyes fixed on the church, his bare feet blistered and bleeding as people gave him a wide berth. "Are you alright?" Joanna asked, instinctively holding out her arms for the child.

The man didn't seem to see her at first, finally dragging bleary eyes to her face and blinking. He smacked dry lips as though he hadn't spoken in some time. "My...my daughter," he said feebly.

Joanna gathered up the bundle of a child without further prompting. Rylan reached her in time to catch the man as his knees gave. He tossed the stranger's arm over his shoulder and turned to force his way through the crowd back towards the church. "Come on, Your Highness," he urged.

Joanna followed, pulling the rags aside to see the child's face, praying to the wolf gods that they had not taken her yet. She found a slumbering girl, pale and starved, but still breathing. The child's hair was matted in twin braids and her eyes purple and puffy with weariness.

The priestess at the front of the church dropped her watering can when she spotted them and ran out to help Rylan get the man to the front steps where they sat him down. "I'm a healer," Rylan explained as he whipped his satchel from his shoulders. The priestess glanced nervously at his sword, but said nothing. She bustling away to fetch some water.

Joanna sat down on a step beside the man, still cradling the little girl. She realized that the stranger was nearer to her own age than Rylan's, though the grime and his thinness made him seem much older. "What's her name?" she asked.

"Ena," the man rasped. "Care for her first, please," he begged Rylan.

"Of course." Rylan unwrapped little Ena from her rag blankets, pressing a gentle hand to her forehead, then checking her breathing.

"What happened to you?" Joanna spoke gently.

The man grimaced. "Our farm was attacked."

"Attacked?" Joanna's eyes flashed. "By Shades?"

The man gave her a confused, searching look. "How did you know that? No one believed me when I told them."

"Papa?" Little Ena woke, squirming in Joanna's grip with surprising strength.

"Shhhh shhh, Papa's right here," the man soothed. "Be still for me, Ena?"

The girl gazed with frightened eyes into Joanna's face as though she wasn't certain she was seeing another human being. Joanna reached into Rylan's open pack and took out the little wolf charm, holding it before Ena's frightened gaze. "Would you like to hold him while we take care of you?" Even as Ena reached for the slender figurine Joanna wondered if it was a good idea to hand a child a death token when she looked as though she had narrowly avoided that fate, but Ena smiled.

"She loves animals," her father said, looking at his daughter with such affection it was almost painful.

The priestess returned with two others, a man and woman in the same robes, carrying water and more medical supplies. They immediately went to work on the man's various hurts as he swigged gratefully from the waterskin they offered him. Joanna helped little Ena take a few small drinks, following Rylan's instructions to go slow.

"The goats are dead." Ena said, almost to herself, as she petted the wolf between its upright ears with her finger.

"They killed all your livestock?" Joanna asked.

"Yes." The man's shoulders sagged impossibly lower. "My wife died last year, and Ena and I were on our own. No family in the area, but we were doing alright. She minded the goats during the day when I went hunting and trapping. We weren't thriving, but we had enough."

"Let me take her?" A priestess held out her arms for Ena, obviously concerned the little girl might not be comfortable tucked against Joanna's armor.

"No!" Ena squealed, jerking towards her father.

"She's fine," Rylan reassured the confused priestess. "Dehydrated and road-sore, but not sick or injured."

Unlike her father, Joanna noted. The man had several shallow wounds that she knew hadn't come from the road. The healers from the church were already applying bandages. "Tell me you didn't try to fight the Shades." Joanna said.

The man shook his shaggy head, looking down. "I've never seen anything like them before. I'd heard a few stories, but nothing like this. There were only three, so I thought...I went for them with a pitchfork, but I guess I'm no warrior." His gaze lighted on the twin swords at Joanna's sides.

Joanna's eyes flicked to the priestesses and healers. There was no doubt they were hearing all this information about Shades, but hid it well on still features. Fortunately, the church steps were otherwise far enough from the market crowd, but she would have to have a word with these people about not causing a panic before she left.

"You couldn't have taken them on," Joanna reassured the farmer.

"They burned the house. The barn," the man said, his voice hollow. "I...I'd heard that the mother and father gods take in those in need. This was the only church I know of, so even though it was far, I knew we had to make the journey."

"Journey?" Joanna raised a brow. "Did you come from near the Serpent's River?" That didn't seem accurate. Any farmers near the river knew the Shades well. Many had seen them firsthand. For this man to claim he had only heard stories...

"I'm from Little Fox. Near mill country."

"Mill country?" Joanna exhaled. "Gods da—" She stopped herself before she swore, glancing at little Ena, who seemed to already be feeling better after her water. She played with the wolf, turning it over and over in her hands. Joanna looked to Rylan. "I thought the first time they went south was when we found them attacking the duke and duchess's carriage. I had no idea they'd gone even further!"

"You didn't travel that whole way on foot?" asked the priest.

"We caught a few rides on farm carts heading to various towns." The man shrugged. "Slept in barns and root cellars, ate what we could forage or beg. I just kept going. I knew we had to make it somewhere safe." He reached for Ena and rested his hand on her head.

"Papa." She turned in Joanna's arms, holding out her hands towards her father. Joanna let her go. Ena folded herself into her father's embrace, still cradling the wolf to her. When the man made as if to free it from her grip Rylan raised a hand.

"Let her keep it." Rylan said.

"Thank you." The farmer seemed to scrutinize Joanna again, as though putting a puzzle together now that he could clearly see her armor and blades. Perhaps this was at odds with her short stature, or the fact that she was a woman, or both.

"Can you walk?" asked a priestess. "We can take you inside, find you a nice bed and some food."

The man nodded, standing with the aid of the three. They gathered around him like white birds around a fledgling, guiding him gently towards the church. "Thank you, Your Highness." The first priestess turned and bowed quickly. "We'll soon have these two fed and comfortable."

"Your Highness?" The farmer's eyes went wide, but the priests didn't let him stop to bow and scrape, much to Joanna's relief.

"Bye bye, lady!" Ena waved over her father's shoulder.

"Ena, do you know who that was?" the farmer asked, his voice going high with shock and alarm. "I think that was the princess."

"The princess?!" Ena gasped. She turned and stared at Joanna with huge eyes until the door of the church closed them both from view.

"Little Fox," Joanna breathed. Her hands strayed instinctively to her swords. Her body tingled with a wild energy that came up the moment she let the child go. Her blood roared in her ears. "Gods dammit, all the way to Little Fox! Rylan! We need to stop this! We need to gather the men right now and ride to—"

Rylan cut her off, standing and grasping her arm. She realized that she had one of her swords half-drawn. A few passersby gaped in alarm. "Highness, it's no use going now. The Shades are long gone. It won't do us any good."

"But..." Joanna choked. The image of a burning farmhouse and that poor, thin man trying to fend of magical enemies with a pitchfork looped in her thoughts. Where was she when he was protecting his child from monsters? Where was the one who was supposed to defend him? Probably sitting on a cushion feasting on exotic sweets. Every step she'd made was a failure. "We have to do something! The Shades are reaching too far!" She jerked free of Rylan's hand, but sheathed her sword. She marched back and forth on the step like a tethered animal.

"Highness..." Rylan's tone was soothing. She ignored him. She was a flurry of trapped energy and anger.

Rylan kept trying. "Your Highness? Princess Joanna? JO!"

Joanna turned, eyes blazing, hands balled into fists. A nearby urchin took one look at her and scuttled in the other direction. "NO! I can't just stand here. I can't stand by while my people suffer."

Rylan flinched. "You're not. I know you feel that way now, but please, be still. You're frightening your people. Mostly me."

Joanna dragged herself to a halt. Already the blast of fire that shot through her heart and every vein was ebbing to embers. "I just...I wish I was of more use to everyone." She let her hands fall open to her sides.

"You are." Rylan knelt to gather the rest of his supplies back into his medical bag.

"Not enough."

"Why don't we find someplace nice to settle down for a bit? I'm feeling shaken, and I know a quiet place to get some lunch." Rylan got to his feet, glancing around. His voice did sound unsteady.

Joanna softened. "I'm sorry. I didn't mean to be so...me." She shrugged. "You're right. There's nothing we can do this minute, and the Shades will have left Little Fox weeks ago. We'll continue our ride tonight." She worked to regulate her breathing, imagining Lyall coaching her to be calm.

"I have to have a word with these priests about discretion, then we can go." Joanna said.

"A gentle word?" Rylan raised an eyebrow.

"A gentle word." She agreed. Amusement bubbled back to her surface. She turned to flag down the nearest priestess.

~~~~~

Rylan led Joanna to a shabby building, squished between two larger ones like an unfortunate child between two plump aunties. The image of a plow horse adorned the weathered sign. The horse was facing away from the viewer so its rump was the primary focus of the sign. Joanna's mouth quirked in a smile, and she followed Rylan inside.

It was like stepping into a cool cellar after a blistering day in the practice yard. The windows at the front of the building were shielded by curtains made of a thin material that let in what breeze found its lonesome way down the busy streets, but kept the baking sunlight out. Joanna had to squint as the shaded interior was illuminated only by slim flashes of light from the windows and a lantern beside the bar.

Aside from the bartender who was sitting on a stool, scribbling in a small ledger, there were only two other people in "The Shire"; a young woman with hair the color of cinnamon, who was sitting on the other side of the bar dozing with her head rested against her palm, and an elderly man at a table gumming his way through a meat pie.

Only he raised his head when the princess entered, dribbling gravy down his stubbly chin.

Though the walk had done wonders to settle her nerves, Joanna took one look at this empty dive and was ready to abandon the relaxation plan. But before she could tell Rylan they ought to leave, the old man got the bartender's attention. "Hey, Will, you've got customers. Snap to, boy!"

Will, who was probably in his forties and looked about as boyish as Joanna's father, took notice and plastered a smile on his face, tossing his pencil at the girl. She woke with a start and nearly fell off her stool.

"Welcome to The Shire!" Will said, tidying the rumpled front of his apron.

It was difficult to tell if anyone recognized Joanna, and in that moment she was perfectly fine with anonymity. It made it harder to feel like she was failing anyone if she was no one.

She thought of picking a spot at the bar, but changed her mind. Instead she strode across to the old man's table and indicated one of the chairs. "Is this spot taken?"

"No, lady." The man looked up with watery eyes that might once have been blue. Joanna suspected he couldn't see her at all. She settled into the chair across from him with a clatter of armor. The old man tilted his head, listening to the clanking metal, but made no comment, digging further into his meal with a blunt fork.

"We have meat pies today," the server girl drawled, sidling over to their table and setting wooden cups of water before Joanna and Rylan. "Lamb and chicken and I think we have a few beef left. They've all got fresh vegetables, just in this mornin'," the girl added, as though to sweeten the deal.

"Two meat pies would be lovely," Rylan rewarded her with his disarming smile. The one that calmed panicking patients and raging princesses. "Chicken will do, don't you think?" he asked Joanna.

"Yes. That sounds fine. Also, whatever cold ale you have to-hand in a *clean* tankard for my friend," Joanna gestured to the old man, then cocked an eyebrow at the girl in warning. She'd found that some establishments did not bother much with washing their drink-ware unless one gave specific instructions. "And a glass of cool barley water for me. Rylan?"

"The same," the healer said dutifully. He knew his princess had no time for alcohol when they were on duty.

"Right." The girl dipped her head and left, meandering as though she half intended to retreat to her spot for a nap before she remembered she had more to do.

"Now then, lady." The old man blinked slowly at his pie, but addressed Joanna with surprising clarity for a man with so few teeth. "Do you play chess?" He reached into a wide shoulder pack hanging from his chair and pulled free an aging board and a leather pouch of pieces.

Moments later found Joanna embroiled in a chess game with a blind man. He maneuvered his pieces with surprising ease. Never once did he need to ask where they were. Occasionally, he would rest his spread hand lightly atop all the pieces, getting a feel for the board, before he would unerringly select one of his pieces and move it into place. For her part, Joanna had only to announce her movements as she took them, and the stranger had no trouble discerning his next move.

He beat her twice before Joanna found her rhythm and took the third game. All the while she chatted with the old man. He willingly spoke of The Ogre, and times past when people were still upset about a creature appearing to take over a castle. "The king did fight," the old man said, sliding a rook into position. "He didn't have much of an army, even then, but he sent what he had. What men survived came back with tales of the monster they faced. A great creature who tore into armor as though it were flesh, and ripped men asunder."

"So my grandfather just decided to leave that monster there? Why not raise a stronger army to help? Why not call for aid from our allies." Joanna leaned forward, her breastplate clunking as it hit the table edge. She knew her father's official answers—not enough willing soldiers, too much loss of life, The Ogre wasn't making any further aggressive moves—but she was interested to hear what this man would recall. He was one of the little people, after all.

The old man shrugged, smacking his lips in consideration. "I was just a lad at the time, but I think it was his pride that foiled him. The king didn't want to admit that he'd been beat. The Ogre settled into the castle and didn't bother anybody for a long while. Nowadays it seems like The ol' Ogre was just biding his time."

"Knight to queen three," Joanna moved her piece, scanning the board for an advantage. The man was a shrewd and ruthless player. He'd sacrifice a seemingly vital piece, only to pull a completely different strategy out of his sleeve. "Everyone forgot about The Ogre?" she asked.

"The mages didn't," Rylan pointed out. He sat back in his chair, arms resting on his belly as he studied the match unfolding before him. The empty bowl that had once contained his meat pie rested before him. The serving girl had returned to her nap and showed no sign of tidying away their dishes.

"No, I suppose they didn't at that. Didn't matter much to me or mine." The old man scratched the back of his neck. "My da never used any of the crop mages some of the other farmers swore by. 'I can grow my fields just fine without any magic interfering,' he'd say." The old man squared his shoulders and put on a deeper voice to imitate his da. "I suppose after a while all those crop mages lost their magic or they left, just like all the others."

"We were never a kingdom renowned for its magically gifted residents anyway," Rylan pointed out. "Or so I've heard."

"Perhaps not," the old man caught one of his pieces between two fingers and slide it into place.

They fell silent for a long moment, focused on the game. Joanna did her best to play more conservatively. She was an aggressive player by nature, and this man managed to capitalize on that every time. Finally, she slid her knight into position, "Checkmate!" she announced. The old man smiled and tipped his king over with a finger.

"Well done, lass. You must have had a good teacher. I'm glad I found a worthy opponent." He bobbed his snowy head to her. "The people around here are so dull. They hardly present a challenge."

"My father taught me, though these days I usually play with my best friend." Joanna said.

"Something happen to your father, lass?" The man asked sympathetically. Perhaps he imagined the man had died.

"We've... drifted apart," Joanna admitted, slouching in her chair. Her armor clattered. She looked up and realize that several people she had not even noticed enter the tavern were now seated around, watching the game and staring at her. She blinked at them in surprise before she raised an eyebrow,. "Chess enthusiasts?"

"Er...of course, Your Highness," said a young man whose pale face turned red the moment he was addressed.

"What time is it?" Joanna looked around realizing how stiff her legs were from sitting for hours. She'd lost track of the day, not something she normally allowed herself to do. Rylan stretched and Joanna suspected he had dozed off watching their game.

"It's getting on dusk, ma'am," the bartender said. He was up and about, clearing glasses and serving his new customers with far more enthusiasm now that he had figured out that there was a princess in his tavern.

"Damn." Joanna stood armor scraping. She winced as her shoulders and knees protested. She should have removed her plate mail before spending the day sitting. She tried to stretch with little success, and she shot a grin at the watching crowd. They gaped as the blades on her hips shifted. "Thank you for the lovely games," Joanna touched the old man's arm.

"Are you off then?" he asked.

"I'm afraid so. I'm to meet my men at the Iron Bull tavern. They're probably already there and waiting."

"It was good to meet you." The man held out a liver-spotted hand and shook Joanna's firmly.

"You as well." She clasped her other hand over the man's gnarled knuckles. Outwardly she nodded to those around her and smiled, but inwardly she berated herself. She'd spent the entire day playing chess rather than investigating.

"I live near The Iron Bull," the old man said after she had released his hand. "I could walk you back."

Joanna chuckled at this, but agreed. "Alright, I'd like that. Perhaps you can discuss some of your chess strategy with me as we walk."

With the old man holding lightly onto Joanna's elbow, she and Rylan made their way from the tavern. The barkeep looked sad to see them go, but those who had come to see the princess seemed contented enough to stay, so Joanna knew he would still have a good night.

The stares of everyone in the tavern pressed on her back as she left. Stares of admiration and of judgment. She kept her eyes forward and ignored them. Thick armor couldn't protect her from the glares of those who agreed with the king, and the Mother and Father deities. That Joanna's place was at a man's side, birthing children.

Once out in the street, which was noticeably quieter than it had been during the day, Joanna expected the old man to keep his grip on her arm, but he smiled his toothless smile and reached for a little nook beside the doorway to take out a walking stick he had secreted there. He held the stick before him and prodded the road and he made his way as though he could see every rut and raised cobble in the street. Joanna hurried to catch up, Rylan bringing up the rear. The healer raised his eyebrows, impressed.

"I've lived here all my life," the old man explained, obviously sensing his companion's curiosity. "I wasn't always blind, and these days I have learned every street as well as I know my own house." *Tap tap* went his walking cane. He poked a loose cobblestone, walked around, and before Joanna could say anything the man carried on speaking. "My sons left as soon as they could, of course. You know how sons can be. Well, I suppose you might not." He chuckled, a dry sound that might have been full and lusty in his youth. "Sons are often eager to be away, to live their own lives."

"Daughters, too," Rylan said, nudging Joanna playfully as he came up beside her.

The old man snorted in amusement and turned down another street with such ease Joanna wondered if he'd been counting steps the whole time. "True enough I suppose," he said. "Though my sons do come to visit from time to time. My youngest was here yesterday as it happens. He's a foreman. Works on building projects all over these parts and lives in the village right near the river."

"Does he?" Joanna asked, interested. "What is his name? Perhaps I know him."

"He's called Roland."

Joanna didn't spend much time with her father's people. Those men, and sometimes women, who toiled for the general upkeep of the kingdom. "Hmmm, I don't think I know him after all."

"Fine looking lad. A bit thin for his mother's liking, but smart as a whip."

"Sorry." She shrugged as though he could see her.

"Ah well, never mind that," The old man shuffled on, pausing only a moment to locate a small puddle with his stick so as to better avoid it. "Do you know the Serpent's River?"

"Of course," The Serpent's River, still named for the snake god of honesty and transparency, cut a swath through the middle of the kingdom.

"You probably heard one of the main bridges went down from the flooding we've had?"

"I had heard that, yes." Joanna had ridden past the bridge on a previous patrol in late winter. It had looked sturdy then, and she would have trusted it with her entire company and their horses. Still, the rains had been intense for weeks that spring and she was no expert on bridges.

"My son was heading up a team to repair it and told me everything was going well when an accident made them lose a whole two days' worth of labor."

"Oh no!" Joanna frowned.

"Well, we're near enough the bridge here in Glen Hollow, so my son came home to have some of his Ma's cakes and to bemoan the trouble with his old Da. He swears he'd blame The Ogre if there had been any sign of him, but there was not so much as a wisp of a Shade. I'd say my son works near The Ogre's land too often. I think he's gone paranoid."

"Perhaps." Joanna's hands were already balling into fists. Even a mention of The Ogre was enough to get her blood up today. Rylan's hand rested lightly on her shoulder, and she settled her breathing as best she could, speaking in a deceptively pleasant tone. "Then again, I too am extra suspicious of The Ogre these days."

"Our journey could take us near that bridge tomorrow," Rylan pointed out, and Joanna caught the warning note in his voice. Maybe he thought she was going to fly off the handle and scare this nice old man. She shot him a warning glare.

"Well, if you do, say hello to my boy for me." the old man came to a stop at the doorway of a house. The door was painted green, and a small bouquet of dried flowers hung upside down from a copper ring. "My wife's doing," the man reached up and touched the flowers, smiling. Joanna wondered how he had known what she was looking at. "A blessing for the house." He turned in Joanna's direction, his watery eyes staring over her left shoulder. "I thank you for the escort, Highness."

"Joanna, please." She shook the old man's hand once more.

"As you wish it, Joanna. Be well." He dipped his head, turned and shambled into his house. Seconds later the voice of an old woman wafted from within, berating her husband for being out so late at "that filthy dive again."

"What do I care if it's filthy? I can't see it!" the man answered before their voices faded.

Joanna let out a full laugh and Rylan joined her as they walked on. The streets were growing darker and the lamp lighters were out, their long tapers in hand. They nodded respectfully or gaped at the princess as she passed.

The Iron Bull was a large and bustling tavern. A well-stocked stable wrapped around it on two sides where their horses were waiting, fresh from their day of rest. Joanna was pleased to see the majority of her men already there and seated outside on the benches before the tavern. They greeted her warmly. Even Jeremy had returned from his visiting with a slightly dopey look plastered on his young face and a fresh love bruise blossoming on his neck. Joanna shook her head at the silliness of romance, but let the man have his pleasure.

Joanna counted heads. When they came up short, Cade went into the Iron Bull and extricated three more who were slightly tipsy, but still managed to stand straight and salute when asked. She furrowed her brow. "Lyall?" she called. "Was Lyall inside?"

"No, ma'am." Cade answered, rolling his sleeves down and straightening his tunic.

"Lyall?" she called again, as though somehow her tall friend was hiding amidst the other soldiers.

"Don't worry, ma'am," Varric gave her a crooked grin, accented by his scar. "He's probably just having such a lovely time with his fellow he is taking a bit longer." He raised bushy eyebrows suggestively at the others and several of them whistled and gave quiet "whoops."

Joanna ignored them. "It's not like him." She spun the cat ring around her finger. "We'll give him another half hour or so, then I'm going to go look."

A few of her men gave her questioning glances, but none argued. They settled in, Cade taking charge of a small contingent to fetch food and drink from the tavern. Cade was younger than Rylan and a few of the other men, but he had a commanding presence and had an easy time getting people to follow his lead. Joanna half-watched with a jealous pang. She supposed if she had shoulders like an ox and looked like a single punch from her would knock you senseless, people might take her more seriously too.

Rylan brought Joanna some dinner. A warm potato generously slathered in fresh, creamy butter and accompanied by a thick slab of oaty bread, just as liberally buttered. Joanna had to tip a bit of the golden liquid from the bread onto her plate before she could take a bite. Rylan also presented her with more barley water and sat down beside her on her bench.

Joanna listened to her men. Their pleasant chatter, discussing the adventures of their day, was like coming home. Even Orin, who was the most quiet and stoic of them, joined in with a few comments here and there.

"I bought a new charm at the market to ward off bad spirits!" said a younger soldier named Bowen, showing off the item in question. It was a tiny figure of the Mother Goddess carved from a green stone, her delicate hand upraised in blessing. It was rare to see one of the deities depicted alone, and Joanna wondered if there was a Father God charm meant to fit together with it.

"I found the best fresh mushrooms from one of the stalls." Varric opened his pack to reveal a goodly amount of brown capped mushrooms. "These will be amazing in stew later, especially with the spices I got to go along with them." If you asked Varric, he would swear that cooking was women's work, but as soon as you turned your back he'd be adding new flavors to the stew-pot.

"I met a kind man and his family near the stables, and I talked with them most of the afternoon. Didn't find out any good information though."

"I took my sweetheart down to the alder grove, and she played her lap harp while I sang."

"Played her lap harp? Is that what we're calling it?"

"Hush up, you! You're in the company of your princess!"

Joanna sighed and kept searching the darkened streets for Lyall, her ears pricked for his voice. Nothing came. She seldom joined in the banter. It was a strange dynamic to be their leader, yet to sit with them on the same wooden benches or the damp ground. In battle she could shout orders without a hint of shyness, but here, in town, she was mute. How could she relate to these ordinary men when she had been raised on cushions and fine food, all her needs met before she even knew she had them? Especially without Lyall to act as a go-between. Where was he?

"Alright." Joanna stood, setting her wooden plate on the bench. "I'm going to track Lyall down before we lose what little daylight we have left. Anyone care to accompany me?"

Several of the men stepped forward at once. Rylan took his place at her side. She noted he had his healer's pack at the ready, just in case.

Lyall was seldom late, but he did have one weakness, and they all knew what it was. None were surprised, as they made their way towards Joshua's house, when they heard shouting.

Joanna picked up her pace, growling in annoyance and dogged hotly by her men. They rounded the last corner and came out onto a wide street to see Lyall and four other men in the midst of a brawl.

It was a bare-fisted fight, as Lyall had not worn his sword to visit his lover. At least the toughs Lyall had involved himself with were kind enough not to draw blades on him.

Joanna stopped and extended her arm to the side, staying her entourage. The men nearly ran into her, like eager hounds falling over one another in eagerness for a hunt. She remained still, coolly pulling on her leather gloves, cracking her knuckles. The right moment to intervene would present itself.

Lyall was holding his own, though his shirt was ripped and his lip bleeding. When he turned Joanna saw a bruise already settling in on her friend's high cheekbone.

Lyall fought with the ferocity of a cornered animal. His blows, while seeming wild and random to the unpracticed eye were, in reality, well placed and timed.

Two men rushed him at once, one meaning to hold Lyall so the other could strike. The bodyguard slipped easily out of the first man's grasp. His attacker might as well have tried to grasp an armload of water. Ducking low, Lyall kicked the other squarely on the knee. The man yelped and fell to the side, grasping his leg. He rolled around on the cobblestones in pain. When his companion paused to check on him, Lyall turned and brought his elbow up against the man's jaw.

Joanna heard the thug's teeth clack from where she stood. She winced in sympathy, even as she was proud of Lyall's skill.

A steadily growing crowd of villagers gathered to watch the fight. Some cheered on one side or another. Most didn't know what they were cheering for, merely that they enjoyed the spectacle.

Joanna leaned forward on her toes, every ounce of her aching to wade into the fray. Her mind was inundated with a memory. *A tall, skinny boy with hair like a haystack and a smattering of pimples on his* chin. *The castle boys and the sons of the guardsmen poked at him with words and fists as the skinny lad struggled to fight back.*

Lyall, swiping blood from his lip with the back of his hand, addressed the other two opponents. These were already sporting bruises and bloody noses, but they were rousing now and looking to redeem themselves. All these men were at least as tall as Lyall, and well built. Joanna guessed they were field laborers in town for the market day and a drink afterward. Their boots were caked with muck and manure. Joanna wondered how much ale they had imbibed before deciding to tangle with her bodyguard.

Lyall bounced on the balls of his feet, putting up his fists, no doubt looking absurd to an untrained brawler used to throwing haymakers and hoping for the best. The man Lyall had elbowed in the jaw stood up to join his two friends, clutching his face and looking as mad as a cat in a sack.

All three rushed in as one. The first to reach Lyall was rewarded with a neat punch to the nose. His own blow went wide of the mark and he staggered into his oncoming friend, giving Lyall a chance to step back and deal with the third charger. This man put his head down and aimed for Lyall's midsection to bowl him over. Lyall danced to the side, but the man threw out his arm, hooking Lyall's lean frame and bearing them both to the cobblestones.

"Now?" hissed Varric in Joanna's ear.

"Not yet." She raised a hand, her eyes still locked on the fight. *A princess coming upon the scene, taking in the taunting boys as they jeered and threw hunks of mud and horse apples. The skinny boy had been avoiding the princess all day to try and win favor with these idiots.*

Lyall and his attacker crashed to the stones with the sound of air leaving them both. Lyall recovered swiftly and rolled away from his momentarily stunned aggressor. He coughed, hauling the breath that had been forced from him.

One of the other men, roaring with annoyance, tried to kick his partner out of his way. Instead of sending the second man clear of the fray, it carried him into Lyall. Lyall let out a little yelp as his leg was twisted, bodies colliding and tumbling sideways.

"Now?" Cade asked. Their tension behind her was tightly coiled as a snake waiting to strike. She was curious how long she could keep them back before their obedience snapped. This was a question she hated to admit plagued her. How much of their deference stemmed from true loyalty and how much from the superior pay and prestige they received as members of her troupe?

"Wait..." she urged them. There was only one man she knew would obey her word no matter what she asked, and that man was scrambling to his feet, favoring his leg and readying for another attack.

The princess rushed into the fray, strong for her size, even then, and fierce as a wildcat. She struck at the boys until she realized they didn't dare raise a fist to her. They backed away, heads lowered. A few bowed. The youngest began to whimper.

The toughs seemed to be rallying for a final assault. Lyall maneuvered himself so none could pounce from behind. The gathered watchers whooped and shouted. They'd taken to encouraging the toughs, who somehow seemed to be the underdogs in the fight. A few wagered coins pinged to the cobblestones.

The man who had been kicked in the knee did not seem as eager to try again. He sat on the ground, nursing his leg and calling encouragement to his friends when he remembered to.

The three remaining men charged once more, better coordinated than before. One grabbed for Lyall, grasping at the man's arms to keep him from throwing any punches. His movements were clumsy, but effective. He managed to grapple with Lyall's arm as the bodyguard ducked a blow aimed for his face and maneuvered himself to face the third attacker, who was trying to flank him.

The man caught Lyall in an awkward bear hug and managed to shift so he was behind Lyall. The other two attackers moved to rain blows on Lyall's unprotected midsection.

Joanna's men pressed forward as though they strained against invisible chains. Joanna raised her hand again, staying them a final time. Her heart thudded a little faster.

The skinny boy turned to the princess, swiping blood from his lip and glaring at her. She would never forget the look of pure loathing in his ice blue eyes.

Lyall, using the man behind him for leverage, kicked out with both feet, landing each kick squarely into the chests of the other two. Once he had propelled the men back, he planted his feet. Twisting to the side he rocked forward with surprising strength for someone so wiry, and threw the man holding him over his head. The weight forced Lyall to a knee, thanks to his weakened leg, but his opponent hurtled to the stones with a *thud* so absolute that several people in the crowd gasped.

Lyall stood, wincing and panting as he placed his weight evenly on both feet and glared at the men before him, challenging them with his eyes. He brought up his fists, ready for more. The crowd goaded the attackers on, but the farm hands looked as though they were reconsidering all the bad choices that had brought them to this end.

Now was her time. "LYALL!" Joanna's voice snapped like a whip across the crowd as she strode onto the street. Her men flanked her and had enough sense to let her take point.

Lyall paused, lowering his bleeding fists and turning to her, brows raised. A mutter rippled through the watching crowd.

The man with the damaged knee recognized her first. "Hey! Isn't that—?"

"Princess Joanna, yes." Liam shouted, a swaggering tone in his voice. Joanna wanted to turn and shush him, but knew it would ruin the image she was trying to project.

"Lyall, what have I told you about street brawling?" Joanna lifted her chin, giving the assemblage what she hoped was her most dominant glare. She knew it couldn't help that all of the men here, and some of the women, were taller than she.

The thugs looked as guilty as dogs who have been caught stealing the soup bone. They knelt where they were and looked up at their princess with baleful eyes.

Lyall stood straight and military, his expression neutral. "I'm sorry, ma'am."

"I should think so," Joanna marched through the crowd. People parted ahead of her, alive with awe. It reminded Joanna of a flock of gossiping crows. Her men fanned out through the assemblage, and she knew she'd lost them. She could only hope they would behave themselves.

"Healer, see to these men." She gestured for Rylan, who was still near her. He was older than most of her soldiers and less likely to wander off. Obediently Rylan moved to check on the beaten field hands.

Joanna marched directly up to Lyall, then remembered with a sinking feeling how much taller he was than she. Lyall must have read her expression because he dropped carefully to a knee, a flash of pain crossing his face as he bent his injured leg. Joanna kept her posture straight and her gaze haughty as she spoke low to her friend so only he could hear. "Thank you."

"You're welcome."
"Anything serious?"

"No. The leg's a bit twisted. It'll be fine by morning."

"Still got all your teeth?"

Lyall paused, clearly exploring his mouth with his tongue. Joanna took the moment to gauge that crowd. They still seemed sufficiently starstruck. She turned her attention back to Lyall. His lip was bleeding and puffy. She drew a kerchief from her sleeve and passed it to him. "Look contrite," she ordered.

"I'm trying." Lyall's smile was discreet, and he was giving her his best kicked-puppy expression.

Joanna raised her voice to be heard by the crowd. "You know how I feel about fighting in the street."

"You're jealous you couldn't join." Lyall whispered, pale eyes glinting with mischief.

She cleared her throat and whispered. "Remember I have a reputation to uphold."

He matched her low tone. "I take excellent care of your reputation. Why do you think I'm kneeling in front of you in a crowded street? For my honor?"

Joanna winced. "I'm sorry." Then her sardonic side bit back. "You know, if you weren't so tall—" She gingerly brushed a finger over the bruise on his cheek. "Not broken, I hope."

"Doesn't feel that way." Lyall answered, still gazing up at her with an expression of false reverence on his face. Joanna hoped no one studied it too closely or they would see the defiant glint in his eyes. She heard her men moving through the crowd, loudly urging them to disperse to their own homes.

"Why on earth were you fighting this time? I mean, I know you think it's great fun, but you'd gone three months without a tussle like this. If this gets back to my father, he'll have another of his famous rants and threaten to find me a new bodyguard...again."

"Those men," Lyall gestured with his head to the farm hands, who sat in a pathetic clump before Rylan. The healer was doling out pain relieving herbs and giving instructions for the care of their various wounds. "They saw me leave Joshua's house. I gave Joshua a kiss goodbye at the threshold. It was...a little passionate. The men followed me for two streets. I could hear them behind me and I caught enough to know what they were talking about. They weren't exactly subtle."

Joanna nodded, then raised her voice so the crowd could hear. "That's no excuse for your behavior!" She turned back to her friend, whispering, "Go on."

"I finally stopped and demanded they say those things to my face, which they did. I didn't like what they said."

"Dare I ask?" Joanna's lip curled in a grimace before she could catch herself.

He rolled his eyes. "You know how the followers of the God and Goddess are. They said some cruel things about myself and Joshua. I made them eat their words."

"So you did," Joanna whispered proudly. "Still..." Her expression grew earnest. "We all have a reputation to look after, and fighting in the street does nothing for it." She raised her voice a final time. "I had better not catch you at this again! It demeans not only you, but your princess, and by extension your king."

Lyall nodded contritely, not meeting her eyes like an ashamed hound.

"Laying it on a bit thick?" she murmured to him between her teeth.

He gave her an impish wink. Shifting to stand, he tilted to the side with a grunt. Joanna instinctively grabbed his hand and propped him up. He got gingerly to his feet, his familiar smile flickering across his face. Joanna had to fight hers back. Staying upset with Lyall was impossible. She helped her friend limp over to a bench so Rylan could have a look at him.

He met her gaze with pale blue eyes, unexpectedly earnest. "Thanks for remembering."

"Of course." She nodded tightly.

The crowd dispersed, and the men returned. Rylan knelt before the bodyguard and Joanna could make out his quiet chastisements as he checked Lyall's wounds. She moved out of the way to let the healer work.

Cade came to stand beside her, muscular arms crossed. "May I ask, Highness..." he whispered tensely. Cade was newer than some of the men. He didn't know the story.

"Why did I wait to interfere?"

"Well... yes." He cut his dark eyes down.

Joanna folded her arms and watched her bodyguard. "I made a mistake when we were young. Before our friendship was forged. I abused power I didn't understand at the time, and I deeply wounded him. I promised after that I would always let him fight his own battles."

Cade raised an eyebrow and she suspected he didn't understand, but he nodded, withdrawing.

With the crowd dispersed and Lyall seen to, Joanna declared they would camp outside of town that night. There were some groans from her men, but no one protested outright. They had had a good day, after all.

As she and her soldiers made their way to the stables for their horses and supplies, Joanna told them of her plans to stay on track and visit a certain bridge the next day.

~~~~

"Let me make sure I understand. Two men fell into the river and the bridge collapsed?" Joanna stood on the riverbank, fingers pressed to her lips in consideration. She squinted at the bridge in progress, noting the disgruntled looks on the workers' faces.

"That it did. I never saw anything quite like it before." The foremen stood beside her, arms folded. He was Roland, the son of the old man she had met yesterday in The Shire tavern. He'd been thrilled to hear that his old Da was friend with their princess.

Roland went on, "Both men didn't fall into the water though. One fell in, the other dove to the rescue and had a bad time of it."

"Brave of him," Joanna commented, though her attention was still distracted by the scene of contained ruin along the riverbank.

The rocks that had fallen into the water partially dammed the river and it had begun to overflow its banks. Now the places where the workmen needed to walk were soggy at best and dangerously slippery at worst. The men struggled in wide, shallow boats to haul rocks from the bottom. Many of the workers were chest deep in the river, dragging smaller stones out or tying ropes so the larger ones could be brought to shore by the oxen. "What happened after the men fell in?" Joanna asked.

"A few others went in when the first two didn't come up and we managed to rescue them both, but in the process the bridge got jostled or bumped wrong or something." Roland rubbed the back of his tanned neck, squinting sun-creased eyes at the workers. "Be careful, Adam!" he shouted to a man who was struggling to pull an especially large rock up the sodden bank. "I'll not have any more injuries on my watch!" He turned back to Joanna. "Thing is, we know what we're doing here. I'm the greenest foreman, and I've repaired three bridges like this with no trouble. It's a balancing game and you have to get everything right, but there was no reason for the whole thing to come down like that. Not that I can see." He sighed, eyes scanning the countryside as if the fields held some answers. "I don't know. I just couldn't seem to find any reason that the whole thing should have come down like that. Not even with the weight of a man against it. A few stones, sure, but the whole damn bridge? That's why I told my Da that I suspect The Ogre's magic. 'Course I never expected the princess herself would come to investigate." He shot a timid, sideways glance at Joanna, and his cheeks flushed.

"It was luck that brought your Da and me together." Joanna spun her cat ring around her finger, still watching the men work. "You didn't see any Shades?"

"No, Highness." Roland shook his head.

"Were there any men working with you that you hadn't seen before?" Lyall asked. "Anyone suspicious?"

"No, sir." Roland eyed Lyall as though uncertain how he should be addressed.

"What about that farm lad?" A sodden worker fought his way from the drenched bank and flopped down for a break nearby.

"Listening in, Andrew?"

Andrew turned scarlet and put his head down, suddenly very interested in retying his boot laces.

"What do you mean, Andrew?" Joanna queried.

Andrew looked up, only meeting Joanna's eyes for a fraction of a second before casting them down to the ground. He was already sitting, now he seemed to be trying to lower himself further, perhaps to sink into the mud. Joanna almost chuckled, but contained herself. She reassured him hurriedly. "It's alright, don't bother bowing, just tell me what you saw?"

"I didn't see anything, exactly." Andrew said, straightening but keeping his eyes fixed on his feet. "We had a couple local farmer's and their sons working with us that day."

"Nothing out of the ordinary there," Roland put in. "We often have help from locals."

"Right," Andrew agreed. "But there was one fellow who said he was a miller's son, but none of us knew him. We're pretty far from Mill Country. Anyway, this lad starts helping and he's strong enough and very keen to be of use, but then when Andrew fell into the river it was the miller who went in after him."

"And?" Joanna raised an eyebrow.

"Well..." Andrew's shoulders slumped. "I realize how silly this sounds even as I'm sayin' it, but it was that fellow trying to pull himself out that made the whole bridge go. I wouldn't have thought anything of it, except after we pulled him out of the water he got really flustered and couldn't leave fast enough."

Lyall folded his arms. "Maybe he was embarrassed."

"He was in a bad way too, that lad. Nasty cut on his arm and a bump the size of a goose egg on his head, but he rushed off quick as he could and wouldn't take our offer of help, or a place to stay."

"And you think that is significant?" Joanna asked.

"Well..." Andrew glanced nervously at Joanna. "Maybe. I mean, The Ogre has never used human agents before, but maybe—"

"Or maybe he was hurting and just wanted to go home to his own family." Roland put in. "I'd have never suspected that lad, Highness. He was a good soul if I ever saw one. You could just look at him and know he'd never hurt a fly."

"Nevertheless…" Joanna raised her voice to be heard by the others. "Any thoughts or leads are welcome. Thank you, Andrew."

Andrew's ears went bright pink and he scrambled to his feet, bowing clumsily before hurrying back to work. He beamed as his friends patted him on the back. Some even looked jealous that he had spoken to the princess.

Lyall turned to Roland. "Did the miller's son come back after that day?"

"No. No sign of him. Probably recovering at home if he has any sense."

"Is there anything else you can think of that might be of interest?" Joanna rested her hands on the pommels of her swords.

"I'm afraid not." Roland turned to watch three of his workers struggle to move a large rock up the flooded bank. The ropes creaked and threatened to slip. Roland called to them, "Bring one of the oxen over! I can't have you hurting yourselves with those heavy ones!" He turned back to Joanna, rubbing his stubbly chin. "Good thing this bridge is based in bedrock, or we'd be out of luck."

Joanna wasn't certain what he was talking about, but she kept that to herself. "Right. My men and I should keep moving on our patrol. If this was somehow caused by The Ogre, we'll ferret it out. We're doing our early summer circuit of the kingdom and we'll have to detour because of the bridge."

"Sorry about that, Your Highness." Roland looked stricken.

She waved away his words. "Don't fret. I understand completely. I have every faith that you will have this bridge repaired in no time at all."

Joanna and her men did a quick patrol of the area, seeing no sign of Shades. Satisfied that the workers were in no immediate danger, she and her men rode out.

The men bantered amongst themselves, not bothering with a formation. This was open country, patched with farmland. Animal pastures, alive with happy goats, sheep and cows, dotted the rolling landscape. The smell of freshly growing crops and the calming sweetness of wildflowers washed over Joanna. She knew how Prince Prosper must have felt when he went to sea to help his own people. These coursing hills with rippling grass were her sea, the lowing of cows her calling gulls, and the squeak of saddle leather her creaking ropes.

They jogged the horses, not pressing them to keep a higher pace. Lyall rode up beside Joanna. "Are we going to take the Almanster bridge?"

"Yes," Joanna answered. "It's upstream, about a day of steady riding from here."

"I know," Lyall gave her a cocky grin. "I have been on patrol with you a few times before, you'll recall."

"Don't you sass me, Lyall. I can have my father lecture you about fighting in the street. You're lucky the men like you and the gossip shouldn't reach the king."

"Gods forefend!" Lyall clasped a hand to his chest in mock terror.

"How's your leg?"

"Much better this morning." Lyall dipped his head, his earnest smile returning. The bruise on his cheekbone was still pronounced, but the cut on his lip was almost invisible, the swelling greatly reduced. "I might even look presentable if we happen to encounter passing dignitaries."

"You had better." Joanna huffed. "This is the time of year the shipments from Ragvah start coming through. You never know when you'll need to look imposing as my bodyguard."

The man beside her, washed in sunlight and resplendent in his armor, might not have looked like the fierce brawler, but Joanna knew him better. Even if she stood in her stirrups, Joanna could never look as grand as her partner. She imagined him as a prince in her place and herself the daughter of some wandering fighter, trained to defend the helpless with no marriage duties placed on her shoulders.

"Personally, I think the bruises help my image in that regard." Lyall sat prouder in his saddle. Sky, his horse, tossed her head as though calling his bluff.

"I think it makes you look like you lose a lot of fights," Joanna countered.

"Cruel, Jo. Very cruel." Lyall put on another wounded expression. He moved to steer his horse away when she stayed him with a raised hand. "What is it?"

"Miller's son..." Her brows came together. She'd been mulling over what the worker, Andrew, had said in the back of her mind like a worry stone.

"What about a miller's son?" Lyall reined Sky even with Willow's longer stride.

"Wasn't it a miller's son we met the day Prince Prosper's entourage were attacked by Shades?"

Lyall cast his pale eyes upwards. "Perhaps. I hardly recall. Wasn't he a cobbler's son?"

"No." Joanna shook her head. "It was a miller's son, I'm positive. He helped us fix the carriage wheel. Sweet lad, just like those men said about the miller's son at the river."

"And?"

"What if it was the same person?"

"Unlikely."

"No. Maybe. Either way…" She waved a hand as if to clear the confusion. "Either way it strikes me as little suspicious. A miller's son is there when a carriage of dignitaries is attack by Shades, then another miller's son appears as a bridge project near The Ogre's land goes horribly awry."

"You're reaching." One of Lyall's eyebrows peaked skeptically. "It isn't the same man. The first one helped us fix the wheel after Shades attacked. If he was our enemy, why would he do that?"

"Stop giving me that look, Ly, it's only a theory." Joanna nudged Willow into a canter, letting the rolling gait of the horse and the warm breeze on her face sweep her away from the world. She needed time to let all her insane theories play out in her head. What had that damn miller's son looked like anyway? She recalled him being blond, well built, not bad to look at, but otherwise she hadn't thought much of him. Her mind had been occupied with meeting another mystery suitor. Though she tried to cut herself some slack, inwardly she was raging. *Pay more attention! Some protector you are!*

~~~~~

The closer they drew to The Ogre's territory, the greater the threat of Shades became until finally they encountered a small band of them worrying a cattle herd. The farmer and his family had locked themselves in their house as the Shades chased their poor cows until the animals collapsed, sweating and rolling their big, dull eyes.

Joanna urged Willow into his powerful gallop, and he cleared the pasture as though he were a wind god himself. Joanna stood forward in her stirrups, giving voice to her battle cry, her eyes and mind filled with nothing but the oily creatures that slunk out of nightmares and into her world. Maybe her twin blades couldn't to kill the creatures, but she could drive them off, tattered and wispy.

Joanna and her men made short work of the Shades and hurried to check on the besieged farmers.

Later that afternoon Joanna's troop discovered what might have been the same Shades attempting to set fire to a field of alfalfa. Shades were rubbish at setting fires and their attempts were clumsy, but given enough time they would have succeeded. Joanna and her men ripped through the Shade ranks like the claws of the badger god, and sent them packing once again, skittering over the ground and melding into one another to get away.

The fighters met the Shades once more, as they skirted close to The Ogre's lands. The creatures rallied and made a more fearsome attack, but Joanna and her men repulsed them, leaving them even more bedraggled than before.

By dusk Joanna was certain the creatures had slunk back to their master at last. Normally dusk was a dangerous time, when the Shades could blend in with their long stretching, less animated brethren, but today they'd been given such a walloping, they certainly wouldn't be back.

The night was due to be moonless, the safest kind of night in these parts. Joanna slumped in the saddle, reins loose in her hands, looking forward to that evening's camp and being out of her armor at last. Her skin itched with dried sweat, and her arm muscles ached relentlessly.

Joanna sat forward alert once more as she took in a copse of trees in their path. She could see part of a pond in the lowland beyond as well as more vulnerable farmland. "We should check in with whoever owns those fields."

The men made weary noises, but no one openly complained. Some of them, like big Cade, were likely even more sore than Joanna. He wielded his heavy ax with seeming ease, but even he couldn't swing that thing forever. Most of the other men chose lighter armaments, though all enjoyed the freedom Joanna allowed them to specialize rather than being forced to use swords, as they might have been in the regular castle guard.

Lyall, beside her as always, leaned up in his saddle to see where she pointed as they made their way into the wooded area, the slim path wending lazily between the trees.

Seconds later he fell back with a yell. Joanna jerked towards him, eyes wide, heart already thundering. Her friend had been borne to earth by a Shade, which had tackled him from his mount.

"FORM UH—" Joanna's order was cut short as another Shade smashed into her. She was driven to one side by the force of its wispy body. Though it seemed insubstantial as smoke, she knew better. Her right foot went through her stirrup as her left pulled free and she found herself hanging upside down from the side of her horse.

Willow spooked, not pleased to have a Shade scrambling around on his back. As the dark creature grabbed at Joanna and clawed for her face, Willow bucked powerfully.

The wrenching motion of the horse slammed Joanna's shoulders and head onto the path with cracking force. She yelped in pain and was stunned for a long second, unable to breathe, lights crashing through her vision.

The Shade was still clawing at her. Her armor scraped and screeched as its fingers raked her chest. She had just enough time to appreciate her dire situation before Willow balked to the side, dragging her along hanging by her right leg from his stirrup.

"Ly—" she choked as her head smacked against a stone and she narrowly managed to dodge one of Willow's flailing hooves. She had no sense of where her friend was—or the rest of her men, for that matter. She could only hope they were having a better time than she was. Focusing with all her being, she managed to roll awkwardly before Willow jerked again and her ankle and knee screamed with pain. She clamped her teeth down hard, glad that in the chaos of spooking and fighting horses, the Shade had been dislodged from her chest, though she couldn't have told anyone when.

She tried to curl towards her snagged foot to free herself, but her armor would not let her bend. "Gods all—curse it!" She choked brokenly between clenched teeth. She sagged back, praying the horse didn't move again. Her head couldn't take much more punishment and her shoulder armor was stabbing her in the neck.

Willow wheeled, taking her with him in a wide circle, like he was using her to sweep the path. She slammed bodily into someone else. The armored figure of one of her men fell on top of her with the clattering of metal on metal. She didn't have time to be glad that his sword had not struck her as she tried to keep her head up off the path and away from jagged stones.

"Willow! Whoa!" she yelled, finding her breath at last.

The horse swung his head around, nostrils wide, the whites of his eyes shining. He didn't understand what she was doing down there, but her order was clear enough.

Joanna shoved at the man on top of her. She didn't have time to wonder if he was wounded or worse. She grabbed his sword from his hand and swung it clumsily at the leather stirrup strap that held her. Her own swords were out of reach in their special sheaths on Willow's saddle.

It took three tries, but she finally hacked herself loose. "Go!" she shouted to her mount. Willow surged away from her, doing as he had been trained. Joanna flopped back, allowing herself three good breaths before she acted again.

Her knee throbbed mercilessly, and her ankle was sprained at best. She knew the warm, abrupt pain of it well enough to understand that she wouldn't be able to move gracefully. Scrambling to her knees, still holding the man's sword, she took in the situation. Her soldiers were fighting off the Shades. They were far more numerous than they had been earlier that day. More numerous and more angry. They attacked with a vigor Joanna had only seen a few times when she ventured close to The Ogre's territory.

By peering through the armored legs of some of the other men, Joanna managed to track Varric and Orin, who were fighting together. Her soldiers seemed to have formed some semblance of a battle line without her, but they were surrounded by Shades. Her mind worked swiftly, taking in all the details she could see. This was where her mind came alive. She could take in a battlefield and see what it needed. How it flowed. How it breathed. This chaos made more sense than any politics or courtly intrigue.

"We need to break to the left!" Joanna shouted, even as she wondered how she was going to carry out her own order.

Only a few of the men heard their princess's command and struggled to obey. Joanna grabbed the armor of the fallen man beside her, noting the red hair and knowing it was Liam. She dragged him as she crawled, roaring at the top of her voice "Don't break ranks! As a unit, move to the left! EAST! Out of the trees! Blast it! MOVE!"

Someone had the sense to parrot her words, and the men finally snapped into proper action. They came together with shields and armor, moving in the indicated direction. The Shades must have also heard, but they had never shown much cleverness when it came to battle tactics. The odd ambush was about as thoughtful as they got, so while a few of them moved to intercept the retreat, most continued their attack on the front line.

Joanna was all but ignored as she scrambled along in the dirt.

"I've got him!" Someone reached down and grasped Liam's breastplate.

"And I've got you!" Someone else gripped the straps of Joanna's armor and hauled her back. It was deeply undignified, but much faster than crawling, she consoled herself as her rear scraped along the dusty road. Her heels bounced over rocks, small pebbles finding their way into her boots.

Whoever was dragging her stopped, and the men formed up around her, outside the trees, ready for their attackers at last.

Rylan squatted beside Joanna, his face a mask of intensity. Joanna knew the healer practically felt every blow inflicted on those he worked to keep alive and healthy. "My knee and ankle got wrenched a bit, and I hit my head, but no dizziness or double vision," she reported before Rylan could ask.

He nodded and moved on. Triage dictated that she was at the bottom of the list for care. She didn't mind. She tucked in her legs as best she could and tried to stay out of people's way. Inside her, rage and embarrassment bubbled, and she had to bite down to keep herself from yelling a stream of unhelpful cursing.

Her men were doing well enough without her and there she was, their leader, knocked off her horse and sitting in the dirt like a child who had fallen from a swing. She didn't even have Liam's sword anymore.

To keep herself from exploding in a flurry of anger that might have involved tears, she settled for watching their lines and shouting orders as best she could. "Shore up that left flank, it's weakening! I see miles of daylight between those shields! Gerald, get your section under control or you'll be overrun! Someone get Avery out of there, he's been injured!"

Finally, the Shades retreated, beaten and ragged like cloth torn apart by age and very aggressive cats.

Joanna heaved out a breath, casting her eyes over her men who were bedraggled but still standing. She inwardly vowed that they would drill for days to prepare for such attacks in future. The Shades so seldom pulled off surprise attacks she had allowed herself to become complacent. Her hands balled into determined fists, leather gloves creaking.

"Jo! Are you alright?" Lyall slammed to his knees beside her, grasping her upper arm.

"I'm fine. Well, no, I'm furious. We completely let them—" She cut off, looking up at her friend. "Gods, Lyall, you're bleeding!"

The side of the man's face was painted dark red and it stained his blond hair, which hung limply over the wound at his temple. "It's not bad." He waved off her concern. "You know how head wounds bleed."

"Rylan!" Joanna shouted, holding her gloved hand to the side of Lyall's head. "Rylan, now!"

The healer skidded in beside the pair, already reaching into his medical bag. "What is it?"

"Lyall's hurt!" Joanna took her hand away to reveal the injury. The blood around it was already dry, and it didn't seem to be producing any fresh. In her mind's eye Joanna had seen a fountain of blood, her friend collapsing to the ground. Instead, he gave her a firm look. Rylan's expression was annoyed.

"Here. Clean him up and he'll be fine," Rylan said, stonily, handing Joanna a wad of bandage. He turned Lyall to face him, squinted at the man's eyes, then held up his hand. "How many fingers?"

"Four," the bodyguard answered at once.

"There. He's perfectly sound." Rylan moved off to help others.

"I'm touched that you're so worried about me," Lyall smirked.

"Shut it!" Joanna grabbed her water canteen and poured a little onto the bandage. "Bring your face over here."

Lyall obeyed, still grinning, hunching down so she could clean the wound on his temple. He winced. "Ouch! Gentle please!"

"I don't think I have a gentle side." She joked. Her insides were still roiling. The battle wasn't over in her mind, and she kept going over ways it could have gone better. Things she could have done to protect her friends from harm. Not getting knocked off her horse would be a start. She was glad to have Lyall's wound to tend to. She needed something to occupy her hands and thoughts.

After Rylan had finished his assessments of the injured and declared that everyone would live, they set about regrouping their bedraggled rabble into something resembling orderly soldiers. Lima had taken a blow to the head that had knocked him out, so he sat sipping willow bark tea, and young Avery sported a fresh bandage on his arm where armor had been torn away. Otherwise it was all minor cuts and bruises. Overall, Joanna agreed with her healer. They had made it through well, considering.

That knowledge did little to slow her internal monologue.

"If this had been a real battle in a real war, we wouldn't be able to just sit around resting in a sloppy muddle like this," she griped, as Lyall offered her his arm for support. She managed to achieve her feet with much clanking of armor and a few throbbing jabs of pain from her knee and ankle. She knew both were swelling. Rylan would check them later, once she was out of her metal suit.

"I suggest we head for the pond," Rylan spoke up, intercepting Joanna's planned tirade. She followed the healer's gesture to the body of water just visible down the path. Tall rushes stood around it, as did most of their horses.

"I suppose they have the right idea." Lyall nodded at the animals, some of whom were drinking and some splashing in the shallows. Lyall cut a glance down at Joanna, who gripped his arm to stay upright. "Please do not start berating the horses for unsoldierly conduct."

"They're supposed to be well trained war horses," Joanna huffed so only her friend could hear. The wind had finally left her sails, and she limped meekly along beside Lyall.

She couldn't keep herself from judging every movement her people made. Why weren't they hobbling over to the pond in formation? What if the Shades attacked now? It was sloppy, it was shoddy, and if her father saw he'd never let her ride out again. She knew she would sound irrational and cruel if she spoke her thoughts aloud, so she settled for grinding her teeth and stepping down just a little too hard on her bad ankle.

The pond was a pleasant place. The men settled in at once without so much as checking with her. Joanna fumed silently. Her head was hurting just enough to be annoying, and her knee and ankle probably did need some attention. Lyall helped her remove much of her armor, even as her insides screamed that she should keep it on in case of another attack.

Lyall looked her in the eye, drawing her attention from herself. "They're not going to attack again. The only reason those Shades fared so well was because they hid in the trees. There's no place to hide out here but in the rushes or behind a few of those rocks. I doubt even they are brainless enough to try that."

Joanna had to agree. The rushes wouldn't conceal more than one or two Shades, and the rocks even fewer.

She sighed in relief when her leg armor came free and Rylan knelt before her to check her joints. She caught sight of Willow across the pond from her. At least the big horse had the sense to look shamefaced as he stood with the others, his saddle hanging crooked and one of his stirrups missing.

"No dislocations or breaks," Rylan announced. "Your ankle will be painful for a few weeks. Your knee should be fine. Go down to the water and get some cool mud to put on both to take down the swelling."

"I'll do it." Lyall stood from spot at Joanna's side and heading for a thick stand of bulrushes. She watched him go, playing the sloppy battle over and over again in her head, seeing herself tossed from her horse like a child who had never ridden before. It was a good thing no farmers saw. As it was, her men would probably tell tales in the next tavern they visited of their heroic leader dangling from her horse's saddle like a sack of grain.

"Meow?"

Joanna turned abruptly. "What?"

An orange cat with white boots on its hind legs strode confidently up to where she sat and butted its head against her arm. "Mer mer!" it announced.

"Ly..." Joanna petted the cat, and it set up a loud purr. "You'll never believe—"

"Jo!"

Her gaze snapped to the bank where Lyall was holding what appeared to be a very ratty, filthy item of clothing. It was so disgusting she could smell dung on it from where she sat. Her eyes narrowed. The hand that was not petting the cat moved to her hip where a sword should have been. "Someone else is here."

At her words three of the other men and Lyall set to swatting at the tall weeds with their arms and sticks. A few moments later she heard a yelp. Her men roared with abrupt laughter. The naked torso of a man emerged from the thickest of the rushes, shedding greenish pond water. He was pale, well-muscled and blond, his cheeks blazing red with embarrassment.

Joanna gaped. "Master Miller?"

"Er....yes," the man said in a voice so quiet Joanna almost didn't hear it.

She tilted her head, a cheeky grin playing on her lips. "Are you....alright?" The way he was blushing, she was certain that behind those rushes there was not a strip of clothing on him.

"I, er, I am, yes. I just got...just got a bit muddy is all...Your Highness," the man stammered, both hands retreating from view to cover himself. He glanced uneasily at Lyall and the other men who stood in the shallows, laughing their heads off. Joanna thought there might be actual tears of mirth in Lyall's eyes. She resolved to keep herself more composed.

"What happened to you?" she asked.

"I was...er..." The naked man floundered for words, turning even brighter red than Joanna thought was possible.

"MEOW!" The cat butted Joanna's arm forcefully and reached out to tap her with a paw.

She looked down and scratched the animal's ears. "Right you are, master cat. Someone please lend some clothes to this man. I think his own are past saving."

"I agree." Lyall brandished the dung covered shirt and tossed it up the bank, far away from them all.

There was some argument amongst the men over which of them seemed closest in size to the soggy stranger. Meanwhile, the miller's son stood in the murky water, blushing from ear-tips to toes and obviously mortified.

Joanna smiled sympathetically. He had seemed uneasy the first time they had met on the road, but being caught nude by royalty would be enough to send anyone into a panic. He cut such a pathetic figure, huddled in the weeds, watched over by Lyall who had finally managed to contain his own mirth.

The men procured a new shirt and trousers, as well as a belt and some dry socks. The miller took these then looked furtively towards the princess. She stared back, blankly for a moment before she understood. With a grin plastered on her face she turned around, back to the pond.

She petted the cat while she waited. He marched back and forth across her lap, his tail striking her softly in the face with each pass. "Are you afraid I'll peek?" she asked the animal, who meowed in her face by way of an answer.

When the miller was dressed, Joanna turned back around and he was led up the bank to sit before her on the grass, hands resting on his thighs, wearing a contrite expression like he'd been taken prisoner.

"Relax...Miller, was it?" Joanna asked. She caught the flash of Lyall's warning look as her bodyguard knelt beside her. He plopped two handfuls of cool mud onto her knee and ankle. She tried to ignore this and gave their new charge an encouraging nod.

"Miller. Yes. Levi. Please call me Levi." The man seemed to find speaking difficult, spitting his words like cherry pips and looking deeply embarrassed. He seemed to be trying to shrink away into the serviceable shirt he now wore.

"Levi." Joanna nodded. "And what was this fine fellow called?" She indicated the cat, who was now going back and forth between her and his master, purring fit to rattle the hills.

"Boots."

"You can look at me, Levi."

"Sorry." He didn't look at her.

Lyall sat down beside Joanna, and the cat began making a triangle between all three to receive the maximum amount of attention. Lyall tilted his head, trying to look the miller in the eyes. "Levi, why were you naked in a pond?"

Lyall's abruptness startled the man enough that he flicked his gaze up to take in Joanna and her bodyguard. His eyes were as blue as Lyall's, though darker—more like the summer sky than midwinter. He swallowed, his hands balling into fists on his lap. "I was...I was robbed."

"Robbed?" Joanna's eyebrows shot higher. "Were you hurt?" She gave him a hasty once over with her eyes, hand already upraised to summon Rylan. She hadn't been able to see him clearly when he was down in the reeds, so she might easily have missed a wound.

"No. No." Levi raised both hands, finally looking her in the face. Joanna didn't think she had seen anyone look so mortified in her life. *One day I'd like to try **not** being a princess, just to see how people would behave.* "You didn't have any trouble with those Shades, did you?" she asked, glancing around in case a few of the nasty creatures were trying to slink in, riding on the long, late afternoon shade. She glanced towards where her horse stood with the others, gathered and looked after by the diligent Liam. The saddles sat in a neat row, her swords still attached, well out of reach.

"Shades? No. Yes? Uhm..." Levi faltered.

Joanna held up both hands in a steadying gesture. "How long ago were you robbed, and how did you wind up in the pond?"

Joanna was certain that this was the man she had encountered the day she had met Prosper, and now here he was in a pond right near The Ogre's territory. She wanted to grab Levi by the collar and shout, "who are you working for?!" Instead, she settled her hands in her lap, focusing on the pleasant cooling sensation of the mud on her injuries.

For the moment, the man before her appeared to pose no threat.

Levi licked his lips. "I w…I was walking by the pond when I…" He hesitated, casting his eyes around as though the grass and sky might fill in the story for him. Boots the cat let out a concerned trill and strutted over to his master to rub his face against the man's knee. "Some men jumped out and grabbed me and took all my things, then threw me in the pond."

"Why were your clothes covered in dung?" Lyall questioned.

"I…they…the men…they took my clothes, and what they didn't want they rolled in a dung pile from one of their horses to ruin them before they left. It was a joke I suppose."

"Mmmhmmm," mused Joanna. "That must have been very traumatic for you."

"Not…not as traumatic as this, Your Highness."

Joanna let out her abrupt bark of a laugh. Levi jumped, then smiled sheepishly. So he wasn't just a soggy piece of cloth, the youthful face and endless blush were hiding an ounce of wit. Try as she might not to, Joanna was already beginning to like this person. If only she could be certain he wasn't up to something. How had he gone untroubled by the Shades? He would have made easy prey.

"Men attacked you, took your things, threw you in a pond, and rolled your clothes in manure for good measure?" Lyall ticked off on his fingers, looking less amused than Joanna.

"That's right," Levi said, though his voice wavered. He looked pleadingly at Joanna, clearly sensing he'd scored points with her.

Lyall leaned in, whispering into Joanna's ear, so close his lips brushed her skin. "Those clothes were too covered in muck to have been rolled in a single pile of horse droppings. It was more like he fell in a whole mire of the stuff"

"So?" Joanna turned to look Lyall in the eye, brows knit. She knew that Levi was watching their whispered conversation with growing concern.

"So? Doesn't his story sound fishy to you?"

"Exceptionally, yes, but we're not going to crack his lie by pointing out that his tunic was more covered in shit than we expected." She cut a glance towards Levi, who was holding the cat to his chest. His expression was so open and worried Joanna softened, whispering to her bodyguard, "I know I was concerned that he, or someone like him, might be working for The Ogre, but look at him, Ly."

"Look at him? Bad people can't be innocent looking?" Lyall sat back on his heels. "How did you do this? How did you get me arguing *for* your crazy idea?"

Joanna smirked, "Skill."

Lyall leaned in again. "Either way, we both know he's lying,"

"He probably thinks we're plotting whether to toss him back into that pond." Joanna had to contain a chuckle as she took in the miller's wide eyes and drawn mouth. Now he was going a bit pale rather than red.

"So what are we going to do with him?" Lyall asked.

"Feed him, I expect," Joanna said, loudly enough that Levi could hear.

"Rew rew!" chirped Boots, who had clearly endured enough of being squeezed and struggled free.

Levi hardly seemed to notice the cat was gone. He gaped at the princess and her bodyguard. "I...no, I have to get home." Levi gestured vaguely in a direction that looked more like he was indicating the pond than any road.

"You said you lived in mill country, didn't you?" Joanna asked, tucking her uninjured leg under her. "That's a long way to go, especially after the day you had. Stay with us tonight. There are Shades abroad...and thieves, by the sound of your story."

Levi grimaced. "Believe me, Your Highness, I have had many worse days than this."

"Really?" Joanna leaned forward. "I wouldn't think the son of a miller would have a terribly eventful life. Did illness move through your village?" To her knowledge there hadn't been any serious plagues or illness to pass through their kingdom since before Joanna was born. Had Shades reached deeper into the countryside than Little Fox?

"No, ma'am." Levi shook his shaggy head, and his damp hair flopped comically. His bangs fell in a thick fringe to obscure his eyes while other sections stood straight up as they dried. It rivaled even the messiness of Joanna's hair after a long day of riding. "I'm just...er, well I'm just a little bit clumsy is all." He pulled up a sleeve to reveal a scar that etched its way from wrist to elbow.

"He's covered in those," Lyall pointed out, quietly.

Joanna looked from the scar to the miller's face. She knew wounds, and the one on his arm must have been deep. "A little clumsy?"

"Very clumsy," Levi shrugged and tugged his sleeve back down.

"Well, you shall have to tell me all about the adventurous days you've had while we enjoy a meal." She raised her voice, getting the attention of her men. "We'll camp here for the night. I'll allow fires until true dusk." With the sunset already casting shadows, it wouldn't make much difference if their cookfires threw out a few more.

"Oh, I really shouldn't," Levi said, squirming. "I...I'm just a little clumsy about fire is all." Levi mumbled, head down.

"Then we'll keep our eye on you," Lyall said, pushing to his feet. He moved off to help the men gather firewood.

Joanna sat with the newcomer, studying him unabashedly. He seemed determined to move as little as possible. Even his breathing was measured. She almost laughed at the absurdity of it. She wanted to put a reassuring hand on the man's broad shoulder, but she suspected he'd wet himself.

Boots seemed to have grown bored and moved on to stroll amongst the men as they laid out wood for fires and fetched food from saddlebags. Varric and Bowen began rigging up fishing lines, eagerly eyeing the pond. The cat received pats and attention everywhere he went.

Joanna smiled as she watched them. She hadn't specifically chosen her soldiers for love of animals, but it was gratifying to see she hadn't picked wrong. The cat and his human were such opposites, one timid, the other self-assured and preening as only a cat can be.

Joanna turned back to the miller. He kept shooting glances from under his shaggy bangs like a spooky horse looking for something to shy at. She cleared her throat and he jumped. "It's alright," she soothed. "We're a friendly bunch—you know that by now. No need to worry. If the robbers come back, we'll see to them." She was certain there hadn't been any robbers, but didn't bother voicing her dubiousness now.

"Oh, no, that's not—" the man cut himself off, his cheeks going red again.

Joanna sent a *help me* look in Lyall's direction.

The tall bodyguard strode over, planting his hands on his narrow hips. "We're not going to hurt you, lad."

"I'm not worried about you hurting me," Levi said, his voice tight. "It's just that I have a tendency, if I stay in a place too long to...hurt other people and you're the princess, and you're nice too. I don't want to hurt you." His words tumbled out so quickly it was a wonder they didn't trip over one another.

"What?" Joanna tilted her head.

"I—" Levi seemed to bite back his words as though trying to keep them under control. No doubt he was considering the humor of this shy miller trying to harm any of them.

"Why don't we settle in for a bit, calm down, and have a nice dinner?" Joanna used her gentlest tone. She was out of practice, and she knew Lyall was one of the few people who had even heard it before. "We'll keep any sharp things away from you, just in case."

Levi seemed to consider. He reminded Joanna of a dog she had seen once. A timid stray who had clearly longed for the mutton bone she had offered, yet was still terrified of her. The animal had trembled with energy and frustration. Judging by Levi's tightly clamped fists and rigid shoulders, he felt the same.

As the camp was prepared Levi sat exactly where he had been placed and didn't move more than to blink or pet Boots if the animal deigned to pay him a visit. Anytime anything went slightly wrong, like a soldier dropping a log, or tripping slightly, Levi would flinch. His expression creased with concentration, as though he were trying to control the whole camp with his thoughts.

It did take longer than usual to set the camp properly, but in Joanna's eyes there was no sign of the doom the young miller obviously predicted. A few of the fires were more difficult to light and no one caught any fish in the pond, though Avery got dangerously close to getting chomped by a smallish snapping turtle.

It wasn't long until everyone was settled, intent on eating while they still had the fires. Joanna's knee and ankle were feeling considerably better, and she was able to limp about without help from Lyall, though her bodyguard watched as though he expected her to collapse any moment. "You're a mother hen, anyone ever tell you that?" she griped as Lyall caught her arm, though she hadn't even tripped.

"Joshua may have mentioned it." Lyall grinned infuriatingly, and Joanna was tempted to trip him herself.

As food was cooked and shared out, Joanna filled a plate for herself with a roast potato, dried meat and a piece of lightly toasted bread, then prepared another for Levi, who was still sitting just outside the ring of firelight having refused to come closer.

His cat, on the other hand, was the life of the party and soon had talked most of the men out of a portion of their meat ration. Joanna smiled and shook her head with amusement as she wove her way through their ranks to join the miller. She handed him his plate, then sat down before him, which caused him to tense again.

She wrinkled her nose. "I think it's time you told me what has you so spooked. You know we're all friendly, and I certainly don't put on airs like a princess. The last time we met you were much less nervous."

He blushed and looked down at his food. "It's just that—"

"I'm the princess?"

"That certainly doesn't help." He looked up through his bangs.

"It's common to have a little...admiration for me. Lots of men do." She tried to infuse meaning into her words with raised eyebrows and a firm tone. She'd let this one down gently. "It's simply that I have no intention of marrying. I don't feel that way about anyone and I don't think I ever will."

"I...er...no..." Levi stumbled over his words so badly Joanna wondered if he'd hit his head in that river. He dragged his hand back through his hair, leaving much of it sticking straight up as he took a moment to gather himself.

"What are you doing to the poor lad?" Lyall took his spot at Joanna's side with his own meal in hand. He plopped cross-legged on the grass like some kind of stick insect folding up its legs.

"Honestly, I'm not sure," Joanna replied earnestly.

Levi seemed to have rallied. "I mean, I *do* think you're amazing and beautiful and...but I don't...Gods!" He threw up his hands in exasperation and in the process launched his dinner into the air. The potato landed in Joanna's lap. Several men turned to stare and a few of them clapped.

Levi looked mortified.

Joanna chuckled, extracting the potato and juggled it between her hands, as it was still quite warm. "No harm done." She righted his toppled plate and settled the potato onto it. Then she slid her own piece of bread from her plate to his. Lyall planted his hunk of dried meat beside the bread and Joanna passed the meal back to Levi.

Levi deflated, shoulders sagging, hands open and limp in his lap as Joanna set his plate into them. It was as though he had been held upright by tight strings and they'd been unceremoniously cut. He gazed at his plate with quiet acceptance. "No harm done this time," he mumbled to his potato.

Lyall cocked his head, a large hunk of buttery bread poised between his fingers. "Is harm usually done when you have dinner?"

"You'd be surprised." Levi answered. "I told you. I'm clumsy."

"You also were not robbed by bandits," Joanna said. "No more beating around the bush, Master Miller. You're a terrible liar."

Levi avoided this statement by wolfing down the bread he'd been given. When neither the princess nor her bodyguard said anything more and he had run out of bread, Levi peered up at them again, looking infuriatingly guarded. Joanna wanted to prod Levi with a stick and demand he speak up this minute. If she did that he'd likely clam up and never utter another sound.

Bluntness had long been Joanna's weapon of choice, as much as it annoyed Lyall, her family, and most of all her suitors. It was time to wield it. "Tell me, Master Miller, have you grown more familiar with The Ogre, since last we met?"

Levi choked on a bite of potato, and Joanna hurried to strike him forcefully between his shoulder blades until the food was dislodged. Once his coughing had subsided and Boots had rushed over to check on his human, Levi gazed at Joanna with plaintive, watery eyes. "Please don't ask me, Your Highness."

"Call me Joanna," she instructed, but she fixed him with a firm stare to indicate that he could not avoid her question.

"I really don't think I can do that, Your Highness."

"Try."

"Uhm... I'll try, J-Joanna."

"There we go. See? Not difficult. Now, please answer my question."

"I've heard a bit more about The Ogre I suppose," Levi said, petting Boots too vigorously.

"Merwow!" The cat yowled, glaring up at Levi with eyes like twin yellow moons. They were beginning to glow in the firelight.

"I'm not...I don't..." Levi struggled.

Joanna wished Lyall would speak up. He was better at conversations than she was. Perhaps she shouldn't have ignored so many of her elocution lessons by daydreaming about swords. For the moment, her best friend was sitting back with a look of bemusement on his features as she dug herself a bigger hole.

Joanna clasped her hands, pressing her nails into her palms as she watched Levi like he was an egg about to hatch. Finally, the miller seemed to realize he couldn't make himself disappear through sheer force of will. He raised his head, startling Joanna with the flash of his blue eyes. "Do you believe in curses, Your Hi- Joanna?"

This was not remotely what she expected him to say, and she wondered how she had botched this conversation so badly. "I've heard of them in tales. The new religion says they aren't real, but..." she hesitated, her mind whirring.

She looked down at Boots, who was nested down on Levi's lap and cleaning the crumbs of the meal from his clothes. She thought she remembered something from the conversation they had shared that day on the road. Granted, she had been distracted by Prosper's family berating and belittling her.

"You still follow the old ways, don't you?" she asked.

"Yes," Levi said, petting Boots as the cat continued to groom him.

"Let's say we do believe in curses," Lyall finally spoke up. He pulled the collar of his shirt down to reveal a tattoo, dark against his pale skin. The image of a bull. The God of power and courage.

A light sprinkling of rain began to fall. It was nothing at first; a cool tickle, almost pleasant against Joanna's skin. What she could see of Levi's expression had cycled back to one of shame.

"I'm not just clumsy," Levi said hurriedly, pulling Boots closer to shelter the cat from the raindrops. "I'm—"

Thunder cracked. Joanna looked up in time for the sky to empty itself onto her head. She laughed as a wild gully-washer of a storm crashed over them. The men shouted, the fires guttered out in seconds, and Levi curled into a ball around Boots.

Joanna got to her feet when lighting flashed. She could see the horses huddled together, and they flinched as one when the night was thrown into day-brightness for that fraction of a second.

"Gather the horses!" Joanna roared, launching herself into the throng of milling soldiers. The men were half-trying to gather food and half simply trying to cover themselves. She snatched at the arm of a passing man and turned him, propelling him in the direction of the frightened animals. "We need to get them all together and head for higher ground! If they spook and scatter, we'll never get then back tonight." Her ankle twinged sharply but she ignored it, grabbing up packs and heading for the tree line.

"Let's go!" Lyall was on his feet. He herded the men ruthlessly as they rushed to obey Joanna's orders.

The princess shot a sideways glance at Levi, who was standing where she had left him clearly wishing he could bolt, but unwilling to leave. The cat had abandoned his human friend and run off to parts unknown. Joanna suspected that Boots was already tucked away somewhere dry.

She was glad that Levi had decided to stay, at least for the moment. Still limping, she turned her attention back to her people. "Head for the tree line!" She had no fear of a Shade attack now. There would be no danger tonight. Already moonless, the darkness was rendered absolute by storm clouds. She doubted the Shades could constitute themselves at all in this black.

The rain continued to assault them with a force that bordered on painful. Drops as large as buttons splashed Joanna's face, and she had to keep swiping water from her eyes if she had any hope of seeing at all. The sodden ground was fast becoming a mire and it would likely take all of tomorrow for her boots to dry if she hung them on her saddle while they rode.

"Should we try to find someplace higher?" A soggy Lyall was at her side. He had to shout to be heard over the maelstrom.

"No. I don't need anyone getting struck by lightning." Joanna shook her head, her drenched, icy hair slapping her cheeks.

"Right," Lyall agreed, darting away to continue guiding the men.

The horses followed obediently, almost without needing to be led, and stood in a huddle, their heads lowered. The soldiers hurried to set up their tents. Treated canvas would keep most of the water out if they could manage to get the tents up quickly and skillfully enough.

Joanna, doing one last sweep of their initial camp, collected Levi and guided the young man to join the rest under the trees. "We have a few extra tents," she reassured him.

For his part Levi allowed himself to be led. Once or twice she saw him begin to move towards one or the other of the men, as if to help, but he would withdraw again. Joanna was too busy with her own tent to wonder much about it, but she resolved to find out the exact details of this curse as soon as possible.

"Ma'am, we have an extra horse here." Liam sloshed through the downpour leading a smallish, plump, dapple-grey mare who wore no saddle. She looked at Joanna with placid, brown eyes as though nothing were out of the ordinary.

"She's mine," Levi spoke up, hurrying over and putting his hand on the animal's neck.

"Ah. Right. I remember you had a horse." Joanna petted the animal's sodden face before she moved to continue helping Lyall with their tents, plus the extra for Levi. "Liam, tether the mare far enough from the high-strung youngsters that they won't bother her," Joanna called over her shoulder.

~~~~

It took two hours to get the camp situated. By then everyone was completely soaked and Rylan went around to all the tents passing out an herb drought that might keep a few of them from catching cold. Joanna, safely installed in her own tent, made a face as she sipped.

"It won't do to have our leader getting sick," Rylan pointed out, tucking his hands into his rain poncho.

"I suppose not," Joanna said, grimacing down into the cup where a brownish green liquid swirled. "Make certain our guest has some too?"

"Already done," the healer dipped his head in a bow that spilled the water that had collected on his hood. He waited to make sure that Joanna choked down every drop of the tincture, checked her injuries one last time, then departed to continue his rounds.

Joanna changed clothes quickly, gathered some blankets, and threw on her own rain cloak. Arranging the cloak so it covered her armload of blankets, she struck out into the downpour.

Outside the rain fiercely pelt the darkened landscape, even knocking down dead branches and tearing green leaves from the trees. Had she been able to see the pond, she knew it must already be overflowing its banks. Lighting raked cruel scars across the sky, illuminating the little camp, the tents like huddled sailors trying to ride out a storm at sea. Joanna hugged the blankets to her chest involuntarily and crossed to Lyall's tent, which was beside hers.

"Ly?" she called, shifting painfully from foot to foot to keep warm. "Are you decent?"

There was a moment of silence in which she wondered if he had heard her over the rain and wind, then his answer, "never!"

Chuckling and shaking her head, Joanna pulled open the tent flap and stuck her head inside. The tent was illuminated by a single candle in a jar with no lid. Her bodyguard had changed clothes and was rubbing a small towel, which was usually used to dry the horses, through his hair. "Come visiting with me?" she offered. "I brought the visiting gift." She nodded to the lump in the front of her cloak where she held the blankets.

"Alright." Lyall finished with his hair, which reminded Joanna a heap of straw. "Let me get my rain gear."

Moments later the princess and her bodyguard had invited themselves into Levi's tent. They'd given him the spare Joanna used as an armory tent. Tonight, everyone would keep their gear with them to keep it dry anyhow.

Levi was a lump in the dark. He hadn't lit his candle, so Lyall did it for him.

"Were your matches wet?"

"No. I just...I shouldn't have fire. Even in the middle of a rainstorm." Levi sat on the cot they'd given him, still wearing his drenched, borrowed clothes.

Joanna clucked her tongue as she extracted the blankets from under her rain cloak and tossed them onto the end of Levi's cot. "At least have that wet shirt off before you freeze. Ly and I will scrape together some dry things for you in a bit."

Levi meekly did as he was told, passing the soaked shirt to Lyall. Even in the dimness Joanna was able to take in all the scars that decorated the miller's torso. Had he been beaten as a child? She'd heard rumors that farmers sometimes took a cruel hand with their offspring. She squinted, deciding that a majority of the wide, white slices on the man's skin didn't look regular enough to have come from whipping. Whip scars tended to be concentrated, while these were different sizes and patterned down every limb, all the way to his hands. Levi settled onto the cot and pulled one of Joanna's blankets around himself. "Thank you," he said, earnestly.

The princess moved farther into the tent. Suspecting that if she were to sit on the cot Levi would become panicked, she stood, trying to look casual. "We hadn't finished our conversation when the rain interrupted us."

"My fault, I'm afraid," answered Levi, glumly.

"Are you trying to take responsibility for the weather?" Joanna's eyebrows lifted. His voice was so earnest.

"In a way." Levi said.

"And how, exactly, did you cause it to rain? Are you secretly the only weather mage left in the land?" Joanna spread two blankets onto the damp floor so she and Lyall could sit. This was likely to be a longer and more involved story than she had first expected. Her heart did an excited little flip. What if this person was like Prosper?

"I'm not a mage," Levi said, dashing Joanna's hopes with one blow. "I'm just unlucky. Very, very unlucky."

As if to prove Levi's point, the tent began to leak directly above him, dribbling a stream of icy water onto his shoulder. He heaved a sigh and moved out of the way.

Lyall gave an amused grunt and stood, digging into his pocket and pulling out a lump of bees wax. "These tents do this all the time. Especially when we need them most," he reassured the miller, rubbing the wax against the tent canvas above the other man's head until the leak stopped. "There we go. You just seal it up like that. If the leak gets too bad, we can patch it when the weather is fair."

For someone who no longer had water falling on him, Levi still managed to look miserable. "I'm not sure how to make you understand." He looked around as though he might find some proof in the tent. Nothing presented itself, so he went on. "The rain started because I was here. Hadn't the day been bright and the night cloudless before I joined you?"

"Storms come on suddenly, and this has been a rainy year," Joanna pointed out, crossing her legs gingerly to favor her injured knee and ankle.

Levi gestured to his little candle, safe in its glass jar. "I couldn't have lit the candle without burning the whole tent down around me. Or at the very least, I'd have ruined the candle and the matches, and broken the jar it's in, cutting my hand in the process." He held up his hands for Joanna to see. She winced at the lattice of little scars. She raised her own hand to compare. Lyall did the same. Both she and Lyall bore an impressive number of scars themselves, both old and fresh, though nothing to the miller's.

"Those are from fighting," Levi said, sitting back and cocooning himself into his blanket. "Mine are all from bad luck. I can't climb ladders or eat with a knife. At best I'm a bother and at worst I'm dangerous." He sneezed loudly.

"Did Rylan give you some of his tea?" Joanna asked,

"Yes. But it doesn't matter." Levi swiped at his nose with the back of his hand. Lyall passed him a handkerchief. Levi blew his nose and sighed. "I used to get sick all the time as a child. When I wasn't falling in wells or out of trees or breaking my family's milling equipment." The words fell from Levi's mouth like the rain. "I know it sounds unbelievable..." Another leak started above him.

Joanna cut a glance at Lyall, who rose, brandishing the beeswax lump. "I think...I think we believe you," she said. Lyall shot an uncertain look over his shoulder but said nothing. She grasped her knees, willing her bodyguard to be silent for the moment. *I need to see where this is going.*

Levi's smile was so wide and genuine that, whatever Joanna thought, it seemed completely obvious that this man *believed* himself to be cursed. Perhaps that was all that mattered. "You understand then? Thank you! You're the first people I've told. I mean, I told The Ogre, but he already knew—" Levi clapped a hand over his mouth, face draining of color.

"You what?!" Joanna burst to her feet, hands reaching for swords she wasn't wearing.

"You what?!" Lyall snapped at the same time, nearly toppling backwards as he stretched up to seal the leak.

"I—" Levi choked. The candle went out.

There was an uncoordinated scramble as both Joanna and Lyall hurried to relight it. Joanna was struck with the irrational notion that if she didn't get it lit soon Levi would disappear and take his information with him. Much bumping and muttered cursing later, the candle was glowing softly once more. Levi had not vanished, but sat looking as downtrodden as a kicked hound.

Joanna stared at Levi. She had to say something, something useful or royal perhaps. Instead, what burst from her lips was a slightly unhinged half-shout. "The Ogre?!"

Levi brought up his hands as though she might strike him with her bare fists. "I know consorting with The Ogre is...probably against some law if not worse, and you're in charge of upholding the laws, so maybe I'm already under arrest..." His shoulders sagged, and he peered at her from under the fringe of his bangs. "Am I? Under arrest?"

It was a struggle, but Joanna fought down her boiling alarm and suspicion, tilting her head and doing her best to look nonthreatening. She was out of practice. Her whole life was a series of struggles to make herself seem taller, more dominant, more imposing. "Just tell us, Levi. You're not in any trouble." The steadiness of her tone surprised even her.

"Yet," whispered Lyall, who had rejoined Joanna on the floor. She surreptitiously smacked his thigh.

"Tell us your story, Levi. Please." She begged.

Taking in a deep, shaking breath, the miller's son explained how he had come to be cursed. How two blessed older brothers spelled a new kind of magic for the third sibling. Joanna's memory prickled as she listened. Something Prosper had said about the way magic begot magic. Levi went on, speaking of a life growing up with a curse always on his back. Of near-death experiences, childhood illnesses and ruining his family's plans and equipment. "My parents stopped taking me to village festivals when I was eight." Levi said. "My brothers would take shifts watching me and enjoying the celebration. They hated it and me. When I was ten, I worked a whole day in the field for the first time and it was a disaster, just like Ma said it would be. At twelve years old I went to fetch water and the well dried up that same day."

"That sounds...frustrating." Lyall spoke sympathetically.

"It was very frustrating. I never knew it was a curse until my father told me before he died. I thought...I don't know what I thought.

That it was just me? That everyone else was better at living life than I was."

All three jumped as the flap of the tent rippled open and something damp and orange rocketed inside. Boots, looking soggy and sour, skittered under the cot and sat, ears flattened with disgust. After surveying the company with a dubious glare, he began grooming himself dry.

"I wondered where he was." Joanna tipped herself to the side to peer cat the grouchy animal. He ignored her.

"I've always been good around animals," Levi admitted. "I can cause trouble *near* animals, but I have never hurt an animal with my curse—that I know of."

"The old gods must favor you," Joanna said earnestly. She spun the cat ring around her finger a few times, like a prayer. This man was a contradiction. Working for The Ogre yet watched over by the old gods? This was a puzzle that only became more complicated the more pieces she had, but she was aching to put it together.

Levi's face lost some of its gloominess and a truer expression shone through at last. Levi was not a frowner. As much as the curse plagued him, his face was clearly made for smiling. It dimpled pleasantly, and his eyes had laugh lines etched deep into the corners.

He visibly gathered himself and pressed on. "I left home after my father died because I knew if I was ever going to be anything but a burden, I needed to find a way to break the curse. Except I wasn't certain how I was going to break the curse. I sought out The Ogre because he was the only person I knew of that had magic. I couldn't think of any way to cure something caused by magic except with magic."

"So you walked up to his castle and *talked* to The Ogre?" Joanna tried not to sound accusatory. "Just marched right up to his gate and had a little chat?"

"He's not as bad as we've been told...at least not in person," Levi assured her.

Joanna snorted, and Lyall shifted beside her.
"He's not a monster like everyone says. He's just a person. Well, he's a mage too. He can use his spells to transform himself and other things. Usually he just does objects. He can transform a chair so I can't break it, or fix something I've already broken."

"He can transform shadows into living creatures," Lyall pointed out.

"So he's just a man?" Joanna leaned forward, elbows resting on her knees. "All the stories describe him as a monster. I never imaged him as anything else." It was difficult to erase the creature she'd had in her head all her life—picture-book images of toothy monstrosities flooding her mind. Could a clever mage with transformative powers truly have ousted an entire family from their fortress? It was during peacetime, so the Carabas family probably only kept a smattering of guards against the occasional bandit. How powerful a mage was The Ogre? "Can he transform into other people?"

"I've never seen him do it," Levi hedged, no doubt sensing her unspoken implication.

The cat had finished grooming and, looking somewhat fluffier, strode out from under the cot and leaped into Levi's arms. Boots settled himself and glowered at Joanna and Lyall as though daring them to upset his human friend further. Levi petted Boot's head.

This gave Joanna pause. She couldn't imagine a discerning cat settling into the lap of a monster. Her gut twisted with unease, but she resolved to continue with her instinct that Levi was what he appeared to be. Beside her Lyall's shoulders tensed, but he said nothing.

Levi petted Boots as he continued his tale. "I've seen him turn into a gigantic creature once, which is where I imagine he got the idea to be called 'The Ogre.' Simon…The Ogre was very interested to meet me and learn about the magic locked inside me by the curse."

"Locked inside you?" Joanna asked. She turned to Lyall. "Prosper said something about that too. How magic can be locked inside a person if it is placed there by a mage."

"Does that help us?" Lyall asked.

"I don't know," Joanna snapped, annoyed at his lack of fascination. "Maybe. Go on, Levi."

"The Ogre took me in and did some research on curse breaking. He wants to help me. He said he found the journal of someone who broke a curse on himself. Apparently, he did it through acts of kindness," Levi said.

"Acts of kindness?" Even with her limited knowledge of magic Joanna thought that last bit sounded fishy.

"That's what he said." Levi shrugged. "He was the first person I told about my curse, and he said he could help me. What should I have done?"

"Wait, what did you *do*?" Joanna leaned forward.

"I..." Levi looked embarrassed again. "I tried to be kind. To help people. The Ogre sent me to help people he heard of in need."

"That doesn't sound like The Ogre we know." Lyall folded his arms. "The one who sends his minions to burn and kill."

Joanna managed to keep her voice steady as she spoke. "The Ogre we know wants to claim more land for himself. He wants to take over this kingdom bit by bit, though my father will never admit it. If he can expand his territory there's probably more magic he can steal." She thought of Prosper and his home where magic was still common.

"He didn't say anything about that to me," Levi mumbled. "He showed me people I could help so I could free myself from the curse. I tried. I really did. I help people, but it always turned out badly." His voice was tinged with a bitter twist of anguish. "I went to help with a bridge—"

"It *was* you!" Joanna crowed, startling both men. The cat rewarded her with a severe glare, which told her just what he thought of such unseemly outbursts. Joanna swatted at Lyall's arm. "It was him! I told you!"

"You guessed." Lyall grabbed her wrists so she would stop swatting and turned back to Levi. "The bridge over the Serpent's River fell because you were there? Because of your curse?" His tone was incredulous. "What then?"

"After the bridge turned out to be a disaster, I went back to The Ogre and he patched me up and gave me a new assignment. I was supposed to help a caravan of traders that was passing near The Ogre's land. They were having trouble with their carts. I'm strong and could have been useful, but I...I made things worse, as usual. Finally, today, I was supposed to help a farmer who had recently lost his son to illness and needed an extra pair of hands. I reasoned that it would be safe because I'm alright with animals, but then other chores got involved and before you know it I had broken a harrow, caused half his corn supply to spill from the crib, and dumped myself into his manure pit."

"That's why your clothes were covered in dung when we found you?" Lyall let go of Joanna's wrists so he could jab a finger at the miller.

"That would be why, yes," Levi said.

Joanna's mind raced around its internal track like a trapped colt. Tangents flew off like sparks, but she latched on to the seed of the idea that was planting itself deep in her brain. "If I might venture a guess as to what is actually going on here." She raised a hand. Both men looked to her expectantly. "I'd wager that The Ogre saw an opportunity with you, Master Miller. He had no way to pull your magic from you because the curse was bound to you so tightly, so he decided to use you to his own ends. He'll send you out like one of his Shades to cause trouble and pave the way for his expanding territory. He wants to ruin the farmers so they abandon their homes, and to stop traders on their way through so the goods never reach the capitol. He's using you and your curse to do it."

"No…" Levi gave a tight shake of his head. "No that can't be right. He seemed so…he was *kind*. He wanted to help me."

"He wanted you to help *him*," Joanna asserted.

"I never wanted to hurt anyone. I just wanted to break the curse," Levi's eyes flashed with anger for the first time since Joanna had met him. He folded his arms in his blanket cocoon, jutting out his chin. "Maybe The Ogre isn't as bad as you think. Maybe if you talked to him…"

Joanna let out an exasperated grunt. "Talked to him? I'd be killed by Shadows before I could get past his front gates. I'm not filled with interesting magic. Doesn't it seem a little suspicious to you? Do you feel that anything The Ogre has asked of you has come close to breaking your curse?"

Levi managed to keep up his glare, though Joanna could tell she'd sown the seeds of worry in his mind too. For all his shy nature, he was no dullard. His mouth twisted sourly, but he spoke. "Well, no, the curse seems the same, but he said it could take a while, and I keep failing. It's like I have to fight against the curse to break the curse."

"Or you're not breaking it at all and you're just doing The Ogre's dirty work for him. Not to mention you're far more subtle than his Shades. He probably never imagined I'd find you and figure you out at all. Did you ever look at that journal yourself? The one he claims has the account of how to break a curse?" Joanna asked.

"Well, no…" Levi hunched into his shoulders.

Another leak in the tent opened up and Lyall stood to deal with it without comment.

Levi groaned. "I think you two should probably get out of here. If I am around other people too long, my curse starts working on them."

Joanna didn't budge from her spot, fixing Levi with one of her more intense stares. "What are you going to do?"

"I don't know." Levi ran a hand absentmindedly over Boots' back. The cat arched happily, purring all the louder.

"Will you return to The Ogre?" Joanna struggled to keep the demanding edge from her voice. Sounding too much like a princess used to being obeyed probably wouldn't help here.

"You'd let me do that?" Levi's gaze flicked up to hers once more. "You'd let me go?"

"Well…yes. You're not our prisoner," Joanna said.

Lyall turned and stared at her like she had lost her mind. "Jo—"

Joanna ignored her friend. She fixed Levi with a firm gaze. "You could go back to trusting The Ogre and hoping he has your best interests at heart, *or* you could help us. You're a way in. A way to reach The Ogre that we never had before."

"Jo—" Lyall tried again and she continued to ignore him.

"If you honestly believe that he is going to help you while he ruins the livelihoods and homes of all the farmers whose lands border his own, then ignore me. Go back about your business. However, if you think there's a chance you might be wrong about him, that he might not be the helpful man you thought he was, then consider helping us."

"I…" Levi shrank away like an hare cornered by a hound.

"Why don't we let you sleep on it and we'll talk again in the morning?" Joanna offered.

Levi was silent for a long moment, looking down. Finally he peered up at Joanna through the fringe of his impossibly messy bangs. Joanna marveled that anyone's hair could be in such disarray. "Alright," Levi said.

"Mer mer MEOW!" Boots announced in an operatic cat voice. Joanna couldn't help but envision the cat in human form, attired in a fine waistcoat, shining boots and hat with a plume, shooing them away like a good servant concerned over his master.

"Alright. We'll talk in the morning." Joanna stood with a grimace, her battle-worn muscles having stiffened from sitting so long in the same attitude. Lyall had to help her as her knee and ankle refused to flex properly. She knew she cut an inelegant figure as she bid the miller's son farewell. "Good night, Master Miller." She ducked out of the tent into the waiting monsoon.

Hopping on one foot to work the kink out of her knee, Joanna tugged the hood of her cloak up tight around her face. The rain pelted as hard as ever, even under the cover of the trees. Was this storm truly the fault of the man they had just left?

Lyall came out a few moments later, having given his wad of beeswax to the unfortunate miller's son in anticipation of further tent leaks. Before they walked on he circled the outside of the tent re-securing the stakes, which had begun to pull out of the soggy ground. Even with Lyall's efforts Joanna suspected the tent might well blow over some time during the night. The real question would be what might cause it. The storm and the muck, or the bad luck of the man inside?

Once Lyall had finished his ministrations and returned to Joanna's side for their walk back to their own tents. She tucked her hands deep into the sleeves of her rain cloak and looked sideways at her tall companion. "So?"

"So? You're mad. What else would you be?" Lyall gestured, splattering water from his sleeve across them both. "We should arrest that man before he goes running back to The Ogre, tail between his legs, and tells that creature exactly where we are and what we're up to."

"The Shades have probably informed him where we are, and he knows what we're up to. It's not as though I'm subtle." The pair wound their way between the trees, checking the tents of the other men. The world was bathed in the deep, almost tangible darkness of rain and tree shadow, but their eyes adjusted. The occasional flash of lightning left them blinking and momentarily blinded.

"Still…" Lyall's tone was contemplative.

Joanna huffed rain from her upper lip as she checked a tent rope. "Still what? If we take him back home as a prisoner, what do you suppose we tell my father? We've caught a very dangerous miller's son, throw him in the dungeon! Do we even have a dungeon?"

"Yes, we have a dungeon." Lyall barely managed to dodge a tree branch that might have put out his eye in the dark. He cursed quietly before speaking again. "I used to play hide and seek down there with some of the other servants when I was a child."

"And you didn't invite me?" Joanna mock-pouted.

"It was not the sort of place you bring princesses. Jo, you're getting us off track again. What do we do about Levi?"

"I think he'll make the right choice," Joanna turned her gaze to the clump of horses that huddled in the thickest tree cover. Generally the animals enjoyed a nice rain, but it was gushing down so hard that even they were not inclined to frolic in it. They blew water from their wide nostrils and swished their sodden tails sullenly. They had even allowed Levi's horse, a stranger to them, into their ranks for the night. Each soldier had taken his mount's saddle and bridle into his tent to keep it dry. Joanna hoped that the rain would lessen on the morrow so she could look for her fallen stirrup.

Willow saw her and sloshed over to put his wet nose against her arm in greeting. She petted the horse and looked back towards Lyall, who was checking more tents; a lanky figure in the windswept woods, almost a Shade himself. Except when he tripped over a protruding root and nearly tumbled face first onto the turf.

The friends came back together in the gloom and made their way to their tents, continuing to check the others was they went. Lyall heaved an expressive sigh. "I still don't know if we should trust this miller's son. He might just be a very good actor. He could play at giving us good information, all while marching us right into a trap."

"He might," Joanna agreed solemnly. "Or he might be a very bad actor, and we're the ones marching him into a trap. If he sides with us and The Ogre finds out…" Her heart twinged at the notion, but the spark of excitement that perpetually blazed inside her refused to be dampened. "Don't ruin my good mood. This might be the closest we have ever come to getting the information we need to defeat The Ogre."

"And that in itself is pathetic, isn't it?"

"Hush up, Ly." Her voice filled with ill-concealed amusement.

"Of course, Your Highness." Lyall swept an elegant bow, and Joanna leaped forward with a wild laugh to flip back his hood, his hair immediately saturated by the heavy rain. He made a clumsy swipe for her and missed.

Giggling like a mad woman, she darted for her tent, barely noticing her complaining joints; Lyall hot on her heels. Several men peeked out of their tents only to see that it was only their insane leader rampaging around.

Joanna made it to the safety of her tent, dampened of body but not of spirit. She sat down on her cot and removed her wet things, listening to Lyall stalk outside the door for a few moments, before he gave up and retired to his own tent.

She arranged dry sleeping clothes, then tried valiantly to deal with the mess that was her hair. She finger-combed, she prodded and pleaded, but only managed to turn the soggy mess into a slightly different soggy mess. If only Hana were here. She sighed, swept the lot back into a tail, and turned in for the night, her dreams alight with battles finally won.

~~~~

"I'm still not certain how I can help you," Levi said.

Joanna stood with Lyall and the miller's son under the bedraggled trees as dawn broke around them. It was still raining, but more gently. Thin droplets slipped through the heavy leaf cover, and a cool mist slithered over the rolling hills, forming grey pockets in the dips and valleys.

Boots stood with his human, looking up at the princess and her bodyguard with suspicious eyes. The cat softened when Joanna secretively dropped a bit of cheese for him.

The princess kept her attention on Levi as her men moved about, packing up the camp. "What can you tell us about The Ogre's lands?" She prodded.

"There's not much to tell," Levi shrugged. "Fields have gone fallow with no one to tend them. Empty houses and rotting barns."

"How does The Ogre eat?" Lyall mused.

"He probably steals everything he needs. Well, has his Shades do it," Joanna said. "What about the Shades? Does he keep them on patrol around his house?"

Levi shook his shaggy head. Even dry his hair was an impressive tangle. "I never saw a single shadow as I made my trip up to his gates. Maybe he could see me coming with magic. He has a magical orb of some kind down in his study. He showed me images in it."

"Hmmmm." Joanna scowled, working to contain her curiosity. She added *seeing magical items* to the list of things she wanted to do in her life, then forced her thoughts back on track. "That's probably how he decides where to send his Shades."

"And me." Levi looked down, shamefaced. "I thought about everything you said last night. How he can't get at my magic, so he just wants to use me until he figures out how. I thought about the way he looks at me sometimes. Like I'm a nut he's just waiting to crack open."

"I suppose I had better be up front with you." Joanna kept her voice gentle. "What we're asking of you…we're using you too. The big difference is that you're volunteering to help us, just like I told Lyall you would." She elbowed her bodyguard playfully.

He rewarded her with a baleful smile. "So you did."

Levi shuffled his feet, which were safely tucked into new boots. "If I can be put to good use rather than ruining everyone's lives with broken bridges and rainstorms, I'm happier for it. I just wish I could be more helpful to you." He rubbed the back of his neck, looking shyly at Joanna.

After a moment of awkwardness, an idea seemed to come to Levi in a jolt and he snapped his fingers, "I know! I draw. I can make some accurate pictures of the layout of the castle. Of any weak points I can find. I can keep notes on The Ogre. Notice anything he does, where he goes and what he gets up to in a day. I'll write everything down, and when he sends me out again to 'help' more people, I'll get someone to take the message to you." He paused. "Maybe several someones, so my luck doesn't keep them from reaching you. As soon as the messages are out of my hands, they stand a much better chance." Levi looked so fully alive and excited for the first time since they'd met. His sweet, uncomplicated expression lit up so much it might have chased away the rain.

"I've never seen plans of the Carabas castle!" Joanna said eagerly, already envisioning the layout and plotting out her way into The Ogre's sanctum. She would root him out and best him in combat, saving the kingdom and proving herself worthy all in one glorious swoop. She cleared her expression with some effort. "Anything you can give us would be immensely helpful!"

Levi beamed. A gust of wind snatched at a nearby tree branch, and it smacked him in the face.

~~~~~

Joanna saw Levi off, back towards The Ogre's lands and his hopeful mission, after Rylan saw to the fresh cut on the bridge of the Levi's nose. As Joanna watched the miller depart, riding on the back of his old horse with Boots the cat sitting on the animal's rump, she heaved a sigh.

Lyall looked down at her. "What is it?"

"I'm trying to convince myself that I made the right choice. I think I did. It's hope, at least."

Lyall's brow creased as he turned to watch Levi move steadily away from them. "Perhaps. I may be willing to buy the whole 'curse' business, but I'm still not convinced he isn't just a clever actor working for The Ogre. Or perhaps he's been magically enchanted to look innocent and simpleminded. He could be a thousand-year-old warlock for all we know."

"Really, Ly? A thousand-year-old warlock?"

"We don't know." Lyall gestured animatedly. "And you just let him stroll out of here with new clothes and a full belly."

"Maybe warlocks are friendly to people who feed them." Joanna tilted a cocky grin in Lyall's direction before it slipped away, carried off on a tide of worry. "You know I follow my gut, Ly. Let's work under the assumption that Levi is who he says and he's not willingly doing evil for The Ogre. Even if he does manage to get the drawings done, there is every chance that The Ogre will see. Or that the bad luck will ruin the drawing somehow. Or that—"

"Jo," Lyall cut her off. "Stop. You made a decision and we must abide by it. Snap your fingers and I'll ride after him and capture him again, but if you don't, then we must let this play out. Things set in motion are often very difficult to halt."

"You're right. I wish there was some way to know for certain. I'm putting an awful lot of faith on a simple farm boy, and that's under the best circumstances. As you say, he could just be evil." Joanna unfolded her arms and held out her hand, spinning the white cat ring around her finger so it looked as though the god chased its tail. She chuckled. "I suppose the god of Luck does encourage us to take chances. I can't call myself his follower if I don't."

"I, on the other hand, must simply be true to myself to please my god." Lyall patted the tattoo concealed behind his clean shirt front. "And I cannot be truer than when I am following my princess." He raised his chin and adopted a noble, self-sacrificing expression.

"Stop that, you," she commanded. "I have a stirrup to find, a saddle to repair, and soldiers to manage. You're going to help me." She strutted away into the drizzling day, hoping that her men would not find her decisions too egregious and her plans too wild. Perhaps it was better that they not know the details. All she intended to tell them was that Levi was a guest and nothing more. An unfortunate that she, as future

Champion of the People, was obliged to feed, clothe, and house on a rainy night.

~~~~~

A week went by with no word from Levi. Joanna and her men kept moving along the border of The Ogre's lands, chasing away Shades wherever they found them. Once they even saw off a group of human thieves who were plundering a farmer's back field at dusk. Those men had been much more easily discouraged by the sight of war horses, armored figures and gleaming blades.

Joanna took careful note as they traveled of anything the farmers reported. It seemed clear to her that The Ogre was snatching up more land at an alarming rate. Three times they met families who were heading for nearby towns, their worldly belongings packed into carts behind them. When she asked why they traveled, all three reported that their farms were simply too much trouble to keep with the nigh constant Shade activity.

Joanna gave each family some money to be getting on with, promising them proper compensation once she returned to the castle and had words with her father, though she knew each coin she could squeeze from him would be hard won. She looked into each weather-worn face as the farmers shared their information, and dutifully wrote it all down.

"We need to do something. If we get no word back from Levi, we'll have to make plans of our own to deal with The Ogre head on,"

Joanna announced to Lyall as they rode along a slim, winding country road. Her men rode in twin columns behind them.

"You beginning to doubt your miller will come through?" asked Lyall.

Joanna ground her teeth. "I don't want to face The Ogre not knowing what to expect. I don't want to subject my men to a hard fight through Shades to The Ogre's keep only to have him slaughter the lot of us when we get there."

"We know he's a transformation mage," Lyall pointed out.

"Right. So he could conceal himself as a caterpillar in the grass before changing into a gigantic beast and murdering us all." Joanna let Willow's reins fall slack, though the well-trained horse dutifully followed the path. She didn't want to speak her darkest fear aloud, even to her friend. That Levi had run back to The Ogre and betrayed them. Blabbed everything he had gleaned about her to the monster.

Behind them the men chatted amiably. They only knew they were over halfway through their kingdom patrol, and once they got away from The Ogre's lands things would be easier. Joanna chewed her lip. Should they stay in the area instead of moving on with their usual route? Could she ask them to stay longer and fight harder until…until when? Until a cat god appeared to her and brought her the message from Levi she was waiting for?

"You're thinking we'll have to chance it, aren't you?" Lyall asked uneasily.

"We're not going to solve the Ogre problem by ignoring it. That was my father's plan and my grandfather's plan. We can all see how well that's working."

Both fell silent, listening to birdsong, the squeak of saddles and the good-natured back-and-forth of the men. Then Joanna's ears detected something else. It took her only a moment to place it. The gentle strumming of an instrument a ways down the road. A voice joined it, emanating from just over the next tree-crowned hill.

"My lady fair, my lady fair,

when will you come to me?

For I have traveled o'er the land,

all through this fair countr-y.

I've seen it east,

I've seen it west,

but your dear face I love the best.

My lady fair, my lady fair,

When will you come to see?

I'm the one who loves you best,

why do you always flee?"

"Perhaps she doesn't appreciate a good tune," Joanna spoke in her clear, princessly tone as she crested the hill and caught sight of the one who produced the music. A skinny bard—attired in clothing that must once have been very colorful, but had since faded to the barest suggestion of greens, reds, and yellows—was seated on a rock at the roadside.

The man, who had a wan face and nose so large and slim he might have been able to slice bread with it, looked up at the approaching riders and whistled low. "Well now. I go into the countryside to practice my new songs in peace and my fans follow me?" He grinned. His teeth were crooked as untended gravestones. Joanna did not want to imagine his breath. His voice, nonetheless, had been exceptionally pleasant and melodious.

"We're sorry to disturb you." Joanna dipped her head.

"No bother, no bother at all." The bard scrambled around for a moment and produced a threadbare hat, plopping it onto the ground before himself. He gave them all an expectant look.

"Hadn't we better hear a full song before we lay down any money?" Joanna rested an arm on her saddle horn.

The man touched the side of his impressive nose, eyes alight. "Right the lady is! Right she is indeed! How neglectful of me!" He gave the stringed instrument across his knees a gentle strum. Though the thing, which might have been a lute at one point in its life, looked to be held together with bailing twine and hope, it let out a tuneful thrum.

The bard took in a great breath to begin a song. Joanna's men eagerly brought their horses around in a semicircle to listen. The bard heartily belted an old story-song about the animal gods and a poor, unhappy peasant who was trying to find his calling in life. In the end, the goddess of music took pity on the sorrowful traveler and gave him an instrument. The beggar at once picked it up and began to play a beautiful tune, which naturally attracted a lovely maid and before you knew it, they had three fat children and a happy life together.

The bard was indeed skillful, managing the fast-paced and overly wordy verses with ease, then encouraging everyone to join him on the choruses.

Finished, the last notes still vibrating pleasantly in the air, the bard let out a long breath and squinted up at Joanna. She expected him to hold out his hand for the coin she had all but promised. Before he could, his face cleared and his mouth fell open. He raised both hands in a halting gesture and began to scrabble around again. "Wait. Wait wait wait!" He stumbled to his feet, fumbling in a wide-mouthed bag tucked behind his rock. "Lady in armor. Lady in armor," he muttered to himself. "How many of those can there be?"

"What?" Joanna swung down from Willow's back. "Are you alright?"

"Blast it, I have it somewhere. When a cat gives you something, you had best not lose it." The man dug more ferociously in his bag.

Lyall and a few of the other men dismounted as well, watching the bard with curiosity and some suspicion. Finally, the bard straightened holding a crumpled wad of paper in his long-fingered hand. "Ha HAH!" he crowed, turning and brandishing the paper at Joanna.

She blinked, uncertain how to react. The bard wagged his find at her. "Here. Lady in Armor. It was Princess Joanna, yes?"

"Er, yes." Joanna finally reached out and plucked the badly crumpled papers from the man. It turned out to be a packet of four sheets, folded and creased so many times she wasn't certain she'd be able to read what was on them.

"I knew it!" The bard looked pleased with himself, puffing out his narrow chest and rewarding them all with a crooked-toothed grin.

"What is this?" Joanna asked, gently folding back the wad of paper, trying not to tear it.

"You'll never believe, especially with me being a bard and a teller of tale," the man said, his unappealing smile not waning. "This note here was given to me by a cat."

"A cat?" Lyall, who was looking over Joanna's shoulder, raised his eyes to scrutinize the bard.

"Aye, a cat." The bard tucked his thumbs into his belt and rocking back on his heels. "Two days gone, I was walking along, enjoying your fine countryside, composing ingenious ballads to myself, when out of the long grass struts an orange cat. Smug as you please."

"Did this cat have white boots on his hind feet?" Joanna asked. She knew Lyall was about to comment on the absurdity of the entire situation, but the bard answered before her bodyguard could.

"Sure he did! Big orange tom with white rear feet. Anyway, I said hello because that's only polite. He came over to me to be petted, and that's when I saw he was wearing a funny little harness."

"Wearing a harness?" Lyall snorted.

"Right. A harness," the bard enunciated as though Lyall might be hard of hearing. "A real cunning one made out of strips of leather. Tucked in that harness was a note for whoever found the cat, as well as that wad of papers that you now hold in your illustrious hands." The bard paused, possibly to see if anyone had questions, possibly for applause. When neither presented themselves, he went on. "The note told me that the cat was carrying an important message for the Woman in Armor, our Princess Joanna, who was supposed to be traveling these roads. There was even a little sketch of your coat of arms. It asked if I would be so kind as to give the paper to her if I came across her, and what do you know, I did!" The bard spread his arms, this time definitely expecting someone to clap. All he received were baffled looks from Joanna's men.

The princess hastily unfolded all four sheets and might have whooped aloud with joy, had so many people not been staring at her. Years of training as a lady at court were called upon to keep her excitement at bay. "You have done well, Master Bard."

"Thank you, lady."

"Highness," Lyall corrected. "A princess is addressed as 'Highness.'"

The bard ignored him. Joanna had met a few traveling musicians in her life and one thing was true of them all: they were unimpressed with titles, ranks, and royalty in general. They came to entertain with songs and stories, not to bow or scrape.

She strode to Willow's side and flipped open one of her saddle packs. With a flourish for the bard's benefit, she pulled three, fat, gold coins free. She returned to the group and ceremoniously plopped the coins into the bard's hat, which was still sitting on the ground at his feet. "If you see the cat again, convey my thanks to him," she said, keeping her tone formal, even as she was laughing inside.

"I'll be certain to." The bard grinned, his weathered face creasing. He picked up his hat and extracted the coins. His eyes went momentarily wide, then he schooled his features. "Blessings! I'd be messenger for you again any old time, lady!"

"Perhaps that could be arranged one day," Joanna said.

"Mayhap, mayhap." The Bard pocketed the coins. He planted the hat on his head, and Joanna caught sight of a small bird expressed in gold thread stitched onto the hat's wide band. The nightingale, the goddess of music, with her wings spread and head thrown back in transcendent song. Joanna understood then why this man would take a note tied to a cat as a sacred duty rather than a practical joke. He was a fellow follower of the old ways.

"Thank you again for your efforts!" Joanna said as she carefully refolded the papers. She could tell the bard had read them, but knew they would have meant little to him. Levi had been careful to ensure that no one would have reason to sell or keep the message for themselves. He had only to hope that people did not throw them into the fire as useless flotsam.

The bard swept a low bow, touching two fingers to the brim of his hat, idly fingering the pocket where his new coins rested. Joanna knew Lyall would think she overpaid, but in this situation she would have to disagree. No amount was too much for the information that would help her finally defeat The Ogre.

As Joanna and her men rode away they heard the bard strike up another jaunty tune.

"I met a lady, fair and good,
who led her men as princess should,
across the land to seek a foe,

and deal to him a mighty blow!
But this lady, proud and strong,
had time to stop and hear a song!
And ride she did o'er hill and flat,
to do the bidding of a cat!"

Joanna fought the mirth and excitement that bubbled in her chest. It was almost painful as she tried to keep her body rigid, her eye keen and severe.

Once they were well clear of the bard. she called a halt beneath a stand of maple trees. "Time for a rest!" she announced. Thankfully no one noticed the way her voice trembled with energy. Perhaps Lyall did, but he made no comment as he slid lightly from the saddle.

As her soldiers milled about Joanna and Lyall secreted themselves away. The princess found a small clearing in the thick prairie grass and sat down with much creaking of armor. Lyall did the same across from her. Without speaking, for she feared if she did she might explode, she took Levi's papers and spread them over the sandy earth before her. The edges of the papers were ragged, and one bore a noticeable ink splotch, but all the information was readable.

After a few moments spent turning the images this way and that, she discovered she could place the first two side by side to create a sketchy map of The Ogre's lands, complete with crude compass points and legend.

The other two papers, when she sorted out the correct orientation, depicted the interior of The Ogre's castle. Levi had also included the walls with the main gate, and the stables. Joanna raised both eyebrows, impressed. Levi had not been joking about his ability to draw. He had included a key for the scale in one corner, so Joanna was able to use her thumb to measure the distances. She was as giddy as she had been when she was five and her father announced that she would begin riding lessons. She'd practically lived in the stable for weeks.

Joanna spent several minutes eagerly measuring various dimensions of the lands and castle with her hand, breathing only when she remembered to. This was better than riding lessons. This was better than all the Solstice and birthday gifts put together. A miller's son had appeared and handed her destiny on a silver platter. She was going to devour it with both hands. This was it. This was what she had waited for all her life.

When she finally sat back, thumb to chin in consideration, Lyall turned the pages over. On the back of one was a list. Confusing to the outside observer, but clear to both of them. He read it aloud.

"Breakfast shortly after dawn.

Retires to his study.

Not seen again until evening meal.

I am ignored unless he has instructions for me.

I can wander freely.

Few Shades inside unless he calls them.

Have seen the Shades come and go.

No more than thirty. Might be the same ones every time. Impossible to tell.

No Shades in the yard or grounds.

Gate is usually unlocked"

"This is amazing!" Joanna crowed, her eyes drinking in the maps and the words over and over as one might the face of a lover. She looked up at Lyall. "And you didn't want to trust him!"

"Neither did you," Lyall pointed out.

"Well I do now!" Joanna might have hugged the pages. She rocked forward again, trembling with nervous energy like a horse about to begin a race. Her eyes were so fierce and wild that even Lyall looked nervous as she spoke. "So, Ly, how do we get in?"

~~~~~

Though it was practically torture to do so, Joanna and her men continued their tour of the kingdom. They found, or were given, three more of Levi's notes, all identical to the ones bestowed by the bard. Joanna figured the miller would have sent out quite a few in hopes that his bad luck wouldn't keep them from reaching their target. She could only hope that The Ogre had not discovered them. She supposed it was the risk they would have to take. Bits of paper would mean nothing to the Shades, so the only danger was if The Ogre found them in his home. Unless he got lucky with his spying orb.

Now that Joanna knew The Ogre had the power to see the outside world with his magics, her skin prickled with the sensation of being watched. She would whip off her nightclothes and leap into her trousers and tunic, even in the safety of her tent. Sometimes, when no one was watching, she made rude gestures to the air, just in case.

When not contemplating how The Ogre might be watching her every move, Joanna's mind was at work formulating various plans. She didn't bring these to Lyall yet, as most of them were half-formed, or too ridiculous to harbor for long. Everything from rallying a massive peasant army to attack, to burrowing in under the castle with a shovel.

She was confident that she would be able to come up with something sound and successful. After all, hadn't her life been leading to this for as long as she could remember?

~~~~~

Finally, their campaign came to a close, and they were once again approaching the capital city. Joanna sequestered herself in a room at an inn overlooking the castle, where she knew her father awaited her return with a scornful eye and a head full of potential marriage candidates.

She cringed at the thought of walking through the doors, her new reports and plans in hand, only to find some fresh suitor waiting to be discouraged. It would be this way until she could march up to the king and announce that The Ogre lay slain and the land once again belonged to their family.

Joanna sent for Lyall, pacing the floorboards smooth until her bodyguard arrived. She hoped that The Ogre could not watch her this far from his own territory. She had no notion of how far his magic could stretch, but if his Shades found it difficult to come all this way, she hoped that the spying would as well. If she'd been thinking, she would have asked the miller for more details, Too late now.

Lyall stuck his head in the door, interrupting her brooding and self-flagellation. "Is this it?" he asked, slipping through the door and closing it quietly behind himself. "Have you got our plan?" There was a tense eagerness in her friend's voice that Joanna hadn't expected. She was prepared for him to take his usual role reining her in, but his eyes were alight with the same fire as her own.

Joanna pulled out a chair at the simple, wooden table where she had laid out the plans as well as her own copious notes. Lyall crossed the room in three strides and sat down, clasping his hands before him like an eager student.

She met Lyall's eyes and spoke. "I think it needs to be us."

"Us? You mean just us?" Lyall gestured from Joanna to himself with a thumb. He puffed out his cheeks, leaning back from her. His chair gave a threatening creak.

Joanna nodded, lips drawn in a line. "You and I. There is no way we're going to sneak all our soldiers onto The Ogre's land, and we already know that we can't charge the gate because have no idea how many Shades The Ogre has at his disposal. It might be thirty, as Levi surmised, or those could merely be the ones he sends on assignment. There are too many variables for me to risk my men that way."

"You could ask your father—" Lyall began, then shook his head ruefully. He'd stood by in enough meetings with Joanna and her parent to know that no amount of begging and reasoning would yield her results. She could have charged into the throne room and declared that she'd found a spear guaranteed to kill The Ogre by itself, no skill required, and the king would still refuse to spare a single soldier.

Lyall cleared his throat, offering another thought. "So, we have our men create a distraction for the Shades, or better yet, we leave the men out of it completely? Is that what you have in mind?"

"Right," Joanna said. "Then you and I creep in and assassinate The Ogre ourselves."

"You? An assassin?" Lyall scoffed. "There are many things that can be said of you, Jo, but I don't think I have ever heard anyone accuse you of being subtle or stealthy."

"I can be quiet," Joanna asserted, glaring daggers at her friend. "It's hard to achieve when you have a band of armored warriors following you around. No, if you and I do it, we'll go in quiet and quick." Her eyes narrowed, eager, like a cat about to pounce. "We could get right up to The Ogre before he has a chance to react. Levi gave us his entire schedule." She tapped the paper.

"Except our spy didn't mention a thing about how much time The Ogre spends with his 'seeing crystal.' He could spot us coming miles off." Lyall rested his chin on a hand, elbows propped on the table.

"If he knew where to look," Joanna pressed. "He won't be expecting another patrol so soon. He knows I stay home and let the men and horses rest before we move out again. Plus, he'll be busy looking for people to trouble with his new patsy, the unfortunate Levi. We're two people who can slip in and out. Gods, even Levi walked right up to the gate without incident."

"So he claims, but you'll recall The Ogre did find him, and only let him live for his own nefarious ends. I don't suspect he will have any of those if he discovers us skulking around in his broom cupboard."

"You make it sounds so adventurous. Do you have a better plan?" Joanna huffed, nudging a table leg absently with her foot. She needed to be moving or all her pent-up energy would explode from her like a wildfire.

Lyall made a show of placing his fingertips on the map, then sweeping it around so it was right side up for him. He flicked his long, elegant hands over the markings and leaned in, studying the map as a jeweler might a rare gem. He muttered under his breath, thin lips moving fractionally.

Joanna let him study in silence. She rested against the equally untrustworthy back of her own chair, lifting up the front legs and balancing by hooking one of her feet on the table's leg.

After several minutes in which the only sounds were the fire popping and a needlessly loud song her men struck up downstairs (something about a beheaded chicken who went on to lead a heroic life, dismembered as he was), Lyall's pale blue eyes finally flicked back up to meet Joanna's. "With the men we have and our exceedingly limited knowledge, there isn't a good way to approach this."

The princess nodded, arms folded. She let the front legs of her chair fall to the floor with a startling thump. "So, what do we do, master Lyall?"

"We can't go alone. We could take one or two more men. Maybe Rylan?" Lyall's face creased in consideration as he eyed his princess. He must have known what she would say to this because he spoke again before she could shoot down his notion. "Say we do manage things your way. How exactly do you expect us to get to The Ogre's castle by ourselves without the men telling your father, or your father becoming concerned over your whereabouts?"

"That is one of the many logistics I am still working on," Joanna admitted.

"We could hire an actual assassin."

"Because our little farming kingdom is swimming in professional killers."

"Hire from outside the kingdom?"

"I wouldn't know where to begin. Do we send out notices? Hold auditions?" Joanna leveled a *be serious* gaze in Lyall's direction.

"I have no idea how you hire an assassin." Lyall admitted.

"Stop suggesting impossible things then." Joanna rested her palms on the map and flipped it back in her direction.

"I'm already out of possible things. Could we get Levi to do it? Kill The Ogre himself?"

She barked a laugh. "Him? Did you meet the same miller that I did? He was about as dangerous as a handshake. Not to mention with his bad luck he would probably end up stabbing himself." Joanna traced one of the lines on the map with her pinky. An old road that led right up to the gate. Once it had been traversed by fine ladies and nobles coming to visit the family Carabas. Now she imagined it nearly covered over with twining weeds and long grasses.

"Right, right." Lyall sighed. He rose and strode to the fire, taking up the poker and squatting to prod the ashy logs.

She spoke low and serious. "It has to be us, Ly. You and I have to go in and we have to kill The Ogre ourselves. I'll make up some excuse for father and the men." She watched Lyall fiddle unnecessarily with the flu lever. If she looked at the map one more time she might scream.

Lyall found a rag at the washbasin and wiped soot from his hands, turning to Joanna at last. "You could always tell the king that a young man has finally caught your attention. Perhaps one you found floundering in a pond near The Ogre's lands." Lyall's face twisted with mirth as Joanna's fell slack in horror. "Perhaps a lad you suspect might be the long-lost son of Carabas."

~~~~

"The lord of Carabas, Father." Joanna repeated as her parents gaped at her. Clearly some creature had devoured their daughter and a doppelganger returned in her place. Joanna ignored their baffled expressions, putting her head down as she might to walk into a strong wind. "I found him in a spot of trouble and we...we became friends. He lives in a village not far from the border of The Ogre's land where I was patrolling. By...by firelight one night he told me of his past, and his family. I believe him, and if you met him, you'd believe him too. I truly think I might have found the long lost son of the family Carabas. A last child who could not make the journey out of our kingdom and so remained, quiet and anonymous, waiting for an heir and a chance to regain their lost fortune."

Behind her Lyall let out a faint snort from which he managed to turn into a cough. She winced. Perhaps she had put too dramatic a spin on the tale. She'd been rehearsing versions of it in her head for an entire day and a half, and this was the one that spilled out.

"And you...you want to see him again?" Her father asked, setting down his dinner fork with an awkward deliberateness. The table was once again lavishly laid out with all the finest trimmings, ostensibly to celebrate her return. In reality, her parents liked to have the excuse for extravagance. This time, however, there was no prince to sit across from Joanna. The chair remained empty, like a threat.

Joanna tried to look shy and sweet. She twirled a coil of her hair around a finger and smiled at nothing. "Yes, Father. I...I think I like him very much. He was the one who sent you those lovely pheasants when Prosper visited us. I didn't know then that I would ever see him again, or take such a liking to him." She attempted to blush, but it turned out blushing wasn't something she could do on command. Instead, she put her head down and hoped it would make her seem besotted. She should have had Lyall give her lessons. Fortunately, her parents had no basis for comparison.

Her father's eyes narrowed hawkishly. Joanna thought to try fluttering her lashes, but decided against it. Her parents still had to believe it was her after all, albeit a version they were not accustomed to. "He was very handsome!" she put in hurriedly. That was something people noticed and mentioned, wasn't it?

The king and queen paused, studying their offspring before they put their heads together, speaking in low, hurried voices. Joanna wished she could hear what they were saying. At least they seemed excited, with several exaggerated hand gestures and fingers jabbed in her direction.

In her imagination their conversation went something like: *"A commoner? Of course our daughter would fall for a commoner. Ever the contrary,"* said Imagined Father.

"No, no. This lad has good blood, he simply had to earn it! If he can spend some time with Joanna and she can bring that out in him, would that be such a bad thing?" Imagined Mother countered.

"He has no land or holdings."

"He could. Perhaps he will be the one to defeat The Ogre. Nothing motivates a lad like a stolen birthright and the hand of a beautiful woman."

"He's only a lord at best. Our child is a princess."

"She will elevate him. Plenty of marriages have gone thus. Besides, isn't a lord better than no husband at all?"

"I had hoped—"

"Better than no one at all."

Joanna struggled not to look towards her brother. She could feel his eyes on her like she was an insect under glass.

"What is he like, dear one?" the queen asked, raising her head from her conversation and resting her delicate chin on her hand. "I mean aside from handsome and possibly a lord?"

"He is…he is very kind and handsome." Joanna cursed under her breath. "I mean hard working. His…his name is Levi and he's…he's tall, though not as tall as Ly. He's got…erm, very strong arms and he's…he's…resilient." She was proud of herself for coming up with that word. "He's seen a great deal of hardship in his life, but he strives daily to make everything better!" She finished strong, locking eyes with her parents.

"And he's kind, you said?" her mother asked. Was she laying a trap?

"What about strong?" her father cut in. "Does he seem capable of taking back his family's rightful land? Is he well-spoken? Would people follow him?"

"Er...very well-spoken, yes. Especially considering his circumstances," Joanna said. She had expected questions, but now that they were flying at her she found herself frustrated by all of them. Keeping her voice pitched high and girly she forged on, "I want to see him again, but trooping everywhere with my men is tedious, and I think it alarms him a little to see me with so many men."

"He wants to see you as a lady." The queen nodded sagely. "He's seen you in armor commanding soldiers. Now he wants to know you have a softer side too."

"Right," Joanna exclaimed, endlessly thankful for her mother. "So this time it should be just me...and Lyall for my protection of course."

"Not Hana?" Mother asked. "To help you with your hair and clothes?"

"Er...of course. Her too," Joanna said. They could bring the maid, then set her up in a nice inn while she and Lyall went on to attack The Ogre. Convincing Hana to go along with their scheme would be considerably easier than convincing the king and queen.

She focused her attention on her meal. Seared salmon with pepper and a squeeze of lemon. She stuffed some into her mouth and cut a sly glance towards Alroy. She was met with a look so searching she turned back to her plate at once. Was he seeing through her already?

"What about these 'Shades' you're always complaining about?" the king asked. "Wouldn't it be dangerous for you to go out with only Lyall for protection?"

Joanna flinched. Did he truly still believe her so unable to defend herself? One day soon she'd show him. She raised her head, trying to look bright and unconcerned. "No, no, Father. We just came back from patrol, and we taught those Shades a stern lesson. They won't be back for a little while," she lied. After all, what was the good of telling her father about the increased Shade activity? He'd ignored it every other time she'd tried.

The king sighed as though she had asked to take his prize stallion for a ride in the back country. The picture of a father giving an indulgence to a favorite. "Oh alright, Joanna. Go and see your young man." He turned to his wife with a shrug. "What could it hurt?"

Joanna bit down on a grin before she gave herself away. Then she remembered that people in love sometimes did grin like fools, so she allowed a toothy smile. She dug into the rest of her meal, only remembering to pause and say "Thank you, Father" when Lyall took away her plate to prepare for dessert.

She pointedly did not look at Alroy even once more that evening.

After dinner the family went their separate ways, though Joanna caught a few snippets of her mother's conversation as she wound her arm around the king's: "I told you she just needed to find someone on her own."

Joanna grimaced and her gut twisted. Her mother tried to understand. The queen supported Joanna's desire to become the People's Protector, but at the same time Joanna knew the woman could never fully grasp a desire not to wed. The queen believed that Joanna wanted to find that "special someone" for herself rather than having men paraded in front of her as though they were cattle at a fair.

Hana was waiting for her in her rooms eager to see whether she should begin packing traveling clothes, or dealing with a distraught princess. Joanna had told Hana something close to the truth. That she and Lyall would be going on a scouting mission to The Ogre's lands. Nothing too dangerous, with the help of an inside man they had acquired.

~~~~~

The stables were quiet except a few confused hostlers, who hurried to saddle three horses for the princess and her entourage. Hana was giddy with the notion of leaving the castle. On her days off she never went farther than Longmark. Her hazel eyes sparkled with excitement as a patient mare was chosen and tacked up for her use.

Joanna glanced down the long, clean rows of stalls, where curious equine eyes watched her. Her heart too was in her throat, though not with the same thrill as Hana's. It looked as though she and Lyall were getting away scot-free as long as—

"Highness?"

"Horse dung," Joanna cursed under her breath.

Liam strode over to join them. Of course he'd be hanging around the stables. He was wearing his thick, farrier's apron and tugging off leather gloves. His pale eyebrows rose as he took in Joanna and Willow, the horse already wearing his saddle and bridle. "What…what's going on? Are we riding out? No one told me."

"No, Liam." Joanna waved a hand in what she hoped seemed like a casual dismissal. "We're just…Hana has had word from her mother in Stone River and she's been asked to come home."

"Nothing wrong, I hope." Liam leaned around Joanna to look at Hana, who tucked her face down into her horse's neck. Unfortunately, in doing so she looked to be on the verge of breaking down. "We should ride with you," Liam said, stoutly, setting his gloves on an empty saddle rack. He tucked his forefinger and thumb into his mouth and blew a sharp whistle before Joanna could edge out another word.

Joanna shot Lyall a pleading look, but he looked to have been caught as flat-footed as she. Cade and Varric trotted around corner, kitted out in practice gear. They looked expectantly from Joanna to the horses. "What's the word?" Big Cade asked. His bare arms gleamed with sweat, and he swiped at his damp brow.

"Get the others," Liam urged.

"NO!" Joanna snapped, too loud. Willow flinched. "No. I…there's no need. I don't want the whole troop. I—" A thought struck her, "Hana doesn't want the whole troop. We're trying to be subtle for her sake, so please don't make a fuss."

Varric frowned, creasing the scar on his lip. He had a long, expressive face and deep-set, sorrowful eyes. He'd come from a rough background with a father who beat him and his siblings. He was a good-hearted man, and he watched her now with an earnest distrust. Was he reading her dishonesty as easily as he might an opponent's movement in battle? Joanna caught herself cutting her eyes downward like a coward.

Liam reached and patted Willow's rump. "At least take a few of us. Cade and I are free. Or Rylan. Is Hana's mother ill? No use visiting a sick mum without a healer."

"She's not ill." Hana's voice was a little too high, but strong. She managed to school her expression and turned to face the men again. Joanna exhaled in relief. They didn't know the maid well enough to read her. "My er...my sister's getting married and I wanted to be at the wedding, but I didn't want to travel alone, so the princess and Lyall volunteered to chaperone me."

"Of course," Lyall put in. "You lads know how bored we get between patrols."

"Right," Joanna said. "I just mope around the castle waiting for my father to announce the next unfortunate prince who is going to try for my hand."

Cade, Varric, and Liam shared a knowing look. They'd fought Joanna in the practice yard enough times when she was in a sour mood over her father's latest candidates.

"So, as we were saying"—Joanna turned to Willow and hauled herself onto his back, an action that was worlds easier today, without any armor—"we'll be off, and be back in a few days. No need to worry." She wheeled the horse to face the courtyard.

Liam seemed convinced, and even Cade nodded slowly, but as she and her little group rode away she could feel Varric's eyes on her back. She sat straight as a blade in the saddle, not daring to look over her shoulder.

Once they were outside the gates and the earshot of the men, Hana leaned towards Joanna. "I lied to your people for you. I hope whatever you're scouting, it's worth it."

"It will be," Joanna said, though her jaw was tight.

~~~~~

The village of Bruen was their final stop before The Ogre's lands. It was a largish village, adjacent to several sprawling farm holdings. It contained an inn, two other eating establishments, and even a small bookshop, which Hana was excited to investigate.

While the maid was nervous for her princess—and for herself staying in a new village for an undetermined amount of time—she reassured Joanna that all would be well.

It irked the princess to no end to pass so many farms and travelers that had clearly been troubled by Shades, but she consoled herself by focusing on the mission at hand and visualizing the map of the castle in her mind's eye as clearly as she could. Soon she had each passage so well memorized she might have walked it in her sleep. She could only hope Levi's maps were as accurate as they seemed.

The Fledgling was Bruen's charming little inn, overlooking the small-town square and the well where women seemed perpetually gathered to gossip and trade. Their children ran about, so intermingled that Joanna wondered how any mother went home with the correct offspring.

They arranged a room for Hana and retired to it.

Joanna leaned out the open window, gazing absently at the dark shape she could make out between the neighboring buildings. The Ogre's castle was nothing but a hump of sharp stone from here, but soon she would be close enough to make out roofs and peaks. She almost salivated at the thought before turning back to her friends, both already unpacking and getting Hana settled in.

"You can wear some of my dresses out if you like," Joanna offered, picking at the puffed sleeve of one of her least favorites. They'd all been brought to fool the king and queen, but now they took up space.

Hana raised her head, wearing a skeptical look. "And what would I do with all the extra fabric up here?" she gestured to her bosom.

"Take it off and sew it to the bottom of the dress," Lyall joked as he strapped light armor over his chest. There was no denying that the women were as differently shaped as two could be. Tall and lean Hana would have simultaneously drowned in, and been too tall for, all of Joanna's dresses.

Both women laughed at Lyall's jab for a little too long. Joanna's head felt like it was full of fireflies, each bursting to light and flying off in its own direction. Lyall looked at them both as though they had come unhinged. "I'm going to walk around and see if I can pick up any last-minute gossip about The Ogre, or a certain miller's son who might still be causing trouble in these parts," he announced, strapping his sword to his hip and buckling his shield onto his back.

"Alright. Meet me in the square at noon. We'll begin then," Joanna instructed. When Lyall had left, she turned to Hana and was startled to be caught in a hug. "Hana, what—?"

"I know you are off to do something dangerous, even if you won't tell me exactly what. Please be careful, alright?" Her voice was muffled against Joanna's hair.

Joanna wrapped her arms around her maid's slim shoulders and squeezed her back. "I will, Hana. I promise. Lyall and I will be alright. We have a plan and a man on the inside, and we'll get everything sorted and be back before you know it."

"If you're not?" Hana asked, still not letting go. "How long do I wait before I ride for your men?"

"Give us a week. That should be more than enough time to do what is needed." She breathed in Hana's smell of soap, armor polish, and home. Finally she pushed herself away, smiling up into her friend's fond face. "Help me get ready?"

"Of course." Hana swiped a lone tear from her cheek and hurried to one of the packs, hauling it onto the bed and pulling it open to reveal Joanna's plate armor.

"Not the plate." The princess raised a staying hand. She selected a different pack and plopped it on the bed, undoing the toggles. "Here. Just the splint mail, like what Lyall was wearing." She pulled out a shirt made of leather and covered in neatly placed plates of metal about the length of her thumb and twice the width. "We're going to be sneaking, remember? It needs to be flexible."

Hana didn't look pleased, but made no comment as she helped pull the armor over the princess's head. Joanna was already wearing the quilted gambeson that would add an extra layer of protection, however small. Hana buckled the straps at the armor's sides, then finished with Joanna's sword belts. Then she stood back, appraising, one slim eyebrow cocked.

"What?" Joanna flexed her body to get a feel for the armor.

"Nothing."

"You think it's too light." Joanna picked up metal bracers for her arms. The maid looked down, saying with her body language more than she could with words. Joanna sighed. "I'll be fine, Hana. I'll wear plate rerebrace and vambrace, alright?"

When Joanna and her maid had finished, she was kitted out in an odd hodgepodge of armor. Her arms to the elbows were protected by plate, while her torso wore the flexible splint mail. Her upper legs were unprotected save for the part of the shirt that hung down, but she wore greaves over her knees and shins. She smiled at herself in the small, grubby mirror. Hana pinned her hair back having braided it tightly so that the princess would not have to do anything with it for days if she didn't wish to.

"Well, do I look like someone about to save the land?" Joanna turned to face Hana, arms slightly spread.

"You certainly look like something." The maid rested back on her heels, two hairpins still clamped between her teeth. "I warn you, I'm not certain I know what someone who is about to save the land looks like, but now I've seen you. I suppose I have a standard by which to judge others."

"And what a standard it is." Joanna turned back to the mirror, resting her hands on the twin sword hilts at her hips. She tried to fix her reflection with a steely gaze, but realized she could never fool herself. She saw the nervousness in her features as plain as day in the lines on her brow and the tight set of her jaw. She took in a long breath, turned on her heel like a soldier, and marched away from the mirror towards the door. "When next you see me, Hana, I shall have saved the kingdom and my father will have to acknowledge that I am worthy of whatever duties I set myself to protect the people." She turned to her maid and saluted with her fist as though she held a blade.

"I know you will, my lady!" Hana's voice was firm and full of a confidence that made Joanna stand a little straighter. At least two people believed in her, even if they weren't her blood. They would do better than blood, she decided.

"Take care of Lyall. That stork is like to get you both into trouble if you're not careful," Hana added.

"I will." Joanna rested her hand on the door latch. "Be well, Hana. Enjoy your vacation and don't let the village men give you any grief."

"As you say, lady." Joanna did not turn back again, but she knew that Hana bowed respectfully.

Having finally managed to leave the room and her dear friend, a feat harder than she anticipated, Joanna clomped down the stairs to the inn proper. She scanned the room, mostly empty as the midday meal would not begin for at least an hour. Her eyes came to rest on a familiar figure at a table near the door, and she sighed.

She strode over to stand at her bodyguard's shoulder, which was rounded with strain as he struggled against the brawny strength of a farmer, locked in an arm-wrestling contest. "You didn't get far," she commented, clasping her hands behind her back.

"I seem to have been distracted," Lyall's voice was tight with strain and concentration. Skinny as he was, Lyall's lithe frame belied the tough, corded muscle concealed by his armor. Joanna watched bemusedly as the farmer grunted, sweat beading on his leathery brow and surprise in his eyes as he found himself unable to budge Lyall's arm.

As she watched, Joanna thought of Lyall as he had been in his early teens. A skinny, bean-pole of a lad, taller than everyone else in his year. He'd had floppy hair and a hungry, lost puppy look in his eyes. Because he was the princess's bodyguard the other castle lads kept him at arms' length. In his younger years he was trained, not to defend Joanna with strength and skill, but to throw his less valuable body between her and an enemy. When she was old enough to understand this, she secretly vowed never to let him do so. He worked hard to become as tough and as wily as any fighter twice his weight, but still, in the back of Joanna's mind, he was ever the boy with wounded eyes who resented her even as he knew he would die to protect her.

Slam!

Lyall had grown weary of toying with the man and had finished their competition decisively. The farmer groaned and rubbed his shoulder as he slid his hand from Lyall's grip. "God and Goddess, you're something else, lad! If you're ever in need of a job working fields, I'm your man. I'll pay you a fine wage and see that you get some color in your cheeks." The farmer took proper notice of Joanna and blinked in confusion at the lady in armor.

"Come on, Ly. No more wasting this good man's time. We have work of our own." She gave Lyall's shoulder a playful shove.

Her bodyguard pushed to his feet, smiling amiably at the farmer. They shook hands. "I'll keep your offer in mind if my current position falls through." Lyall leaned down to the man and stage whispered, "I'm not well treated, you see."

"Get!" Joanna ordered, pointing to the door.

"Yes, lady!" Lyall slouched his shoulders like a beaten man. The farmer laughed and scratch the back of his neck in bafflement. He'd have a story to tell his friends when they came in for lunch that day,

"You couldn't find any street brawls to get into?" Joanna asked, taking a few jog-steps to walk beside her bodyguard once they were on the street. He had straightened up and was striding along normally, the sun shining golden on his hair. He might have been a noble's son, not the child of a sellsword.

"No good fighting in this sleepy little burg. I made a friend instead." Lyall tucked his thumbs into his sword belt.

As twitchy as Joanna was, Lyall looked calm as a summer day. His chin was raised, pale face turned to take in the sun. He breathed deeply, closing his eyes for a moment. Joanna couldn't decide if she wanted to swat him on the shoulder or beg him to teach her how she could find such an air of ease. Her heart was already thundering like she was in the thick of battle, and they hadn't even stepped onto The Ogre's lands yet.

She and Lyall made good time to the edge of town. It was freeing to go somewhere outside the palace without her troop of men, as much as she missed their rowdy chatter. She and Lyall would be leaving their horses behind as well, and both wore laden traveling packs to be abandoned somewhere near The Ogre's walls.

The Ogre's walls. Just thinking those words sent another lance of nerves through Joanna's chest, but she marched on with as much calm as she could muster. "I wish we had a way to communicate with Levi. Let him know we got his messages and we're coming."

"I know," Lyall agreed. "Anything we sent would probably be intercepted by The Ogre."

"Especially considering Levi's luck. We'll just have to hope that he stays well clear of the fighting, if there is any."

"Right." Lyall swatted at a low-hanging sign sticking out from a building.

"This is exciting, right?" Joanna cut a sideways glance at her bodyguard, even her skin prickled with anticipation.

"Very." His tone did not agree with his words.

"Well, *I'm* excited," Joanna said firmly, trying to ignore the strange looks some of the townsfolk were giving her. She guessed a few must know her as the princess. She certainly was no stranger to the area.

No doubt they wondered at her lack of entourage or why such a royal personage might go on foot and wearing an ugly mismatch of armor. One day, she vowed to herself, they'd watch her because she was a noble inspiration, and not because she stood out as an oddball no matter where she went.

The pair made their way out of the village, heading up a path that grew steadily narrower, eventually giving way from paving stones to the packed earth of a cattle trail. She knew all they had to do was crest a few more tree-dotted hills and they would see The Ogre's castle again. No. Not The Ogre's castle, Joanna reminded herself. Her castle. Carabas's castle. Levi's castle? She wondered who might claim the place after she had finished her deadly work. She had no idea if a single member of the true Carabas family remained in the kingdom. She'd heard rumors that when their land was snatched out from under them by The Ogre and the king had been unable to help them, what remained of the family had departed for far-off climes. She had no idea how much of this was true, but she suspected that most of the Carabas family had been killed when The Ogre first arrived. She wondered if any had been mages; the first to have their power sapped and used against them by their attacker.

"You're sure you want to do this?" Lyall came to a stop so abrupt she walked on past him for several strides.

Joanna spotted what had stayed her friend's steps, in plain view now: the castle looming, dark and abandoned on the horizon like a hollowed-out stone. A shiver that was mingled anticipation and fear careened up her spine, and she hugged herself—something she would never do in front of her men. In a few steps, she would officially be setting foot on The Ogre's land.

She spotted a bedraggled sign that folk had put up, warning her away. They'd seen no Shades, faced no trials thus far. Was this too easy? Was The Ogre letting them walk right into his waiting claws? She set her jaw. Even if he was, what did it matter? She was closer than she'd ever been, and this time she was going to end him.

"This is your last chance to go back to your father, let him marry you off, and have a normal life," Lyall said.

"You always know just how to motivate me."

"You're welcome." Lyall tipped his head, then he followed his princess onto The Ogre's land.

The pair slipped off the road at once, sliding into the jungle of long grass, which, if she kept low, concealed Joanna nicely. Lyall was obliged to crawl much of the time, which slowed their progress more than she liked.

"Why'd you have to be so tall?" She griped, as she waited for her friend to catch up to her for the third time. She straightened to peer over the top of the waving grass, getting a sense for the landscape before ducking down again. There was no sign of any Shades stalking them. The sun was high, a poor time for the creatures to be about.

"I'm sorry. I'll work on that," Lyall grunted as he joined her, sitting down and panting from the effort of crawling for hours. He swatted grit from his gloved hands against his thigh.

"We could cut a few inches off your legs. That'd do the trick."

"Might." Lyall pulled out his waterskin and took a few gulps. Sweat shone on his brow and upper lip. "Might make me a little grumpy though."

"Hmmm. I suppose so. You're no good to me grumpy." Joanna plopped down beside him, her nose tickled by the thick pollen that filled the air. Summer was truly beginning, and the world was alive with growth, sweet smells, and the promise of fine harvests and fat animals.

"Do you think we'll reach the castle by nightfall?" Lyall sat up a bit, checking their path as Joanna had done.

"That's my hope." She took out her own water and sipped with trembling hands. Her whole body was alight with energy like electricity through every limb and digit. She wondered if this was what having magic was like. She hardly noticed the sweat that dampened her curls. "We'll sneak in under cover of night and get the lay of the land. According to Levi, The Ogre does sleep, so we should be safe to investigate."

"If he's right about there not being many Shades around," Lyall pointed out, and he continued to study the landscape.

"If he was right," Joanna agreed soberly. "He wasn't entirely clear about how many Shades are in the house, but I am hopeful we can meet up with him to discuss plans before dawn."

"And at dawn we strike?"

"We strike whenever we see an opportunity." Joanna capped her waterskin and adjusted her position back to a crouch to keep moving.

Lyall's eyes went wide. "Down!" he snapped and tackled Joanna to the dusty earth.

She swore under her breath as her cheek ground into the dirt. "Ly, what?" she sputtered, his weight on top of her keeping her prone.

"Shades. Moving fast not twenty paces from us," her bodyguard hissed in her ear. His lips were so close his breath ruffled the loose hairs at her temple.

Joanna stopped breathing altogether for a moment, listening with every fiber of her being. This was pointless; Shades never made a sound, yet listen she did. There was only the gentle hiss of the grass and the sweet tune of a distant bird. Somewhere nearby a cricket set up an early song, looking to get a head start on his fellows before dusk.

"Where…where were they headed?" Joanna choked, spitting grit from her mouth as she did so.

"Not towards us," Lyall assured her. "Away from the castle. I think they were moving out to get up to their usual mischief. Mischief we will be unavailable to thwart."

Joanna's lips curled in a frustrated grimace. She and her men could have hunted down those pesky Shades before they caused any harm. Would the farmers wonder where she was? Would they blame her for loss of crops or livestock? She reminded herself grimly that when she was finished here, there would be no Shades at all. Wouldn't it be glorious to see off the occasional band of highwaymen rather than this constant, losing war against monsters who couldn't die? This thought calmed her, and she waited patiently until Lyall eased the pressure off her back.

"Is it safe?" she asked.

She remained still as her friend checked the terrain. "We're good." he whispered. "I don't see them."

Joanna sat up cautiously, wiping grime from her cheek and freeing a stone that had slid down the front of her armor and lodged somewhere uncomfortable. "I suppose we should be glad to see those Shades go. It'll mean less to worry us at The Ogre's castle."

The pair got moving once more. As the day wore on towards sunset, Joanna was glad she had decided against her plate armor because she would have been cooking like a hen in a stew pot. As it was, she was sweating like mad and her armor pinched in awkward places as she moved. The padded gambeson was soaked through, and her first waterskin was empty. She gritted her teeth in a fierce, if silent, snarl. *Don't complain. This is your mission. You wanted this.*

Lyall soldiered on with his shield on his back like a turtle's shell. From above he must look like a gigantic beetle scuttling through the long grass.

The sun settled deeper into the horizon like a mother hen on her nest when the pair finally reached the wall surrounding The Ogre's home. Joanna and Lyall crept along it towards where they knew the gate was located. "I hope it's unlocked as Levi promised," Joanna mumbled.

Lyall's face was paler than usual from sweating all day, and his hair hung in limp strings. Joanna didn't like to think about what her own hair was doing. Lyall's eyes were steely when she met them, and she smiled. Her excitement surged again. This was really it. She was touching The Ogre's wall and soon she'd be inside it. She tried to memorize the cool feel of the mossy stones under her palm. She wouldn't forget a single detail of this day.

Joanna crouched at the edge of the path leading up to the wrought iron gate. It was a fine thing, with the Carabas crest still emblazoned on a placard in the middle: a tree with roots that reached almost as far as its branches, like a mesh of tendrils. Perhaps if they had chosen the cat god as their emblem, they wouldn't have had such troubles.

One hand drifted to her sword hilt. The other idly spun the cat ring around her finger. "God of Luck, be with us," she whispered, her lips barely moving. In that moment, just as she was about to step out into the open, something brushed against her leg. She turned, looking around in alarm. All she saw were Lyall's questioning eyes and long, swaying grass. He couldn't have been the one that brushed up against her leg. It had felt like… "A cat?"

"What?" Lyall hissed.

"Nothing." Joanna shook her head then squinted up at the gate. This was no time to be hallucinating cats. It must have been the grass brushing against her.

She slid her fingers between the bars, the solidity of them grounding her. She shot a look back towards Lyall, held her breath, and pushed. The gate swung open. Joanna wanted to cheer, but instead she slipped silently inside, Lyall on her heels.

Now they were in the open, completely exposed in The Ogre's courtyard. Joanna picked up her pace to a run, darting to the left where she knew the stables waited. She didn't need to check to know that Lyall was keeping up.

They reached the stable easily and scuttled into the dusty, cobweb-adorned interior. Joanna finally allowed herself to breathe normally. Her every breath had been short and shallow as she had run, and now she gulped air greedily, ignoring the dust.

Lyall leaned against a beam and collected himself, flush with exertion and exhilaration.. "The Ogre doesn't take very good care of this place, does he?" Lyall coughed as he disturbed a thick patch of dust.

"It would seem not. I suppose the Shades have no need of horses." Joanna rubbed at a stitch in her side. She limped around the stable a bit to loosen her rapidly tightening muscles. "Wait, Ly—Levi has a horse, right?"

"He does." Lyall nodded.

Joanna gestured to one of the stalls. The door was open and inside the cobwebs had been cleared. Straw bedding was laid on the floor and fresh grass was in the feeder in lieu of proper hay. There was a pile of droppings that did not look more than a day old in the corner. "No horse." Joanna folded her arms.

"No tack either." Lyall checked the hook on the stall door where bridle and halter were meant to hang.

"Levi's gone?"

"Seems so. Probably out on another ill-fated mission for his taskmaster."

"Damn. I was hoping to have his help." Joanna swatted the open stall door so it swung lazily. "Maybe this will be better, anyway. With his bad luck we might have put him in more danger."

"We sound like a pair of lunatics." Lyall strode to one of the shuttered windows and unlatched it to peek at the courtyard. "Bad luck curses, missing miller's sons, assassinating The Ogre. This is insane."

"You saw that rainstorm. How the tent leaked even when you waxed it," Joanna countered. She walked down to the far end of the stable, getting a feel for the place. In a pinch, it was always a good idea to have a bolt hole. Any of the stable's many crannies might be a decent place to hide if things went sideways.

"Alright." She turned to the stable door. It was partially ajar, and she could see through across the courtyard to the waiting servant's door Levi had marked on the map. It was strange to see it in real life when she had pictured it so often in her mind's eye. "There's our way in." If the door was locked there was no way to tell from their side. "You ready?"

"As I'll ever be." Lyall crossed to stand beside her.

Joanna's heart thundered against her ribs like a horse ready to bolt as she bent her knees, braced for a moment, then dashed out of the stable towards the small door.

She slammed against the wall beside the door, reaching down and testing the latch. The latch gave under her hand and the door swung open. She gave Lyall a look that she hoped expressed her elation. *We're going INSIDE The Ogre's castle!* It was exceedingly difficult not to charge down the hallway like a child about to discover a lifetime supply of cakes. If she had only known it would be this easy all those years. All that time wasted chasing Shades when she could have done this.

Lyall shut the door with meticulous quiet, and the pair moved on. Already Joanna could sense something was off. It prickled at the edge of her mind, but she couldn't put her finger on what it was. The hallway seemed completely ordinary. Joanna had seen ones just like it in her own home. She blinked, wondering if a mote of dust had found its way into her eye.

It was Lyall who put his finger on it. "The shadows…" he breathed.

"What about them?" Joanna grabbed her sword hilts. She had her blades half drawn before she followed her friend's gesture with her eyes.

"Wait…no. You're right!" She squinted. The hallway was poorly lit and shadows should have stretched behind each small table or sconce. Instead, there were odd gaps of impossible lightness where shadows should have been. Joanna's heart tightened like a fist. She spoke so quietly she wasn't certain Lyall even heard her. "That's where he gets them. He uses real shadows to make his soldiers. He magics them to be something else, just like Levi said he could transform chairs…or himself."

"It must be." Lyall let out a slow breath. He extended a hand, checking that his own shadow was still intact. "I don't think I like magic, Jo."

"Come on," Joanna hissed. She slid her twin blades from their sheaths as silently as she could. Lyall pulled his own sword free, but didn't unsling his shield just yet. He knew it could hamper his movement in the narrow hallways.

Joanna laid out Levi's map in her mind's eye. She had hoped to make for Levi's room to rendezvous with the man, but she guessed they would find it empty. Perhaps they could still hole up there, in case they were unable to deal with The Ogre that night. The thought of slinking up behind the long-hated mage as he slept, raising one of her twin blades and driving it down into his spine, surged in Joanna like ice water under her skin. Equal parts anticipation and revulsion. The image in her head of his very human blood bubbling up around her sword's edge was unsettling. She had always pictured herself slaying a monster, and thus far had allowed her excitement over the plan to override the knowledge that she'd have to kill a man while he slept. She swallowed the glacial lump in her throat and set her jaw.

Lyall grasped at Joanna's shoulder and met her eyes, then flicked his sword tip upwards asking if they intended to head towards Levi's room or down to seek out The Ogre in his workroom. Joanna thought for a long moment. Every minute they stayed in the castle was another minute they could be stumbled upon by the Shades or The Ogre himself. She knew it was risky to head straight for his sanctuary. The Ogre left his study for dinner, and Levi had neglected to leave an exact time for the meal written on his instructions. Perhaps it varied.

Joanna paused. Raising her nose, she tried to seek out the scent of baking bread or meats fresh from the oven. All she smelled was the cool odor of the disused hall and candles.

She kicked herself inwardly that she had not imagined a scenario in which the miller's son might be away. Between Levi and the Shades, The Ogre was going to do a lot of harm to her kingdom without lifting a finger. This made Joanna's heart pound all the faster with anger. And anger fueled her resolve. Her hands clenched around the hilts of her twin swords, the metal thirsty for their first drink of Ogre's blood.

"We're going to find him *now*," she hissed.

Lyall raised both eyebrows but didn't argue. Silently she thanked the gods for Lyall. She couldn't imagine creeping through a dangerous castle seeking a deadly foe without him.

The servant's hall was long with plenty of doors leading off and down to various rooms. Joanna knew most of them by heart thanks to Levi. This one led to dormitories, and this one to the kitchen, another led to a laundry room. It was strange to be in a castle that was so utterly still. No maids hurried about their tasks, chatting to one another. No guards patrolled or footmen bustled. The castle was as dead as its owner soon would be.

No Shades leaped from behind half-closed doors or snatched at them from hiding places. Joanna stopped, reaching the end of the hall at last. A white door whose panels had been decorated with fading painted flowers stood between her and the castle proper. She knew it led to the grand entrance. The massive room with few furnishings and access to the main stairs would leave them completely exposed, but she planned to dart across and reach another servant's way beside the stairs before anything could spot her.

Pushing the door open with her shoulder, the copper knob cool against her palm, Joanna peered out. Her eyes went wide. "Gods…" she exhaled.

"What?" Lyall pushed closer and peered through the gap over the top of Joanna's head. "Gods indeed. That is…unsettling."

The room was darkened without the sunlight that might stream through the high windows during the day, but was somehow completely without shadows. "It doesn't look real," Joanna breathed. "Like someone drew a picture and forgot the shading to give it depth." She blinked, shook her head, her mind struggling to process what her eyes took in. She half expected to step out and run into a painted wall instead of an opening.

"Jo?" Lyall asked.

Joanna squeezed her eyes shut. She was here to kill The Ogre. No amount of odd magic and missing shadows could stop her.

Her skin prickled, and she barely recognized it as magic. It had been there before, on the balcony with Prosper, though The Ogre's was different. Like frost on bare flesh. Taking a big breath, she opened her eyes and stepped into the strange room. The urge to keep close to the walls was strong, even though there would be no darkness to conceal her.

There was not a scrap of shadow in this room. She only had her gentle footfalls and her fingertips brushing the plaster to assure her that the wall was real. Her thoughts were so muddled and disoriented by the place that she didn't notice they were not alone until a stranger's voice rang out.

"Hello there."

Joanna's head snapped up, and she followed the sound to the grand staircase. A man stood at the top attired in a fine, green velvet coat with white ruffled sleeves, several years out of fashion. He looked to be only a bit taller than Joanna, with a slim build and stern glare on his inscrutable features. His black hair was slicked back with some kind of oil, which only added to his stern countenance. He watched Joanna curiously and clasped slender hands before himself.

"Jo," Lyall whispered. Grabbing the back of her armor, he made to pull her out the way they had come.

"No." She stayed him with a gesture. Her swords were in her hands, and she was filled with a wild confidence.

This fellow was nothing! A slip of a creature who could pose no threat. Now she wouldn't have to stab him in the dark. She'd face him like a warrior, and it was better than she could have imagined. Somewhere inside, a wiser part of her screamed for caution. That this man was in possession of powerful magics. But that logical voice was overridden by her wild, deadly side that cried for blood and destiny.

She strode towards the foot of the stairs, fearless and commanding. Lyall came along, but she could sense his uncertainty. He had pulled his sword from his back and strapped it hurriedly to his arm.

"What brings you to my home? And why, may I ask, did you elect not to use the front door?" the stranger asked.

How could this be The Ogre? True, she had not met many mages, but this was a strikingly unimpressive specimen. Could this man truly have ousted the entire Carabas family? Levi had said that the monster took the form of a human, but why would he choose such a nonthreatening one? She raised her voice to match the man's confidence. "We were hoping to catch The Ogre unawares."

"Jo..." Lyall cautioned again. She could see him readying his shield out of the corner of her eye.

"Were you?" The green-clad man raised an eyebrow and smiled faintly. "Brave of you. No one else has come to visit me in some time, and certainly not with such malicious intent. No one dares." Joanna made a quick study of the man's waxen face. There was not so much as a twitch or a tell when he lied about not having visitors. She knew better than to mention Levi. "Perhaps if you were more hospitable," she suggested.

"I have no desire to be hospitable to people who are of no use to me." The man leaned casually against the railing, his coat draping dramatically. "The pair of you are useless. Not a shred of magic in you. Instead you brought swords? You planned to attack the only mage in the land with simple blades, did you?"

"We do with what we have," Joanna said, letting a smirk cross her lips. *Play it confident. Plan your next move.* She sidestepped slowly, centering herself at the bottom of the stairs. Lyall stayed where he was. If The Ogre charged down at them now, he could only strike at one of them and the other would flank.

She could feel the mage's attention on her. It was like being watched by a venomous snake. Her blood thundered in her ears.

"I've seen you, you know?" The man dismissively examined a fingernail. "You must have guessed who I am, and I know exactly who you are."

"Who am I?" Joanna calculated how fast she could make it up the stairs. Without shadows, the steps lacked dimension and it took more focus than usual to plot her path.

The Ogre waved his hand dismissively. "You're the meddler. The troublemaker. *The People's Protector.*" He spat the last words as though they were a hunk of phlegm in the back of his throat. His nose wrinkled and his face twisted with disgust, losing its flawless smoothness. "I don't know why you bother. All those people? Useless. All of you so painfully ordinary."

"You've been doing a great deal of harm to those ordinary people," Joanna pointed out. "And as you said, I am their champion, so I intend to stop you. In any way necessary." She narrowed her eyes, raising one of her twin blades for emphasis. This was enough talk. She had to act before her enemy did. She could almost hear her old fighting teacher shouting, *"Move, girl!"*

She should charge now, perhaps surprise him with a straight-on assault, but there was magic to contend with, and she wasn't certain what powers he might have besides transformation. What if he could blast her back with a fireball to the chest? She's seen that kind of magic in stories.

"I can see we can dispense with these insincere niceties." The Ogre smiled once more before his face twisted again, this time unnaturally.

Before Joanna's eyes, the small man began to change. To transform. Her breath caught in her throat, and she took an involuntary step back, eyes and mouth wide with awe and horror. This was no simple wind magic practiced to amuse, this was the whole hurricane. What once had been an unimpressive human being was now a grotesque mass of roiling flesh and jutting bones. Halfway between what it had once been, and something deeply horrifying.

Joanna could feel the magic around her, like frost on her skin. Was Lyall still in position? This was it. This was when she would slay The Ogre. Even as she braced to fight, her muscles warming to the familiar stance, her resolve drained away replaced by unwelcome fear.

Magic like talons of ice sliced across her skin, though they left no mark. She clenched her jaw so tightly it was painful.

The mammoth creature at the top of the stairs looked down at Joanna with small, green eyes like pinpricks of emerald in a mask of fleshy wrinkles. Huge tusks sprouted from The Ogre's lower jaw and one of its hands looked as though it could fit all the way around Joanna's ribs. It was apelike, leaning forward on meaty knuckles, huffing hot breath from a boar's nose.

A Shade struck Joanna from the side.

Its slim claws raked her armor, and several metal scales ripped free, scattering to the floor. The attack did not reach her skin, but Joanna staggered and nearly fell. It shocked her into motion at last, but not soon enough. She raised her blades, pivoting instinctively to follow the Shade. In that moment The Ogre barreled down the stairs like a boulder down a steep hill.

The sound of its coming was like a stampede of bulls rather than one beast, and it crashed into Joanna, smashing her to the floor and sending the air from her lungs.

The monster's momentum carried it over the prone princess. It was a miracle its heavy limbs missed her. Sliding across the smooth marble, The Ogre collided with the heavy front doors. It was a testament to their construction that they did not splinter.

It was all Joanna could do to roll onto her side, struggling for a breath. She heard The Ogre near her head. Each step of its heavy paws was thunderous, and too close to her ears. She was certain each vibration meant her death. She still had her blades, she realized gratefully, and if she had any air inside her she might have been able to lash out towards the foe. Her vision swam, and she struggled to angle herself so her swords at least pointed at the creature.

The Shade that had attacked her dove again, and Joanna rolled once more, finally catching a good breath in the motion. She scrambled to all fours and slashed at the Shade. She only managed to catch its tail as it slithered along the ground.

She heard Lyall's battle cry and the rattle of armor as he charged The Ogre's exposed side. She caught the white flash of metal as his sword came down.

The Ogre swung a tree-trunk forelimb and slammed Lyall back, sending him crashing to the floor on his side. He sprang up at once to charge once more. If he had been wearing heavier armor, this would have been impossible.

Another Shade appeared, and a third, rushing in from doorways, slipping through windows, slithering gracefully and silently into the fray.

Joanna collected her legs under her, leaping towards one of the approaching Shades and driving both her blades into it. It writhed back, the holes where eyes should be seeming to stare in bafflement as she yanked her swords away from one another and sliced the creature in two

She was used to fighting Shades. Used to how they moved, their every attack. Fighting them was muscle memory. The first Shade was nothing but wispy remnants in the air; tattered cloth caught on a breeze. Even as she turned to the next two Shades, she did her best to keep an eye on Lyall and The Ogre, and she didn't like what she saw.

"Jo!" The Ogre had pinned Lyall against the wall and floor and was pressing its giant paw down on the man's desperately upraised shield. Lyall snarled with effort, bracing both arms and legs against his shield so as not to be crushed.

Joanna stepped artfully, disengaging from the Shades with a few expert flicks on her twin swords. She let out a roar as she charged, slicing The Ogre's side, sliding as its blood splashed onto the already slick floor. The Ogre's blood was red as any human's. She had half expected it to be black, or perhaps a putrid green, the color of pond scum.

The Ogre swung an arm back, swatting at Joanna like a bothersome fly. It was a clumsy try, and she ducked the flailing limb easily, thrusting a sword upwards, slicing the monster's palm.

A Shade smashed into Joanna's back, shoving her down onto all fours. She cursed as she landed hard. She could fight one or the other, but battling The Ogre and his minions at the same time was proving impossible.

Her swords clattered against the floor, but she kept hold of them, crushing her fingers under her weight. She somersaulted to her left as The Ogre turned, still holding Lyall down with one hand, swatting at Joanna with the other. A blow glanced off her hip, and she grimaced as more of her armor was torn away. Every movement, every blow, echoed in the grand hall like thunderclaps and rattled in Joanna's skull. Some twisted part of her was still elated, and she almost laughed. She'd hurt it. She'd wounded The Ogre!

Before her eyes The Ogre's skin roiled, bones shifting and cracking below the surface of his flesh. And it wasn't The Ogre anymore. It was a massive hound the size of a pony. A square-headed, slathering thing with teeth as big as her hand. This was so unexpected Joanna staggered back. The hound grabbed her arm in its mouth. It was faster than The Ogre's previous form, and graceful.

Its jaws were like a vice against her armor, but there was no way it could penetrate the plate she had chosen to protect her limbs.

Her mind hadn't quite caught up with the transformation. That the dog was scrabbling at her with claws that had moments before been blunt, monstrous paws. The Shades used her bafflement to their advantage. One swiped at the back of her head, and she gasped in pain as blood trickled from her hair and down the back of her neck.

Lyall, free now that The Ogre had changed form, scrambled to his feet and surged towards Joanna and the dog. He smashed the creature to the side with his shield.

The dog yelped and skittered across the floor, claws struggling for purchase.

"Jo?" Lyall asked, checking her with a quick glance before he stabbed an oncoming Shade and sliced it apart in a single, deft motion.

She met his eyes for a bare moment and nodded. Her head throbbed, but it was only a cut. It could be ignored. The pair pivoted, back to back as they defended themselves from the Shades' latest attack. This time the creatures dove in as a unit, lashing with their claw-hands, reaching for any part of the fighters that wasn't armored. Joanna and Lyall slashed them to cloudy ribbons in moments.

Lyall let out a snarl of pain and bumped clumsily into her. Joanna turned and grabbed his arms as he tilted sideways.

The dog had become a huge boar, charging in and burying a tusk into Lyall's side. His armor did little to stop the tusk, and the boar swung its head, ripping the wound open further.

Joanna darted to the left and brought her sword down with all her strength on the creature's head. She opened an ugly gash across its face, and it squealed, recoiling, trailing hot blood. Lyall sagged, hand to his side, gasping.

Joanna grasped at his arm and angled them both so she stood between him and the boar. She caught one of the Shades out of the corner of her eye and lashed at it without needing to look. She saw fragments of it fluttering free. It retreated like its brethren, too tattered to fight on.

The boar transformed again, this time into a bull. Blood still ran from its wounded face, but its green eyes flashed with deadly intent.

Joanna cursed, pushing Lyall behind her as she tried to maneuver them into a better position. The bull lowered its great head and charged.

Joanna kicked behind herself, knocking Lyall's feet from under him. She heard him land with a grunt as she too dropped to her knees, blades upraised. The bull's horns missed her entirely, though one of its hooves smashed into her thigh and she slashed up towards its throat.

One of her swords lodged in the creature's chest, and she let it go, managing to keep hold of the other as the bull flailed with club-like hooves, inches from her nose. Joanna roared in pain and rage when a hoof caught her leg. She tucked her legs in and had the notion that she should grab for Lyall's shield, which, like her friend, was beneath her body, but she did not have time. Another hoof came across her face. Her head exploded with pain, her vision blurred and tilted drastically before everything went black.

Part 5

Boots

Some time earlier.

Boots was in a fine mood when he and Levi returned to The Ogre's castle. This was especially surprising considering their latest misadventure had involved animal dung, Boots nearly being stampeded by some especially cross sheep, and Levi capping the whole thing off by landing himself in a pond. After that more rain had come, but with it came the princess-human. She and her people pulled Levi out of the pond and gave him a nice shelter. Boots enjoyed visiting with the men, who all adored him appropriately.

Boots hung back, ears flattened and tail lowered, as Levi opened the little side door to The Ogre's home. It wasn't likely that the cat-hating mage would meet them, but he didn't care to risk it. Boots was ever vigilant to hide from The Ogre. The magic that followed the man around stung like frostbite and made Boots' skin crawl and his whiskers twitch. Not to mention that any time The Ogre caught sight of a cat, he had a tendency to shout and throw things. Boots had nearly been taken out by a well-aimed goblet one day when he had been unwary about his napping spot. The breakfast room had such good sunbeams.

Levi crossed the room, glancing down at Boots following on his heels. "Sticking with me today?"

The cat ignored him, picking up speed and heading for the bedroom before their hateful host could make an appearance.

Boots spent the rest of the afternoon and into the evening snoozing on Levi's bed, flopping around to follow the last rays of the sun and taking breaks from his naps to groom his fur into a fiery sheen.

By the time Levi joined him it was well onto dusk. The human slouched into the room looking weary and in need of some attention from his truest companion. Boots bounced lightly onto the floor and rubbed against Levi's legs as the young man attempted to reach his bed.

"Simon had a few questions for me," Levi grumbled as he pulled off his shirt, letting it fall to the floor, where Boots gave it a careful sniff. "I'm no good at lying, but I think I managed to omit enough that, if he was suspicious, he didn't know of what."

"Mer mer?" Boots chirped. *Did you bring me any leftovers from dinner?*

"I tried to play up the mess I caused at the farm, and thank the gods he didn't ask me about my clean clothes. He did seem a little distracted tonight." Levi's face brightened. "Maybe it's because Princess Joanna is beating his Shades all over the countryside."

"Mi mer?" *No dinner then?* If he was honest, Boots didn't mind. He'd go on a hunt later that night. This castle was filled with plump mice. Boots would even dine on the odd roach or spider, if the mood took him.

Levi sat at his desk and drew for a short time before hauling his mattress, which the Shades always returned to the bed while he was out, onto the floor and flopping down with a tired groan. Boots knew he could spend a few hours tucked up against his human friend before Levi's bad dreams and flailing began. As soon as Levi became too challenging to cuddle with, the cat would be off to explore the castle, raid the kitchen, and perhaps leave a few choice rewards for that Ogre scattered about the house.

Levi was not quite asleep. He petted Boots' head with a heavy hand. "Tomorrow I'll start charting the castle."

"Mer mer," the cat answered. He wasn't certain what Levi meant by this, but he hoped it would not end with more ponds or rain.

"Once I get it all drawn out and memorize Simon's routine-" He yawned cavernously. "Then I can help the princess." Boots scooted up Levi's chest and rubbed his nose against Levi's chin, purring. "Could you ever have imagined it, Boots? You and me? Two nobodies from mill country mixed up with The Ogre and the princess?"

"Mrrrfff," the cat said as he rubbed his cheek across Levi's jaw. The human had stopped petting and was staring thoughtfully at the ceiling. This was no good.

"I'll have to figure out a way to do all this without getting caught, and with my luck I probably will be spotted. Or lost. Or some combination of both."

Levi rolled onto his side, dislodging Boots who gave a disgruntled chirp. *Must you have these crises right now? I was trying to snuggle.*

The man groaned and raked his hand through his hair, making it stick up again. If Levi had a mama cat she could have smoothed his hair down for him. "How am I supposed to do this, Boots?" Levi's voice was a raspy whisper. "I can't. There's no way. I won't be able to draw the maps, and I have no idea how I am ever going to get them out of here and to the princess without Simon noticing. This is never going to work. I can't believe I said I would do it."

Boots sat still for a moment, then butted his head against Levi's arm. "Mer mer MEOW," he announced encouragingly. Whatever human problems his friend was having, certainly a pleasant, purring cat could make everything better. He attempted to tuck himself into Levi's arms once again. It was an awkward process.

Levi did not seem appropriately moved by the pep talk. Instead, he curled into a ball. The cat huffed and jammed his face between the hands that now covered Levi's face. This done, the cat wedged himself into the lee of the man's curled body, completely unwilling to be dissuaded until Levi was chuckling silently. He opened his arms and let Boots slip in before he heaved a final, dramatic sigh and closed his eyes.

The cat dozed for perhaps an hour before he was rudely wakened by Levi flailing an arm and shouting something about not wanting to go for another swim. Boots heartily agreed with this sentiment as he extricated himself. This human had proven himself entirely too prone to falling into bodies of water.

Safely clear of the miller's thrashing limbs, the cat took some time to groom himself until he was satisfied that he looked the picture of a sleek hunter.

Levi always left the door to his room slightly ajar for Boots, though the cat had no real need of this. He learned early that he might also exit and enter by way of the window. The latch was just a little hook and eye, which Boots could swat with a paw and open with ease.

He had always been good with simple, human latches. Paw at something long enough and he'd soon have his way.

Once outside on the sill, the cat might go left or right, as the distances to the next windowsills were not far for one as skillful as he. From there he could reach some thick ivy, which was good for climbing up or down. Finding another open window had posed some trouble until the cat discovered a broken one which someone had stuffed a rag into. He pushed the rag out and encountered an area for which The Ogre had little use, but which would allow the cat access to any part of the castle he wished. The family quarters.

The room the cat let himself into that night had once belonged to a little girl. There were numerous dresses and dollies—and dollies wearing dresses—all around this room. There was a miniature baby crib with two neglected dolls inside, which the mice had chewed. The mice took a liking to the stuffing inside the small mattress and had taken to gutting it. They'd had run of the whole family wing before Boots had come to ruin their fun.

Tonight he had his heart set on a particularly wily mouse.

Several hours of hunting and one dead mouse later Boots made his rounds, stopping by the kitchen. The Ogre's larder was well stocked and, as usual, not watched or tended. The cat helped himself to a shank of meat that hung to drain over a vat. It did take some effort to tear off a reasonable hunk, but it was well worth it, and the cat squatted on the stone floor, enjoying his prize.

Afterward he lapped up some cool water from a bucket beside the cookfire, which still guttered faintly. Even Shades needed the fire to prepare food, though the cat could tell from the faint, electric tingling along his skin that more than a little magic was used in the preparation.

He jumped onto the scarred preparation table and swatted at several drying herbs hanging above it, until he had dislodged and scattered them to his liking. He spent several moments gleefully chewing a bit of mint and not thinking of anything in particular.

When he was finished in the kitchen, he decided he had better check in on Levi. After all, the human had been particularly glum that evening, and his dreams might wake him. It would be best if Boots were there to calm and soothe the unfortunate with his sparkling presence. That, and Boots was in the mood for a chin scritching, and Levi was decidedly skilled at it.

Boots used the open bedroom door rather than the window this time.

He strutted around the corner and stopped short, blinking in surprise at what he saw. His fur raised and his tail puffed to twice its normal size, as he encountered not only his human, but another cat in his room.

The other cat had whiter fur than any Boots had ever seen. The stranger must spend all his time grooming. Boots stiffened his legs and made himself known with a low, throaty growl. The white cat looked up. It was sitting near Levi's head, neck gracefully dipped, one paw daring to touch Levi's temple. At least the human was still slumbering innocently.

Boots drew nearer, ears pinned, whiskers tight to his cheeks in warning. *You had better not bother that human.*

The other cat's eyes were the same reddish yellow as Boots' fur, and they glinted as though embers were trapped within. Boots stopped, stayed by those eyes. Never had he encountered another cat who could halt him in his tracks with a look.

The other cat blinked languidly, spreading its whiskers. *Hello, little brother.*

Boots lowered his head, though he maintained his defensive posture. He stood sidelong to the stranger, back arched and legs stiff. *What do you want here? This is my territory. That is my human.*

Your human?

Yes. Mine. I have been watching over him for some time now, and I would thank you to step away. Boots hissed, showing all his keenly sharp teeth.

Something about this other cat was off. It took Boots a moment to realize that the stranger had no smell. No odor at all. The most Boots could detect was the faint whiff of a spring breeze, but nothing more. *What are you?*

I am called Luck. I am the god of cats. The stranger twitched an ear as though this impossible identity was nothing to be concerned over.

You may claim to be the god of my people— Boots snarled, still not daring to attack. The stranger cat held him at bay with his stare alone. *But do not expect me to bow.*

The white cat chuckled in the feline way, with the twitch of his skin and the upward swish of his elegant tail. *You would be no true cat if you did. My feline brothers and sisters bow to no one, not even their gods.*

Boots scoffed, but hesitated. *You say you're the god of Luck? If you are, then perhaps you can help my human. He has been cursed with very bad luck. Prove you are a god and cure him.* Boots sat down, letting his fur settle. If he could not attack this other cat, then it was time for bravado.

I know of your human's affliction, the cat god said with a sad swish of his tail. *Alas, I am unable to cure him. What happened to him was natural magic, placed there by another human. The magic is buried deep and wound all around inside him like a tangled thread. Even I cannot tug it free...especially now.*

Well, what use are you then? Boots huffed. He wished he dared take his eyes from this so-called god long enough to groom himself disdainfully.

This part of the human world has been robbed of its magic. We gods, protectors of the power, must guard what still remains in the spirit world. I carry very little with me. He paused, tilting his head, considering Boots. *You may be able to help your friend, little brother.*

More than I have been? Boots asked, curious in spite of himself.

Oh yes. You have been willing to be this human's companion. So many cats do not take up such a noble calling.

Well, I am very noble. Boots puffed out his chest.

Indeed you are, the god agreed. *Do you wish to help your human and help free the land of this creature called The Ogre? The one who loathes me so much that he hates all cats? The one who steals magic from the people and keeps it as his own? The gods have hoped and hoped that a human would finally stand up to this monster, and now might be the time.*

Boots flared his whiskers. *I hate that Ogre. He kicked at me and threw things. He says he is going to help my friend, but he doesn't. He's lying about the whole thing, just like the princess-human, Joanna, said.*

Yes. I have watched over the princess as well, the cat god blinked slowly. *She is one of my sisters without fur or whisker. In her soul she is a wild cat. She will help you be rid of this Ogre, but you must aid her, and your human.* The god stood, long, well-muscled body shining iridescent white like snow in moonlight. Boots almost had to squint to look at him.

He eyed the luck god as he leaped down from Levi's mattress without making a sound and stepped gracefully up to Boots, tail raised in friendly greeting. *Will you vow to help your human overcome this Ogre and free his land at last?* the god asked again.

Er...is it hard work? Boots backed away a few steps. *Because I am already very busy.*

Nothing a fine cat like you cannot handle. The god was grinning. *Do you so vow?*

I vow. Boots said, surprised that the answer came so quickly and easily. Perhaps it was the way the stranger seemed lit from within, or that he still had no smell, even when he stood so near.

Boots might have thought himself dreaming, but he never dreamed of such things. Whatever this was, whoever this cat thought he was, it was as real as Boots' paws. If the being before him truly was a god, well then, he was about to be blessed and there could be nothing more special than that, could there?

The white cat stopped directly in front of Boots, stretched out his head, and kissed Boots between his ears. Almost as a mother cat might. *Little Brother. Fire Cat. Boots. So you may help your human and aid in his quest I grant you the gift of understanding. Understanding of the humans' ways. Understanding of their words. Understanding of their world, that you might better help them.*

Boots shook his head vigorously. It was like tiny insects tingled across his scalp where the god had kissed. He raised a paw and swatted at his ears. There were no bugs.

When he looked up there was no white cat either.

Boots stood alone in the doorway, looking across at Levi on his mattress on the floor. The only evidence that the god had been there was that Levi was sleeping peacefully for the first time. Boots groomed his ears just to be sure, and wondered what the god of luck had meant about "understanding." He didn't feel any different.

After a thorough sniff, Boots was satisfied that both he and Levi were unharmed by their godly visit. He flicked his tail in a rude gesture at the spot where the cat god had been. He might not have dared to insult the god in person, but now he was gone Boots was happy to show what he thought of the intrusion.

Finally, he settled against Levi's side and set up a robust purr, letting his eyes fall closed for a nap.

The cat did not notice anything different about himself until Levi returned from breakfast the next day. In fact, Boots had all but decided that the encounter with the impossible cat god had been a dream. He lay on the bed in a patch of morning sunlight that washed in from the window with the open latch. He was quite contented, and might have lain there all day if it suited him, but when Levi entered the room, Boots opened his eyes and raised his head.

Levi chatted away to the cat, as he went about his day. This human loved to narrate his every thought to whatever animal happened to be in earshot. Boots listened, and after a moment he realized he was truly *listening* today instead of enjoying the drone of Levi's voice.

"Simon told me he is going to be in his study all day trying to find me a new mission, so we have at least today to begin our own." The human bustled as though preparing for an expedition. He found a satchel in one of the wardrobes and stuffed it full of paper, filling a little pouch on the side with drawing implements. "I'll just be taking notes today, but who knows how long all of this will take, so I might need more paper," he explained as he worked.

The cat sat up, studying his human friend. Normally the sunbeam would be too beguiling for Levi to coax him from it with the promise of damp corridors and stalking Shades. Today, however, Boots yawned and stretched, grabbing the comforter with keen foreclaws as he arched his back before joining his human.

"I think we should be systematic about this." Levi dropped several pencils to the floor with a clatter. He bent to pick them up and thumped his head on the desk. He little seemed to notice, just rubbing the spot on his head as he continued to prepare. "I'll start in the southeast corner maybe. Should we begin at the bottom or the top of the house?" He looked at the cat as if he expected an answer.

Boots pondered for a moment, picturing the house in his mind's eye. He had never done this before, and it was an interesting experience. He envisioned himself strolling down each hallway in turn, planning the best route. It was unusual to have this kind of focus outside of a hunt. Why spend your time plotting when you weren't about to act? Today his mind wouldn't stop rolling over images of hallways and winding stairs.

He jumped to the floor to illustrate that a bottom-to-top system might be best. Levi did not seem to notice. "Mer mer!" Boots announced. He flopped onto his back and wormed around. Certainly, this would make sense to the simple human.

Levi turned and chuckled at the cat. "I know. You would rather we stayed in here and napped."

No. Start at the bottom. Down. Like this, you—! Boots rolled onto all fours again and scowled at Levi with whiskers tight against his cheeks. Were all humans so slow? He supposed that yes, they all were, only he hadn't minded until now. Before, the only thing he had needed Levi to understand was when he wanted to be petted.

What's wrong with me today? Boots wondered.

The man took in a big breath and exhaled a despondent sigh, dragging a hand through his perpetually messy hair. "I am going to get very lost today."

Boots trotted over and rubbed back and forth between Levi's ankles to encourage him. He was rewarded when Levi reached down and scratched his ears just right. The cat purred and closed his eyes, but Levi grew tired of petting long before Boots did and stepped over him. He took up the haversack stuffed to the laces with art supplies, squared his shoulders as though about to face a difficult foe, and marched out the bedroom door.

Boots sat in the young man's wake for a moment, pondering the sunbeam and why it held so little sway this morning. His mind was busier with human affairs than it had ever been. He had been contented to let Levi and the princess-human figure out this Ogre situation, but now it was obvious that he would have to actively intervene. Of course, he was a fine cat—possibly the very best cat for the job.

Levi did start at the bottom of the castle, as Boots had advised. "The lower part has more rooms." Levi took a narrow servant's stair, marking at intervals on a piece of paper. "I figure we'll start with the hard stuff, so it will only get easier."

"Mi," Boots agreed before trotting to the bottom of the stairs and waiting for Levi to join him. The human was especially careful about steps. This time there were no head-over-heels spills, but the cat was prepared to rush in with much comfort and purring once the unlucky human reached bottom.

As the pair made their way through the dark and the damp, Boots found himself guiding the human along. He knew Levi had much poorer ability to see in the low light. They had a lantern intermittently, but it kept going out. Levi burned his fingers afresh every time he tried to relight it.

The cat took to meowing to guide Levi's steps. It did not take the miller long to catch on to that, and Boots was impressed.

Even with Boots' guidance Levi had two bad falls, smacked his head against a low outcropping that neither of them saw, and managed to slam himself nose first into a wall.

Levi sat down on the dusty floor, spreading out his tattered and battered piece of paper to mark the route, and also to allow his nose to recover from its latest blow. Boots trotted over and sat beside him to receive petting as the human worked.

"I think we've seen most of the old servants' rooms on the floor above this one. I'm pretty sure those last two rooms were root cellars. One probably used to house casks of wine, judging by the smell." Levi sat forward, squinting into the gloom. "Ouch," he muttered, gingerly touching his nose. "I had better not let myself get too beat up. The Ogre will want to know where I was and why I'm black and blue."

"Mer meow mi," Boots agreed, curling his tail to rest over his feet. He did not appreciate how filthy and damp it was down there. The thought of the waiting sunbeam and a warm, dry bed was calling like a siren. If this new determination to wander dank passages was the "gift" the cat god had given him, Boots was beginning to wonder if he should ask to return it. His coat was going to take hours to adequately clean.

Their lamp was lit for the moment, so they could see a little way down the winding path ahead. The walls here were old stone that smelled of earth so long undisturbed it almost seemed to breathe. At higher levels, the castle was divided into rooms with wooden walls and panels, but down here it was all thick, well-cut stones. The true bones of the castle.

"What time do you suppose it is getting to be?" Levi asked, folding his paper as neatly as he could. "I don't want to be missed."

Boots gave his human a meaningful glower with half-lidded eyes to express exactly how ridiculous it was to ask a cat for the time.

"Perhaps just a bit more exploring," Levi said, pushing himself up from the floor and dusting his trousers, an action that only smeared the grime around more.

The pair moved on down the path, Boots in the lead. Levi whistled low and rocked back on his heels when they came to the end of the passage. "A dungeon? Well, I suppose every castle has one, eh Boots?"

The room before them was rectangular and segmented into four cells along one side. The bars looked rusty, but sturdy enough to hold, though the door to the dungeon itself was missing all together. There were still a few dented slop buckets discarded on the floor, as well as a very rickety table and chairs. Each cell housed what might have been a cot and a few rags that had perhaps been blankets. The cat could guess by the dank, earthy smell that this foul place was disused long before The Ogre took ownership. There was no scent of anything human down here. Plenty of rodents though.

Levi shuddered and rubbed his arms as he scanned the room. "Another dead end to mark on my map, I suppose." He took out his notes, which were about as crumpled, torn, and smudged as a paper could be and still be read. "There we are. Now…time to get out of here. I think I had better make an appearance someplace we're supposed to be, shouldn't I, Boots?"

"Mer mer," Boots agreed. He twined himself back and forth around the rusted cage bars. It gave him a sense of demonstrating how no one could hold him. This urge satisfied, he trotted back to the human, tail raised to say *let's go*.

"Right." Levi made a passable attempt at folding the paper, then tucked it neatly into a pocket before the lantern went out. It took an interminable amount of fumbling in blackness to get it going again.

Finally, the pair made their way back up the hall, out of the depths of the castle. As soon as the paths branched, Levi was lost, but Boots patiently guided his friend back the way they had come, with very few stops to sniff this or that mouse hole, or scent-mark some cranny. The cat mused with satisfaction that soon he would have scent ownership of the whole castle right under The Ogre's nose.

Levi followed Boots willingly, even if he was a little baffled by the cat's ability and eagerness to lead him out. Boots caught Levi staring at him with one eyebrow raised and vowed to act more like a cat for the rest of the afternoon; to sleep in whatever patch of sun suited him for as long as suited him. At this rate, people were going to start mistaking him for a dog. What a horrifying thought!

~~~~~

It took the pair over a week to map the entire castle. It might have gone faster if Levi didn't have so many luck related issues. He'd gotten caught snooping twice by The Ogre, but managed to pass it off as being lost in the castle. The cat, hiding under a table or chair, had to grudgingly admire his human in those moments.

Levi played a country dullard with uncanny accuracy, his expression vacant and sad as he apologized to The Ogre each time. Boots wasn't certain if it was Levi's acting abilities or The Ogre's willingness to see his charge as an idiot that made it easier for Levi to get away with things.

Levi toiled day and night to get the maps and The Ogre's daily schedule written up for the princess. He refused to give up. He managed to spill ink, even with his special inkwell. He tore pages so badly there was no hope of pasting them back together, and once he somehow swept an entire day's work into the fireplace where they burned to cinders in seconds as a despondent Levi could only watch. Yet each time, he returned to his desk and set to scribbling again like an insane automaton.

Boots tried to be encouraging. He sat on Levi's lap while he worked, and rubbed against his shins or demanded petting when Levi grew too frustrated. It took a great deal of time and hard work, but several copies of the documents were finished and a few of them didn't look half bad, at least as far as Boots could tell.

Levi folded them with meticulous care, as though they were made of gold leaf, and put them in a satchel. This he hid in one of the smallest castle libraries to keep them away from his bad luck until he needed them.

"Now all we have to do is find a way to get the information to the princess," Levi mused. He sat at his worktable, which was stained with ink, gouged with long scratches, and leaning very slightly to the left. The cat didn't even know how that had happened.

He jumped to the table and walked back and forth as Levi absently petted him. "I'm sure I can distribute some when Simon sends me out on my next 'mission.' He's been making rumblings about it all week, and I've been putting him off. There must be other ways I can distribute the letters so there's less chance of me destroying them."

"Meow, mer," Boots said. *I'm sure you'll think of something.*

Levi looked up, seemingly finding a different meaning in the cat's comment. "Boots? Wait! You roam all over during the day and I have no idea where you get to at night." Levi snapped his fingers, his elbow knocking the desk and sending three pencils clattering to the floor which he ignored.

Boots twitched a skeptical whisker. He did like to roam, though usually it was to hunt or to find a good place for napping. What did this insane human have in mind?

"If I make you a special little harness, next time we go out I can go one way and you another, and you can carry the papers to the princess…though she might be far away by now. Better still, you carry the message to another human with instructions to pass it on to the princess! Everyone must know what she looks like. Well—" He paused to ponder, and to breathe.

Though the rapid fire delivery of Levi's idea made Boots' head spin, he found that he understood the plan. It sounded like a lot of work on his part, and that didn't seem like a good idea. Boots didn't spend much thought on the fact that human's words made so much sense. It was like before, when he had envisioned the castle's corridors separate from himself for the first time. This new, deepening comprehension made Boots twitchy, but he listened on. What else could he do?

"Maybe I had better add a description of the princess, just in case. I wish I could draw people." Levi was ignoring Boots again, snatching a few bits of paper and and fumbling with a pencil.

"Mer mi mi, merwow MEOW!" Boots yowled. *Now just hold on! I think you're getting a little carried away!*

"It's alright, Boots. We'll figure this one out." Levi scratched Boots in his favorite spot, right at the point of his jaw. The cat closed his eyes in blissful happiness, his protest forgotten, paws kneading at the tabletop. He purred loudly. He couldn't help himself. A purr was like a song. Some cats could be stingy with their purring, but never he.

~~~~~

Levi got to work on the harness right away. He tried twine from the barn and string from the kitchen. Neither could withstand his bad luck. Boots wasn't thrilled to spend his time letting the human tangle strings around him, but he tolerated it.

The Ogre was out and about more the past few days, smiling unconvincingly and becoming more insistent that a new mission for Levi was at hand.

"Soon the curse will be broken," he assured Levi over and over. The cat watched with disgust from his hiding spot as the little mage fawned over Levi as though the miller were a jewel to be collected. Couldn't Levi see that he was being coveted rather than helped?

It was straps of leather that finally got the job done. Levi repurposed some old bridles he found in the stables and managed to make a serviceable harness. He even figured out how to add a pouch constructed from a pocket he ripped out of one of the fine coats in his wardrobe.

Boots felt very silly wearing the contraption, but the leather was durable enough. "Now you see, if you get the harness caught on something," Levi explained, grasping one of the straps that looped behind the cat's shoulder, "all you need do is wriggle out backwards."

Boots blinked at the human for a moment, then lowered his head and slithered free of the harness with ease. Feeling very clever he strutted around on the bed, refusing to be caught to have the harness put back on until Levi gave him more chin scratches.

The Ogre announced over breakfast the next morning that he had found a new job for them. Boots watched jealously as the human and mage ate, keeping himself concealed behind a large potted plant with no shadow.

The Ogre gestured enthusiastically with his fork. "One of this kingdom's main exports is wool. Sheering season is upon us, and farmers are scrambling. I know you like…"—the Ogre grimaced—"*animals,* so this job is perfect for you."

Later, as Boots followed Levi out the side door towards the stables, the human looked glum. "He was right about me and animals I suppose…but sheers?" He cut an uneasy glance at the cat. "Maybe if I just help catch the sheep."

"Mer mer!" Boots agreed as he trotted along.

"I have your harness and the papers ready for the princess." Levi patted a satchel that hung at his hip. It was only a matter of time before the shoulder strap would give way, but it was holding for the moment.

"Mi," Boots agreed.

"Once we're clear of the castle I'll put it on you and you can go your way to try to find someone. Alright? You can hunt all day and maybe someone will notice you. Hopefully you'll have given out your letter by the time you come find me in the evening." His voice was pitched high with desperate hope.

Boots thought this human was putting an awful lot of faith in a cat. Then again, Levi didn't have much choice in the matter. Perhaps his friend also had some notion that Boots was more gifted than usual these days. No ordinary mouser would be this helpful or understanding.

The man, cat, and horse made their way down the path away from the castle. Once they had crested a hill and were mostly out of sight (at least the non-magical kind), Levi stopped the horse and pulled Boots onto his lap where the cat balanced while the man fitted him with his harness. Levi tucked the papers into the pocket-pouch and closed it with a button. "There we are. Now then, Boots, off you go! Good luck!"

Boots sat for a few moments longer, contemplative. No cat likes to be told what to do, not even cats who are blessed by gods. Levi watched, hands on hips, as Boots cleaned his face, jumped from Molly's back, scent marked a clump of grass, and spent a solid minute chasing a grasshopper. As he ate the bug, he shot a look towards his human and was satisfied with the dismay on Levi's face. *Good. Let him know he can't boss me.*

You're a naughty cat, Molly huffed, glaring. *A horse knows when to do as we're told.* She leaned down and snorted warm air in Boots' face. *Be off before I step on your tail!*

Boots flopped his ears in mock disgruntlement, but trotted away into the grass, tail held high.

Humph. Gift of understanding indeed, the cat grouched as he wove through the long, green stems like a forest around him. *Some blessing this is. It's all well and good to talk about making me do this much work, but doing it? I should show him and find a sunny spot to nap instead.*

Even as he said it, Boots knew he wouldn't go through with it. He thought of Levi alone on his adventure with sheers. Hopefully the human would come back with all his fingers still attached. No, he would find someone to give this paper to as quickly as possible and hustle off to follow his unlucky companion before things got bloody.

The trouble was that The Ogre's lands were expansive, especially if you are a smallish animal, and the cat had to trot half the day to find a single soul. He came out of the grass feeling ratty and warm, into a farmer's field of beet sprouts. The field was lousy with mice, and he took some time to catch a few, enjoying a well-earned snack. He wondered what the farm cats in these parts were like if they could not be bothered to deal with the infestation. *Lazy,* Boots mused as he polished off his second mouse.

He moved on, feeling a bit better after his meal. He jogged through the field, giving the farm buildings a wide berth. There would be people there, but he also smelled a dog and had no desire for an encounter with such a creature.

Boots found the road and made his way down it, sticking to the edge in case a horse or carriage came rushing by. He needn't have worried, for this road turned out to be a quiet, country lane. The cat supposed it made sense, so close to The Ogre's lands. No one was in a hurry to travel around here. Not with so many of the nasty shadow creatures about.

"Alas the day, oh my lady fair,

I shall not see thy face,

nor touch thy golden hair!

I travel far o'er these lands

to find my fortune fine

'cross fields and golden sands!

And then I will return to you

with glittering treasures in hand,

and...

and...

what shall I rhyme with 'you'? Shoe? Blue? Askew?"

The cat pricked up his ears. The human voice was male, and it rose and fell pleasantly in song. The cat had a bit of an ear for human music. Enough to know that Levi was terrible at it, and this new fellow had some skill.

The cat left the road to seek out the voice.

He soon found the man. A lean, scarecrow of a figure in clothes that might once have been brightly-colored, but had seen too much sun and rain. He sat on a rock with a parchment draped over his thigh and a stubby pencil in hand. He mused quietly for a moment, tapping his stubbled chin with the pencil.

"Mer-wow." Boots made himself known.

The man looked down, blinking owlishly. His smile was filled with crooked teeth, but his eyes wrinkled pleasantly at the corners. "Hello there, puss puss," he said. His speaking voice was almost as melodious as the one he used for singing. He reached out a long-fingered hand, and Boots butted his head against it. "What a fine-looking cat you are. And what an odd thing you're wearing." The man tilted his head.

Boots stood still and allowed the singer to investigate the harness and then to pull the papers free. "Huh. Well then. You certainly don't see this every day." He unfolded the bedraggled pages with care, reading. "I'm to give this to the princess…a lady who carries two swords and fights Shades? The lady in armor?"

"Mew mer," Boots affirmed.

"I have to say—" The man scratched at his jaw, studying the map of The Ogre's castle with a raised eyebrow. "I have seen many odd things in my travels, but this ranks quite highly. A messenger cat. Or are you something more than a cat?"

Boots cocked his head. "Mi?"

"Are you...a god, puss puss?"

Boots puffed out his chest, smiling a wide, cat grin. "Mer meraw, mi mi," he explained in his best operatic meow. *I'm blessed by a god. What do you think of that, human?*

"You have a fine voice to boot." The man grinned again. "I suppose you aren't a god. Isn't the Luck cat supposed to be white?"

"Mrrrph," Boots huffed. He sat down and wrapped his tail around his feet. *Yes he is. And rather pushy too.*

"Well, whoever your human is, they have a very good friend in you, fine cat." The man petted Boots' head.

The cat couldn't help but let out his big purr. He'd chosen well to give his note to this human. Cat lovers were the finest people. He was certain this stranger would finish the task and see the letter get to the princess.

That was, of course, assuming the man ever happened upon the princess. Perhaps luck might favor the note now that it was away from Levi. If the cat god wanted his tasks done, he should speed things along with a little more of his power.

Boots stayed with the raggedy man for a little while, receiving petting and listening to the song he was working on, then decided the poor fellow looked half starved.

He strode off into the tall grass, following a smell he knew. A fat pheasant was picking the grasses clean of their seeds not far from where the bard was sitting. Boots made quick work of the dozy animal, clamping tooth and claw around the bird before it had a chance to fly. Though the fowl was almost as large as he was, Boots still managed to grasp it by the neck and soon he felt the snap and give of breaking bone in his powerful jaws. The bird went limp.

He dragged this prize laboriously back to the man, who looked down in utter bemusement.

"Well gods all bless! The day only gets stranger! Is this for me?"

Boots plopped the bird in front of the man and made the trilling sound that hunter cats make when they return with food for the clan. Boots' own mother had made such a sound. She had been a skilled hunter. Of course, Boots fancied she had never been skilled enough to so easily catch a pheasant. "Meow!" Boots yowled to assure his new friend that the bird was indeed a gift.

"Well thank you very much, you fine cat you!" The man picked up the bird with one hand and petted Boots' head with the other. "You wouldn't like to come with me and be my companion would you?"

"Mer mer." Boots tinged his voice with a little sadness. Once he might have taken such an invitation. Alas, now there was an unlucky man out there who might very well be chopping off his own toes this minute. Levi needed to be supervised.

"No, of course, a fine cat like you already has a human. Clearly, or you would not have come bearing letters in a special carrier. Your human is very inventive."

"Mew!" Boots agreed.

"Then, Puss with White Boots, I hope one day I shall meet you again." The man stood and swept off his patched hat in an elegant bow.

Boots swished his tail in response, spreading his whiskers magnanimously. What a pity he already had Levi to look after. This man certainly knew how to flatter a person. Levi didn't do nearly enough praising of Boots' cleverness. He butted his head against the bard's knee by way of a goodbye and sallied forth.

Feeling as smug as if he had personally seen off every mouse in the county, Boots went on his way, tail high, chest out. He knew how to get back to the main road that Levi would have taken, and would pick up the human's scent from there. He even sang himself a little tune as he strutted along.

It was dusk when Boots spotted his first sheep. It was running full tilt, bawling its head off and kicking its heels like a lamb. It rushed by too fast for Boots to stop and question it, so he picked up his pace, knowing full well where the escaped animal had come from.

Moments later Boots hid behind a squat shrub as two men on horseback and a pair of herding dogs came charging into view, their wooly quarry fleeing in every direction before them.

"Look, Grey, there's one!" the first man shouted. He whistled shrilly, and one of the dogs broke off, swerving through the long grass. "Get 'im, Sandy, before the beggar runs any further onto The Ogre's land!" He whistled again, twice this time. "Come bye, Sandy! Come bye!"

"There's two more!" the other rider shouted. "King, get 'em up, boy!" At the man's words the other herding dog shot off in the direction of a pair of sheep who obviously thought they were hiding in a patch of wild blackberries. Boots shook his head at the dimness of sheep.

He slithered from his hiding spot and moved on, belly low to the ground, ignoring both sheep and herders and keeping a lookout for a shock of blond hair and Molly's dapple grey coloration.

Several stray sheep later, Boots found his dejected-looking friend sitting astride Molly and heading in the direction of The Ogre's castle. He wasn't making any attempt to help the other men catch their escaping livestock.

Boots sprinted over and meowed up at his human. *Things went well?* At least he couldn't smell any blood on Levi.

Levi drew Molly to a stop so the cat could jump on.

"I'm sure you notice that my curse isn't broken." Levi's voice was surprisingly light for someone who had released hundreds of wooly vagabonds over the countryside. "No surprises there. Maybe I should ask Simon again why this isn't working?" He shot a glance at Boots, and the cat was taken aback by the impudence in the human's eyes. He pricked his ears forward in approval. Levi wrinkled his nose. "It's not even getting better little by little. If anything, it was worse today. I leaned against one fence and before you know it, chain reaction. Sheep everywhere. This isn't curing me." His mouth twitching in an ill-concealed smile. "On the other hand, I think the sheep were happy about it."

"MEOW!" Boots agreed heartily. He butted his head into Levi's back.

Levi's face grew more contemplative. "Of course, if I start to act suspicious, Simon might guess what the two of us have up our sleeve with the princess." He paused, reaching back and pulling Boots onto his lap. The cat let out a chirp of annoyance, but didn't fight as Levi fished his fingers into the pocket-pouch on his harness. "I see you got rid of your note. Did you give it to someone or just snag it in a shrub?"

Boots let out a trill. He'd forgotten he was wearing the harness, but now he found it annoying. He hooked a hind foot against a strap and wriggled free. The harness rested on Molly's broad, swaying back. Boots absently gnawed one of the straps until Levi took it away.

"You are a very clever cat," Levi said, stroking Boots' head. His tone was contemplative, and when Boots tipped his chin up to look at his human friend, he found an odd look in Levi's eyes. "And you seem to be even cleverer lately. Have you been holding out on me until now?"

"Mer mer." Boots gave the cat equivalent of an evasive shrug

Are you hiding something from our master? Molly asked, both her ears swiveled back to listen in.

Boots bristled. *Master? No one masters a cat and don't let anyone tell you otherwise.*

Oh, my mistake, Molly snorted sarcastically. This seemed to have distracted her from the line of questioning and Boots tucked himself more comfortably against Levi. He didn't feel like explaining his godly visit to the horse. Sure it might be fun to rub it in that he'd been "blessed" and she hadn't, but as this gift seemed only to come with more work for him, and Boots decided to keep it to himself.

~~~~~

The three returned to the castle and The Ogre sat Levi down in the parlor with the big fireplace to hear his report. Boots hid under a chair in the next room. It was dusty and the cobwebs were troublesome in his whiskers, but he wanted to keep a close eye on the mage.

He could just make out both humans through the open doorway.

"How did it go?" The Ogre asked. His magic tingled in the air in an unpleasant aura and it made Boots' nose twitch.

The kind of magic that the cat god used was like someone lightly brushing their fingers over his skin. But this stuff was like thousands of needles. As if someone was dragging claws down Boots' spine. It took all his will to stay in place. He wanted to dart out to spook that vile mage-creature and make him flail around and shout. He settled for imagining the scene, complete with The Ogre somehow falling rear end first into the coal scuttle and coming out filthy.

"It went…it went well. I think I'm closer to breaking my curse." Levi answered, blinking earnestly under The Ogre's gaze.

If he had not been hiding, Boots would have let out an un-catlike groan. Levi's words were about as convincing as a drawing of a mouse. The Ogre seemed to agree as he fixed Levi with a questioning look and one of his tight-lipped smiles. "Really?"

Levi hung his head. "No. It was the same. No change, no cure yet."

"You simply must keep trying," The Ogre insisted. Even Boots had to admit that the mage sounded encouraging.

He put a pale hand on Levi's arm. "You'll do it! Soon you'll find just the right act of kindness and your curse will be over for good."

Levi didn't respond and the cat was glad.

The Ogre looked to the fire for a moment, contemplative. "I'll find you another place to help soon."

~~~~

Boots was relieved when dinner was finished, and Levi retired to his room at last. Boots was already on the bed when the human entered.

Levi took the little harness out of his pocket and set it on his desk. "I have to make a few repairs." He opened a drawer and selected some of the small tools he had found and made. Even with such harmless tools as these, he still managed to pinch his fingers and cut his hands. He little noticed, stopping once or twice to hold a bit of cloth to his newest scratch before he pressed on with his work.

Boots hopped up and sat on the desk, watchful. For someone with such large hands, Levi was fast and skilled with his. There was always that little pang of jealousy for someone who had thumbs. If not for the bad luck this human could be a wonderful bridle maker, or architect, or anything else that suited him. The cat saw little need of those jobs when there was a warm patch of sunshine and enough food to be had, but humans liked to keep occupied.

He wrinkled his nose at the thought. More of that "understanding" that the god had given him? Now he was contemplating human jobs? Disgusting. To take his mind off such things, Boots thrust a hind leg into the air and began to give his nethers a good cleaning.

"Here we go." Levi raised the freshly repaired harness. "Let's try it on to make sure it's right."

The human rudely grabbed Boots away from his washing and set him on all four feet. The harness was slid over Boots' head, the straps fitting behind each foreleg. Boots wished he could just slither back out and continue his washing over on the bed, but instead he tolerated the situation.

What did that god do to me? he thought bitterly, as he was jostled this way or that while Levi looked for flaws or breaks in the leather strapping.

"There." Levi took his hands away. "Tomorrow I'll give you another note to take out and whenever you are ready to go for a roam about, you can find another human to give it to." He slipped the harness off the cat and set it carefully aside, crossing the room to get as far from the project as he could.

Boots leaped away and sat on the windowsill to finish grooming by moonlight. As much as he wanted to continue helping Levi, he had officially reached his threshold for being manhandled.

Levi dragged the mattress down to the floor and settled in to sleep. Boots sat glaring for what he decided was sufficient time to make the human sorry for being so demanding, then he hopped down and tucked himself into Levi's arms.

For a week or more the cat was sent out with messages. While Levi awaited his next assignment with trepidation, Boots had mild success with his delivery system. Once he got caught on a branch and was obliged to wriggle free of his harness and return home empty-pawed, but Levi didn't seem to mind.

In his spare time he perfected the creation of several more harnesses. This was nothing to the small pile of failures he burned up in the fireplace to destroy the evidence, but it was enough to keep Boots able to continue his missions.

Fortunately, The Ogre had little to no interest in what Levi did with his free time. The miller's son still made certain to be seen sitting in the library reading or sketching and sometimes raiding the kitchen all the while causing mild destruction with his bad luck. The Ogre had to tidy up using magic.

As much as it rankled Boots, the mage behaved like a kindly friend. He smiled his thin smile as he cleaned up after Levi's messes, never complaining or belittling. When that happened Levi's blue eyes were so sad and solemn. Like those of a reprieved prisoner, someone certain of their own disastrous fate being told everything was alright and they could be happy again after all.

Even the cat understood the allure of someone who could make all your troubles seem like mild inconveniences that could easily be repaired.

Still, Levi put messages for the princess into the little pouch on Boots' harness time and time again, and the cat went out.

~~~~

As the early morning sun shimmered through the window, Boots lay curled on the bed enjoying a nap with his harness freshly emptied from his latest mission, when the human came in, dragging his feet and slamming the door.

Boots looked up. "Mer mer?"

Levi grimaced. "I have my next assignment."

"Mew?"

"Simon found a healer's house in a nearby village that is shorthanded. They're troubled by a sickness and Simon wants me to go lend a hand." Levi made a scoffing sound as he moved glumly to his wardrobe. "He says that this 'might just be it.' This might be my final big act of kindness."

Boots sneezed.

A small snort of laughter escaped Levi. "You're right. This is just another thing he's hoping I ruin. I'm better than Shades. No one can blame The Ogre for the messes I make. Who knows, perhaps I can manage to burn a hospital to the ground. Or carry the sickness to all the nearby villages."

"Mer mi?"

"You're right." He jabbed a finger in Boot's direction. "I could catch it myself. Some horrifying version that is ten times worse than what everyone else has. I'll add to the healer's tasks *and* infect everyone with this new plague." Levi took out his traveling pack and halfheartedly dumped clothes and supplies into it. "I can try to help with bridges or moving logs…but letting me near sick people?" Levi turned to the cat, his expression defeated.

"Mew mew raw," Boots agreed glumly.

"I could just go out, but not actually go where I am supposed to go."

"Mi!"

"But Simon will expect to hear reports of the disaster. He probably sends Shades out to check my work or watches me with his spying glass." Levi heaved a sigh and sat down hard on his chair. The seat gave a little groan, but it held.

Boots strutted over, jumped into Levi's lap and stuck his head and shoulders under Levi's arm.

"I wonder how long Simon thinks he can keep using me without my figuring it out. He can't imagine I'll keep going on these useless missions forever."

Boots flattened his ears and his whiskers back. *I would have stopped after the first time. You fell in water, remember?* He shuddered.

Levi looked at his hands. Boots followed his gaze, tracing with his eyes the little scars that were etched over the man's knuckles like tally marks. Levi grimaced, curling his fingers into fists. "I wish…I wish he hadn't been so kind to me. It's not very nice…being tricked with kindness." His face twisted as though he tasted something sour, and he sniffled. "My family was kind too, of course, but they…they were tired of me. I could tell. They've been caring for me all my life all by themselves, and they were tired. The Ogre…he can fix anything I break with a wave of his hand, and he doesn't mind. It's nice not being a bother."

"Mew mer mer mer," the cat said. *It's just that you're so sweet and trusting that people will trick you easily with kindness.* In a cat that sort of nature would be a weakness, but Levi managed to make it endearing.

"The princess was nice," Levi pointed out, as though countering an argument Boots had made. "At least she asked me to help rather than demanding I do what she said. She could have. She's the princess after all. Do you think she got any of my letters yet?"

"Mer."

"I suppose. We've no way to tell. She could never send a message back to me. It would be intercepted. I'm guessing you haven't met her in your travels, or she might have sent some note back with you."

"Mi," Boots scrambled onto Levi's lap to receive petting. *No princess-human.* It was too bad. She was nice to cats and might have been inclined to reward him with sweet cream and cheese for his troubles if he had brought her the message personally.

Levi scratched Boots in his favorite spot at the point of his jaw, and the cat purred, closing his eyes dreamily. "We'll figure it out, Boots. For now I need to decide what I am doing about today." Levi rose, dumping Boots unceremoniously from his lap. He finished stocking his traveling pack, including several bandages and a packet of pain relieving herbs he had pinched from The Ogre's supply.

Levi still had a cloud over him as he prepared Molly and they rode out from the castle.

Boots sat on Molly's rump as always, glowering up at the looming building, hoping The Ogre could see him. Hoping it would drive the mage mad to be flouted by a cat.

Levi hadn't put Boots' harness on him yet, and the cat reveled in the lightness of being without it. He let the gentle, summer breeze ruffle his whiskers. The air smelled of thick-stemmed plants growing tall and fat. The world hummed with the gentle melody of the bees at work and the ceaseless calls of songbirds. Even with his bad luck, the bees had better things to do than sting Levi, so Boots did not bother to bat at any of them.

Boots considered making a jump for some of the birds that gamboled and flirted just overhead, but decided against it. If he fancied a snack, there was no need to work so hard for it. The grasses were teeming with mice and plump shrews. Even a baby rabbit could make a meal if he could sniff one out.

He was so wrapped in his thoughts of summer and what he might like for lunch that when Levi brought Molly to a stop he nearly fell off. He just managed not to use his claws on the horse's unprotected rump. He knew Molly would never forgive him for that.

Why have we stopped? he asked.

I don't know, Molly tossed her head to free enough rein that she could snap at some grass tops. *There's nothing around here but a few wild apple trees.*

Levi slid down from Molly's back. "Oh dear," he said, too loudly. "I think I have lost the way! I had better…I had better climb a tree to check my position." He glanced at Boots and shrugged, whispering, "I don't know if he can hear with his spying crystal."

Boots cocked his head. What? Climb a tree? Lost? What was this mad human on about this time? "Mew meow?!" Boots jumped down and followed Levi, who was making his way to the tallest of the apple trees.

"Don't worry, Boots. I figured it out." There was a tremble in Levi's voice and his hands were shaking as he dropped his supply pack to the ground at the foot of the tree. He unbuckled the bag's main pouch and flipped it open before looking up. He took in a long, shuddering breath.

Boots watched in disbelief. Was this fool human seriously considering climbing a tree? This was pure insanity and clearly Levi knew it as he stood staring at the shimmering leaves above him like a man looking on his own gallows.

The cat trotted around to stand in front of Levi. "MEOW?" *Have you finally cracked?*

"I have to do this, Boots," Levi said, his voice still quiet as though he didn't want someone to hear. "I can't go to that hospital, and I can't just *claim* to have gone. I have to have some other reason. If he's watching me, he'll see that I stopped to check my direction and…had a spot of bad luck."

Boots huffed, swishing his tail. *This is a terrible idea! Come up with something else. You'll crack your idiot head open and I'll have to sit by your corpse until someone comes to collect you and... and...stupid human, what are you doing?!*

Levi stepped around the cat and grabbed the two lowest branches of the tree. He braced a foot against the trunk and froze. Boots could feel the fear rippling from his human friend like a fog before a rain.

Trees had always been a place of safety for him. He had never looked at those sturdy branches and concealing leaves as a death trap until that moment. Boots rushed to the tree, trying one more time to talk some sense into the human. "Merowow! Mer mer! Meow mi mer raw!" He scolded. He even hissed. Nothing seemed to get Levi's attention.

Fine, Boots said. *Wait a moment.* He swarmed up the trunk, stopping on a low branch. The climb was easy, and he wished that Levi had claws to hold him instead of his useless, stubby fingers. A tail wouldn't hurt either.

He yowled to get Levi's attention. *Here, stupid, grab this branch to pull yourself up.*

To Boots' surprise Levi did grab the branch in question. Though his face turned an unhealthy white, Levi chuckled, a sound completely without mirth. "I haven't climbed a tree since I was a child."

"Mer." *Stop talking.*

"I fell out, of course. Mother had to rush me to the healer. Or was it father? I think they took turns carrying me."

"Meow!" *No talking. Only climbing!*

"I suppose you have been climbing trees for a long time." Levi heaved himself up aand hooked a leg around the branch. He had strong limbs for all his lack of practice and pulled himself into place with ease.

He paused, one leg on either side of the branch, calling out again to no one. "I need to go higher to get a better view!"

What is he doing? Molly whinnied from the ground, tossing her head to watch cat and human climb.

Something foolish, Boots bounced onto the next good branch, showing Levi where to place his hands.

He could fall off of me, it would be safer! Molly said.

I don't think he wants safer! Boots yowled.

Levi climbed higher, his arms shaking. His eyes looked haunted, but he struggled upwards. Each time he came to rest on a substantial branch he breathed for several moments before continuing on. Boots was unexpectedly impressed. Levi had gotten considerably further than he would have thought, especially for someone without claws and a tail.

Levi's foot slipped and he grappled for purchase with a yell. Boots wove back and forth on the branch above, meowing encouragement. Levi hung by his hands for a moment before hooking his feet on another branch. Perhaps he should have just let himself fall. It would have been a painful landing, but not too bad. Clearly Levi was determined to get as high as possible.

Up here, human. Put your hand here!

With the cat's instruction, Levi managed to get impressively high into the tree. He was even smiling as he neared the top.

No amount of careful leadership by the cat could keep Levi's curse at bay forever.

What Boots had judged to be a perfectly healthy branch must have been dead on the inside and it snapped under Levi's feet. His falling weight jerked his hands free of their grip and, as Boots watched in fascinated horror, the human tumbled to earth like a sack of grain. His attempts to catch himself on other branches made things worse. He hit the ground with a thud and a sickening crunch.

Levi yelled in pain, writhing on the ground, kicking up dust.

Boots scrambled down at speed, and Molly hurried over and put her nose against the human, rumbling gently. Levi clutched his shoulder and alternated growling between his teeth and yelling senselessly. Boots didn't know what to do. He stood clear of the human's writhing legs, watching with deep concern. The horse was more helpful, allowing Levi to twine his cut and scratched fingers into her mane and tug, even though it must have been unpleasant for her.

"Ow. Owowowow hahahahaha!"

Is he laughing? Boots asked, ears pinned. *I didn't think he landed on his head.*

He didn't, Molly agreed, brushing her soft lips across Levi's face and through his hair, checking for blood like a mother mare with her foal.

Levi's laughter had a hysterical edge and was punctuated with bursts of "Owowowowow!"

Both animals watched him with confusion and worry. Finally Levi took a deep breath and stopped, using Molly to help himself sit up. "I think I broke my collarbone," he told Boots between gritted teeth.

Yes. Probably. And why? Because you're an idiot! The cat yowled in Levi's face.

411

"This is good, Boots," Levi whispered, nudging his traveling pack closer to himself with his foot. "I can go back to Simon and tell him that I would have completed my mission, but I hurt myself. He'll fix me right up and I won't have to go to that healer's house. At least not today. Ow. Gods that smarts." Levi paused and rocked forward, hand clasped to his shoulder. Sweat beaded at the ends of his hair and dripped with each motion of his head. His arms were latticed with shallow cuts where branches had lashed him in his descent.

Boots trotted over to the traveling pack and stuck his muzzle inside, pulling out the little pouch of herbs. He dropped it on Levi's lap.

The human looked up, face twisting in confusion rather than pain. "How did you—? Never mind. Don't ask questions," Levi said, seemingly more to himself. He took the packet in his good hand and pulled the little leather string with his teeth, dumping some of the contents into his mouth and the rest down the front of his shirt. Then he sat for a few minutes, chewing reflectively.

Boots glowered, tail tip twitching with disgust.

Finally, Levi spat a green wad of well chewed herbs onto the grass.

With a determined grimace he grabbed the back of Molly's neck and, with help from the horse, levered himself upright. "If I had been smart I would have made a sling before I climbed," Levi rasped, almost as if he were whispering sweet promises in Molly's ear. "I suppose I had no way of knowing I'd hurt my arm."

Exactly, Boots huffed. *What if you had broken your legs? Or your idiot neck?*

Levi scooped up the traveling pack. After some fumbling, he managed to get one of the straps off and buckled it to itself to form a loop. Boots was reminded of his own harness as Levi put the loop over his head and tucked his injured arm into it. "I suppose this will snap eventually, but for now it'll do. Now…how to get back onto the horse?"

They had no saddle for Molly. Boots jumped easily to the tree, then to Molly's rump where he chattered grouchily at the human. *If you hadn't been so determined to hurt yourself, you could have jumped back on just like that.*

Of course, even Boots knew that wasn't true. Levi would have still ended up on his backside in the dirt if he had tried to be so graceful. Still, the cat was in a berating mood. Levi began hunting around them in the long grass. "Here we go," he called, waving at the two animals from a little distance away.

Molly plodded over to join him, Boots still perched on her back like a judgmental decoration. Levi had found a tallish rock concealed by the grass. Once the horse was near enough, he used it as a mounting block. He nearly slipped off Molly's other side, but the horse was ready. She stepped and rocked her weight gently to right the clumsy human. Boots doubted Levi even noticed her efforts. "Alright, Mol, let's go back," Levi urged, his voice tight with pain.

Boots butted Levi's back to give him a little encouragement before letting him know exactly how foolish he was with a fresh bout of yowls. When Boots was in full form he could put even baying hounds to shame.

All the way back he sang operatically about Levi's folly.

By dusk the slow threesome reached The Ogre's castle again. The sun had turned rusty red and gold as it slid away behind the hills, leaving a star-dotted trail of deep oranges that faded into majestic purple in its wake.

Boots, facing backwards on Molly's rump, enjoyed the sunset. He spread his whiskers and soaked up the warm glow as only a cat can.

Levi dismounted before he entered the front gates. He took Molly's bridle off one-handed. By some miracle his sling was still in one piece, though the traveling pack had nearly fallen apart completely, and for a while they had left a trail of clothing and food along the path.

The cat knew his human friend was in a great deal of pain, though he was doing a fine job of bearing it. Courage worthy of a cat, Boots decided as he watched the human set the horse loose in the long grass to graze for a few hours, too weary and injured to tuck her away in her stall.

Cat and man made their way through the gate and into the courtyard. As the pair neared the main doors at the front of the house and Boots prepared to hurry off and find his own, sneaky way inside, he hesitated. Something was up.

The air crackled with magic. The same, cold, unpleasant magic that The Ogre used. The atmosphere near the doors was so saturated that it made all Boots' hair stand up. "Yeow!" he warned.

Levi ignored him. Oblivious as usual. Boots flattened his ears. There was a smell now. An odor he knew well. Blood.

"YEOW!" Boots said again, trotting around to get in front of Levi.

The human nearly tripped over him, but caught himself on the door. He looked down, brows creased. "What is it, Boots?"

"Raw raw meow!" Boots darted back and forth over Levi's feet. *I don't like this. Don't go in! Let me check it out first!*

Levi didn't understand. He watched curiously as Boots, whose fur was puffed to make him look twice his normal size, marched like a sentry in front of the door. He yelled and growled, hopelessly. There was no saving some humans.

Even as Boots considered biting his friend as a viable option, Levi grasped the handle of the big door with his good hand and pushed it open.

The door swung lazily, and the cat stared, completely stunned, at the scene spread before them in the front hall. Magic coiled around the room in thick, stinging clouds that made Boots shudder.

The smell of blood was everywhere and now he knew why. Two humans lay in a heap on the floor in the far corner of the room. It took the cat a few moments to recognize them as the princess-human and her tall bodyguard. The Ogre's Shades flitted around them, making Boots ache to hiss and run for cover. Instead, he stood between Levi's legs and stared. Of all the times the princess-human could choose to make her attack on The Ogre, of course she would pick now.

Without the benefit of a keen, feline nose, Boots wasn't even certain Levi recognized the unfortunate people on the floor.

The Ogre stood over the fallen humans, a look of consideration on his narrow face. The mage too was bleeding from several places. The worst wound was a deep stab just above his collar bone, what looked to be scant inches from his jugular. The Ogre held a piece of cloth to the spot, but the rag was already completely saturated.

Levi made a sound. It may have been intended to be words, but all that escaped his mouth was a strangled, "Uuuh—"

The Ogre looked up, his eyes seemed unfocused for a moment. Boots took advantage of this, finally motivated to hide before all this magic was aimed at him. He darted in to slide behind a hanging curtain and peered out.

Levi took a few unsteady steps into the room.

"What…?" The miller managed. He had grown even paler and looked about ready to pitch over in a dead faint. The cat could only hide and hope the human managed to keep his feet and his wits. If only Levi had not been so determined to hurt himself, he could have had a clear head for this situation.

"Ah, Levi," The Ogre said in a voice that was trying to be casual, but audibly trembled. "Back so soon? What happened?"

"I…I fell. What happened here?!" Levi took a few more faltering steps. Boots let his eyes rove over the destruction. Tables were overturned and a few were utterly crushed. Streaks of blood decorated the monochrome floor. A carpet was wadded up and shredded near the wall, and the walls themselves were scoured with deep scars that looked like impossibly huge claw marks.

Shades flitted here and there trying to right the situation, but they seemed aimless. Some hovered near the ceiling, arms hanging limply at their sides, heads drooping. One repeatedly bumped itself into a fallen table and another attempted to get a three-legged chair to remain standing. The continual falling of the chair was almost rhythmic.

"Ah, yes. This." The Ogre's voice was still shaky, but he stood straight, trying to put on an air of collectedness. Boots recognized this act all too well. When a cat did something clumsy, they knew to act as dignified as possible. Boots wasn't fooled. "These people broke into my home and attempted to assassinate me. Naturally I had to deal with them." He gestured at Joanna and Lyall with a blood-smeared hand.

"I...I see," Levi managed. Boots could see that Levi's eyes were now fixed on the princess and her bodyguard where they lay. There was blood pooling around the pair, but the cat could smell that both were still alive. If only there was a way to communicate that to Levi, who still looked like a stiff breeze could send him crashing to the floor.

"Who... who are they, do you think?" Levi croaked.

"I know exactly who the woman is." The Ogre turned his sharp gaze back to the fallen pair. "That meddlesome princess who has been nothing but a thorn in my side for years. She simply must insinuate herself into all my work, and now she has taken it into her foolish head to do me in." The Ogre's face creased with deep lines of hatred.

"The...the princess? The king's only daughter?" Levi was floundering. Boots might have rolled his eyes had the situation been less dire.

"I'm afraid so. Poor, misguided, girl." The Ogre said, not noticing the miller's poorly disguised distress. "Naturally I overpowered these two imbeciles. They seem to have come alone. I cannot fathom what made them believe that facing me would be a viable option."

"Er, yes. Very foolish," Levi said. He cleared his throat. "What...what do you intend to do with them now?"

The Ogre's lip curled. "I ought to kill them. A reasonable punishment for two would-be assassins. And it would serve double purpose of reminding the king that I won't be bullied. Especially not by little girls playing at being warriors." He prodded Joanna with a toe, her tattered armor jingled faintly.

Boots twitched a whisker. The Ogre was one to talk when he bore several near deadly wounds. In cat culture both males and females were equally fierce. Boots had once known a tiny calico called 'Bloodpaw' who had won so many fights that no cat dared try her in combat. Fortunately, she had fancied Boots and he had left her with all his skin intact. Joanna was like Bloodpaw.

Boots wished he could have witnessed the battle himself as he tried to piece it together by following the scratches on the floor and the patterns of spattered blood.

"You'll kill them?" Levi clasped his arm to himself and swayed. His pale face had taken on a greenish hue.

"That is what I said, yes." The Ogre shot Levi a questioning glance.

"I was...I was just wondering if perhaps we should imprison them instead. A living princess could be a more powerful tool than a dead one." His speech slurred, but he remained standing, much to the cat's admiration.

"Oh yes?" The Ogre cocked an eyebrow. He paused, raising the saturated rag from his collarbone to check the wound. Blood oozed sluggishly from the hole and the Ogre pressed the rag back into place with a grimace. Boots wondered why he didn't heal himself.

"Are you an expert on strategy now, young Miller?" The Ogre asked.

"P-perhaps in a way. After all, I have lived my whole life finding better ways to do things so I can outwit my curse. Ways other people maybe didn't think of."

"I suppose you have." The Ogre dipped his head in ascent. "Well then, what is your plan, oh master tactician?"

Levi hesitated, clearly not expecting to have convinced The Ogre to listen so quickly. "The way…the way I see it is that the princess would never have just come here with only herself and her bodyguard. She must have had someone to ride back to her father if things went wrong. The king will be told, and he might decide to launch an all-out attack. R-revenge for his slaughtered child."

"I have my Shades for protection." The Ogre waved a hand towards the dark creatures that were still milling aimlessly around, but Boots caught a hint of unease in the mage's tone.

Levi pressed on, though he paused to pant for breath more than once. "If the king *was* to attack, he might cause serious damage to your home and definite inconvenience to your plans. He might be able to besiege you for months. We don't have unlimited food without the Shades stealing from the farmland. But if we had the princess alive, we could threaten to harm her. Show the king what we could do to his only daughter until he is forced to submit and do as you say." The words fell from Levi's lips like boulders rolling heedlessly down a hill. His eyes were wide with a desperation that an uninjured Ogre would have spotted.

Boots' claws came out involuntarily. His ears lay flat against his head, and it was all he could do not to charge. Only instinct held him back. He was the patient predator. *The cat who waits receives reward* his mother told him when she was teaching her kittens to hunt.

After an agonizingly long moment The Ogre said, "perhaps you are right." He looked almost as unsteady as Levi. "It might be better to keep them alive, at least for a while. Perhaps part of me knew it, which is why I did not slay them immediately."

"That must be it," Levi agreed, exhaling and sagging where he stood.

"I'll have them taken to the dungeon." The Ogre snapped bloody fingers, and three of his Shades swept down to hover beside him. All three were looking a bit wispier than usual.

"They need medical attention," Levi pointed out. "No good them dying a few minutes after you put them in the dungeon."

The Ogre made an annoyed harrumphing sound. He snapped at two more Shades who slithered away and returned in moments with packs of healing supplies. Boots doubted the medical capabilities of these creatures, but suspected Levi had plans to sneak down to the dungeon later.

Boots hoped everyone could last that long.

With Princess Joanna in the arms of the Shades and Lyall being supported between two more, they were carted away towards the stairs that led down into the underbelly of the castle.

The cat stayed rooted in his hiding place. Though he longed to follow and keep an eye on the pair, Levi was his main responsibility. The cat god may have given him "understanding" enough to worry, but had said nothing about actively caring for anyone extra. He had his paws full as it was.

"Clean this place up," The Ogre ordered his other Shades, who were still floating around the room like untethered kites. They moved sluggishly into action, righting fallen tables and sweeping up broken glass with their hands.

"Come along, Levi." The Ogre gestured the miller's son towards the parlor.

Once the mage was out of sight, Boots scuttled from his hiding place. The Shades little noticed him. One did turn its empty eyes in his direction, but did not approach as the cat slunk, belly to the marble, keeping close to the wall. Boots slithered unnoticed into the room where Levi and the Ogre had each found cushioned chairs to flop down upon. Both looked spent as the cat installed himself under a smaller chair by the door to watch and listen.

"They just came in and attacked you?" Levi asked, gingerly maneuvering his injured arm so it didn't brush against the winged back of his chair.

Boots could see bruising already spread across Levi's collarbone and up his neck.

"They did indeed. The insolence!" The Ogre snarled, glaring at the low fire as though he saw Joanna's face in the embers. "You would think, with my being established in this castle for so many years, people would be more accepting. Instead, they barge in here and try to kill me!" The Ogre winced, his pale face registering true pain for the first time.

"Forgive me, but," Levi spoke tentatively, "why don't you heal yourself?"

The Ogre heaved a sigh and leveled a scornful look at Levi. One that an adult might give a child who has not been paying attention at his lessons. "Magic, Levi, is not infinite—not even mine. And large magic begets large consequences."

"But surely healing the worst of your wounds—"

"Oh, I shall, lad, but I must wait a bit. The magic I use to heal is the same as my transformation spells. I do not repair a broken bone, I transform it to a whole bone once more. All magic has a price and a penalty, like a spring ever tightening, ever coiling until it cannot take the pressure and it snaps back. Use too much, spread your power too thin, and you flirt with disaster. I was obliged to transform several times defending myself from those attackers. Not to mention keeping so many Shades active. If I were to use my powers now, the magics would rebound on me."

Levi sat forward slightly, worry lining his gentle features.

Boots huffed. Why should Levi worry over the man who had just been contemplating killing the princess-human? "If you don't mind me saying," Levi said, "you should at least clean your wounds. I get hurt all the time, so I'm used to taking care of myself, and I don't know how your magic deals with infection but…"

It was all Boots could do not to yowl again. *You great idiot! Don't give our enemy advice about keeping himself alive!*

"Perhaps you're right." The Ogre whistled and a Shade slithered into the room. "Fetch us some more healing supplies."

Boots' growl began deep in his chest, but he fought it back. He pictured his mother demonstrating how to wait out a vole who had gone into its den. He imagined himself quietly perched above the hole of The Ogre in rodent form, waiting for the vile little creature to get too confident and come poking his head out.

He had caught that vole. He could turn the tide here too. *Wait. Just wait.* The end of his tail twitched a frustrated rhythm.

When the Shade returned, the cat watched with disgust as Levi tried to help The Ogre see to his injuries. Mostly the miller instructed, sometimes using his good hand to help. "How long will it be before you're able to heal us?" Levi asked.

"Some hours," The Ogre replied. He carefully spread a foul-smelling herb concoction over his wounds.

Levi slumped back, his face ashy as he clasped his arm. Levi had undoubtedly expected to be cured of his hurts as soon as he returned to the castle, but as usual, nothing was going to plan. Boots supposed that his friend was more used to things going awry anyway, but the poor man did look very uncomfortable.

The conversation died, and both Levi and The Ogre seemed content to sit and await the time that would bring their healing. Levi looked ready to fall asleep in his chair. Boots decided he was not going to wait around. It was time to investigate.

With careful slowness, he padded from under his hiding spot and slipped from the room. He trotted across the main hall with his tail unabashedly raised, ignoring the Shades that were still trying to tidy. A few drifted in his direction this time, but lost interest as the cat trotted on by.

Boots made good time to the dungeon.

Having guided Levi there to make his map, the cat had memorized the route better than he might have if he had explored it alone. Best of all he was finally free of the icy prickle of magic that pervaded the main floor. Boots decided he would rather have the dank smells and damp walls than the constant needle stabbing of The Ogre's magic.

He found the two prisoners locked away in the best cell. The little cot seemed to be mostly intact, and the bars looked sturdy, if rusty. Both humans were awake, the tall blond man sitting on the floor as the princess knelt before the medicine bag The Ogre had left them.

The princess-human, Joanna, was agitated. She did not need to have magic for the cat to feel her energy spiking. Her hands were clumsy as she sorted through the supplies, and her face was twisted into an expression of disgust and rage. At first Boots assumed that she must be furious at The Ogre. Her words proved otherwise.

"Idiot! Imbecile! What was I thinking?! You and I could take on The Ogre by ourselves when his henchmen alone have caused so much trouble for us? I'm so used to things going my way that I didn't even THINK!" She withdrew her hands from the bag and smashed the wad of bandages she was holding to the stone floor as if she meant to drive them through.

"Jo." The man called Lyall spoke. His voice was quieter, raspy. He looked small, slumped in the corner with his back against the damp wall. He held his hand to a deep wound in his side, a little blood still oozing between his pale fingers.

"Why am I such a fool?!" Joanna fell back onto the healing pack, tearing items from it without rhyme or reason.

I don't know, Boots thought. *My human fell out of a tree intentionally. You two can have a contest to see who is the bigger fool.*

"Jo, I went along with you. I'm as big of a fool as you are," said Lyall. "We need a new plan now that—"

"New plan?" Joanna snarled, stopping her digging to grasp at her hair. "Because the old plan was such a success. I shouldn't be allowed to come up with plans."

"Well one of us has to."

"It shouldn't be me. I can't believe I didn't bring more men. We could have made it work. We could have gotten four inside instead of two. Just adding two more fighters could have turned the tide. But oh no, I had to be cocky! I had to go in thinking I was going to assassinate The Ogre all on my own. I'm not an assassin! I'm the least subtle person I can think of!"

"You are certainly not being very subtle right now," Lyall pointed out, his voice thick with pain.

"The Ogre knows our plan."

"I imagine the whole countryside knows our plan the way you're shouting." Lyall's sassy grin turned into a tight grimace. "Is your new plan to shake the bars apart with your voice?"

She looked ready for another retort, but her face softened as she took him in. "Gods," she whispered. "I'm sorry Ly. I just…I just…" The fury behind her eyes seemed to die like candle flames going out. She put her head in her hands. "This is all my fault."

"Well, what are we going to do about it?" Lyall asked.

Boots approved. No use raging over something that had already happened. Time to come up with solutions.

"I don't know," Joanna returned her attention to the medical supplies. This time she took items out one by one and set them neatly on the floor. "If we live, Father is never going to let me leave the castle again. Mother will know she was wrong, encouraging me to follow my own path. They'll take my swords, my armor, my men…not that I deserve the men, since it seems I couldn't be bothered to use them."

"Jo. Stop." Lyall struggled to prop himself straighter against the slimy wall. "We're still alive, which probably means The Ogre plans to taunt your father. He's been hungry for more land for years, stealing it slowly, methodically. Wouldn't it be wonderful for him if he could snatch it up all at once? If the king *gave* it to him? We need to think of a way to work with that ambition."

"Why couldn't he have killed us?" Joanna selected some bandages and a packet of herbs from the bag.

"Speak for yourself," Lyall huffed. "I, for one, am pleased to still be alive…though if you insist on taking forever with those healing supplies, I might just shuffle off anyway."

"I'm sorry, Ly."

"Can we talk about you and your problems once we fix the hole in my side?"

"Right. Right. Gods, I'm useless today!" Joanna gave him some of the herbs to chew. The Shades had left a metal cup full of what Boots hoped was clean water. Joanna poured more of the herbs into her cupped hand and doused them in water, making a thin paste, which she gingerly applied to Lyall's wound. "I suppose we can thank Rylan for giving us all lessons in emergency healing, just in case we got separated from him."

"And we can thank The Ogre," Lyall said, breathing in jerks through his teeth, doing his best to sit still as Joanna worked. "He clearly had enough sense to know that he wouldn't have two living prisoners for long if he didn't send some supplies down with us. How's your head, Jo?"

"Fine."

"It probably isn't." Lyall reached up to brush back her hair.

Boots leaned, trying to see how bad her head wound was. He couldn't tell from his position by the door. Without thinking he took a few more steps into the room. Into the wan light of the torch that one of the Shades must have lit. He supposed if those creatures could light cookfires, they could light torches.

"You were knocked out cold," Lyall persisted as Joanna tried to shoo his hand away. She pulled him towards her by his shoulders in what almost looked like a hug. He linked his hands around the back of her neck as she wound the bandage about his ribs.

"I don't think that tusk hit any vital organs, or you wouldn't be nearly as able to keep up the back talk." She finished her bandaging and eased Lyall back against the wall.

Lyall grunted in pain, but fixed pale eyes on Joanna. "I'm serious, Jo. Take some of these herbs. We'll take turns sleeping because if you pass out and won't wake up, we'll have a larger problem."

"Fine. Fine." Joanna took a pinch of the herbs that remained and chewed them, making a face. She sat down beside Lyall against the wall. Her eyes roamed the room then came to rest. It took Boots a moment to realize she was staring at him. "Well hello there, cat," she said. "Boots, was it?"

"Mer mer," Boots raised his tail in friendly greeting. The princess's voice was no longer tinged with fury, so he felt safe approaching.

"I'll be damned." Lyall noticed the cat as well. "Was that miller here in the castle after all?"

"Mer mew mer mi," Boots explained, knowing full well they couldn't understand a word. He wished that some god would give the humans a gift of understanding as well. He trotted over to them, slipping easily between the bars.

"Hello again, master cat." Lyall petted Boots' head.

Boots butted his head into Lyall's hand appreciatively. Joanna folded her arms, tucking one of her legs up to her chest as she leaned against the damp stone. She kept the leg Boots guessed must still be paining her, stretched before her.

"If Levi was here, where was he hiding and why?" she demanded of no one in particular.

"I don't know." Lyall shrugged as Boots climbed gingerly onto his lap. "Perhaps he wanted to keep himself out of harm's way. I doubt someone with his…troubles would be any good in a fight."

"Meow," Boots agreed. The thought of Levi with a sword was horrifying. Boots envisioned himself being accidentally beheaded. His whiskers trembled at the thought.

"What if he betrayed us?" Joanna asked. "Set us up to face The Ogre? Told his master everything?"

"I suppose that is possible—ow! He bit me!" Lyall shook his hand, which Boots had given a gentle squeeze.

Don't be so sensitive, human, I didn't even draw blood, Boots huffed. He turned to the princess and fixed her with a stare. She blinked back at him, clearly surprised by the intensity of his gaze. Perhaps she could sense the intelligence behind his eyes.

*As for you, Miss princess-human. You had better be careful whom you accuse of being traitorous. You met my master. I've never seen anyone so idiotically loyal in all my days. He fell out of a tree for you…well, alright, not for **you**, but still.*

"He's in fine voice today, isn't he?" Lyall chuckled as the cat perched on his knees, giving the princess a piece of his mind.

"Alright, alright." Joanna raised her hands before her in surrender. "I am officially scolded, Master Boots."

"Mer," Boots finished. *Good. There will be no more speaking ill of my human.*

Joanna wrapped her arms around her knee and looked expectantly at the cat. "Well then, do you have a plan to get us out of this mess, Boots? As you have so many opinions this evening."

Boots sighed, nestling onto Lyall's lap to ponder the question. It was a thorny dilemma indeed. It was stupid of the humans to be injured and captured, but here they were and it couldn't be helped. Perhaps Levi would have a plan when he finally managed to drag himself down there to join them. To pass the time, Boots groomed himself as the princess and her bodyguard continued to speak in low, more reasonable tones.

~~~~~

Boots had grew weary of waiting several hours into his vigil and gone to track Levi down. He'd found the young man in his room, sitting quietly, waiting for the coast to clear. At least The Ogre had finally healed him.

"I think he's gone to bed." Levi told Boots as soon as he spotted him. "Lead the way down to the dungeons, master cat."

With arms already laden with blankets they stopped in the kitchen for Levi to fill a bag with what prepared food there was.

Boots helped himself, as usual.

Then the pair made their way down. The food pack developed a hole about halfway and several hunks of bread and some fruit fell out before Boots, who was leading the way, noticed. The floor down there was so filthy that even the cat was not surprised when Levi left the food where it had fallen. No doubt rats would carry the spoils away before the night was out. The thought made Boots' claws come out. He was not over-fond of rats. Mice were one thing, but he had seen rats almost as big as he was and had no intention of trying one in battle, especially as they often came with reinforcements.

With Levi hugging the remaining food to keep the pack in one piece, they finally came out into the thin, lonely light of the dungeons. Both Lyall and Joanna sat up excitedly. Boots watched the humans interact with a careful eye. If either of the prisoners again implied that Levi might have betrayed them, Boots was fully prepared with another lecture and perhaps more biting, if it came to that.

Levi explained to the captives where he had been all day as he distributed food. The princess claimed she was not hungry, but a glare from everyone including Boots induced her to eat a bit of bread and drink some water.

Levi settled down to sit in front of the cell, his knees touching the bars as Lyall and Joanna sat opposite him, inside their cage. Boots walked back and forth between all of them to nuzzle here or cuddle there whenever needed. The mood was somber, and Boots knew that it was up to him to keep whatever shreds of morale remained intact.

"How badly were you hurt?" Levi asked after he had finished recounting his side of the story and apologizing endlessly for not being around when the princess had arrived.

"Ly was stabbed." Joanna gestured to her friend. "I got my leg a bit stepped on, but I don't think it's broken. The muscle is just a bit…tenderized." She gingerly touched her thigh and winced. "I also got a good smack to the temple, but I'll recover. I have a hard head."

Lyall chuckled at this. "Lucky thing too. I've seen men taken out by less."

"I'm sorry the plan didn't work," Levi mumbled.

"Don't start that again," Lyall cut in. "Jo was already having a wonderful self-blame party today. I don't need two of you. I didn't bring my party clothes."

"Ly." Joanna fixed her friend with a warning look.

"What?" Lyall asked innocently, petting Boots, who had lighted in his lap for the moment. "I am the victim in all this." His attempt at a snarky grin was undercut but the greyness of his features from the loss of blood. His lips were almost purple. Still, if Lyall was conscious and able to make conversation, he must not be too bad off, Boots reasoned.

The cat knew a bit more about wounds and bleeding than any of the humans might have expected. He had been well trained in the traditional hunting method of feline-kind. It was a time-honored way that had been passed down from cat to cat to ensure minimal risk to the hunter and ultimate death of the prey. Boots' own claws and teeth were deadly sharp and tapered to very keen points. One calculated blow would puncture a vital organ. The prey would bleed on the inside as the cat artfully kept it moving, encouraging it to run, tossing it about to speed the bleeding until the animal finally weakened and died. *Perhaps the assassin should have been me, not the princess.*

"Will someone alert the king?" Levi asked of Joanna. Boots brought his attention back around to the conversation.

The princess grimaced, this time not from pain. "Yes and no. We brought my maid, Hana, with us. She will go back to fetch my father…in a week's time."

"That does give us something to work with," Lyall pointed out, resting his hand on Boots' back. "If we know the king won't come for a week, we know how long we have to keep ourselves alive."

"Oh. Grand." Joanna waved her hands then flopped them onto her lap. "What will we do exactly? Our weapons are gone and even if we did have them, are we even fit enough to fight?"

"You could," Lyall pointed out. "I might be able to help, a bit." He glanced down at his side. "I haven't soaked through my bandages yet. That's a good sign."

"You won't be healed in a week," Joanna countered. She turned to fuss over Lyall's bandages like a very angry mother hen. Boots stayed out of her way, but managed to remain on Lyall's lap.

You're very negative. Even for a cat you're negative, Boots yowled at the princess. He supposed she was used to getting her way. She defied her father daily to ride out with her men. Kittens were supposed to grow up and defy their parents. A cat that did not cause trouble for his kin was considered to be lacking in survival skills. It seemed to be different with humans, where obedience and compliance were desired traits. Boots could not imagine why.

"Maybe I could convince Simon to heal you too," Levi said, though he didn't sound as if he believed it.

Joanna laughed in a dry, choppy way that reminded Boots of a dog barking. "I somehow doubt he'd go for it. Wait—" She hesitated, hands still poised over Lyall's bandages. "You said The Ogre made you wait for healing. That's why you were so late coming down here."

"Yes," Levi said, brows creasing. "Because he'd used so much of his magic to...to fight you."

Boot's watched Joanna's face. He'd spent enough time with Levi to see the gears working behind a human's eyes. "Believe it or not," the princess said, "I've met another mage and he gave me some very interesting information about magic and what happens when too much is used."

Levi scooted further forward, grasping the rusty bars. "Yes! Consequences! Simon said something about that. That's why I had to wait so long." It was almost as though he and the princess were communing on another level, their eyes locked across the space between them.

Share with the rest of us please! Boots huffed, tucking his tail tighter around his paws and glaring at the excitable humans.

"Prosper, the mage I met before, told me that when too much magic is used and a mage spreads himself too thin, the power snaps back and could cause something disastrous."

Even Lyall was nodding along now, and Boots bristled, annoyed. He tipped back his head and let out his most operatic yowl. *Will someone tell me this plan you're cooking up in your silly, human heads?*

Levi's tone was musing. "We have a week. A week before your maid rides for the capitol. I assume it will take a few days for the king to return with soldiers?"

"Yes." Joanna nodded once. "If he comes at all. Perhaps he will figure it serves me right. Disobedient daughter that I am."

"You know your father isn't like that," Lyall snorted. "He'd come for you in a heartbeat. If for no other reason than to scold you in person."

"I know." Joanna looked at the floor. "And that would be the end of all my hopes to become the Champion of the People. If my father could even get us back from The Ogre. Father isn't a fighter. He'd throw a bunch of soldiers against the Shades, and he might win, but people will die."

"I still have a plan." Levi raised his hand tentatively. "A thought, really. An idea—"

"Yes, right!" Joanna's eyes flashed with a fiery intensity Boots found he quite enjoyed.

"I could…" Levi's cheeks flushed, and he looked everywhere but Joanna's eyes. "I could maybe help out by using my…my bad luck."

"Using your bad luck?" Lyall asked.

"Yes. I could go around the castle and try to do things." Levi shrugged, still not meeting anyone's eyes.

Joanna burst out laughing and both men stared at her. She got herself under control waving her hands in their directions "Hahaha…no no, It's just the way he said it. 'Try to do things.'"

Levi's thick brows came together. "Yes. Exactly. I'd go to the library and try to organize the books. I could head to the kitchen and try to cook something. Walk the halls and lean against some tables. Try to polish the fixtures."

"Sit in every chair!" Lyall joined in, his own pale face brightening with mirth.

The princess seemed to get her laughter in check just in time for Lyall's comment to send her into a fresh fit. It took her a good minute to stop, groaning and holding her head. She took a long breath. "So, you'll break things. I'm certain it will annoy The Ogre, but what else will it do?"

"The Ogre likes to fix the things I damage. Keep the place tidy. Any time I start to destroy something, he transforms it so it is safe for me to use. He doesn't even blink, just transforms whatever he needs." Levi explained.

Boots grinned his wide, cat grin. *That's using your head for once, human. Far better use of your "gift" than falling out of trees!*

"You'll make The Ogre use up all his magic," Lyall clarified. "Keep the well dry, as it were. One step away from whatever side effect happens if he uses too much."

"Right." Levi nodded. "I could try to push him over the edge, but he seems too careful for that. He sat with a stab wound on his neck for over two hours to spare his magic. He doesn't use it blindly."

"At least I wounded the bastard. Even if he did heal it." Joanna smirked, her hands balled into fists as though she still held her swords.

A sad expression replaced the victorious one on Levi's face.

"Mer mer?" asked Boots, abandoning Lyall's lap for his best friend's.

"I wish—" Levi ran a hand slowly from Boot's head to the white tip of his tail. "I wish there was a way without hurting him."

"Him? The Ogre?" Joanna asked.

Levi's look was as baleful as a kicked puppy's. "Yes. I know. I know he's a bad person. He hurts farmers and traders and takes people's livelihoods without a second thought. He almost killed you and Lyall. Still…"

"Still nothing," Joanna snarled. Boots was inclined to agree. "He needs to be stopped, and the only way we can keep him from slowly taking over the whole kingdom is to end his life. Even if we were to banish him, he'd just run off to another land and stock up their magic for himself. We can't imprison him. He'd transform the bars of his cell into spears and the Shades around him to soldiers."

"It's just that he was…he was kind to me when everyone else finds me annoying and troublesome." Levi admitted, still petting Boots distractedly.

"I don't find you troublesome," Joanna said. Her voice was firm. An anchor in a storm-tossed sea. Her dark eyes were more stoic than he had yet seen them. "I find you very helpful and sweet."

Levi looked up carefully through his bangs, which managed to hang over his face and stick up at the same time. Boots had to struggle not to bat at the man's messy hair like a tuft of grass.

"I rather like you as well." Lyall raised a hand weakly. "You have a bit of a luck problem, but that isn't your fault."

"It really isn't," Levi said, a bashful smile tugging the corners of his lips. "Everyone thinks it is. People think I angered the luck god or something."

If only you knew, Boots said. *Those damn god creatures seem to think you're worth keeping an eye on.*

"So." Joanna clapped her hands, drawing all the attention back to herself. "About this plan of yours. You tax The Ogre's magics and probably his patience and then what?"

"I break you out and you finish him off when he hasn't got any magic," Levi said, shrugging.

"Ah. Here I see a snag." Lyall said. "We're locked in here, and as helpful as you are, your luck is a real issue. If you tried to break us out, you would probably only hurt yourself. Perhaps you might jam the lock or otherwise render out escape more difficult."

"You're right." Levi sat back thoughtfully, resting his palms against the floor. As if to prove Lyall's point, he planted one of his hands in a moldy puddle and it slid from under him, toppling him sideways with an annoyed grunt. Boots was dumped from his lap in a highly undignified manner.

The cat scrambled to regain his composure, scuttling to the inside of the cell and sitting down to groom his paws, glowering at Levi.

"You alright?" asked Joanna.

"Fine." Levi waved off her concern. He wiped mucky water from his palm on his pant leg. His sleeve, up to his elbow, was also smeared with the stuff. "I have a lot of fresh clothes in my room. I'll toss these in the fire, so The Ogre doesn't know I was down here."

"You must go through a lot of clothes." Lyall's brows peaked sympathetically.

"I do." Levi's shook his head ruefully. "I suppose I will just have to get you the key so you can break yourselves out."

"Our weapons?" Joanna asked.

"And I'll…have to find where those are being kept and guide you there because I won't be able to carry swords and a shield without chopping off my own arm."

"How are you planning to get the key?" questioned Lyall.

"Well…I'll…I haven't figured that part out yet."

"I see."

Levi sighed, unfolding himself from his sitting position with care so as not to slip on more puddles. "Right. I'll keep thinking and planning. Don't worry. Right now I should probably get to my room. I don't want Simon suspecting I was down here talking with you, and if I am bleary-eyed tomorrow…"

"Right. Of course," Joanna started to rise to see Levi off, but as she did, she clasped her head and sat back down.

"Jo?" Lyall asked urgently.

"I'm fine. I've had head wounds before. Just a little dizzy is all." She leaned against the wall, looking towards the ceiling and blinking.

Boots strode over and butted her knee encouragingly. Then he crossed to Lyall and did the same to him.

"At least this cat is on our side," Lyall said.

And that is all you need. Boots spread his whiskers, tail raised.

"Highness?" Levi's voice quiet and small.

"I told you—" Joanna scolded. Her eyes seemed to focus again, and she limped to the bars, supporting herself against them. "Call me Joanna."

Levi didn't speak, his shoulders tense. He wavered, as if he was fighting the impulse to leave without another word.

"What is it, Levi?" Joanna urged.

"I...I didn't know there were other mages. That I had any option besides Simon."

"You didn't," Joanna soothed, her gaze soft. "Prosper left almost as soon as he came, and there was never a chance for you two to meet. You didn't fail us. You're helping us."

Levi hesitated a moment longer, then nodded tightly, a half-smile flickering on his lips.

Joanna limped back across the cage and made a monumental effort to get Lyall onto the little cot. They both ended up on the floor once again, but managed to find a dry patch to lay down a layer of the blankets Levi had brought.

"Boots," Levi turned to the cat, "stay down here and keep them warm. If anything happens, come get me, alright?"

"Mer mer," Boots agreed.

"Gods, if I didn't know better, I'd say that the cat understands you," Joanna remarked as she made Lyall more comfortable.

Levi looked at Boots for a long moment, considering him. Boots gazed back, blinking lazily. "I suppose he and I have just been together long enough that we each almost know what the other is thinking."

"Mi meow. Raw raw." *If that were true you never would have climbed that damn tree.*

"I've never seen a cat quite like Boots," Joanna commented thoughtfully. "We've had palace cats to keep down the mice, but they were never one this...intelligent seeming. You're sure he's an ordinary cat?"

Madam, I have never been, and shall never be, an ordinary cat.

Joanna's full lips quirked in a smile. "I think he knows what I'm saying too."

Boots slipped between the bars and joined Lyall on his blankets. *I'll sleep next to this one. He has the sense to keep his mouth shut.* He made a show of yawning and curling up in the crook of Lyall's elbow against his uninjured right side.

The bodyguard grinned. "Seems I'm the favorite."

Boots reached up a paw and patted Lyall's ribs. *Hush. You were doing so well.* He looked back to Levi. *And you, try not to get lost on your way to your room.*

"Goodnight, Boots," Levi said. "Take good care of them."

"He will." Joanna reached over and scratched Boots' ears. The cat raised his chin so she would find his favorite spot. As Levi disappeared from view in the dank corridor, the cat set up his biggest, most comforting purr.

"I'll sit first watch," Joanna said, needlessly arranging Lyall's blankets for the fifth time. "You sleep. I'll wake you when I need you to take over."

Lyall heaved a sigh. "Normally I'd argue, but..."

"Shhhh," Joanna soothed, touching his brow. She wore the faintest smile, though it looked like an effort. "No need to pretend you're big and tough around me. I know the truth. Go to sleep now. I have to get you back to your man in one piece."

"He will be rather annoyed already, what with you getting stab wounds put in me," Lyall said, nestling down into the blankets. Boots cuddled tighter, still purring thunderously.

"I'll have to beg his forgiveness. Perhaps I'll bring him a gift. What do you suppose he'd like?"

"Me. In one piece."

"Perfect. I happen to have one of those. Getting it to him is the only issue." Joanna pulled her good knee to her chest, looking down at Lyall's pale features with a quiet kindness Boots had not seen before.

"Ah well…if you can't get him one of those, he also likes nice hats. Ones with feathers in the brim. Says they make him look taller."

Joanna chuckled. "Right. Feathered hat. Very tall. I'll work on it."

"Good…" Lyall's voice was growing heavy.

"Go to sleep, you," Joanna instructed. "You're wasting your turn."

"Yes…Princess." Lyall's head lolled to the side. In moments his breathing changed to the slow, deep breaths of slumber.

Joanna gingerly brushed her friend's hair back from his face. "He's really just a big puppy, you know?" she told Boots.

The cat, who had been resting his chin on his tail, raised it and gazed sleepily at the princess. "Mi?" he chirped. He kept one ear turned towards the doorway, in case Levi should shout that he needed assistance.

"He pretends to be so big and tough, but you should see him with Joshua. Sweet enough to make your teeth hurt. He'd never let me say it, but I look out for him just as much as he does for me. He's my responsibility."

"Mer mer?"

"I was the first person he told when he realized that he was in love with Joshua. One of the only people he told for a long time actually, because some folks who follow the God and Goddess aren't very…understanding. My mother and father don't even know. Ly's the only person who ever truly listened to me about…about my not wanting to be married."

Boots cocked his head. Her voice was husky and quiet now. She reached over and scratched Boots' jaw again, and he kneaded his front paws into the blankets with pleasure.

Joanna chuckled as she went on, as though talking to the cat were the most natural thing she could do. "There was a time when Lyall and I didn't get along. He resented me. Why wouldn't he? Forced to be the friend of an odd, spoiled little girl that he was supposed to die for if the need arose." She wrinkled her nose at the memory. "My only friends were the ones my father assigned to me, and I was so lonely and desperate for someone. I didn't even have Hana back then, just an older woman who didn't have much to say to me. I used to follow Ly around. Sad eh?"

Mer wow? Boots asked, blinking lazily.

"There wasn't a single moment that forged us as true friends. It happened slowly. I guess I proved that all I wanted was a companion and he...well, it turned out he needed a friend just as much."

That's how cats make friends, Boots agreed, sagely. *Hatred turns slowly to trust.*

Joanna sighed and leaned her head back against the wall, watching her bodyguard's slumbering face, seemingly lost in memories now.

Boots settled in to fall asleep when something ruffled his fur. He looked up as a gentle feeling of warmth spread over him. Standing just inside the cell, calm, amber eyes unblinking, was the cat god. Boots looked to Joanna. She had not taken her eyes from Lyall. She didn't notice the celestial creature in their midst.

The cat god of Luck crossed to them on feet that did not disturb a single drop of water on the floor. His fur was, as always, immaculately, impossibly white.

These are my humans, said the god, smiling at Joanna with spread whiskers.

It was obvious Joanna did not hear his voice any more than she saw him. *Your humans?* Boots asked.

The ones who defy tradition. Who don't do as they're told. A cat does exactly as she wishes. She always finds a way. The god nodded towards Joanna. *Like your human upstairs.*

Defiant humans are all well and good, but they still seem to be a bit stuck, Boots pointed out.

So they are.

You could help them. You're a god.

The Luck cat smiled, blinking slowly. His eyes flashed like the sunset each time he opened them. Boots almost had to look away. His own eyes, merely yellow, seemed ugly compared to this cat's. He tried not to think about how dirty his own fur was.

Sadly that is not how the arrangement works, said the god. *Especially now.*

Arrangement?

Yes. We watch over the humans. We ensure balance, but seldom can we interfere directly. With all the magic drained from this land, we have even less sway. We are part of the magic, and it is the life-breath of the land. We gather it, flow through it, guide it into human vessels.

How? Boots tilted his head.

The wolves of Death are the masters of magic's river. They take the magic that is inside a human when he dies. Then, as a new child is born, we gods find them worthy or not of a drop of magic. If they are, the wolves place that drop inside the human and a new mage is born.

Do you place any magic within humans anymore? Since the Ogre?

Oh yes. We tried for many years, but no humans here can wield what they were given because The Ogre steals all but the kernel, the seed that was planted and can never be removed. Rarely, there is an anomaly like your Levi. The curse is an especially large piece of magic stitched up tight inside him, which The Ogre hungers for but cannot have.

I know all that, Boots dismissed, twitching his ears. He glanced at the princess. Even defeated, he could still see the wildness behind her eyes. *How do we help these humans succeed? Or have you simply come to sit and watch?*

You must keep helping them, the cat god said. He stepped artfully around Joanna, stopping to touch a paw, with perfect, pink pads, to her arm. Then he moved on and touched Lyall's head. *This is all I can do to help them for now, but you, Boots, can do much more.*

I suppose I need to find that key they were talking about, don't I? If it would help them.

I'm beginning to wish that you hadn't given me this "blessing," griped Boots, settling himself more snugly, wedging his body tight against Lyall who slumbered on, oblivious.

Ah, many special animals might resent their greatness at first, the god said sagely.

Flatterer, Boots harrumphed.

The god grinned. *I flatter because it works.*

Boots hated to admit it, but even if he was being manipulated, being deemed "great" by a god was bolstering for his ego. He ruffled out his fur, forgetting how dirty and matted it might be. He thought of it in the sunlight where it shone like flames. *You needn't have come to tell me. I would have found the key on my own.*

Oh, I have no doubt. I merely wished to check on the humans, said the god. *And now I shall leave them in your capable paws.*

Before Boots could answer or protest the god took two bounding leaps straight towards the wall, vanishing like mist before he so much as tickled stone with a whisker.

Boots shook his head. Some gods were simply mad. Still, finding a key sounded easy enough. He was certain he could complete it with no trouble at all.

The princess did not wake her friend to take watch a few hours later. Instead, she sat up the rest of the night in near silence. She only spoke when Boots reached out and tapped her thigh with a paw. "Sometimes a bump on the head keeps me awake instead of making me sleepy," she explained, shrugging. "And Ly needs the rest."

Boots uncurled himself from his nest at Lyall's side and crawled onto Joanna's lap, where he established himself, pushing her limbs out of his way. She chuckled and gave his jaw another good scratch. "Am I finally worthy of you, master cat?"

"Mer."

"Ah. Good."

When golden dawn light pushed through the tiny window near the ceiling—a window so small that even Boots would have had a hard time slithering through it—Lyall woke and scolded Joanna for allowing him to sleep the full night. He accused her of punishing herself. She only smiled, then turned and curled up to sleep at last.

Boots stayed with the pair for a few more hours, cuddling against Joanna as she curled around him like a crescent moon.

Finally, the cat decided it was time to find some food, relieve himself, and figure out what Levi was up to. No doubt the foolish human was attempting to fulfill the new mission he had set himself.

"Good luck, Boots," Lyall called encouragingly to the cat as he trotted away, between the bars and up the dank stairs.

"Mer merwar!" Boots called back. *You too, human.*

He stopped in the kitchen to help himself to a fresh slab of bacon that was still tinged with magic. A few Shades lingered, cleaning up from breakfast, so he had to be careful, but for the most part they still ignored him. Apparently, the uncanny servants didn't share much of their master's hatred for cats.

Boots smiled to himself with a flourish of whiskers and tail as he chewed the thick bacon and watched them from behind a coal scuttle. The Ogre was accustomed to using his powers for almost everything in his life. It was casual: as easy as snapping his fingers to get what he wanted. It would be a hard habit to break when Levi started ruining his home.

The cook fires guttered as the Shades scraped what was left of the meals into a bin. When they vanished, retreating into corners and becoming again what they truly were, Boots slipped out of his hiding place and dangled his head and forepaws into the slop bin to help himself to eggs, hunks of ham, and buttery bread to go with his bacon.

After a good grooming session to remove both food and dungeon grime, Boots hurried up the stairs. He paused near the top where he would come out into the main hall, hearing voices. Lowering himself to his belly the cat sneaked along the wall, keeping under tables and behind low hanging tapestries.

"I would send you out again, naturally." The Ogre's voice echoed around a corner and Boots' froze, ears cupped forward and tail wrapped tightly around his paws. "But with the princess here, I cannot risk you being captured by the king's men."

"Why would I be?" Levi's voice. Boots could hear the extra innocence that the young man added when he wanted The Ogre to remember he was but a humble miller's son. Boots smirked. Levi might have been a bad liar, but The Ogre was clearly foolish about people. Perhaps it was because he had been alone in his castle for so long. Or his tendency to believe himself smarter than everyone else.

Wouldn't he die at the thought that he'd be outsmarted by a cat? Boots mused with a feline smirk as he listened.

"It is a risk I would rather not take. With your luck and all," The Ogre said, his voice a little breathy. Agitated? Boots could even hear the mage's light footfalls. He was pacing.

"I suppose you're right," Levi's voice agreed, still thick with false innocence. Then there was a crashing clatter.

Boots dared to creep closer, tucking himself behind a porcelain statue of a lady carrying flowers. Now he could see a slice of the main hall. Levi had knocked over a candle holder, breaking candles and sending them spinning loose across the smooth floor.

"I'm sorry!" He knelt and scrambled around trying to pick them up, only crushing them further and making an ever-growing mess.

"Never mind." The Ogre smiled indulgently. Boots had seen humans wear such an expression when looking on a favorite pet. Levi never looked at Boots that way. The cat's stomach clenched with displeasure.

Magic thrummed briefly, like a lute string being plucked, and the candles were whole again. The Ogre gathered them in his slender hands and replaced them in the candle holder. "No harm done, lad."

"If I cannot go out, how will I perform my act of kindness and break my curse?" Levi asked. His tone struck Boots as overly dramatic, but The Ogre didn't seem to notice.

He resumed his pacing, his expression—when Boots could see it—intense and focused as a hawk that watches for a rabbit. It made Boots' skin prickle with more than just the magic still buzzing in the air.

"Never mind. We will deal with the issue of the princess and the king first, then we can worry about breaking your curse. Once that is all over, I will have much more power, much more control over the whole kingdom. You will have your pick of good deeds you wish to do." The mage stopped, patting Levi's bicep, which was twice the size of his own, in a comradely gesture. "You can be my lieutenant! That's what I've been missing! Or, perhaps even general if you play your cards right!"

Levi was clearly struggling to keep his expression blank. His mouth twitched. He managed to play it off with a wide, simpleton smile that did not reach his eyes.

The Ogre went on, a bit gleefully. "I've always wanted a loyal lieutenant! Most of the humans here about are so disloyal, but not you. You remember that I helped you when no one else would. When others treated you like a monster and a liability. Even your own family." The Ogre was rambling now, barely talking to Levi, twisting his pale hands together with either agitation or excitement, the cat couldn't tell.

"Right. A lieutenant." Levi's shoulders sagged, but he managed to keep the pain The Ogre's words had obviously caused him from his face. Luckily, The Ogre was too lost in his own world to notice Levi's lack of enthusiasm. "Is there anything I can do right away?"

"No. Not at the moment. I must keep an eye on my scrying orb and ensure my Shades are ready to fight. I must know the moment the king and his troops enter my territory."

"Alright. Perhaps I'll just...study some military tactics in the library?" Levi said, jabbing a thumb towards one of the larger libraries and taking a few shuffling steps in that direction.

"Excellent, excellent." The Ogre waved vaguely, and Levi hurried away.

Boots trotted from his hiding spot and rubbed against Levi's calf to let the human know he was there. He looked down at his cat companion. "This might be easier than we thought. Especially the part where I abuse his powers."

"Mer mer," Boots agreed, walking back and forth across Levi's feet.

"Of course I still don't know how I am going to get the dungeon key. I don't even know where The Ogre keeps it, but it isn't hanging on a peg in the maid's quarters like the rest of the keys. I suppose that would have been far too lucky for me, eh Boots?"

Don't worry about that. Boots tilted his head to look up at his human. *I'll take care of the key. You just use your very special talent to ruin as much as possible. Look. I'll help.*

Boots bounded over to the table where the candles Levi had knocked down were perfectly restored. With one swat of his paw the silver holder and candles tumbled to the floor. Boots sat in the vacated spot on the table and twitched the very end of his tail in victory as he watched the shattered candle pieces roll away.

Levi began to laugh and caught himself, glancing around nervously in case The Ogre returned to investigate the noise. When nothing happened, he gave Boots his big, eye-crinkling smile, scooped the cat up, and headed for the library for some fun.

~~~~

The next three days went by a routine. Meals with The Ogre, then time spent alone in the castle, punctuated by moments of high chaos. In the library, Levi tried to get the books down from the very highest shelf. This had ended with the entire, heavy, hardwood shelf toppling over. Unfortunately, Levi was under it, but the noise was great enough to bring a Shade to investigate.

The Ogre used his magic to restore cracked shelves and Levi's cracked rib.

There was a great deal of drama when Levi attempted to warm his own water for a bath.

Boots decided that the less said about the "kitchen incident" the better. It had involved an entire rack of lamb somehow ending up wedged in the chimney, filling much of the lower house with a greasy smoke before The Ogre was forced to investigate. Boots had to bow to Levi's skill for disaster. It would have made even the sassiest cat proud.

By the end of three days the castle was so alive with freshly used magics that Boots was constantly on edge. His only respite was when he went down to the dungeon to check on the prisoners.

While Joanna and Lyall's wounds improved bit by bit, the mood of the two captives did not. The princess was inches from a rage most of the time, while her partner was more prone to deep fugues.

A few days seemed more than the pair were able to bear locked away in the dark and cold. Boots couldn't blame them. Like cats, they hated to be trapped. Joanna especially. She limped back and forth behind the bars like a caged tiger until Lyall convinced her to sit down before her injured muscles stiffened up.

Levi was careful not to be seen going to visit the prisoners, only venturing down when Boots deemed it safe. If Levi thought it odd that he was taking advice from a cat, he didn't mention it. Instead, he'd look to Boots, who would either begin his walk to the dungeon, or commence washing himself as a signal that they would be staying where they were.

Sometimes Levi would send the cat alone with messages tucked into his special harness, or dragging a leather satchel of extra food. Boots found the second task deeply demeaning and was only willing to do it a few times.

The Ogre's mood grew almost as bad as the princess's. His smooth, easy nature was gone, replaced with worried gazes into the distance and bouts of snarled curses under his breath. Bur he still used his magic as freely and casually as a lord might ring for a servant.

When they weren't spending hours knocking over every valuable item The Ogre owned, Levi and Boots had located Joanna and Lyall's weapons piled in a small anteroom that might have once been an armory. There were empty weapon racks and what might have been a practice dummy. It had fallen on hard times with sagging limbs and its head missing.

Levi didn't dare enter, cutting a sidelong look at the cat. "You know if I got near one of those blades I'd trip and stab my eye out."

"Mer mer," Boots agreed solemnly as Levi shut the armory door.

The key issue remained the stickiest of all. Levi still searched for it daily, with no success, especially as he steered clear of The Ogre's study. Boots did not dare enter that sanctum any more than the human did, but as the days went on and the end of the week approached, the cat supposed that he would have to risk an investigation before Levi tried it.

~~~~~

Boots trotted down to the dungeon to check on the prisoners, lost in thought. A frustrating side effect of his "blessing" from the luck god was a tendency to daydream. Today he plotted his next night hunt in his mind's eye. If he waited by this or that mousehole he could catch the little creatures by surprise.

He trotted into the dungeon, still lost in thought, and stopped short. There was someone down there with the princess and her guard, and it wasn't Levi. He stopped and backed behind the opened do to watch, fur bristling and whiskers twitching.

The Ogre paced back and forth at the bars of Joanna and Lyall's cage, hands clasped behind his back. He reminded Boots of a mother cat about to reprimand her kittens for slopping hunting.

The prisoners stood, Lyall clasping Joanna's shoulder to remain upright. Both glared defiantly at their captor.

"Where is your father? Why hasn't he come?" The Ogre demanded.

"It'll take time to mobilize his troops." Joanna's tone was level, steady. Boots swished his tail in approval. "If you haven't noticed, your land is a fair journey from the castle, and my father doesn't keep his army in constant readiness."

"You're his daughter. One might think he'd hurry. I should be able to see them in my glass by now," The Ogre said. Magic flared and Boots backed a little further up the passage, ears flat against his head. He peeked through the crack above the door's hinge.

"I don't know what to tell you," Joanna shrugged.

"Perhaps he doesn't plan to come after all. Does he love you so little?" The Ogre rounded on the princess as though he'd found a soft spot to poke.

"He's…overly cautious," Lyall answered instead. Even injured he towered over both Joanna and The Ogre. "He knows you won't kill Joanna if you plan to ransom her, so he'll want to be prepared. He never does anything without a plan."

"You *know* the king will come?" There was a wheedling tone to The Ogre's words this time. Boots suspected he was trying to convince himself. He imagined that someone so used to success, slowly gaining power over all these years, would find it difficult to imagine things not going his way. Joanna had promised that his victory would march right up to his gate, after all.

"Of course he'll come." Joanna exuded confidence. Boots half believed her.

The Ogre's shoulders squared. "If he does not, or if you found some way to warn him, I will not hesitate to put an end to you." He raised a hand, crooking a finger. The stones at the back of the cell transformed. Once smooth rocks, now jutting spikes as keen as a spearpoints. They elongated, reaching towards the prisoners. Joanna and Lyall pressed themselves against the bars to avoid being impaled. "Do not doubt for one moment that you are completely in my power," The Ogre hissed.

Boots' fur bristled and he drew his whiskers back in an angry grimace.

"My father will come. How dare you question me!" Joanna's voice boomed this time, the word of a true princess and military commander. It echoed off the walls.

The Ogre's hands twitched before he collected himself and, with a flick of his fingers, returned the wall to its natural state. "The king had better start making the journey, or I will have you and your servant begging for death." The Ogre spun on his heel and marched of the dungeon.

Boots hugged the wall with his whole being as The Ogre passed, footfalls clapping rhythmically on the damp floor. The mage did not so much as glance at the cat.

Alright. Boots' claws inching out to meet the cold stone floor. *This can't go on. It's time to find that key and I am just the cat for the job.*

~~~~~

Boots waited until Levi and The Ogre settled down to a tense evening meal. Boots lingered in the doorway long enough to hear the shattering of a drinking glass and Levi's fervent apologies. Satisfied that his human was still doing his job and The Ogre was distracted, he ventured down the stairs towards The Ogre's study.

As he drew nearer to The Ogre's sanctum, he sensed the latent magic like a snake's discarded skin. It made his nose twitch.

He found the door to the study was closed. This might have daunted the cat once, but tonight he sat down, tail curled over his feet, and studied the mechanisms. It wasn't locked, merely shut. The Ogre knew Levi wouldn't invade his privacy, and he had no idea of a cat doing so.

After some consideration, Boots stood on his hind paws, forepaws against the thick wood, reaching up and fiddling with the latch. It was a tricky one, requiring pressure from above to open. Any easy task for someone with thumbs, but Boots had wit on his side.

He wrapped one paw around the handle part of the latch, then braced his hind paws against the door and dug in his claws. He half pushed, half pulled himself upwards, grasping the latch with both forepaws. Once he had a firm grip on the smooth copper, he let go with his hind claws and allowed his weight to dangle. A click from within and the door swung inward with the cat hanging from the handle like a bizarre decoration.

He dropped to the floor, wedging his face into the crack to open it further, then strutted inside.

Books were stacked all around, towering in piles like a forest of misshapen trees. It was nearly impossible to resist the temptation to knock them all over on his way, but he reminded himself that he was an extraordinary cat, and thus should not be doing silly, ordinary cat things…at least for the moment.

The room was poorly lit, but this bothered him little. His keen eyes took in each cranny and crook with ease. His nose, however, was befuddled by dust, and cobwebs caught in his whiskers. *The Ogre should try to be tidier. If he sits around in here all day, the least he could do is dust.*

Boots followed the rounded outer wall of the room, seeking any special key receptacles or hidey-holes. He checked pegs on the walls, tipped glass bowls, and peeked into mugs. Anything that a careless mage might drop a key into. It seemed The Ogre was not careless. Too trusting of Levi, perhaps, but not careless.

He wove his way inwards, towards the center of the room where most of The Ogre's magic was concentrated. There was less dust here than amongst the towering stacks. A clearing in the forest of books revealed a massive desk with feet carved to look like claws. It was accompanied by a battered armchair, and a faintly glowing orb on a pedestal. Boots could feel a gentler magic drifting from the orb, unlike The Ogre's own. He surmised that wherever the orb had come from, it was not The Ogre's creation. Perhaps he stole it from some other magical person long ago.

The cat jumped onto the desk and almost slid off the other side. The surface was covered in papers, scraps of cloth, and candles whose wax had seeped down onto the whole mess. Sheaves of paper slipped and slid under-paw like snow over ice.

Spraying a few more stray sheets onto the floor, Boots righted himself, looking down with disgust. Perhaps now The Ogre would do a bit of tidying.

The red wood of the desk was scored deeply with carved symbols and designs and Boots' paws tingled with magic if he stepped on them. The pages of thick books splayed open in every direction, ink marks and blots indicating what Boots assumed must be important lines of text. He was amused that, for all his new "understanding," he still had no idea what the ink-scratch symbols meant. The god must not have deemed reading to be crucial to his quest.

Boots swatted some more of the papers aside. Thanks to watching Levi, the cat could tell the difference between drawings and writing, and he paused to take in a colorful illustration of several animals cavorting across a page in tableau. Gods, he suspected.

A doe with a silver coat stood in a stream, head lowered to the water, apparently in conversation with a fish who had scales the bright golden hue of morning sunlight. Several rainbow-feathered birds flew above the Deer and Fish gods. Boots wondered what they were the gods of.

There were trinkets on the table as well. Necklaces with huge gemstone pendants the size of his paw nested in silver and gold beds with ponderous chains. They all looked uncomfortable to wear. There was what appeared to be a carved twig which Boots was tempted to chew on the end of beside a goblet half-filled with a crimson liquid, which smelled fruity and a bit spoiled. Boots wrinkled his nose and rifled through pens. Ink. Wax from both candles and for sealing. Two bronze seals. No key.

He might have yowled in frustration, but contained himself. *The patient hunter always gets the mouse.* Mama cat had taught him that lesson.

He centered himself, rubbing a cobweb from his whisker with a paw, then put his head down and kept searching.

Wait. There was a small, carved box at the far end of the desk he assumed would be full of more pens, as it was surrounded by them, but now he wasn't so certain. He strode confidently across the papers and books, leaving an inky track or two.

The box was about the length of his foreleg and half as wide. It was made of some white material he suspected might be bone. There were more designs he couldn't identify etched into the top and sides of the box.

He batted the lid with a paw. It wiggled but fit snugly in place. It really was a pity the god hadn't seen fit to bless him with thumbs. There was nothing for it. He would have to use the time-honored method passed down through cat generations.

After judging the trajectory carefully, he swatted the box with his paw. A good, hefty slap that scooted the box several inches.

He pricked his ears with excitement as he batted at it again, three small taps this time. There was a distinct pleasure in this impending destruction. With a wide, feline grin, he inched the little box to the edge of the table.

Bap bap bap.

He paused to savor the moment, then whacked the damned box to the floor where it landed with a satisfying clatter and the lid fell away. Boots looked down, scanning the scattered content.

There were a few little baubles, a nib for a quill pen and…there! So grey and rusted it clearly didn't belong among the other trinkets. The key!

"Damn you! I knew a cat was lurking around!"

Boots' head shot up. His heart jumped into his throat, and the fur along his spine stood up straight as straw.

The Ogre stood in the doorway, magic crackling around him, sallow face twisted with deadly rage. Boots knew he had seconds to react before he was transformed into a dead cat. He leaped from the table, scattering papers and the cup of red liquid. He landed beside the box on the messy floor. A thrown book hurtled past him, and he dove for cover.

He scooped up the key in his teeth and did his best to ignore the flavor of copper and pocket lint as he ran.

The Ogre was still shouting, but Boots wasn't paying attention. The air around him prickled with magic like knives poised over his skin.

He darted left and right through the stacks of books, feeling like electricity was jumping between each of his whiskers.

Around him the shadows peeled themselves from corners and from behind each stack. Then took on their vaguely human shapes, reaching for Boots with wispy, half-formed limbs that stretched unnaturally far.

The Ogre stopped yelling and the magic surged to a crescendo.

The cat zagged to the left, just out of the reach of the grasping tendrils of the Shades hands, his breath coming in gasps as he inhaled dust and blinked it from his watering eyes. Something big was in the room now. Boots could sense it rather than see it, just as he would know if there was a hawk overhead. He was prey and he was hunted.

It smelled at once animal and very much not. Like flesh that had been half-charred.

Boots darted around a small bookshelf, trying to make his way towards the door.

To his horror the creature he smelled was there, looming directly in his way. A hound, enormous and brown-furred, with slathering jaws and fangs the size of his paw. It sniffed the air, seeking him as the Shades coalesced all around him.

Boots paused just long enough to swipe at a reaching Shades. The wispy creature ripped like thin fabric, and the cat yowled a victory cry around the key as he dodged into the maze of books once more.

He'd hoped the hound would follow, but it remained by the door. Boots doubled back to face it, peeking from behind a marble pedestal.

The hound lowered its wedge of a head with muscular jaws, perfect for crunching a cat to bits, and waited.

Boots struck at more Shades, on the move again. He darted from cover to cover, tearing his claws through the creatures' forms, sending shredded bits of them drifting in the air like ash.

He couldn't keep up this pace, even as fit as he was. A grasping Shade managed to snag his tail. He jerked to a halt with a chirp of pain, almost dropping the key. He whipped around, claws fully extended, rending the Shade apart like tissue paper. The bit that had been a hand clung to Boots' tail for a few more seconds before drifting away, disembodied.

Boots panted around the key, his eyes wide and wild. There were no windows, no visible escape except the Ogre-guarded door. There was not so much as a mouse hole and The Ogre knew it.

Gods blast it, he was going to die in here, holding a nasty key and running around like a frightened rabbit. Worst of all he was going to die covered in dust, deprived of any dignity.

Boots turned, putting his tail to the wall, facing the oncoming Shades. He arched his back, puffed his fur as far as it would go and laid his ears so flat against his head they almost vanished. He drew back his lips in a grimace that showed off his keenly sharp teeth, clasped around the key. If he was going to go out, he would do so fighting.

I am the bane of every rodent throughout the lands! I am the firecat! The god-touched! Friend to the princess! Look on me and tremble!

He set the key at his feet and lunged for the nearest Shade, leaping into the air, flailing with all four limbs and yowling his war cry.

The Shades had never faced anything like a frenzied cat. Boots was a blur as he jumped and dove, ripping with all his claws and biting where he could. He was a tornado of blades, all edges and points. He tore a Shade to ribbons while another pulled his fur, nearly getting hold of his scruff. He shot a glance towards the door and saw that the hound-Ogre was no longer there. Hope sprang to life in his chest, but then he realized it was missing because it was coming for him.

A Shade grabbed Boots' hind leg and jerked him into the air upside down. He yowled and doubled up so he could flail with his forepaw. He left his attacker's limb in tatters, It dropped him and he landed on his feet.

Another Shade managed to score a deep scratch on the cat's hip. Boots screamed in pain and struck out wildly. Where was the hound-Ogre? Did he have time to grab up the key and run again?

"Boots!" Another voice echoed in the room.

The Ogre-hound yelped.

Levi?! Boots turned on a Shade that was trying for his tail and sliced its hand to bits. *You idiot, what are you doing here?!*

"Boots, run!" the human yelled from the doorway.

Boots scooped up the key in his mouth and rushed around several stacks of books, unable to get a clear view of the door. One of the Shades knocked a pile down, and a book struck Boots' flank. It knocked him off balance, but he scrambled up, ignoring the sharp pain that coursed up his spine.

As he rounded another pile, he was finally able to see the door. Levi was there. The foolish man had thrown himself bodily onto the

Ogre-hound and was struggling to hold it down with his weight. It writhed under him, magic sparking off in random directions. Boots knew he only had a few moments before Levi's luck kicked in and the situation turned from bad to disastrous.

Boots put on a fresh burst of speed, ignoring his injuries. He whizzed past the struggle in the doorway, barely dodging the swipe of a paw that was as big as his head.

He tore down the hall faster than he had ever run, heading for the stairs, a streak of orange fur. Shades peeled off the walls, reaching for him. He dodged right and left, gasping around the key, narrowing his eyes to slits as he focused. Behind him he heard Levi cry out in pain.

Boots zigged and zagged down each turning, hoping he remembered correctly. The Shades eventually stopped chasing and he tried not to think about why.

He came careening into the dungeon so fast he almost smashed into the cell bars. He skidded to an undignified halt, though he still had the presence of mind to be disgusted at the state of his coat. His beautiful fur was matted with dust, streaked with blood, and stuck out in unsightly clumps.

"Boots?" Lyall was awake, sitting on the little cot. He rose unsteadily, hand clasped to his side. He lurched more than walked to the bars to see the cat, who sat panting, key deposited on the floor at his feet. "Jo! Jo, get up! Something's happening!"

The princess shot awake from where she curled in a tumble of blankets in a dry spot on the floor. Boots was taken aback by her hair.

Some of the warlike bun remained, but most of her hair was a frizzled mass around her face.

"What is it, Ly?" She clearly noticed Boots yet and he was too tired to scold her about it.

"The cat. He's back and he brought us a key."

Joanna and Lyall paused and looked at one another. They must have known it wasn't in the nature of an ordinary cat to retrieve keys. "What—?" Joanna began.

There was a loud thud from above them and the princess's eyes turned flinty. Rather than question the bizarre situation she crouched, her leg obviously still paining her and reached between the bars, She snagged the key between her two longest fingers, drawing it to her.

"I hope this is the right one." Lyall took the key from the crouching Joanna and moved to the door as the princess eased herself up to stand.

You and me both, panted Boots. He was certain his heart would never beat at a normal rate again. No matter how much understanding he had, he wasn't going on another mission like that. If it was the wrong key, these humans were on their own.

He watched Lyall fumble with the key for a moment, struggling to get it into the hole without being able to see it, though the tall man's long arms snaked easily around the bars to fiddle with the lock.

Come on! Boots huffed. *My human is in serious danger upstairs! You're the one with the thumbs, work that key!*

Lyall stuck out his tongue, brows coming together. There was another thundering sound from above and Boots flinched. He imagined poor Levi being beaten to a pulp. The Ogre furious to find that his right-hand man was in league with the princess, and worse still, with a cat. Boots paced, resisting the urge to rush back up the stairs to help his human all by himself.

Boot's attention snapped back to Lyall at the sound of a satisfying *click*. The tall man grinned victoriously. He gave the cell door a shove and it opened with a sound like a wailing woman. Even had hope blossomed at last, Boots could tell that the bodyguard was hardly in fit condition to walk, let alone fight.

That was a human issue, Boots decided. He would just worry about getting theses two warriors up to help poor Levi.

"I think I remember the way," Joanna frowned, scanning the room, "but to be safe—Boots, lead us out?"

Oh, of course. I'm needed for everything. Boots shook dampness from his paws and ignored the creeping ache in his hip where he'd been clawed. *Come along, let's go*, he instructed with his loudest chirps and trills.

Joanna and Lyall followed as best they could. "Boots, do you know where our weapons are?" asked Joanna. Clearly, she had not only figured out that the cat was unusual, but she had taken it in her stride. Perhaps she even thought he *was* the cat god. This notion made Boots walk a little more heroically, and he couldn't keep a feline grin from his face as he guided them to the armory.

The way was dark enough for Shades to erupt all around them at any moment, but they did not. This should have been a relief, but instead Boots wondered what the mage was up to and what he might be doing to

Levi. He could still feel the icy crackle of The Ogre's magic around them, even down in the dungeon.

The arming room was just as Boots had last seen it. Joanna's twin blades as well as Lyall's sword and kite-shaped shield were tossed carelessly into a corner. Joanna limped inside and distributed their weapons as Boots stood watch by the door.

Once she had her weapons in hand, she looked down at herself, picking at the armor that hung off her in tatters. Strips of leather and links of chain jangled against small, metal plates, many of which seemed to be missing. "I suppose it's better than nothing," she muttered.

Lyall hissed in pain as he strapped his shield to his arm.

"Alright?" Joanna turned and grasped the bottom edge of the shield to take some of the weight.

"I can wield it, but not well," Lyall admitted. "Better my shield arm than my sword, I suppose."

"Try to stay back from the fighting. Defend yourself if you have to, but don't come flying to my rescue."

"Right," Lyall lifted an eyebrow. "I'll just ignore a lifetime of friendship and training and let you face an Ogre and his army of Shades alone."

"Ly," She reached up and grasped the back of his neck, pulling his head down so their foreheads touched. "If you die I'll go mad, alright? Stay alive. Those are my orders."

Boots watched in impatient puzzlement as they stood, forehead to forehead. Like two cats butting heads in friendship, then forgetting to move on. Humans were very odd.

He flicked his tail and let out a low "meow," just to remind them that they had a mission here.

When the two broke apart, Lyall looked resigned. He arranged his shield on his arm, lifting it with obvious strain. Boots wondered if he should lead them to a servant's exit to flee into the countryside instead. They might get away if they were quick enough.

But then what would become of Levi? He had no idea where his human was, but he knew the unlucky miller needed more help than one cat could provide.

Joanna's face was set like stone. One look and Boots had no doubt that she intended to defeat The Ogre now or die trying. He wondered at her sanity, but decided he liked her better fierce, wild, and a little insane.

"On we go," Joanna strode past Boots. She barely limped now, and her twin swords glinted with deadly intent.

Boots guided the pair up and out towards the main hall.

The two humans did their best to keep their footfalls quiet as they approached the final door, but each step sounded thunderous to Boots. Though his gait was uneven thanks to his throbbing hip, the cat still moved as silent as smoke, his ears on a constant pivot. How could he fight an enemy with no scent? A foe so powerful he could become any monster that suited him?

The princess-human had better have a plan.

When they reached the door, Joanna made several hand gestures to Lyall, who nodded. Some sort of understanding passed between them. She crouched, her ear to the door. Boots listened as well, though even he couldn't tell what was behind it. If The Ogre was there, he was being quiet at last. Their enemy was no fool. He must have realized that Boots had escaped with the key. Would he believe a cat would be intelligent enough to bring the key to the princess?

There was only one way to find out.

Joanna drew her lips from her teeth in a grimace and shook her head tightly. She pressed her palm to the door as though she might be able to feel the magic on the other side. Boots looked between the two humans. Their expressions were so intense even he felt like he could understand them. Whatever was on the other side of this door, Joanna was ready to fight it.

Boots took a big breath and trotted to Joanna's side. He flared his whiskers forward.

Do it, human.

Joanna turned the nob and shoved the door open, her twin swords back in her hands in seconds.

As she faced the massive room, her intake of breath was audible.

The great hall was swarming with Shades, so thick it looked like dusk had fallen, though fractions of splintered sunshine sliced between their bodies like knives. The Ogre stood in the middle of the swirling, coiling tornado of Shades. An even darker shape with an even darker purpose. His venomous smile shone too bright.

Boots crouched low on Joanna's feet, ears pinned and fur raised. He drew his whiskers back in a grimace of hatred.

The Ogre's green eyes narrowed with loathing. "Did you plan all this? To be taken prisoner then get free for another surprise attack? I knew you were lying about your father." His voice echoed eerily, as though the cavernous room were empty.

Boots tilted his head back to see Joanna's reaction. She managed a grin that impressed even Boots. "You're right. My father was never coming," she said. Only Boots was close enough to hear the unsteady rasp in her voice.

"Well, it's all over now. I don't know how you enchanted that *cat*, but it wasn't enough." The Ogre took a moment to glare down at Boots as though the cat were the one who could transform into a monster. "I thought it was the magic of Levi's curse that I was sensing, but it's the damned animal as well! I didn't think there was power enough left in this kingdom to enchant a caterpillar, let alone a cat. And who would waste it on a filthy animal? Seems I was wrong."

"Get to the point," Joanna snapped.

Lyall chuckled faintly, his pale eyes fierce even as he leaned against the wall for support. Boots guessed that the bodyguard might have liked to stretch the conversation, but Joanna seemed determined to march them ever faster towards their doom.

Boots looked at the princess again from his spot on her feet. It was a true testament to the understanding the cat god gave him that Boots was not wishing these humans luck and fleeing the castle, never to be seen again. Oh, to be an ordinary cat again. He glared as only a cat could. Dispassionately and without blinking, as though he could see right through to the mage's bones. It was immensely satisfying to see The Ogre flinch in response. His Shades flinched with him as if they were attached to him by fine threads.

Boots, bolstered by the effect his glare was having, gingerly stepped from Joanna's feet, head up, tail raised like a victory banner, eyes still locked on The Ogre's.

The mage took a step back. "What is your spell, you damned beast? Why can't I draw the magic from you?"

Boots imagined a light shining on his own brow, where the cat god had kissed him.

"You are right that this is no ordinary cat." Joanna spoke up, her voice gaining confidence by the second. "The animal you see before you *is* the cat god Luck himself. We are his humble servants...you have displeased him."

Boots hesitated, but there was nothing for it but to go along with Joanna.

"Yeeeoooowwww..." Boots let out his most haunting yowl. It echoed gratifyingly, just as The Ogre's voice did.

The Ogre took another step back. With ever growing confidence, Boots watched as the Shades rippled and coiled to and fro, uncertain. He opened his mouth and let out another throaty cry. "Yeeeeeeoooooowwwwww!"

The mage raised a slender hand and magic sparked at his fingertips. Boots struggled not to shy from the tingle of power that filled the air.

"Cat god? We shall see." The Ogre's voice dripped with soft menace. His grin spread wider, showing very many alarmingly sharp teeth.

He gestured to something on the floor behind him, in the middle of the room where the Shades swarmed thickest. The dark creatures withdrew like horrible black birds on silent wings, to reveal a figure slumped on the marble floor.

"Levi," Joanna breathed.

The miller's son was crumpled in a heap. Boots smelled blood before he saw it. His human friend's blond hair was thick with matted crimson. Boots' fur rose, not with fear this time, but with anger. Feline rage filled his little body. How dare The Ogre hurt his human. *How dare he?* It was all Boots could do not to charge into the room, claws out, ripping at anything in sight.

The Ogre raised both eyebrows. "Now then, little cat god, or whatever you are. If you want your pathetic human pawn to live, you will come to me. Let me have a little look at your magic."

"I don't think so!" snarled Joanna.

"Jo," Lyall warned as the Shades began to swarm in, stopping just short of them, near enough to touch. Lyall was still mostly in the hallway and Boots wondered if the soldier would grab Joanna by her scruff and drag her away to safety.

"This is your last chance, Ogre." Joanna raised her chin. Boots thought that, if she lived, she'd make a marvelous queen. "Release my friend by order of the crown or feel its wrath."

The Ogre laughed and it sounded like branches scraping glass. "I have no respect for your crown, you whimpering *child*. You are a nuisance to be batted aside and it will please me to be rid you. I should have done away with you sooner, but I am too soft hearted."

He drew a slim knife from inside his fine coat. It glinted, almost blue in the hall so clogged with Shades. "I will kill you and leave your body for the crows. Then I will stroll across your lands and take what I please, before I walk up to that feeble king and snatch away everything that was his. Once I have killed a god, if that is indeed what this creature is, and taken its magic, nothing can stand in my way." His attention was once again on Boots, and his eyes shone with a hungry intensity Boots had never seen from him. Like a snake eying a fat mouse.

Damn you, princess-human, for coming up with that cat god story. Now The Ogre won't just kill me, he'll experiment on me first. Boots braced, ready to fight or flee, whatever he needed to do to get to Levi.

The Ogre took a few steps backward, eyes still locked on the cat as though he knew Boots could bolt and be gone into the bowels of the castle faster than a blink. He stopped over the limp figure of the miller's son on the floor. He reached down and, still daring Boots onward with his eyes, he grabbed Levi by the hair. Levi let out a little groan. The Ogre jerked his head back and placed the blade against his throat.

Boots yowled his war cry, claws out and ready, fur bristled to its fullest extent. His whole body tremored and a thousand invisible bees swarmed his skin, but now he didn't dare move.

"We're going to have to do this," hissed Lyall. "We'll have to charge him."

"Gods defend us," Joanna agreed, raising her swords. Boots could smell the fear rolling from her just as strong as the rage. "OGRE!" she thundered.

The Ogre's head snapped up, eyes widening.

"Death comes now!"

She launched herself at the nearest Shades, driving her small body towards the mage.

Boots surged into the fray, keeping pace with Joanna. Lyall did his best to take up a defense at the rear. The cat wasn't sure about the injured man's chances, but he didn't have time to stop and ponder as he leaped, claws outstretched. He tore directly through the first Shade. It shredded like so much useless paper. He could hear the princess fighting, roaring her own battle cry to his left. At least it would be easy to keep track of her.

Boots' success was short lived. Shades encircled him in seconds, snatching at him. They clawed with fingers like knives. One gouged his flank. Boots yowled in pain and ducked low, skittering under the Shades. He could get his back to something. Once he regrouped he would make another try for Levi.

He ran so fast he skidded and slammed into the wall. His breath left him in a painful huff.

He scrabbled madly at the slick, too-smooth marble, and made it under a table. He peeked out at the swarming Shades. They were thick in the air as hornets, though they were eerily silent. The only sound was that of Joanna fighting and gentle footsteps of The Ogre moving through his crowd of minions.

Boots' ears soon told him that The Ogre was headed in his direction, leaving the princess to his Shades. Boots tucked himself up as small as he could. He tried to become one with the wall as sharp, hateful magic coiled around him.

"Where are you, little god?" The Ogre crooned, his feet stopping near the table. His boots shone with an unnatural polish. Boots could see his own terrified face reflected in them. "Not so powerful now, are you, cat? Not since I took all the magic in the land for myself? You cannot hoard it and feed it to these useless peasants anymore, can you?"

The mage bent down to peer under the table, his green eyes like drops of venom in milk. His lips drew back in a sickening smile.

Boots hissed, ears pinned, tail wrapped around his legs. The Ogre's hand swept under the table, reaching and grasping like a talon. Boots lashed out, raking the mage's skin with his claws. The Ogre withdrew for a split second, then struck again, ignoring the bleeding scratches.

The Ogre's blood was too dark, almost black, and it oozed sluggishly from his wounds. He grabbed for the scruff of Boots' neck.

The cat managed to wriggle free with the aid of his hind feet, but he was well and truly cornered.

Joanna's voice grew distant. He guessed she'd retreated to the far side of the room. At least she was still alive. Boots hissed and spit again, showing all his needle-sharp teeth before he bit The Ogre's hand as hard as he could. The other hand shot down, grasped Boots' scruff, and this time is clamped like a vice. It hauled him from under the table.

Boots couldn't struggle. Being scruffed was an old technique even mother cats used. When he was held like this, by only the skin of his neck, all he could do was tuck up his limbs and hang uselessly. He managed to emit a low growl as The Ogre raised him to make eye contact, smirking "This is a god?"

More of a god than you, rot-breath! snarled Boots. His claws were fully extended, if only he could use them.

"Perhaps you are not a god after all? You don't look like much, do you, pussy cat? Someone must have put an enchantment on you. Who and how is the true question."

If I could move I would claw your throat into ribbons and show you who is a 'pussy cat'!

The Ogre gave Boots a firm shake. Pain shot through the cat's body, and his head swam. If he was about to die here, that blasted Luck god could at least make an appearance.

"I have never successfully transformed an entire living thing besides myself," The Ogre mused, raising his bitten hand into Boots' view. His dark blood slid down his wrist in little streams like ink against the parchment of his pale skin. "Perhaps I should try again…this should show me what you really are." His voice was low, almost sweet. A disgusting imitation of how most folk spoke on animals.

Boots didn't close his eyes, he kept them focused and filled with hatred, staring deeply into The Ogre's.

He was drowning in a river only this time there was no Levi to save him. This time they would all be swept under.

Wham!

The Ogre grunted and dropped the cat to the marble floor. Boots landed on his feet, his sore muscles absorbing the shock with a painful jolt. He turned and saw a blade protruding from The Ogre's side. He followed the path the blade with his eyes. Joanna. She had seen her moment and lobbed one of her swords with extraordinary accuracy.

Boots scrambled to get clear of The Ogre before the mage recovered and grabbed for him again.

Now Joanna only had one sword. As Boots skidded to a stop under another table, he saw that she had retreated to a corner with Lyall. The man was guarding her as best he could with his shield as she fought using the mismatched pair of her remaining sword and Lyall's. The two humans battled with the grace and skill possessed only by those who have spent a lifetime at each other's sides. As if each could read the other's movements before they even made them. But Boots knew that even Joanna and Lyall couldn't keep up the fight forever. For every Shade they rent to shreds, two more pushed in.

The Ogre roared in rage and pain, and the air thrummed with his magic. Boots flinched as it washed over him. Where a man had stood The Ogre now loomed in his favorite, monstrous shape. The wound Joanna had inflicted was nothing but a scratch to this massive creature.

The Ogre turned, tree-limb arms sweeping Shades out of his way like they were rags in a stream. Small, green eyes sought their prey and Boots could smell the monster's rancid breath from where he crouched. It was an unholy, unnatural smell, like rotted meat and magic.

Boots' eyes desperately sought out Levi, still crumpled on the floor. An abandoned plaything. Could Boots reach his friend's side before they were all killed? Coiling his limbs, he prepared to sprint for it.

BOOM!

The front door of the castle crashed open in a shower of splinters and piece of the broken lock. Boots startled so badly he abandoned his charge and dove back under the table.

Men came pouring in through the freshly opened door. Joanna's men. Armed and armored and shouting battle cries of their own.

"FOR THE PRINCESS!"

"DEATH TO THE OGRE!!"

Boots scooted back against the wall, making himself small. The warriors moved in formation, driving towards Joanna and Lyall with impressive precision. The princess looked so shocked that two Shades nearly took her down before she remembered herself and hacked them to bits.

The Ogre too was baffled for a moment, giving the soldiers enough time to reach Joanna and encircle her before he did more than blink and gape.

Boots hoped that Joanna was giving her people the order to go rescue Levi. As if they had read his mind the formation began to move again, pushing towards the fallen miller. Four men hung back, keeping Joanna and Lyall safely surrounded.

The Ogre roared, rattling the castle to its very foundations. The beast transformed again, this time into a dragon. Boots had seen one in one of the library books Levi had knocked to the floor during his days causing mayhem. This dragon fit the image very well. Green scales, leathery wings, and arrow-shaped head adorned with curved horns. It had a lithe, muscular body covered in glinting green scales.

The dragon slashed out with a mighty forelimb and sent the rank column of Joanna's men flying in a clatter of armor and shouting. As it moved its tail, so long it scraped along the wall, came around and crashed into the stairs. Hunks of wood and even chips of marble scattered across the floor.

Joanna's men were fearless. They collected themselves, pulling their wounded into the safety of their ranks. "Is this all you have, Ogre?"

Through all the chaos, Boots kept his eyes on Levi. The soldiers were drawing the fight away from him, and the Ogre seemed to have forgotten him, focusing on his attackers. This dragon was powerful, but unwieldy, unable to maneuver to attack the nimble humans at its feet.

The Ogre must have realized the flaw in this form as the soldiers slashed at him with blades. They cleared his Shades easily. Boots supposed they'd had plenty of practice.

With another ripple of frigid magic, The Ogre transformed again, taking the form of a giant boar, taller at the shoulder than any of Joanna's men, but more maneuverable than the dragon. It lowered its head and charged, scattering warriors with its tusks and herding the rest out of its way.

"That was rubbish!" One of the soldier's mocked. They formed up again, blades bristling between shields like a gigantic hedgehog.

They really are Joanna's men. Boots flared his whiskers in amusement in spite of himself.

He noticed that the Shadows were beginning to falter. They had become thinner, wispy. Some had vanished all together, or slithered back to the walls and crannies from whence they were born, reforming themselves into what they had once been. Now Boots understood what Joanna had told her men to do. Not to rescue Levi, but to get The Ogre to use his magic. To keep him transforming again and again until the magic was all used up and it snapped back on him.

Boots heart rattled to life and his energy returned. *Hiding under the table letting the humans do all the work? What kind of master hunter does that?* "Raaaaaaoooooooowwww!" Boots bellowed at the top of his lungs.

The Ogre's ear twitched in Boots' direction. The air popped and seared with a satisfying stab of magic as the creature's rage grew. *Transform again, you idiot mage. Do it again!*

The boar swung around, making another sweep with its head, trapped three of Joanna's men and pressing them against a wall. The other soldiers were shunted aside, falling to the left and right of the creature like flies being shaken from its flesh.

"SIMON!" A new voice shouted.

Boots' heart gave a happy leap. Levi was awake! The miller's son had managed to crawl away from the fight to the far wall while Boots had focused on the chaos. Had the human had been awake for a little while, subtly inching himself clear?

Now he had pulled himself up using a tapestry. His face was tight with pain and half-covered in blood, but his voice was clear. "I betrayed you, Simon! I was a spy! I told the princess exactly how to find you and how to kill you!"

The boar's small eyes glinting emerald. It released the men it had pinned, wheeling on hooves that looked as sharp as blades. It huffed a gust of steaming breath, bracing to charge.

Joanna's men wasted no time launching a fresh attack. They sliced at the boar's sides and crashed against it with their shields. The creature squealed in in pain and rage, flailing with limb and tusk alike.

Its skin seemed to ripple unnaturally.

Boots knew The Ogre was trying to transform again. His Shades were all but gone and the magic in the air was as taught as a drum. It tightened in Boots' chest, a warning even he could understand, but which The Ogre ignored.

Stretch your magic too thin and it spells disaster. Boots' lips curled in satisfaction.

There was terrible a sound like a whip cracking. A perfect pain of glass shattering.

It was so loud that Boots' ears rang and the humans all clamped hands to the sides of their heads. The magic in the air rushed towards The Ogre, then out again, crashing so hard into everyone that several men were knocked flat, and Boots was pinned against the wall, like being struck by a wave in a storm.

And then there was stillness.

Boots collected himself, shaking his head to clear it. There was no longer a great boar standing in the middle of the room, nor a dragon, nor even a man. It took the cat a moment to locate The Ogre at all.

The magic had stretched too tight and rebounded, just as Joanna and Levi had predicted. Too much transformation, too many Shades to maintain after several days of dealing with Levi's sabotage.

Now there was not a single Shade in the room. They had all returned to their natural state, tucked under tables and trailing harmlessly from people's feet. As deadly as motes of dust.

Boots spied a flicker of movement on the marble floor where the Boar had been. The humans were still collecting themselves, baffled by the rush of powerful magic. The cat did not hesitate. Gathering his strength one last fight, every muscle protesting, Boots lunged. The Ogre, trapped by his own magic in the form of a plain, brown mouse, did not stand a chance. The cat was there, deadly jaws and claws digging in. The mage's neck was broken in seconds and he sagged limp in Boots' mouth.

Boots let the dead mouse fall from his jaws and lie before him on the floor, beady green eyes staring at nothing.

Before anyone had time to investigate Boots' fresh kill there was a new sensation of magic. As different to the Ogre's as summer to winter. Boots looked around. The humans were all staring, some with mouths open in complete awe.

Boots puffed out his chest. *I know I'm impressive, but really, it was nothing. I've been killing mice for years—*

Boots turned to follow the humans' gazes then flared his whiskers, his eyes going wide. Standing in the ruined doorway were four wolves, their fur the silvery color of moonlight, their eyes shimmering like stars. They had no odor save for the faintest scent of a summer breeze. Beside them, carelessly grooming a foreleg, was the cat god.

The wolves began to move with an uncanny grace that no animal could emulate, not even a cat. Like mist sweeping over a darkened prairie. Boots scurried out of their way. He could sense the power of death on these beautiful creatures as they trotted soundlessly past him. It wasn't unpleasant or cruel, but it was cold and left Boots shivering.

The cat god came and stood beside him, fixing with a calm gaze.

The humans all backed away as the wolf gods crossed the room. *They can see the gods?* Boots asked, tilting his head towards Luck. *I thought only animals could see them.*

The wolves wish to be seen, Luck explained, dipping his head and blinking placidly. This is an important moment.

The gods of death stepped gingerly around splatters of blood, making their way to where the humans had dragged their fallen. As the humans flinched back the wolves wove in and touched their noses to the still figures of three men. With dismay Boots recognized each one. The lean man with a scarred face that had given him the largest hunk of his meat. A younger fellow who had petted Boots shyly. The third had talked of how silly he found the animal gods to be, but had let Boots sit as long as he wanted in his lap.

The spectral forms of the fallen humans leaped from their bodies. They looked around at their living comrades with pupilless, shining eyes, as though to say goodbye. The spirits did not seem the least bit distressed, each placing a hand on the head of the wolf who had called them from their bodies.

The wounded on the other hand looked horrified any time one of the wolves drew too near them, but the animal gods showed no interest in the living. They did not even swivel an ear in the direction of the injured men.

The fourth wolf split off from the others and trotted to the tiny corpse of The Ogre, still locked in the form of a brown mouse. The god lowered her head and touched her nose-tip to the delicate corpse. The air around them stirred, as though a wind rushed in, ruffling hair and tugging at garb. Boots skin tingled too.

Magic. Not the cruel, needle-magic of The Ogre, but a wild magic that had no master nor keeper and was eager to be free. It burst from the tiny corpse and coiled around the room in a golden ribbon, touching everyone and everything like a child exploring a new world. Joanna pushed to her feet and reached out, swishing her hand through the glittering stream. Her fingers swirled it like water, but the magic slipped onward, up and around and away before it drew back towards the wolf who stood over the mouse.

Beside the wolf, a spectral creature tentatively emerged from the mouse. Boots cocked an ear in interest, his feline confidence steadily returning. The gentle warmth of the cat god beside him was like a reassuring hand on his back.

He had expected The Ogre's spirit to resemble the man he chose to be much of the time, but the thing that stood beside the wolf goddess was a small, feeble being. Shorter than any grown human, it was a withered, skeletal. It rubbed its semi-transparent hands together nervously, fear in his large eyes as it studied the wolf. The goddess of death was ignoring it for the moment as the wild magic circled and wrapped around the wolves. The energy built and boiled, then absorbed into each wolf's porcelain body.

Boots wondered what the humans understood of this scene. Some had made hasty signs of their various gods over their chests or before their eyes.

What was The Ogre? Boots asked, turning to the luck god.

Human once, long ago. He was born with a very rare magical gift.

The transformation power? asked Boots.

That is indeed a rare and special ability. The god dipped his head. *But the one that sealed his fate was the uncanny ability to detect and absorb the magic of others. We gods had never seen such a thing before. We believe it was a magical mutation, unique to this individual. We were not prepared for what it could do.*

Can you not control what magic people will be born with? Boots twitched a whisker.

The magic does as it wills. The wolves only reclaim it when a mage dies and recycle it back into the world as new mages are born.

Could something like The Ogre happen again?

Perhaps. The cat god dipped its head, though he did not seem especially concerned.

Could he have stopped himself from stealing other people's magic?

He could resist, if he wished it. He did not wish it. He soon gained a taste for the magic of others and the power it gave him over them. He learned to take what he desired rather than asking. He stole without consequence and found himself a home from which to steadily rob all this land of magic. The power inside him kept him alive for an unnatural time, but perverted his form until he was obliged to use his magic to appear as he wished to be. By that time, we gods had realized what he had done, but it was too late. The humans of this land were robbed of their magic and slowly began to disbelieve in us. They chose new, human gods to worship as we continued our silent duty to them and to you animals, our children.

Are the human gods false? Boots asked, only half curious. He wondered if seeing their gods at last would give Joanna, Levi, and the others some comfort.

No more than we are. The luck cat's teeth flashed in a little smirk. *The magic which creates gods is ancient and powerful and cannot be stolen, not even by this unfortunate mage.* He gestured with his head towards what had been The Ogre.

Boots' attention was drawn to the wolves who seemed to have finished absorbing all of the freed magic in the room. It swirled in the god's semi-transparent body like water rippling in a quiet stream. *What will become of the magic The Ogre hoarded?* Boots asked.

It will be redistributed to the kingdom. Some will be placed as seeds into new life as babies are born. The rest will be set free to find all those who yet live with a seed of magic inside them, for it was always theirs.

Do I have any magic besides what you gave me? Boots looked down at himself as though he might see this undoubtedly impressive magical gift already beginning to manifest. He imagined himself with power over fire, or the ability to make humans do as he desired with a thought so he might sit on a cushion at be fed fresh fish all day.

I am afraid you do not, Master Boots, the god gave him a sympathetic look. *And I can take back my magic from you, if you would like. Would you like me to remove your understanding?*

Boots thought of his life before. Of simple days enjoying sunbeams and feeling no compulsion to snatch keys from deadly monsters. "It would be nice to go back to those days of leisure. Yet…he looked at Levi, propped against the wall taking in the scene with his wide, sky-blue eyes. This poor human needed all the help he could get. *I think I shall keep my understanding. Magic is magic, even if it wasn't mine to begin with.* He puffed out his fur, attempting to look a bit regal. He knew he failed, but didn't much care. He glanced at Levi again. *What about my human? Can you take the curse from him now?*

The god looked apologetic, well, as apologetic as a cat could manage. *I am afraid not. It is as much a part of him as his heart or his mind.*

But *I thought once we had defeated The Ogre—* Boots huffed.

I am very sorry, young fire cat, but your human is the way he is forever. There is nothing that can be done about that. We gods distribute the magic. What humans and animals decide to do with their gifts is their business. Blessings and curses, once placed by humans hands, cannot be removed. But it shall not be so bad for your friend, I think, from now on. The god's tone was gentle and reassuring.

The last wolf began to move off, taking with her the soul of The Ogre, who shuffled along behind looking very small and ashamed. Boots supposed everyone looked ashamed if they had been cruel in life, when they met the Death wolves and the bill came due. Perhaps The Ogre had never expected to face this moment.

Now then, my fine cat, I leave you to your long and prosperous life. The god of luck bowed.

Boots had the sudden urge to beg the god to stay, but he could find no reason.

The wolves were gone, the dead were dead, the alive were alive, and the world moved on. He watched as the white cat strode daintily across the floor towards the humans. Boots could tell he had made himself visible to Joanna, Lyall and Levi at the very least. Joanna's eyes lit with the excitement of a child as the white cat stopped before her, sitting on its haunches and looking up at her as though stopping to converse.

When he finished Luck stood and trotted over to Levi. The miller's son extended a hand, and the god of cats butted his head against in. It was the sweet gesture of greeting someone as an old friend.

Finally, light as a breeze, the cat god followed the wolves out the doors and into the shimmering countryside.

Then the god was gone and all that remained were the humans and the orange cat with white hind paws.

Part 6

Levi

Levi's head thundered with pain. He had no idea how long he had been out before he finally wakened on the floor of The Ogre's study and tried to make his slow and painful way towards where he hoped to find Joanna and his cat. The Ogre returned for him before he could get far.

He must have passed out again because when he woke there were Shades all around and the sounds of fighting. Instinctively, he had started to scoot away from the action, knowing that any large movement might attract attention. He wished he knew where Boots was, though he thought he heard a very angry yowl, as well as what he hoped was Joanna's defiant war cry.

At least Boots was alive.

Now he leaned against the wall on the opposite side of the room from Joanna and her men. He was still trying to make sense of the chaos of battle. The Ogre's magic rebounded on him far worse than Levi had predicted, reducing the once powerful mage to a rodent that could be killed by a cat. To make matters even more confusing, before Levi had a chance to collect his thoughts a pack of spectral wolves and a silver cat with red-orange eyes appeared.

Perhaps he was hallucinating. He inched a hand up to his hairline to touch the nasty wound the Ogre had given him. He regretted it instantly as fresh lances of pain sliced through his head and his vision fractured like stained glass. He gritted his teeth and breathed through the waves of splintering pain.

He had little choice but to sit where he was and watch as the wolves moved to some of Joanna's fallen men. Then the fourth wolf took what must have been The Ogre away. His arms and legs were made of stone and his body was that of a scarecrow.

Perfectly content to be ignored for the moment, he sat. At least no wolves were coming his way. At last, before all these strange animals with their wild magics departed, the white cat trotted over to him on silent feet. Instinctively, he extended a hand to what he only vaguely realized was a deity. It rose up slightly on its back legs and butted its head into his palm. The simple gesture filled him with momentary light and warmth.

Hello, companion of cats.

"What? How can I understand you?" His lips were chapped and raw, his words slurred.

It's better if you do not worry over such things. Only know that I am watching over you. You are a friend to my people an no cat will ever harm you so long as you live. And your children will never find themselves without the good company of a friendly cat.

With a slow blink of its sunset-colored eyes the god turned and trotted away.

Levi gaped after it, unconvinced he'd seen or heard any of it. He squeezed his eyes shut and when he opened them Boots was limping towards him, tail raised in greeting.

Levi gingerly reached for his feline friend, investigating Boots' injuries with his hands. The orange cat had cruel scratches along his sides that were no longer bleeding, and he was lame on his left hind leg, but still bore an expression of confident dominance. "Mer wow!" Boots proclaimed.

Levi winced as even this sound made his head throb, but he petted Boots as carefully as he could.

Across the room Joanna spoke to her men. Her voice was raised, echoing off the walls.

"What are you doing here?!" she demanded. Levi could just make her out through his foggy, swimming vision. She was surrounded by a semicircle of soldiers. Levi wasn't certain he knew when or how they had arrived, and part of him thought he was hallucinating during the fight, but there they were. For her part, Joanna was clearly feeling well enough to plant hands on her hips and address her healer, whose name Levi couldn't remember just then.

"It was your maid's fault," said the healer. He did not appear to be the least bit cowed but Joanna's obvious displeasure.

"I told her to wait a week before getting help!" Joanna threw up her hands.

"She disobeyed." The healer moved to check each wounded soldier in turn. Joanna's people were armored, but Levi could see that several were badly hurt from the fight. Lyall had lowered himself to a sitting position and was clasping his side. Levi worried he must have reopened his wound.

"You should not have come." Joanna's voice was lower, tinged with something like sadness.

"Because you clearly had everything under control?" one of Joanna's other soldiers asked. Levi vaguely remembered this man. A big fellow with tanned skin and wielding an ax.

"If we hadn't come, we would have lost our princess and commander," the healer pointed out, hands working quickly with his medicines and bandages. "And lost our jobs into the bargain."

Levi wished someone would come over and check on him, but he barely had the energy to pet Boots, let alone call out. He little noticed the subtle, warming sensation spreading up his arm as he ran his hand over the cat's back.

"Did you tell my father?" Joanna asked, the wrath already bleeding from her voice. She turned to kneel beside Lyall, putting her hand on his shoulder.

"No," the redhaired soldier said. He'd been injured and sat awaiting the healer's attention. "You know he doesn't have any say over what we do."

"He does. He's the king." Lyall's voice was raspy.

"He's not our commander." The ax wielder said.

"You're all a bunch of idiots." Emotion slurred the princess's words.

"We're *your* idiots, Commander," a youngish man with brown hair said. He grinned widely even as the healer assessed a nasty cut across his brow.

Joanna seemed at a loss. She stared around at her people as though seeing everyone for the first time and trying to memorize each man's face.

Boots set up a purr in Levi's lap, and the miller could no longer ignore the strange, but not unpleasant heat that engulfed his hand. He made a small noise of surprise as he looked down at the cat. Boots was…better. His ruffled fur was smoothed, and was it Levi's imagination or were the cuts along the cat's sides less pronounced?

He removed his hand and Boots looked up, blinking big, yellow eyes as if to ask, *"why did you stop?"*

The warmth subsided in Levi's hand. He frowned, which made his head hurt, but he ignored this for the moment. There was something else now. The gentlest tugging sensation against his palm as Boots looked expectantly at him. A surge of *knowing* poured into Levi's head, and he almost doubled over as his senses were overwhelmed.

He let out a little "Mmff!" of alarm.

The cat…the cat wished he would go back to petting. Of course, this might have been gleaned by the expression on Boot's face, but Levi knew it as clearly as if Boots had spoken the words. It was certainty rather than supposition. He settled his big hand onto Boot's back and the warmth returned. Not burning, but definitely more than the cat's body heat alone. "Huh," Levi said more loudly than he meant to.

Joanna and her men looked up. No doubt they'd forgotten him completely. Just his luck, he reasoned with a small smile. The hateful magic inside him had tugged to be free when those strange wolves were in the room, but the curse held fast. A fist twined tight around his insides, never to let go. He supposed a part of him had always known there would be no cure, though for the first time in a long time he allowed himself not to worry over it. In that moment he was perfectly, almost pleasantly, resigned to who he was.

"Levi!" Joanna gasped. She limped hurriedly over to him. The princess knelt at his side, her dark eyes filled with concern. She pushed back his hair with gentle fingertips, wincing in sympathy when she saw the wound on his head. "I'd ask if you were alright, but..." She gave him a kind smile.

"Yeah," Levi agreed. He had been distracted from the pain by his strange moment with Boots, but now it came flooding back. The princess's brows were peaked with worry as she held his chin in her hand. She looked like a goddess herself, he thought groggily. Like a warrior goddess come to save the day.

"Rylan!" Joanna called over her shoulder.

It took a few moments for Levi to realize that this was the healer's name. Seconds later the man with the trim beard and kind eyes landed on his knees beside them.

Levi felt appropriately fussed over for the first time in his life as Joanna clasped his hand and the healer saw to his wound. He feared he squeezed the princess's hand harder than was polite, but she did not show a hint of discomfort.

Once his head was bandaged and feeling less like it was going to shatter apart, Joanna and Rylan eased Levi's arms about their shoulders. Even injured the princess made herself useful, though Levi tried to put more of his weight on the able-bodied healer.

Boots was forced from his lap and trotted along beside the group as Levi joined the other wounded. Lyall welcomed the miller with a warm pat on the back.

Levi glanced down at the cat, who seemed to be miraculously as hale and whole, as if he had never been in a fight. He no longer limped, and his cuts were all but gone. His fur was shining like fire. Perhaps Levi had been wrong about the severity of the animal's injuries. Maybe most of the blood had simply been his own running into his eyes. Levi had little time to consider this, however, as the princess finally allowed Rylan to treat her injuries and they discussed their next plan of action.

It was decided that, with some of the men badly hurt, there would be no use in trying to leave immediately. The princess and her men would set up a little base of operations in The Ogre's castle.

Levi was able to give them some direction, and Boots willingly led the soldiers about the place like a furry little tour guide. Levi heard people remarking at the cat's clearly superior intelligence, and he smiled to himself. As baffling as that was, he had come to accept it. Boots was special and that was all there was to it.

The men eventually deposited Levi in his room and onto his mattress, which he convinced them to leave on the floor. They wondered at this, but didn't question it. Joanna had made it abundantly clear that Levi was to be treated with the utmost respect and care. Someone was even assigned to sit with him at all times, to watch over both his health and his bad luck. The men were all willing to believe in Levi's curse now that they had seen transforming Ogres and wolf gods roaming around.

Levi was in and out of consciousness for a while after that.

Sometimes he woke to find a cold cloth placed over his forehead and his guardian of the moment quietly reading beside him. Joanna even took a turn on watch. He woke to find her doing stretches across the room, flexing her bandaged limbs.

"Should you be doing that?" Levi croaked.

Joanna looked over and smiled. She moved stiffly to fetch a cup of water before coming to sit on his mattress bed. She expertly slid her hand under Levi's neck as he took the cup and sipped. The princess did everything with confidence, her every movement like a dance.

Boots, who was installed on Levi's other side, looked up and purred. Contact with the cat spread a soothing warmth through Levi's arm where it brushed the Boots' side.

"How are you feeling?" Joanna asked, easing Levi's head back to the pillow.

"Much better," Levi said, and he meant it. His head throbbed dully instead of stabbing at him with shards of pain that caused nausea and dizziness. "How many days has it been?"

"Two."

"Then I am pretty sure you should not be moving about so much." Levi wondered where his boldness came from. Perhaps it was because Joanna seemed so personable, like a friend rather than a royal.

Joanna's smile flashed. "Don't tell Rylan. I'm already going crazy, cooped up in here. Now that The Ogre is dead I can't wait to go home and tell my father. Maybe he'll finally understand who I am. What

I can do…" She paused and corrected herself with a hint of unexpected emotion in her voice. "What my men and I can do."

"You were all very remarkable." Levi gazed admiringly up at her.

Joanna sighed. "I could have done without the capture and Lyall being hurt."

"How is he?"

"Better. His wound was infected, but the fever is clearing, and he's been lucid all morning. I'm visiting him next, after I have finished my turn with you." Joanna gave Levi another warm, almost motherly smile.

"I'm sorry about the capture thing too. If only I had been here…my luck I suppose."

"Or mine." Joanna shrugged. She pulled one of her legs to her chest, wrapping her arms around it. The other she kept straight. Levi guessed it still pained her.

"What happens now?" he asked, his hand absently petting Boots' head, enjoying the warmth that tingled in his fingers at the touch.

"I've been thinking about that a lot, as it happens," Joanna said. "I've been thinking about this castle, and about you."

"Me?" Levi raised his head slightly, pleased when he wasn't greeted with a jab of pain.

Joanna turned and grabbed some extra pillows, helping Levi prop himself up so he was nearly sitting. One of the pillows kept sliding out and Joanna was obliged to put it back each time. If that was as bad as his luck would get that morning, Levi would gladly take it. Perhaps the curse too was battered and bruised.

"Yes. You see, I told my family that I had found a long-lost son of Carabas. They were the family who owned this castle long ago, before The Ogre. Lords and ladies who were under my father's rule, but oversaw these lands." She paused, a thoughtful look on her face. "I saw your drawings. Your ideas for mills and the machines that would run them."

Levi blushed. "They're...they're just ideas."

"Good ideas." Joanna gave Levi's arm and encouraging squeeze. "I've been thinking. What if we use my lie and you play the part of the long lost Carabas? That family isn't coming back. What remained of them left our kingdom before I was even born, when their castle was taken by The Ogre."

"What?" Levi spluttered, his pillow slipping out and falling to the floor. "I'm not...I'm a miller's son. I'm nobody. I...those drawings, those were only dreams. Shouldn't we try to...to track down the real Carabas family and—"

"You were honestly hoping your dreams would never come true?" Joanna's brows came together, her dark gaze intense. "You don't think you've worked hard enough to earn them?"

"Well, of course I was hoping, but I never...I never imagined—"

"That you could have what you wanted at last?"

Levi shrugged, knowing his cheeks had turned as pink as a summer sunset. "Well...with my luck and all. I could never— This castle will fall down around my ears before I'm able to get a single one of my ideas off the ground." His head was beginning to hurt again. She was insane. What could she possibly be thinking offering him something so absurd? The best he could hope for now was to go back to his family and plead to be allowed to help with the mill after all.

"You won't be alone here." Joanna was utterly undeterred by his unease. "You'll have helpers. Men I hire until you have enough success to pay them yourself. The farmland around here is untended, but fertile. Farmers will clamor to work it. To work for you."

"But…I…" Tears threatened, and he had no idea why. There was a stone the size of his fist lodged in his throat, and he pressed the heels of his hands to his eyes. Everything he ever wanted was being set at his feet and he was too cowardly to look at it?

Joanna went on, her tone bafflingly merry. She had no idea what she was talking about. She had no ability to offer him that life…did she? "The people we hire will know about your curse and you can tell them every detail of how it works so they can help you. With The Ogre dead, magic will soon be a reality in our lands and your predicament will not seem so farfetched." She paused, studying Levi's face as though finally noticing his distress. "Are you alright?"

Levi's mind was a swarm of bees, and he dropped his hands to his lap and clasped them, unable to meet Joanna's insistent eyes. Even though every part of him shouted that she had lost her mind and this plan would never work, a tiny, but glowing vision in his mind was already showing him as the master miller he had always pictured. Those had been fantasies too implausible to entertain, but now he could envision himself overseeing shining fields from his own castle, surrounded by people who were there to help him and understood his curse. He could invite his family to live here, and they would never have to work again. He winced, a fresh flash of pain fighting for dominance.

Joanna moved with surprising quickness, fetching a rag soaked in cool water and placing it gingerly on Levi's brow. He was glad when a trickle of water streaked down his cheek because then if he cried, she might not notice.

He had seen the white cat, which he hoped was indeed a god and not a hallucination, go over to the princess too. Perhaps there was one person whose own luck could counter Levi's, and perhaps she was kneeling beside him now. He glanced at her hand where he knew he'd find her ring, a cat with tiny amber eyes chasing its tail around her finger.

Friend to cats…

"Mer mer mi meow!" Boots announced. He sat up, taking a clear interest in the subject as well. Levi knew at once that the cat was instructing him, on no uncertain terms.

Go on, you foolish human! Recognize something amazing when it's staring you in the face for once!

"Alright." The words came out as a trembling breath. "Alright, I suppose you can talk to your father about it. That couldn't hurt anyway. Would…would I have to meet him?"

"Eventually." A huge smile spread over Joanna's face, dimpling her full cheeks. That smile injected courage directly into Levi's soul. Joanna went on, talking fast in her enthusiasm. "I've already told Father that you have spent much of your life as a peasant—" Levi grimaced faintly, and Joanna backpedaled. "Sorry. I suppose that is a bit of an insulting term."

"If a true one," Levi shrugged. Tears were still threatening in his eyes, but they were rapidly becoming ones of happiness rather than fear and disbelief.

"My father won't expect you to have any courtly graces, and we'll keep the meeting short, so your luck won't have a chance to do any damage."

"Good." Levi grinned, though his lip wobbled.

"Alright." Joanna cheered, clapping her hands, eyes bright and dancing. Levi wondered if this was an expression Joanna's parents and friends had learned to dread. She reminded him of a cat who had finally caught a tricky bird. "Oh…" she stopped her celebration and frowned at some memory. "I also told my father I wanted to marry you, so you'll have to pretend that you turned me down."

Levi spluttered, the rag falling from his brow. Beside him Boots huffed at being displaced. "Marry you?!"

"No." Joanna said, firmly, picking up the rag as well as his fallen pillow. There could be no question of her feelings, her eyes no longer sparkling, but steady as stone. "You will *not* be marrying me. I will not be marrying anyone. However, my father believes I had an infatuation with you, so play along and assure him you're not interested. Use whatever excuse you like." She waved a hand dismissively. "I'm too difficult, too noisy, too short."

"Right." Levi's head was still swimming. Marriage? Certainly he considered Joanna beautiful an enticing. Being around her was exhilarating, like standing beside a fast-moving river. But she was right. Marriage was taking this Carabas scheme a little too far. No. This princess was not the sort that you kissed, or married, or professed your love to. She was a whole different kind of princess, and Levi found it hard to imagine her any other way. "I'll tell your father I fancy men if you like," he offered, hoping to bring her smile back.

"Then you'll get Lyall's hopes up." Joanna laughed, rewarding Levi with her confident grin once more. "Of course, he is very loyal to his Joshua, but I know he thinks you're handsome."

Levi flushed. By now even his ear-tips must be crimson. If not the princess, at least someone found him good looking. He didn't believe anyone had ever thought that about him, but then he had spent most of his life beside Brodie, whose handsomeness made everyone else look like filthy farm laborers beside a lord.

Joanna settled back, talking animatedly through various plans and options for how they could implement things for Levi. What men she would leave as temporary helpers for him, once she was ready to return home. Levi watched her talk, his own mind miles away as he envisioned himself standing tall and proud on his new castle wall, overlooking the farmland that he owned (as a helper stood behind him so Levi didn't accidentally pitch off the wall.) His new mills were thriving using his machines and techniques, and he was on speaking terms with the princess.

~~~~~

Levi recovered over the next few days, and before he knew it, two weeks passed in a blur of activity and discovery. In that time Joanna's soldiers made themselves at home and helped with any number of chores and duties.

Word of The Ogre's defeat was sent to the king by fastest rider, as well as Joanna's plans to stay and help young "Lord Levi Carabas" settle into his freshly recovered lands.

Levi did his best to stay out of the way and not cause trouble. Joanna's men were endlessly kind to him, and he was baffled by how they took his luck in their stride. If he lingered too long in a room and things began to go wrong, no one insisted he leave. They simply modified what they were doing to be more careful and watchful. Still, Levi avoided places like the kitchen and armory altogether, and to be safe, he never tried to reshelve any books.

He found he most enjoyed spending time out in the sun with the company's horses. The redhaired young man, Liam, was more than happy to introduce Levi to each one, and to regale him with endless details about their personalities.

Boots was his constant companion, but also enjoyed a good nap in the sun while Levi communed with the horses. Levi happily brushed, picked hooves, and turned them out daily. Liam playfully griped that he had better watch out or Levi would steal his job. Joanna's mount Willow followed Levi around like a puppy.

More and more, Levi was coming to understand that something about him had changed, and for once it was for the better.

With the morning sun already shimmering pleasantly in the sky promising a warm summer day, Levi helped Liam turn the horses out to graze before it grew too hot. Molly lagged behind. Liam moved to check her, but Levi raised a hand. "It's alright. I'll see to her."

"Right, I'll keep an eye on this lot." Liam herded the rest of the animals towards the gate as they trotted and nipped bossily at one another, jostling like foals.

Levi doubled back to Molly, following the insistent pull in his chest. Not like the tug of his curse, which was nagging and uncomfortable, but a gentle, leading hand guiding him back to the old mare. "What is it girl? Not feeling well today?" he soothed as he petted her nose.

The warmth and pulling sensation rippled through his hand and up his arm. Curious, he allowed it to guide his hand to rest on Molly's hip. Understanding snapped into his mind as though it had always been. As if it were the most obvious thing in the world. Her arthritis was paining her. Of course.

He pulled his hand away and looked at his palm. There was nothing but a bit of grime from the morning's work. He set his hand back against Molly's flank and petted her gently. Warmth eased down his arm and from his fingertips into Molly's skin. Like heat from a sun-baked stone. After a long moment he stopped petting, his hands going cool again.

Molly looked around at him. Once again, the knowing came into his mind as easily as if the horse had spoken in a human voice. *My hip feels much better now!*

Levi looked at his hand again as Molly moved off after the other horses, trotting happily, flipping her tail in greeting to her fellows.

"Mer mer?" Boots asked, striding up and butting his head against Levi's shin.

Levi's voice came out in a breathy rush. "Boots... I...I think I have magic. Proper magic!"

~~~~~

He experimented carefully over the next few days. All he had to do was touch a muzzle or a flank to know exactly what mood the horses were in. He prevented squabbles before they occurred, and if any horse should have the smallest complaint or ailment, he was able to make it go away with a touch of his hand.

"Animal magic?" Joanna when they gathered for dinner and Levi told her of his findings. The princess perched on the arm of her chair, peeling an apple with a keen little blade.

She set the knife down when Levi drew near, a precaution they had all become used to taking.

"I think so." Levi explained what had happened with Molly and his interactions with the other horses. "Sometimes I don't even need to touch the animal. Sometimes I can even tell when the birds in the trees are upset. Not just by the way they're chattering. I can feel it. I just *know* it."

"It's uncanny," Liam confirmed. "I've seen it. It's like the horses talk to him. They tell him their ills and he cures them with a touch." He had been eager to see Levi share this power with the princess as well, though he'd been willing to wait and let the miller do it himself.

Lyall draped himself languidly in another chair, long limbs seeming to overflow it in every direction. "I imagine we'll be seeing more of this. More people showing magical gifts."

Joanna considered for a moment. Her men peppered Levi with more questions. No one else owned up to manifesting any sort of powers, but now that they had seen a bad luck curse in action and defeated an Ogre, they were perfectly willing and excited to learn of more magic.

Joanna pursed her full lips. "I haven't experienced anything unusual, myself." She sounded disappointed. "Ly, have you shot any lighting out of your fingertips or found yourself able to fly?"

"No more than usual."

"I believe you, Levi." Joanna smiled encouragingly. "Just be careful. Remember what happened to The Ogre. How the magic snapped back when he used too much, and it spelled disaster for him."

Levi nodded, brows knitting as he settled into his chair. It was the thick-legged, sturdy one The Ogre had transformed for him. He had also continued to use his special dishes, so there was considerably less breakage. "I'll be careful. I have a lot of experience with caution after all. If I went wrong and hurt an animal, I'd never forgive myself."

"Pity your magic power wasn't self-healing abilities." Joanna gestured to a fresh cut on Levi's forearm that he had earned that day by tripping and catching himself on a sharp stone. He hadn't even noticed it. "Do you think your animal healing works on people too?"

"I...er..." Levi floundered.

"Try," Joanna commanded. Before Levi could stop her, she picked up her apple knife and pricked her thumb, setting the blade back down hurriedly.

Lyall sat forward with a jerk. "Jo!"

Levi hesitated, then tentatively touched a fingertip to Joanna's outstretched thumb. There was no strange heat, no bolt of understanding. His new magic settled in him like a cat curling up to sleep. Just to be certain, he pulled her entire hand to him.

No warmth, no tug of magic. Levi shook his head and let her go. Joanna shrugged and grabbed a napkin to stop the little trickle of blood that ran from her thumb.

"Ah well, we can't have everything." Lyall slouched back in his chair, calm completely restored.

Levi found he liked the steady, thoughtful Lyall. He suspected of himself that if he did fancy men, he would have found it difficult to resist the bodyguard's easy charm.

These days Joanna's hand maiden Hana had joined them at the castle, and she had taken to looking at Levi with blushes and smiles. He didn't know what to make of it yet, but she was very pretty, and anyone Joanna valued had to be someone of great worth.

Two of Joanna's soldiers burst into the dining room pushing trollies with that evening's dinner. According to Joanna, their best cook, Varric, had been slain by The Ogre. The other men took turns preparing the meals. Having no Ogre to magic them their food, the fighters were obliged to hunt and forage the countryside. If anyone complained, Joanna insisted it was good practice.

Tonight they all enjoyed fresh rabbit and pheasant with wild onion and mushrooms. Levi had showed a few of Joanna's people how to make his small animal snares, and Boots even deigned to help by finishing off an animal from time to time, leaving minimal blemishes on the kill.

The group was rowdy and noisy and broke almost as many fixtures as Levi did. He supposed he should be insulted, as this was going to be his house, but it was only a matter of time before his bad luck produced the same results. Why not get it over with? Besides, it was difficult to think of the decorations as anything but The Orge's. It wasn't as if Levi picked those delicate vases or ornate candlesticks. Once the house was his he would decorate more practically.

He watched the men celebrate, petting Boots curled who up on his lap so as to enjoy treats from his human friend's plate. The cat liked the chatter and company.

Levi couldn't help but smile. This was how he wanted to live the rest of his days. No more wandering alone, no more feeling unwanted, inconvenient. Even when he repeatedly knocked his glass of water to the floor, someone always picked it up and refilled it without breaking their conversational stride. As though it were no bother at all.

"What's on your mind?" Joanna asked, perhaps noticing Levi's fond expression.

"This. This is good," he said. "When I was growing up it was only my parents and brothers to keep an eye on me and my luck. We didn't have a much money, and they grew dreadfully weary of me. With so many people here, always on the move, all of them keeping an eye on me, I think it'll be better."

"Of course it will be better." Joanna gave his arm a companionable squeeze. "Even when the lads and I have to move on, we'll hire you an excellent staff that all understand your luck issues."

"If my farms are as successful as you say they'll be, I'll hire craftsmen to design special furniture for me. So it lasts longer." He rested his arms on the table, slowly so as not to disturb anyone else's meals. His sleeve trailed in the gravy from his own plate, and he glanced down. "And I'll have to hire some tailors because I go through clothes faster than a rowdy child. The Ogre isn't here to magic me new ones."

"Very true," Joanna agreed. "We'll be leaving soon to return home and present our case to my father. Do you think there is anything you need before I go?"

Sadness prickled in Levi's chest. Joanna would leave several men for the time being, but he would miss her bombastic company. Not to mention Lyall's steady grace and sweet Hana. She was sitting at the far end of the table, and when Levi looked up she blushed and cast her eyes down at her plate. He did his best to give the princess a confident look. "I'll be alright. Cade, Orin, Justin and I will do well enough, provided they don't tire of dealing with me."

Joanna shot warning glances at the men in question. Cade, who was nearest, gave a serious nod while Orin and Justin, both younger soldiers, ignored their princess as they arm wrestled enthusiastically.

Lyall looked on sorrowfully, as his wound prevented him from joining their fun.

Joanna leaned towards Levi again, her tone confidential. "Just don't let them give you too much lip. Remember, you're a Carabas now. This is your castle."

A blush rushed to Levi's cheeks and he looked down, unable to hold Joanna's steady gaze any longer. Instead he busied himself trying—and failing—to wipe the gravy from his sleeve. It only spread further. "If your father goes along with our plan."

"He will," Joanna replied, firmly. Her hands balled into fists on the tabletop. "If this doesn't get him to respect me, nothing will."

Part 7

Joanna

Confident words to Levi were one thing. Knowing what her father's reaction would be was quite another. She put on a good show for the men, but Lyall and Hana knew that their princess was one step away from flying into an anxiety-fueled breakdown that would send her soldiers scattering.

She could hardly bring herself to eat, and her smiles were pasted on facsimiles of her true ones. She stayed outside the group gatherings at night, lingering in the shadows and picturing all the ways her victorious homecoming could go terribly awry.

Of course, she had promised Levi the Carabas castle. They'd just won the day and she was feeling magnanimous. But what if the king, upon hearing that The Ogre was no more, decided to claim the freshly liberated castle and lands as his own? Perhaps stationing some random lord in the old Carabas fiefdom. What if he used the lands and holdings as more collateral to entice eager suitors for his stubborn daughter.

Even with all these fears, Joanna was eager to spread the good news to the farms and villages they passed. Most folks guessed that something had happened at the castle Carabas, as they had seen no Shades in weeks, but Joanna took immense pride in informing all she met that The Ogre would trouble their lands no more. She was also careful to include the fact that a new lord, who had been instrumental in The Ogre's defeat, had taken up residence. As it was, she knew the farmers were already plotting to expand their lands back to what they had been. Like someone who has worn a belt too tight all day and was finally able to take it off to draw a proper breath. After the summer had been so harsh, with the rains and the increased Shade activity, the people threw parties and held small festivals. Some hung black rags with eye holes poked in them from trees and passing children would beat them with sticks.

Joanna put on a good show for her subjects, riding tall and proud in her shining armor. Discomfort be damned, she wanted to look the part of the conquering princess, though her men griped and complained that they had no need to wear their plate.

When Joanna and her soldiers finally reached the capitol city, spreading from the castle like a blanket at the feet of a seamstress, Joanna had gathered a following of civilians who trailed along, keeping the party mood going. They carried hastily made banners with Joanna's sigil, and even images of her leaping into the air, twin swords drawn and aimed towards the face of a horrible beast. The artists had made a guess at what The Ogre looked like. No two artists could agree, but Joanna enjoyed all the interpretations.

It didn't feel right to mentioned that the creature that had so haunted their lands for so long had merely been a selfish mage. Instead, the soldiers played up the horror of the creature. By the time they reached the castle gates, The Ogre was nine stories tall, vomited acid, and could turn a person to stone with a look.

It was this way, banners flying, armor gleaming, hair perfectly in place thanks to Hana's ministrations, that Joanna rode into her father's courtyard. Lyall flanked her, looking almost as resplendent, if a bit paler than usual. His wound troubled him with all the riding. You would not know it at a glance, for he sat straight—less a humble bodyguard and more a lord in his own right. Joanna would have offered to give him lands and title after this, but she knew what his answer would be.

"Someone, fetch the king!" Joanna shouted in her loudest, most reverberating voice. She knew that guards on the walls would have announced her return already, but she wanted her father to have to come to her rather than waiting for her inside.

Several moments passed in which Joanna was supremely glad she was wearing her armor. Hana had suggested a fine gown, but the stress sweat stains she knew she was sporting now would look anything but regal. She shot an uneasy glance towards her handmaiden, who had selected a fine dress for herself—one just on the cusp of being too elaborate for her station. Joanna hid a grin as she spotted several of the workers in the courtyard making eyes at Hana. A pity for them that the maid only blushed and looked at a certain miller's son these days.

The king took his time coming down. Joanna might have complained if she hadn't been the center of so much attention. She focused on remaining calm and confident looking, even as she wanted to roll her eyes.

Finally, her father strode into the yard, the queen on his arm, Joanna's brother and his wife in tow. Kathleen looked ready to have her baby any day, but she still managed to keep up with the others, and a genuine smile spread across her beautiful features.

What a pity that Joanna's father didn't wear a similar expression.

"Daughter, where have you been? You told us you were riding out to meet a beau and instead I hear that you battled The Ogre?" The king's voice was metal against stone. Joanna had to try very hard not to flinch.

She looked to her mother. Under normal circumstances the queen would have wrapped Joanna in a hug and look her over for injuries. Today she clung to her husband's arm as though it were the only thing keeping her from flying to her daughter's side. At least there was no anger in her eyes.

"Father, I have defeated The Ogre." Joanna's powerful voice hitched, but it was covered by her train of followers who waved their banners and cheered. Some even tossed flower petals for emphasis. Joanna wondered how long they had been carrying those.

"You have done *what*?" The king's bushy eyebrow rose. "I heard the rumors, but *this*...by yourself, you defeated the beast?"

"No, my men helped me..." She faltered under the king's steely glare. He thought she was lying, clearly. Centering herself, she spoke all the louder. Volume could hide her lack of confidence like her gleaming armor hid her trembling. "As well as the long-lost son of Carabas, Lord Levi."

"So, this person was not a fiction you made up to appease me?" His voice was laden with skepticism.

"No father. Lord Levi aided greatly in the defeat of The Ogre, and has already installed himself as master of Castle Carabas, as is his right. Soon he will send for his family, who have been living as peasants in mill country all these years."

The king pursed his lips, and Joanna silently prayed that her father had not been in secret correspondence with some distant member of the family Carabas all these years. And then there was the fact that she had no actual proof to bring back. She couldn't very well bring her father the head of a mouse. He would have to take the word of her men… of his people. The lack of Shades was proof enough for them.

She spun her cat ring with her thumb, recalling the white cat with eyes the color of sunset and embers that had greeted her when she defeated The Ogre. It had sat before her, and she knew without it speaking a word—knew that she was truly chosen of the god of luck himself.

Luck be on my side now.

Perhaps years down the road her father would be amiable to the notion that her victory was approved by some forgotten animal god, but not this day.

"Come inside, daughter," the king urged, his voice low, his teeth clenched. "We will discuss this further."

"No, Father." This time there was no tremble to her voice. Her words were so loud and commanding that a few of her entourage startled. "I wish you to acknowledge my victory here. In front of all these witnesses. I wish…I *demand*, that you allow me to take up my place as official Guardian of the People, and that you will no longer attempt to marry me off." This was the only way.

"Joanna," the queen spoke, her tone gentle, though her eyes were worried. "This is hardly the time nor place—"

"This is exactly the time and place, Mother." Joanna's grip on Willow's reins was so tight that her fingers were starting to cramp. "I will no longer be a useless, second born princess. I will fulfill my duties to protect these lands, as I would if I were a son."

Her father set his jaw. Joanna could see his hands balled into fists and he worked his jaw back and forth like he was gnawing a bone. His eyes might have bored through metal and Joanna thought she felt the heat of them on her skin. Her father had not raged in many years, but she knew she was the most trying thing in his life. Harder than running a kingdom was raising a daughter such as herself. The king's lip twitched, but still he said nothing.

"But now that The Ogre is dead, what use have the people for a protector?" Alroy spoke, eying Joanna as though he wasn't quite certain he knew her. As if some strange knight wearing his sister's armor had wandered into their courtyard.

The train of peasantry cheered and waved their banners again when he mentioned The Ogre. Joanna raised a hand and was deeply gratified when they fell silent at her gesture.

Her father seemed to have become locked inside his thoughts, his teeth clenched so tight it looked painful. Joanna decided she might need to snap him out of it. Her voice this time was quieter, though no less commanding. "Father, you are a good and fair king. Other than The

Ogre, your lands are safe enough, but bandits and those who mean us ill will still threaten. You have many alliances, but most know that we have no true defenders. Now that magic has returned to the land, as I suspect you may also have noticed, we will need to keep those mages who have less than wholesome intentions under keen observation." The king did not respond, so Joanna pressed on. "Your legacy is safe. You have a son, and soon a grandchild. Your trade routes with the surrounding kingdoms are as strong as ever, and will only become stronger with The Ogre gone. All I ask is that you let me do what I have always known would be my destiny. Let me learn, let me protect my people, let me—"

"Joanna." The king's voice was hoarse, like it physically pained him to speak. Was he regretting every time he had given in to her over her lifetime? Her first sword, her first battle-master, her first horse? Every concession he had made for his strange daughter's happiness. "You know what you're doing. Putting me in a spot like this, and believe me, we shall discuss your tactics later…however…I fear I am outflanked." He finally dipped his head, his iron gaze falling from Joanna's face.

Joanna had not realized how mightily her heart was beating until that moment, when she could have sworn it was throwing itself against her armor breastplate. Lyall moved his horse in beside her and caught her arm, as she was about ready to tip from Willow's back. "Are you saying…?" She didn't dare hope, even as ever fiber of her being vibrated with the knowledge of it. He couldn't take it back now. Could he?

"Yes," The king looked up again, his expression marginally softer. "I may be stubborn, but I am not beyond reason." He raised a cautioning hand before Joanna's train could start cheering once more. "However, I shall personally be handling a few more things from here on. I will be sending some of my own agents to investigate Castle Carabas, and to meet this young man…" A faint smile flickered on his lips. "I take it you were lying about falling in love with this long-lost Carabas?"

Joanna's cheeks heated, and it was her turn to drop her gaze. "Er, yes. He, uhm, wasn't interested and my affection faded. It was only a passing fancy."

Joanna looked through her lashes and caught sight of her mother's smile. She had to fight not to laugh. Relief was flooding her veins and making her giddy, like she'd had too much wine. She was thankful that Lyall kept his hand on her arm.

"Please, Daughter," the king said, gesturing towards the keep, his own bearing restored in a movement, "come inside and we can discuss this further."

Joanna turned and met Lyall's pale eyes. She gave him a nod. He let her go and she dismounted, her knees almost buckling when she hit the cobblestones. Her men dismounted as well and surrounded her, cheering and thumping her on the back.

She wondered how she had ever doubted these men, even for a second. They could be rowdy and obstinate at times, but they were unfailingly loyal in the end. Now she knew they would never leave her side. Even if she ordered them not to come, she thought wryly.

Once she had extracted herself from her own soldiers, some of the guards and servants from the castle, and those men and women who had followed her, banners still waving, she went with her family into the keep.

It was impossible, but she had won.

She kept wondering if she should find a gap in her armor and pinch herself.

Though her father grumbled about being ambushed, and loudly bemoaned plans he had to let Joanna meet some new prince he had recently discovered, Joanna knew he was already coming around to the idea of her new role. After all, it was not truly a new role at all. It was only a culmination of all she had been doing for years.

Her brother even joked and jabbed her with his elbow. "Perhaps you don't need a lady's maid at all," he joked. "Just have Lyall dress you and see to your armor like a proper squire."

~~~~~

Joanna wasted no time taking up her mantle and new title. While her father sent his people to check on Levi and ensure that all was well, Joanna sent messages to other kingdoms. Her father agreed that they had to deal with the magic situation. Abilities were awakening in people all over the kingdom, and they needed to bring in teachers and experienced mages to train everyone.

Joanna insisted on contacting Prosper, and soon she got word back that he would come personally, bringing some mages from his kingdom who were willing to set up the first of many magical colleges.

Joanna called in fighting teachers for herself and her men. She was intent on increasing her skill and honing her talents to become a well-rounded warrior, seeing as no magical power had found her.

Before her father could protest, Joanna sent word that she would be accepting female candidates for her unit. These ladies would be trained and armed as well as any of her men. To her surprise there was very little grumbling from her men, though she gave them a stern warning about flirtation. She had places in her ranks to fill.

She rode out personally to inform the families of Varric, Bowen, and young Avery of their deaths. Varric's father had not heard from his estranged son in many years, but he teared up when she shared the news. Avery's sweetheart wept on Joanna's shoulder, and the princess did her best to be comforting, though it did not come naturally.

The miller's son-turned-lord was still inexperienced, nervous, and communicated with the outside world almost exclusively by letter for some time, lest close contact cause his luck to pass to others. But one day Joanna received a note from him saying he had begun riding out on the new horse she'd sent him. Molly had officially retired to a life of leisure.

The farmers that were taking up residence on Levi's new lands were eager to meet the lord to whom they would swear loyalty and pay taxes. Levi reported that he planned to keep this luck issue a secret from the general populous for fear that no one would want to serve a cursed leader. However, he was more open with his magical gift and happily recounted tales of visiting injured animals on the new farms. It did not take long for his new tenants to call on him to see their newborn livestock, simply to ensure that the youngsters got the best possible start.

Now that he was established, Levi planned to send a letter to his family in mill country to ask if they wished to come and stay with him in his new castle. Joanna did him one better, riding out herself to deliver it.

She found Levi's mother and brothers on their little mill near a shallow, pleasant river.

Joanna was impressed by Levi's brothers. Her friend had not been joking when he had explained his siblings' blessings. Fergus looked as though he could pull a young tree out of the ground on a whim, and even she could tell that Brodie was incredibly handsome.

As impressive as these people were, it was nothing to a princess riding into their homestead, clad in fine traveling attire and flanked by her men. Levi's mother nearly fainted.

After Joanna dismounted and they had all settled in the yard (there was not enough room in the house for everyone) she explained the situation as best she could. Mrs. Miller looked completely at a loss. Her eyes were huge, and as Joanna related the tale, she kept mumbling "Levi? *My* Levi? No. This can't be right. Not my Levi."

The two brothers stared, saying very little. They were also joined by Brodie's wife, who seemed to be taking things better than anyone else because she had less experience with Levi.

"My...my son defeated an ogre?" Mrs. Miller spluttered for perhaps the tenth time.

"He had help," Rylan commented good-naturedly. The healer sat beside Joanna on the dusty earth. Chickens strutted around them, investigating who far more boldness than their human counterparts.

"Indeed, he did have some help." Joanna tried her hardest not to laugh. "He had assistance from myself, my men, and of course his cat. Boots."

"His...wuh?" Brodie finally spoke.

"Darling, I think they're messing about," Brodie's wife assured him, gently touching his arm.

"Oh no, the cat was instrumental. Without Boots I doubt I would have survived." This time Joanna was unable to keep her expression under control. The looks on the faces of Levi's family were too much for her to handle. Several of her men lost their composure at the same time and there was momentary chaos as Joanna tried to settle them while also keep herself from bursting into laughter as tears of mirth ran down her cheeks.

Mrs. Miller stared as thought she'd been struck by a bolt of lightning. Her mouth moved a bit, but no words came.

"Oh yes." Joanna turned her attention from her men to the woman's round, motherly face. "Bad luck and all." She looked around the little farm. It seemed cozy, well-loved and much lived in. "He was hoping that you would come join him at his new castle."

"My brother owns a castle." Fergus spoke at last, his voice much smaller that Joanna expected from such a giant. "My little brother...owns a castle."

"He's a lord," Joanna said. Levi's family gaped like stunned frogs. "For assisting in the defeat of The Ogre, I bestowed the lands and holdings that had belonged to that creature on him. He's called Lord Carabas now."

"And…he can handle that?" Mrs. Miller asked, tears shining in her eyes. "When he ran away from home, I feared he might find a place as a beggar. Or perhaps he would live on the outskirts of some village with a job doing minor tasks. We searched the area, but we couldn't find him. We couldn't leave the mill to hunt. You're telling me that somehow *my son*, who could hardly walk across a room without tripping, is a lord?!"

"He still has trouble with the walking, but he has people to help him now, and I'll be checking in to make sure everything is going well for him. He won't have to manage alone," Joanna said.

"Your majesty—" Brodie raised a tentative hand. "I know what you must think. How could we abandon our brother to the world when he was so…different?"

Joanna made a calming gesture. "That is not my business. If Levi is forgiving and wishes you to come live with him, then I respect his decision."

Mrs. Miller began crying in earnest, and it took quite some time to calm her.

Joanna spent most of the day and late into the evening with the Millers, who promised to settle their affairs in mill country and set out for their son's new castle as soon as they were able.

Part 8
The Bard

The bard strode into town on festival day. He smiled up at the flapping rainbow of banners hanging from every eave and fence. This usually quiet, sleepy town was as alive as a hive of bees in summer, and the scent of cinnamon and freshly cut lilies filled his nose.

He headed for the center of town, his lute tap tapping gently against his back. This was a smaller village, but he wouldn't reach the capitol until the next day so there was no harm in earning a few coins here. Besides, these little towns always hid the best foods. He was certain that somewhere here would be a woman who made the best sweet bread he had ever tasted. All he had to do was find her.

Just as he expected, the square was all set up for dancing and performing. A small, wooden stage already stood at one end with torches and lanterns waiting for night. A young man distributed chairs, but the bard was looking for someone else. There he was. The inevitable man with a clipboard.

The bard marched up to the stout fellow.

He waited his turn as a different performer spoke to the clipboard-man. "Any slots free tonight for stories or songs?" He leaned to peek over the man's arm.

The man considered his list. "I can fit you in for stories. I have enough musicians."

"Very well." The bard gave his most winning smile. Fortune had been kind these last several years, and he'd been able to replace his garb so he looked the part of a fine, traveling performer. The sort you would want to see on any stage, large or small.

He gave his name and took note of his spot on the list. Before a trio of singers and after a puppet show. There were only a few other story tellers, and he was up before them. Good. No one would tell inferior versions of the tales he planned to tell.

He turned to wander the town until nightfall and nearly ran into a small boy. The lad was no taller than the bard's thigh, and so slight in build he would have easily been knocked to the ground. He looked up at the bard with eyes so blue he might have borrowed them from the summer sky. The boy munched what looked like a baked apple on a stick and the bard made a mental note to track down that vendor later.

"Can I help you, my lad?" The Bard squatted to be eye-to-eye with the boy.

"You're the storyteller?"

"I am. How can you tell?"

The boy pointed at the nightingale stitched into the front of the bard's multicolored tunic.

The bard smiled and his eyes twinkled. "You're a fan of the old gods, are you?"

"I like the animals." The boy paused to crunch sloppily on his apple. Juice and streaks of cinnamon ran unnoticed down his chin.

"Which one is your favorite?"

The boy reached into his pocket and extracted a bit of fabric with a white cat stitched onto it. Perhaps it was an older sister's sewing practice.

"Luck! Good choice! I am rather fond of that god, myself." He paused, looking into town where he knew he could find more home cooked food than he could possibly eat, though he was willing to give it a try. But when he looked back into the little boy's sticky, hopeful face his heart melted. "How about you get some of your friends and I'll tell you all one of my favorite stories? I need to practice for tonight anyway."

The boy grinned, revealing a missing front tooth, and darted away.

He collected his friends in record time, and in twenty minutes the bard was surrounded by eager little faces. They sat around him in an imperfect circle and cheered for a story.

"Do any of you know the story of Puss Named Boots?"

"Puss *in* Boots?" a little girl asked, raising her hand as though she were in school.

"No, silly," said the blue-eyed boy. "He didn't wear boots!"

"He did!" She folded her arms.

Both children looked up at the bard, expectant.

"I'll start at the beginning, shall I?"

He spread the tale before the children as he would for any audience. A tapestry of beginnings and endings, of danger and kindness. They listened, wide eyed, as though he held some magic in his words, though he was not one of the lucky ones gifted with magical ability when The Ogre was defeated.

He wove the story of a miller's son, cursed with bad luck.

"Lord Levi!" the children cried excitedly. This village was near enough to the castle Carabas that the bard wondered if any of them might have met the lord in question.

He told of a brash, determined princess, which earned more cheers from the assemblage.

He told of an orange cat, "who did not wear boots."

"Awwwww..." the girl whined as her friends nudged her and giggled.

The bard held up a hand. "Before you ask, he didn't speak either."

"I didn't think he did that," the girl said defensively.

Before the others could poke more fun at her, the bard pressed on. He wound the story up and around, recalling everything he knew, and some things he embellished. Though he would never outright lie as some of his fellows clearly had regarding the abilities of Boots the cat. It took him over an hour to reach the end, but the children never lost interest.

At long last he finished, "the famous Boots sired many kittens and the demand for his progeny was high in the lands ruled over by Lord Levi."

"My cousin has one of his grandchildren!" One of the children cheered. The others looked at him in obvious jealousy.

The bard gave him a toothy grin. "It was believed that these kittens in particular, brought extremely good luck. Especially the orange ones. The mighty Boots lived a happily until the day of his death, though he did live considerably longer than was ordinary for a cat. He seldom had to make use of his "understanding," but it came in handy from time to time. He did, however, refuse to ever wear his little harness again."

The End

Printed in Great Britain
by Amazon